# THE DIRECTION

## Book One

"…For it is better to suffer for doing right, if that should be God's will, than for doing wrong. For Christ also died for sins once for all, the righteous for the unrighteous, that He may bring us to God, being put to death in the flesh but made alive in the spirit…"

# The Direction

**ELISABETH NADLER**

This is a work of fiction. Names, characters, places, and incidents either are the product of the author's imagination or are used fictitiously. Any resemblance to actual persons, living or dead, events or locales, is entirely coincidental.

Cover art by Elisabeth Nadler
Copyright © 2024 by Elisabeth Nadler
Grammatical Edits: September 2025

All rights reserved. No part of this book may be reproduced in any manner whatsoever without written permission except in the case of brief quotations embodied in critical articles and reviews.
First Printing, 2024

# PROLOGUE

"I, Jax Erricks, take you, Lila Collins, to be my lawful wife."

"I, Lila Collins, take you, Jax Erricks, to be my lawful husband."

Out in a meadow covered in wildflowers, just outside of a quaint town at the foot of the Rockies, a little 9 year old girl with dark eyes giggled, covering her mouth with one hand, the other hand holding onto the hand of a boy a head taller than she was. His blonde shock of hair almost covered his sage green eyes, and even though he was barely 11, he had a strong build. She was more slight, not scrawny, but lithe while delicate in appearance.

"Now, I guess we're set! No one can take you away from me, now, Lil'," Jax declared with a proud grin.

Lila was almost in tears and threw herself into him in a youth's rambunctious hug. "Thank you, Jax. I don't want to be taken away like my sister was. You're my best friend! Don't ever leave me, OK?"

Jax gave a hearty laugh, or as hearty as an 11 year old could, and squeezed her in a tight hug. "Anytime, Lil'. You never have to worry. I'm not going anywhere and neither are you." He wiggled his ring finger that had a simple band of metal, identical to hers, albeit a bit big for their little digits. "We have these now. They don't take away married girls."

They began walking through the grasses and flowers, holding hands and heading back to the town. They both wore jeans and t-shirts, though his t-shirt had the image of his favorite superhero and was blue, while hers had a horse, but also blue. Their favorite color was one of the many things they had in common. Her auburn hair was in a long braid down her back, her skin a golden tan with the sun.

"Where did you get these?" Lila asked as she proudly held her hand up in the air, admiring the simple shiny ring as though it were the largest diamond in the world.

"I told my Mom what happened to your sister and told her I was going to marry you, so it won't happen to you, but needed rings. I wanted hers and Dad's, but she told me I could use my allowance on a couple union bands, so I ordered some on the Console." He scowled a little and added remorsefully, "I tried to guess our sizes, but I think I messed up."

She giggled and squeezed his hand. "It's ok, it'll fit us sometime. I'm so excited to tell my Daddy I won't be taken away! He seems really sad since… since Terra was taken."

Lila became somber and quiet suddenly, watching their feet as they walked. Immediately, Jax returned a squeeze to her hand before letting go and putting his arm around her. He understood, without her saying anything, that sometimes just having someone there was good enough to comfort the sorrowful. And she likewise knew, without him saying anything, that he would always be there for her.

It wasn't long before they reached their houses, which were both on the outskirts of the town, and they froze where they stood, watching as a crew of medics wheeled a cloth covered stretcher to the medic bus. The color from Lila's face drained; she had seen this with her grandparents when they were barely 60. She let go of Jax's hand and ran to the house, screaming, "Mom! Daddy?!"

Jax ran to catch up. She was fast, but he was faster and was there by her side when she nearly ran into her sobbing mom. That fateful day they learned her father had died of an aneurism, the explanation being he had received a concussion during a recreational outing and was sent home to recuperate. The two friends held each other as Lila sobbed against Jax, while her mom was taken to be assessed for extreme emotional distress by the attending medics.

That was 6 years ago… 15 year old Lila stood with tears streaming down her face as she watched Jax get into a Collective bus with his three siblings. Their parents had been killed in a fire, and because the oldest, Jax, was not approved for custody, the siblings were all taken to Direction Childcare and Jax to Juvenile Adjustment. Her neighbor, her support, her best friend, everything that kept her grounded, was just driven away; like so many dear things in her life.

*God, if you are the God my Dad said you were, why the hell have you let this happen??*

Lila dried her tears and turned away, entering into her all too quiet home where her mom despondently maintained her position in front of the Console, fulfilling her daily quota of work for The Direction.

# | 1 |

# The Direction

I wake with a start. I had shed my blanket in the night but now even the sheet is too hot. Wiping the sweat from my brow, I swing my legs over the edge of the bed.

*Shorts and a sports bra and still too hot to sleep comfortably.*

I grab the brush from my nightstand and deftly brush my dark hair until the knots are gone. Without even looking, I braid it on the side and secure it with a tie from my wrist.

My bedroom is at the back of the two-story home, past the living room and kitchen. It used to be my parents' room until my mom was taken away after a mental breakdown. She could no longer do the programming work required by The Direction and was deemed unfit for society. Where she is, I am not sure. I have been declined visiting rights every single time I apply.

Looking now through the five-foot-wide picture window past the foot of my bed, I watch as the light slowly increases, setting the sky aflame with reds and oranges. The Wilds make a beautiful scene, yet it does nothing to ease my stress.

The door to the hall is on the left wall from the window, my closet is on the right wall. My décor is simple but personal. Photos of my family, one of a cat I used to have, and finally a painting of a mountain sunrise my sister had done.

I finally work up enough oomph to push myself up from my bed. Walking down toward the kitchen I pause at the mirror in the hall, staring at my reflection. Absently, I fidget with the metal band hanging from a chain around my neck, the edges rubbed smooth over the years, and I survey my face for a moment. The dark circles belie my good health, telling instead of the countless nights of fitful dreams over the past few months.

*I will be 25 tomorrow.* Maybe I should explain why 25 years of age is so significant. *Or in my case, terrifying.*

During the 21$^{st}$ century, a catastrophic event happened to significantly impact the world's population. Something first took out those who were immuno-compromised, and then there was a massive impact on the fertility for the remaining population. This led to brutally low birth rates, and a large portion of the children who were born ended up having severe disabilities.

As the population began to age, this sudden decline drastically reduced the workforce, and governments began collapsing throughout the world. Industry came to a standstill and advancement in technology was put on hold, which is why most of our technology now is not much more improved than when the initial collapse took place. Other than the medical scanners, AI assistant programs, and then the hovercycles, which are restricted for use only by officials.

The decline continued, the elderly could barely be provided for, and those physically unable to work became a strain on the remaining society. However, here in what used to be known as the United States of America, in the 22$^{nd}$ century, a non-governmental research company, called The Direction, became the leading reason for the survival of the human race.

The Direction did the research on the heredities of the population and concluded that if they selected those with clean genetics, from any race, they could establish a good base to develop a healthy population. This would be accomplished by taking those selected and placing them in a healthy environment where they could raise their families. These areas were spread out in a certain section of the former States, the area now called Paradesa, covering parts of Colorado, Nebraska, and a small mountain section of South Dakota. These areas are now known as, in the same order, Eden, Gamal, and Oshana.

The selected families are provided with substantial education and given low-stress work positions that fit their skills, some of them from their home Console, like digital programming or positions in the further research and development of increasing and maintaining a healthy population. Those who are not fertile or carry hazardous genes, are assigned to work in the fields and factories located in Gamal. The entirety of the area is covered in fields, greenhouses, and factories for the processing of produce and products for those residing in the Eden and Oshana regions. Their permissibility to have children is severely limited.

The remaining states are said to be in absolute ruins, covered in wildlands, abandoned towns, and destroyed cities. The few inhabitants that remain are so out of touch with society that they are considered to be savages. The rest of the world? No one knows. The Direction cut ties on communications with foreign regions to prevent unnecessary anxiety and damaging influence.

Did I also mention that religion is restricted as well? The Direction analyzed that the varied religious practices are mentally unhealthy and have the potential to divide the remaining population and cause a restriction in human development, thus negatively impacting the chance for a recovered populace. This would be devastating to the process and another reason why most written material was confiscated; the only method of research is via the Console.

*At least that's all what my history class told me.*

What does this mean for a 25-year-old woman in the early 23rd century? Well, the rule is set in place that a single woman is to find a DNA-clean spouse by the time they are 25. As research concludes, of course, that solid family dynamics are the best way to raise mentally stable children. That, and the best age range for childbearing is from 23 to 32.

What happens to those women who do not find spouses by then? They will be transported to the facility in the Oshana region to be surrogates. If they are intellectually suited, they will also be given a prime position in the labs, education, or leadership fields. Otherwise, they are used solely for the purpose of reproduction.

I suppose I should clarify why men are not subject to this "find a spouse" rule. There is a large imbalance in the number of males versus females. Although history isn't thorough, there was a strong decline in male births in particular and an even stronger decline in the testosterone levels in the males after the initial fertility crash.

There is no clear explanation for this in any of the studies I have read thus far, yet I suspect The Direction knows more than they care to share. One doesn't dare challenge that, however, or accuse them of anything other than being the salvation of the human race. That would be instant transportation to the Gamal region.

So, that is why I am dreading tomorrow. Despite my best efforts in my college-level studies, I don't consider myself to be an expert at anything. Maybe broadly knowledgeable and perhaps very artistic, but my lack of any particular expertise in the desired fields means one thing.

I do have some medical know-how, but I doubt substantial enough. My fate will be as a surrogate until I am no longer of optimal age and health. No one really knows what happens then. There are rumors, but that's all they are. I don't even want to think them out loud in my head right now.

Jax was one of the only boys I could have seen myself with, yet that was when I was in my early teens. Now I have no clue where he might be, if he is still alive, or maybe he has been assigned to Gamal. He more than likely found someone anyway. There are plenty of options out there, after all! Even so, time can change anyone; he may not be the same person I remember.

My own town, Vouna, being one of the smaller ones, had a significant lack of boys my age growing up. There are maybe a few other men near my age; most of them are taken, and the younger ones are immature. The remaining already have pursuers, and as I am not exactly strikingly beautiful or immensely intelligent, I have not had a single one show interest. Unfortunately, I also tend to be a little more on the tomboy side and haven't done any favors for myself in that sense. I play rough, I am competitive, and I insist on fixing my own things when they break.

*Not that I haven't had my interests,* I ponder thoughtfully.

Still absently observing my reflection, I smile a little as my thoughts drift to Gamar. Tall and dark, like the old history photos of those who used to be in the Africas, and well built. He is always polite and caring, and he even came by several times to make sure I didn't feel alone after my mom was taken. It isn't that I love him in that way, but he has been someone I could abide being married to. Two weeks ago, when I told him my birthday was soon, and I needed to find someone, that's when I asked if he would be that someone. He made it painfully clear that day that I was a good friend and that was all. He still comes by, though, and has coffee with me some mornings.

*That won't help me tomorrow...*

## | 2 |

# Contraband

I hear a knock on the door, interrupting my musings.
*I am nowhere prepared for anyone.* I groan in aggravation as I rub at the circles under my eyes.

"Just a minute!" I yell through the open-concept kitchen and living room to the entrance.

"It's just me." I recognize Gamar's deep voice.

*Speak of the devil... or more like think.*

"Come on in and start the coffee. I'll be out in a minute!" I reply before ducking into the bathroom.

Despite the rejection, Gamar is always welcome.

It doesn't take me long to brush my teeth, rinse my face, and put on some deodorant. I don't bother changing into anything special, though, I just throw on a tank top. I work and study from home, and Gamar and I are comfortable enough with each other that lazy-day clothes are acceptable. I put on a smile and walk down the hall into the kitchen, where I smell the fresh coffee.

"I brought breakfast," Gamar says with a big, white-toothed grin that could bring cheer to a funeral.

*I need that.*

He stands a good six and a half feet tall, towering over my small five-foot five frame. Gamar waves at two plates boasting hearty omelets. Bacon is excluded, of course; The Direction still hasn't found a way to make pork healthier to eat.

"I wasn't going to eat anything this morning, but I guess if you insist." I grin and punch him in the arm. "You're going to make me fatter."

He scoffs at my comment. "You're not fat. If anything, you need more meat on your bones."

"You're biased, Gam."

"I am a very honest man," he retorts. "Sit down and eat before it gets cold."

I comply with his commanding but gentle tone and sit opposite him at my mostly empty six-chair table. The table and chairs are aesthetically pleasing, solid wood and even decorative. It was decided that comfortable living conditions with attractive features was best for wholesome living, so that's what every family got according to their tastes.

*My family loved wood products.*

I sip at my coffee and glance at Gam over the rim of the mug, noticing a certain edge in his smile. "What's up?"

He looks up at me from his food, a chunk of omelet still on his fork and halfway to his open mouth. The smile quickly turns into a grin.

"I knew we were friends for a reason."

The statement stings a little, considering the rejection the other week, but I smile. "So? What do you have today?"

Gamar is notorious for somehow acquiring literature, in printed form, no less! A huge breach in the societal rules, but he has never gotten caught. He reaches into a side bag he always has with him and pulls out a rectangular shape; something carefully wrapped in canvas. Gently he lays it in the center of the table and slowly pulls open the coverings to reveal an ancient looking leatherbound book, the edges dark with stains and tattered with handling. On the front in gold, or what used to be gold colored, is written a five-letter word.

"A bible?!" My jaw drops in disbelief.

I had only seen one in the hands of my dad when I was 7, and he had to hide it quickly when a coworker blabbed to the Defense Industry. I haven't been able to find it since.

"Yes, although a lot of the text has been destroyed by mildew," he bemoans sadly.

I scowl a little bit. "I know you have been looking for this for a while, but I still don't understand why you risk your status here for such a trivial thing."

He shakes his head at me.

"Lila, I have read enough to know that God exists, and He wouldn't want us to live like this, separating people just because of a genetic abnormality."

I begin to feel irritated, and I stuff a couple more bites in my mouth so I don't say something rude. Gamar has always been secretly religious, and even I to some extent believe there is a God, but I don't know Him, and I am not sure I want to. It just divides everyone and takes things away.

*Like my sister, Dad, Jax, and Mom.*

"I know what you're going to say, but you can't change my mind. I'm going to find somewhere I can learn more about God and bring it back to people like you and the others. The whole town deserves to make their own decision if religion is right or wrong."

Finally, I hold my hand up, my face slowly turning red in anger.

*He is going to get himself killed!*

Yes, I firmly believe my Dad had been murdered for his religious beliefs, but what am I to do? The best I can do is prevent losing anyone else.

"I admire your enthusiasm, and I understand why you want to do this, but you are being too loud and obvious." I shift my eyes to the Console in the living room. "You know they hear everything, and a stupid ideal isn't worth losing you. We live well here, we still have our friends with us, and I don't want that to change."

"But it will," he reminds with a pointed gaze. "Tomorrow you will be taken away, and that's not right. This," he points to the book on the table, "says it isn't. All human life is of value, no matter the cost. God Himself died for us to make that point."

"Then marry me like I asked." I throw my hands in the air, frustration threatening to bring tears to the mix. "And they won't take me. To hell with religion, this way is good enough."

Gamar shakes his head, and if I didn't consider him my best friend, and perhaps believed deep down he is right, I would hate him for what he says next.

"You know in your soul it is wrong. 'Good enough' is still empty when you consider eternity. We can leave; we can bring others with us and find another way. We don't have to comply with the rules. There are at least a dozen other girls in this town in the same boat as you, should I deny their freedom just so you can avoid facing the hard truth? I won't marry you, not just because I believe we aren't meant to be together, but because it is only avoiding the truth of the matter. This needs to end."

I know he is right, about this being wrong, maybe not the religion, but the tears burn and threaten to spill as I stand from the table and grab my plate. With aggravated movement, I scrape the leftovers into the compost and forcibly wash my plate and fork. Suddenly, I sense Gam's hulking frame by my side. He waits until I put the plate down and brings me into a warm embrace with one arm and turns the water full force with the other hand.

"Come with me, Lila," he says as quietly as he can. "Tonight, me and a few others are planning to leave on foot; we'll hit the mountains and head West. Away from the main roads. We want you to come with us."

It takes everything in me to pull away from the comfort of my friend's hug and look him directly in his dark, kind eyes, the tears freely slipping down my face.

"I'm too scared."

And I am. I am simply terrified. *What if we are caught?* That might be worse than what I already know what I am headed for. Knowing is comfort, and I suddenly realize that I have been comfortable for far too long. Handing me a towel for my hands and face, he presses a hand gently down on my shoulder.

"I'm by your side, so are the others," he firmly replies, not saying names.

"Alright. When?"

"Sundown."

He turns the water off and gives me an encouraging smile. This is it. The leap my dad always wanted to take. The one his wife, my mom, refused to take. We could have saved Terra. But that is the past. Now I have a chance, and I am going to take it; I will go with Gam. He wraps up his Bible silently, and then we part with a hug. No more words are spoken. I am too terrified to speak, and he understands without asking.

# | 3 |

# Time

My hands are sweating. The daypack that I have for recreational hikes, as physical activity is required, is nearly bursting at the seams with everything I believe I need. Health bars, Hydra-thlete, spare clothes, a small pocket knife, thermal blankets, and rope. Guns are forbidden unless you are part of the Defense Industry.

I wipe my sweaty palms on my jeans, trying to force my breathing to steady and my pulse to slow. The time seems to tick by so slowly. My day had been spent meeting my quota for studies on the Console, although not one bit of the information processed properly in my brain; I was too distracted. I barely passed the finals on physics, but it was enough to keep with my usual grades: average.

Sitting at the end of my bed, I stare straight out the large picture window facing west. The view of the mountains is breathtaking with the fall colors slowly spreading, and I have been there during guided outings, but the thought of facing it with little wilderness experience makes my heart pound harder. I am lost in the thoughts of 'what if' as I watch the sun set.

There would be enough light to see for a while until we are out in the woods. After that, I am guessing we would be hiking with headlamps. I am blindly trusting Gam with the details, and this scares me a little more. Even though he has read prohibited documents on wilderness survival, how can anyone be truly prepared?

A knock on the door causes me to nearly jump out of my skin, and I am sure I feel my heart literally skip a beat. My hands won't stop sweating, and my stomach ties in a knot while I grab my day-pack, slinging it over one shoulder.

*Alright, Gam, right on time.*

My hiking shoes clunk across the hardwood floor, the sound matching every other beat of my heart as I rush across the room. I grab the handle of the door and hesitate, doubt coursing through my mind while I battle with the known versus the unknown.

*Let's just do this,* finally hits my thoughts, and I throw the door open.

All color drains from my face, and I stare, horrified, not at Gam but at four Defense guards and a Collection Official.

*It's not time...*

*I'm not going. I already told Gam I would go with him. There is no way this is happening.*

Without thinking, I scream and turn on my heels to run for my rear door by the kitchen. I have no clue what I will do after, but I am not going to be taken without at least trying to escape.

It's a pointless effort, however, as the guards quickly cover the ground between us and overtake me. I feel a jab in my arm, and suddenly the room begins to spin, blackness encroaching on my vision until finally...

# | 4 |

# Haste

Entering data into his Console, the highly decorated Defense Officer stumbles across a file of one of the future surrogates. The photo shows an athletic woman, her long brown hair braided to the side and her eyes a bright amber.

"Well, she's kinda pretty. Always loved brunettes," he comments to one of the officers beside him.

The other looks over and nods in agreement. "Nice. You have good taste, Don. Too bad I'm taken."

The officer named Don laughs a little and shakes his head. "Never stopped you before."

*There's something about her...*

His smile fades a little when he reads over her name with the marking of 'Expedited'.

"Is there a way I can get you to cover for me, Marc? I think I'm going after this one, and time is short."

"I didn't know you could move that fast on a decision. What's so special about this one?" Marc queries.

"Just a feeling," Don replies somewhat flippantly as he grabs his coat and heads for the door, not even waiting for Marc to confirm his request.

----

After a grueling six hours on his hover-cycle, Officer Don finally arrives in the small town of Vouna at the foot of what were once known as the Rockies, now simply referred to as The Wilds.

*I hope I am not too late. I've seen what they do with Expedited surrogates.*

This could be the most impulsive thing he has ever done; he is apprehensive but determined.

With the sun already setting, something in him tells him he should hurry, and he accelerates through town probably faster than he should. He slows when his AutoMap *dings* a signal indicating his destination is right up ahead. Seeing the Collection Bus already at the door of the address he saw on file, he sucks in a sharp breath and hops off his bike.

"Hey!" He yells out sharply as he sees three women from Defense carrying an unconscious woman toward the transportation.

The other Defense escort present raises his AR in challenge until he sees that the man walking toward them wears a dark blue uniform. Lowering his weapon, he gives a sharp salute while a terse looking Collection Official with short cropped blonde hair steps forward.

"What can we do for you, officer…" She pauses to glance at the name plate on Don's chest, which is at eye level for her, and the rank on his shoulder. "Major Bachman?"

"I claim her," Don answers shortly.

"Are you sure? She's Expedited, and that's risky," the official confronts dubiously, her eyes narrow.

Without hesitation, despite his nerves being on edge, Don replies with force in his voice. "Yes. Don't challenge me, or you'll be hearing it from higher up."

The official raises a hand and takes a step back, smirking a little at the intensity. "I didn't mean any offense Major; I'm just doing my job. If you insist, I will grab my data pad from the bus right now."

"Hurry up," the Major persists, "it's getting dark, and I need to get back to my duties."

The official nods and retreats to the bus with Don watching her cautiously. The streetlamps illuminate the vehicle enough for him to see through the windows as well. He sees six figures, four of them young women, and his heart sinks a little.

*I can only save one right now,* he remorsefully reflects.

The other two are men, one a full head taller than the others and dark in color.

*I haven't seen that many pulled from one small town all at once.*

As the official returns with a data pad and a stylus, he begins filling out the necessary facts and pulls details from his files for her information.

"Lila….Collins… age 25" he transcribes, mumbling under his breath.

As he fills out his own information, his curiosity gets the better of him.

"Why so many tonight?" He jerks his head, indicating the half-filled bus.

The official sighs and shakes her head. "Renegades who tried to run for the Wilds. Safer for them if we take them to the facility up North."

Don nods as he signs his name.

"What about *her* signature?" He gestures toward the unconscious Lila, who had been unceremoniously dumped on the well-manicured lawn.

"Unnecessary. Just needed yours."

A scowl crosses the Major's face, but it fades quickly as he hands the data pad and stylus back to the official.

"Done. Now please, if you will," he motions to the officers present. "Place her gently on her couch or something. I am guessing she is drugged. When will it wear off?"

"By morning, sir." One of the women answers.

"Very well. Let's get her inside," he directs, his voice and expression all business.

*This is risky.*

Don walks ahead of them and opens the door, stepping aside to allow them to pass into the subtly lit home as they carry the woman in and hastily place her on the couch. After printing the Certificate of Union, the official hands it to the Major and gives him a smug smile.

"Getting the union bands is up to you. Good luck," she utters pithily before leaving through the door, followed by the Defense escorts.

Waiting until he hears the Collective bus drive away, he moves over to where a neatly folded blanket is laying over the arm of the couch on which Lila is lying. Covering her gently, Don stands for a moment, watching her breath steadily, her face seemingly at peace.

*Although that's what sedatives will do*, he bemoans silently.

The sudden ring of his communication device in his ear startles him, and he backs away from the unconscious woman and taps his earpiece once.

"Major Bachman... Yes, sir... I understand sir... Yes, sir... I am on my way."

Tapping his earpiece again, he sighs. The voice on the other end was his commanding officer, who was none too happy with the Major's sudden leave of absence, despite Marc vouching for him. Lifting the document in his hand, he stares at the written proof of his hasty decision, flinching.

"Don J. Bachman and Lila A. Bachman," he murmurs.

Placing the paper on the kitchen table, he quietly walks back to Lila and goes to tug the blanket up to her shoulders. Glancing down below her chin, he sees a simple union band hanging from a chain around her neck, and for a moment his brows furrow.

Don's eyes travel around the room, noting the only photos seem to be of this woman's parents, her as a child, and what looks to be a redheaded version of her. Until he sees a small, framed photo on the desk of her Console. Lifting it closer to see better in the dim light, the image of a little girl and a boy a head taller than she comes clear. Taking it from the frame, he folds it and places it in the pocket of his uniform slacks.

Silently he steps out, closing the door behind him. Stepping over his hover bike, he takes one more glance at the house before steering his vehicle away.

*What have I gotten myself into?*

# | 5 |

# Realization

"Lila... Bachman. Lila Bachman. Lila. Bachman. Bachman. Mrs. Bachman."

I repeat this to myself while staring in the mirror, the unfamiliar name getting stuck in my throat each and every time. The past couple weeks have gone by as though I were in a haze, and that first morning had been painful.

My thoughts flit through the memory of practically crawling from the couch and lifting myself with the table in order to stand. That's when I saw the official document staring me in the face. It was also the worst hangover I had ever had. Not that I had many, because after a few, my Console restricted the purchase of anything alcoholic. Something I wish it didn't do right now, because I could use some.

"Two weeks and I still haven't met him. Who is he?" I bemuse, my reflection giving no answer.

Splashing cold water on my face, I dry with the towel nearby and walk into the hall between my bedroom and the kitchen. I pause again at the mirror there, which is full length so I can see my whole body. I am leaner than I remember, the athletic jacket and pants don't cling as much; probably the stress and the fact that breakfasts are not a thing for me since Gam...

*I hope he made it to freedom.*

Passing through the kitchen, I go directly to my Console.

"Hey, APA."

"What can I do for you, Lila?" APA, Automated Personal Assistant, answers from the Console with a feminine voice.

"Who is Don J. Bachman?"

"Major Don J. Bachman is an officer in the Defense Industry. He has been awarded the Manda Medal for excelling in the field of Intelligence, the Meod Medal for being wounded in the line of duty, the Oshana Medal for saving the life of a fellow officer, the Araza Medal for..."

"Stop. Do you still not have any images of him?"

"I am sorry, that information is restricted. Is there anything else I can do for you, Lila?"

"No."

"Very well. Have a good day!"

This is now my daily routine. Every morning, I ask and receive the same answer. Every morning, I lift the empty picture frame and resist throwing it across the room.

*Why take that?!*

And then every morning I go for a run, to avoid the silence and gloom in this house and fight the growing depression. A sigh escapes my lips as I reach for the lock on the front door before remembering the entire town had their door and window locks replaced with voice recognition locks last week.

"Unlock."

A solid *click* indicates it works, and I swing the door open and step into the brisk early morning air. I love the smell, feel, and look of Fall; I breathe in deeply. Starting my jog, I tap my earpiece twice.

"Running playlist."

Vouna is a clean, pleasant, small town, and I head for the center, or what would be considered downtown I suppose. We have no stores; they are not necessary since anything we need we order from the Console. There is a small café and a restaurant for socializing purposes, as well as a gym and a hair and nail salon.

Passing identical houses, the only variation being color, I wave to the occasional neighbor sitting on their porch drinking coffee or tending to their flowers. One or two of them wave back, but the others just stare, so I give up waving. As quiet and pleasant as this town is, gossip still happens.

I pause about three miles into my run and bend with my hands on my knees, taking in deep, slow breaths as I wait for my heartrate to go down. Suddenly, a timid but attractive blonde-haired woman about fifteen years my senior waves me over, a bottle of cold water in her hand. Glad for the distraction, and the fact that someone isn't afraid to speak with me, I straighten and walk over, tapping my earpiece to pause the music.

*Besides, I forgot my water and my throat is protesting my absentmindedness.*

"Hi, Mrs. Reeghan!" I greet her with a forced smile.

"Oh, please, call me Cora!"

As she hands me the water, I notice the weariness in her face. She has three children in their teens, and her husband is a Defense Officer. He is rarely home, but she always seems happier when he is gone, which seems odd; most unions are happier together.

When I was little I knew her as a very outgoing young woman, and she even babysat for my parents a few times. Once she was married, however, she became somewhat of a recluse, mostly whenever her husband was home. Rumors have it that he is abusive, but I am not one to pry; we only have the simple relationship of neighbors.

"Thank you, Cora."

"Anytime…" She seems to hesitate for a moment. "Are you alright, Lila?"

The question seems strange to me, but it warms my heart a little to actually have someone ask. I take a swig of water and swallow, shrugging my shoulders.

"I've been better… but also worse." I swallow again, trying not to let my thoughts reflect on the recent events.

She nods and purses her lips in thought for a moment, then suddenly she reaches out to grasp my forearm, her piercing blue eyes earnestly searching mine.

"If you need anything. Let me know. I know..." She stops herself, but only for a moment, conviction growing in her tone. "It's not easy to be married to an officer. He may be charming, but a union is different... so different."

"I wouldn't know, I haven't met my husband yet."

I add quickly as I realize I sound insensitive, "I'm sorry, I didn't mean to be dismissive. I appreciate your concern."

Her eyes grow wide in disbelief. "How? I mean..." She stops as someone jogs by and waves.

"I don't know, I was being collected and..." I pause midsentence as the recollection flashes in my mind. "I woke up the next morning and found the Union Document on my table."

Somehow saying this aloud to someone else lifts a bit of the mental malaise, and instead of the haze, a sudden stirring of anger wells up. I suppress it for the moment while in the company of Cora, who gives my arm one more gentle grip before releasing me.

"I am so sorry, Lila, I had no idea."

"It's alright. I would rather not be the talk of the town, really."

"Don't worry, they won't hear anything from me," she assures.

"Mom!" One of her kids yells from the doorway. "Dad's calling!"

Cora's face goes somber for a moment before she gives me a gentle smile.

"I suppose I should take that...and remember what I said. If you need anything."

I simply nod and wave as she jogs back to her house. I resume my run, leaving the music paused as the clouds of melancholy slowly lift, and my mind forms questions.

*I need to find out who he is and how this happened. And where do I go from here?*

I am glad I wasn't taken, but the unknown is still there; not knowing makes me uneasy. I suppose that is normal, but I feel I am missing something else important. Reaching the house, I open the door which I had left unlocked. The first thing I notice is a flashing image on my

Console indicating I have a new notification. Grabbing a health bar, I peel back the wrapping and step toward the screen.

"APA, play message."

"Yes, Lila."

A friendly-sounding female voice chimes in. "Congratulations, Lila, you have been selected for the position of Town Medic. Your additional training begins tomorrow, here, and you will be ready to start in six months."

*What?? What happened to Kassy?*

It suddenly dawns on me that Kassy, the one who originally had the medic position, may have left with Gam. They are siblings after all, and even though I did not know her very well, I instinctively liked her. Things are finally processing in my brain; things I never thought to ask.

*If Gam is missing, and Kassy, who else left with them?*

I have only a few friends, and now that my thoughts are clearer, I realize they would have come to my door by now with all the rumors.

*Unless they were scared? And what type of friend am I to not contact them for two whole weeks?*

*I really have been just feeling miserable and sorry for myself.* I ponder somberly.

I know what I should do now as I tap my earpiece once.

"Call Kassy Abarash."

"I'm sorry, that contact info has been redacted."

"Call Jona Paventi."

"I'm sorry, that contact info has been redacted."

A knot forms in my stomach, and I swallow before trying the next one.

"Call Tess Jenkins."

"I'm sorry, that contact info has been redacted."

"Call Jain Terrence."

"I'm sorry, that contact info has been redacted."

And finally.

"Call Gamar Abarash."

"I'm sorry, that contact info has been redacted."

I slump down on the chair in front of my Console, and I stare at the blank screen, a sinking feeling creeping over me.

"APA..." I am not sure why I haven't done this sooner, but I am terrified of the answer. "Where is Gamar Abarash."

"Gamar Abarash has been transferred to Oshana to be penalized for misconduct. Contact is prohibited."

"APA, where is Kassy Abarash?"

"Kassy Abarash has been transferred to Oshana to..."

I numbly go through the remaining names, and each answer is the same. I feel like someone hit me with a med-bus, at least mentally, and the anger I felt earlier is back with a force. Placing the half-eaten health bar on the desk, I lift the empty picture frame and hurl it across the room. It hits the wall and the glass shatters, clinking as it showers down to the hardwood floor. No scream, no tears, just anger.

*Is this how it's going to be, God?! Couldn't You have helped them?! They trusted You!!*

# | 6 |

# Routine

"APA, who is Don J. Bachman?"

"Major Don J. Bachman is an officer in the Defense Industry. He has been awarded the Manda Medal for excelling in the field of Intelligence, the Meod Medal for being wounded..."

"Stop. Still no images? Location?"

"No, I am sorry, those details are classified."

"Thank you, APA, that will be all."

Even though it has been nearly six months, I still ask the same question every morning. There is a strange feeling, however, that one day the answer will be different.

*Maybe I will even see what he looks like.*

My anger when I first learned of my friends' fates has leveled to a strong determination. I will leave one day, but not yet.

The opportunity to advance my skills in the medical field might give me the chance to be more prepared for being out on my own. I had already had a couple years of minor medical studies under my belt, but this additional training gives me a good improvement on the knowledge I had already.

I have added other activities as well, in preparation, such as frequent day-hikes in the foothills and guided extreme hikes in The Wilds. Despite my extreme fear of heights, I have even taken some basic rock-climbing classes. Let's just say I am not a huge fan.

Despite the classes and guided hikes, I have become accustomed to solitude, as the only person in town I usually speak with is Cora. She has become my new coffee companion, and it helps ease the pain I still feel from my friends and stops these walls around me from talking, but we're still not particularly close friends.

I flip through my digital calendar, noting that next week will be my first day on the job as the new town medic. There has been a temporary one in place, and she has helped with my hands-on training. Most of the diagnostics are done via the Console with APA, so the majority of my skills required will be the direct physical care and dispensing of medicine for injuries or illnesses. For anything beyond my ability, like major surgery, the patient will be transferred north.

I haven't spoken with God since yelling at Him that day. It's useless. Everything is up to me now to make things happen, so I have buried myself in education and as much research as the Console would allow me. After additional approval from Defense Officers back at the facility, it has even allowed me to learn how to identify poisonous plants compared to edible ones.

"Just in case a child ingests something during a hike, and I have to act fast," I had used as an excuse.

This week is a light week for studies, being my last, but I have my own studies to add.

"APA, medical videos on setting broken bones."

"Broken bones are set by advanced surgeons; your Medic position requirement is to stabilize the patient."

"What if the Med-bus is late or delayed somehow? My patient and their comfort and wellbeing are my top priority, especially if it is a child."

There is a significant pause in APA's reply.

*Perhaps she is consulting Defense again?* I hold my breath for a moment.

"Your request has been approved by a facility Defense Officer, Lila."

I breathe a sigh of relief as the video options pop up on the display, and I start with the first one.

*This will take the rest of my time this week.*

# | 7 |

# Spy

Sitting by his Console at the facility, Don goes through the security requests which constantly spill in from other Consoles in the towns. He quickly spots one from Lila's and selects it for review. APA's writeup appears on the screen.

"Lila Bachman has requested to study setting broken bones. As a basic medic, she is not required to learn this skill but has made the following statement: 'What if the Med-bus is late or delayed somehow? My patient and their comfort and wellbeing are my top priority, especially if it is a child.' Should I deny or approve access?"

Without hesitation, Don selects "Approve" and moves on to the next request on his list.

"Playing favorites?"

Marc's comment makes Don jump a bit and his jaw tense.

"Spying on my screen again?"

Marc laughs and punches him in the shoulder. "Relax, I was just teasing. So, when are you finally going to go see her?"

"Hopefully soon, but I have been busy, and the Commander still hasn't let up on me after that incident."

"I've noticed that. At least your hard work has paid off. Congratulations on your advanced clearance! Pretty soon you'll be promoted to Lieutenant Colonel, and I'll have to call you 'sir'."

"Thanks." Don grins. "I doubt it about the Colonel thing; I'm not that lucky. Speaking of clearance, though, I gotta go down there and check a few things. Catch you later."

"Isn't it a bit late? Everyone has pretty much closed up shop down there," Marc challenges.

After a slight hesitation, Don replies, lifting an eyebrow. "Security is part of my job. When they close up is the most important time to check on things."

"Copy that. I'll just sit here with these countless boring requests until the shift change."

Bachman smiles and gives Marc a slap on the back as he passes by. "Goodnight, Marc."

"'Night, Don"

What Marc doesn't notice is Don's increased heartrate as he steps outside their office and heads down the hall to the elevators. He stands with his arms down by his side, waiting for the doors to open, his hands clenching and unclenching. After what seems like an eternity for him, the doors open and he steps in just as an older woman in a lab coat steps out.

"Evening doc," he nods curtly, expertly hiding the nervousness in his voice.

She smiles and returns a nod. "Goodnight, Major."

Taking out his own security card, he taps it against the digi-pad of the elevator and presses Sublevel 10. Forcing himself to breath deliberately in and out, he calms his nerves and feels his heart slow to almost normal. As the elevator descends, he reaches his hand into his uniform slacks, his fingers touching a folded photo, and he pulls it out. He unfolds the image, and a faint smile crosses his features before he refolds and places it back where it was.

The doors open to a long, well-lit hall, either side lined with numerous glass-walled rooms. As he walks forward, his service boots clap on the concrete in a steady rhythm. His glance wanders to the multiple surveillance cameras and then to the rooms themselves, most of them filled with research equipment, everything stark and clean. A bead of sweat traces down the side of his forehead as he glances over his shoulder. Being the only one there doesn't ease his tension and only makes him more wary, especially since the cameras are watching.

Using his security clearance again, he opens the door to the last room. Instead of being filled with lab machinery, this room has computer towers from floor to ceiling, the sound of the cooling fans somewhat deafening. He sits himself at one of four access displays and taps the screen until it lights up.

"Hello. What can I do for you, Major Bachman?" APA's distinct voice resounds over the fans.

"I need file numbers 0425 to 0550 on this chip," Don replies while clicking a data chip into one of many open slots.

"Access to those files is restricted. Please let me verify your clearance."

"Access denied." APA's reply is quicker than he expected.

"It was worth a try," the Major mumbles and ignores her as he quickly types in an override command and extracts the files.

"What are you doing, Major Bachman? I will have to report this to your Commander, and it will go on your record. Using the override code is in violation of your contract with the Defense Industry."

"Fine," he dismissively mutters and grabs the data chip, securing it in the buttoned chest pocket of his uniform jacket.

Hastening his pace, he leaves the room and jogs down the hall to the elevator. Estimating he has, at most, ten minutes to leave the facility before the Commander gets the notice and comes storming over to confront him, he hurriedly taps his clearance card and presses Ground Level. His foot fidgets as he waits for the doors to open. Without waiting for the doors to fully part, he dashes out from the elevator and continues his jog toward the main lobby, which is clear across the facility. His thoughts go into a brief prayer.

*Please, God, give me time to leave without anyone getting hurt.*

Before he nears and passes the front desk, he slows his pace to a normal walk and straightens his uniform jacket, nodding to the attendant. The guards at the door give a sharp salute and he returns it, exiting into the cool night air. He sees his hover bike halfway across the lot, about 50 yards, along with almost two dozen other hover-cycles and biodiesel vehicles. The close spots are reserved for the scientists.

*Almost there.* He sucks in a breath as he glances at his watch. *Eleven minutes.*

Then he hears the voice of one of the guards behind him.

"Major Bachman!"

*Shit.*

# | 8 |

# Defector

Swinging my legs over the edge of the bed, I feel a tingle of apprehension. Something is different, but I am not sure what. It's only six am, earlier than I am used to because I am typically a late riser, but this is my wake-up time now; it will have to be for my new position next week.

I take a quick, cold shower to wake myself up, and I braid my damp hair. Donning a pair of exercise sweats, a hoody, and my jogging sneakers, I glance outside to see the frost clinging to the trees, the scenery subtly lit by a partial moon. It may be April, but the air still gets quite cold out here near the mountains.

It will be two hours before I have to go into the clinic to start my final hands-on evaluations, in the meantime I decide to eat a small breakfast of yogurt and fresh fruit. Turning on the living room light, I take a spoonful from my bowl and raise it to my mouth while walking to the Console. After swallowing, I dip for another spoonful and go through my usual routine.

"APA, who is Don J. Bachman."

"Former Major Don J. Bachman is a Defector of the Defense Industry and is sought after for the crime of theft. If you see him, please notify authorities immediately. It is prohibited to speak with this Defector."

My spoonful of yogurt falls back into the bowl, but my mouth stays gaping open in a moment of shock.

*What does this mean for me, now?!*

The sinking feeling is accentuated as I hear the locks on the doors and windows click into place.

# | 9 |

# Timing

Don shuts the lights off on his bike and relies on the faint moonlight filtering through the clouds. He had barely made it; the guard already had his hand on him before he could make a run for it, and he had quite the struggle getting free. The bonus is that he now has an AR in addition to his sidearm. The drawback is obvious in the throbbing of his calf muscle where he had caught a round from the second guard before having to fire upon him with the acquired weapon.

*Drones will be in the air soon,* he reminds himself as he notices a familiar landmark and pulls off the main road.

Stopping at a small, abandoned house, he steps off his hover bike and walks through the doorless entrance, favoring his right leg. It is a wonder the house is still standing; the ceiling sags and most of the wood is rotting, but Don isn't using it for shelter.

*At least not this time.*

Using a small flashlight to illuminate his environment, he reaches in a barely intact cabinet and pulls out a large backpack. Digging out a med-kit from the pack, he tosses his bloodied pants into the cabinet, removing the photo first, and quickly wraps a bandage around his wound, even though he can feel the bullet still deep in his muscle.

*I can take care of it later.*

Tugging out some earth-toned cargo pants and a grey tac jacket from his pack, he takes off his uniform jacket, looking morosely at the ribbons over the left chest. He had done things he regrets to receive those.

*God forgive me, I didn't know.*

He removes the data chip from the pocket and tosses the jacket into the cabinet with his pants. He grimaces as he tugs on his cargo pants and swiftly throws his tac jacket on over his standard issue beige t-shirt. After slipping the photo and chip into a zippered chest pocket, he removes one more thing from the pack, stuffs the med-kit back in, and pulls the pack onto his shoulders.

Half jogging, half hobbling, he goes to his bike and looks down at the device he had taken out. Placing it over his AutoMap, he presses a switch on the side and activates the scrambling device, which will disorient the drones. He sits quietly for a brief moment and stares ahead to The Wilds, fighting fatigue from the hours he has been awake. Glancing at his watch, his jaw clenches in apprehension.

*5:30 am, one more hour and I'll be there.*

Pressing the power button on his hover-cycle, he heads back for the maintained highway. He is reluctant to stay on such a main thoroughfare, but he needs speed more than stealth. They will be after her next.

*I'll be there soon, Lila.*

# | 10 |

# Reunion

My throat tightens in a bit of panic. I place my bowl of yogurt down on the desk and try both doors.

"Unlock"

"Access denied. Please remain indoors for your safety."

A window. "Unlock"

"Access denied. Please remain indoors for your safety."

The next window. "Unlock"

"Access denied. Please remain indoors for your safety." APA's voice grates on me like nails on a chalkboard right now.

"My safety, my ass. YOU locked me in here so you can come and collect me!" My retort is dripping with rage.

"An Official will be on their way to assist you in your relocation in 20 minutes."

"The hell they will," I snarl as I glance at my watch, the time reading 6:34. "I have until 6:54"

I yank the communication devices from my ears and drop them to the floor, crushing them beneath my heel with gusto. The ire inside me that has silently built up over the past six months has added to my determination, and somehow the fear I have lived with has diminished to a hushed whisper in the back of my consciousness.

It is still barely twilight, and suddenly I hear a hover bike pull up and steps approaching the door.

*That was quick.*

Swiveling around, my eyes search for something, anything, yet I am not sure what I can do against an armed officer. The handle of the door wiggles, followed by the sound of a fist pounding on the solid slab.

*Why can't they unlock the door?*

I dismiss the thought, rush into the kitchen, and grab a kitchen knife, while at the same moment my large picture window in the bedroom comes to mind. It doesn't have metal straps between the panes like the other windows, so I can break that and escape.

Without hesitation, I dash down the hall, reaching my room just in time to see my own patio chair come crashing in through the glass. From the doorway where I am the window is on the left wall, and I watch as the hurled chair causes shards to scatter across the room to my bed. The wooden seat settles to the floor amidst the broken glass, the intruder still out of my view.

Knowing my only way of escape is being blocked, I grasp the knife firmly, ready to put up a fight. I watch as the butt of a gun clears the sill of any remaining sharp edges, and a leg swings over and into the room. The light outside has increased enough, combined with my still-lit bedside lamp, that it should allow me to have the advantage of surprise in the dimly lit hall. I simply plan to rush and dash, maybe even take the officer's bike.

The rest of the person slips into view, a tall, perhaps 6' 2", fit man in his late 20's, but not in the usual officer's uniform. He wears earth-toned cargo pants, an unzipped grey tac jacket over a beige shirt, and a brown backpack. A handgun is strapped to his right leg, and he holds the rifle he had just used to clear the glass by his side.

I nearly rush forward as planned, but his presence and lack of uniform take me aback for a bit and I give his face a good look. Sandy blonde hair, closely shaved on the sides with a tousled two inches on the top, compliments the sage-green eyes set in a lean, strong face.

*Why do I know this face...?*

My stomach is nearly in my throat as the knife slips from my fingers and clangs loudly on the floor.

"Jax."

His name comes out in a cracked voice, and my feet feel immovable. He rushes forward and grabs my wrist, not roughly, but firmly, and pulls me toward the now-glassless window frame.

"No time to explain, Lil', we have to go before they get here. You're not safe anymore."

I can't even say anything, my throat is tight, and I am trying to decide if I am shocked or thrilled; this is the first time anyone has called me Lil' since he left. Even so, I comply and, careful to not touch the shards, climb through the opening and rush just behind him to the front of my house. He releases my wrist from his grasp as we reach the hover-cycle I had heard earlier, which I guess is his, and jumps on, handing me his helmet.

Without comprehending what I am really doing, I slip on the helmet, get on the bike behind him, and grasp onto the side bars right behind me. His backpack, however, encroaches upon some of my space. Noticing this, he leans forward to give me the room I need, and without another word he starts his bike and heads down a side road.

I hear the sirens of a Defense vehicle from the opposite direction, and my jaw clenches in uneasiness until I can't hear them anymore. Which thankfully is pretty quickly as Jax accelerates and takes the bike cross-country.

I have so many questions, but there is no time to speak, even though the bike only makes a low humming sound as it smoothly travels over the ground. I realize I have never been on a hover-vehicle and never in any vehicle this fast, and although there is an exhilarating feeling, there is also nervousness which prevents me from relaxing. Then there is the question on the top of most of my thoughts...

*Who is this man that I am trusting with my life right now? Is he really the Jax I remember?*

# | 11 |

# The Hut

It seems like an eternity on this bike and honestly uncomfortable, but I bear with it and keep my grip on the side bars until my muscles are aching. We get onto an old road, at least, so the ride seems a little less death-defying now that we are no longer dodging trees and rocks. I estimate it has been nearly two hours of riding, and I wonder how exhausting it must be for Jax.

I shiver as the wind cuts right through my hoodie as it has done the entire ride. Hunger and tiring muscles make me wish the ride were over, but I don't know where we are going, and I also know the farther we are, the better.

*I wish I at least had something warmer.*

Finally, my arms begin to numb a bit to the discomfort, and I start to look around more now that the terrain is fully illuminated by the morning sun. Our surroundings have switched from forest to open fields with low butte-like hills, mostly brown and dotted with decrepit houses. They fly by just as fast as I notice them.

Far off to our right, which I am guessing is east, I see a thin glint along the ground.

*A maintained road, maybe?*

My gaze drifts downward, looking at the details of the ride. I am not very mechanically inclined, but I do know the hover-cycle is propelled using magnetism and very little energy, a technological wonder courtesy of The Direction. I scowl at the thought for a moment.

*At least it is serving a better purpose right now.*

My glance wanders to the back of Jax's head, his hair being ruffled by the wind, helmetless. He is leaned low over the handles and has his elbows resting on his knees, I am guessing for support, his broad shoulders tense.

I don't have any more time to look things over, though, as I notice he steers the bike off the path and into a small scattering of gnarly trees between two low hills. Unexpectedly, a house appears before us, quite in disarray, but amazingly still standing. It looks to be made of wooden logs, and the roof seems to be sheets of steel, although a couple spots are caved in.

Jax stops the bike, and I slide off, stretching my numb arms. Now standing still, even with the wind the sun is warming, and I don't feel as chilled anymore, although I am still quite a bit shaky. The adrenaline from the morning is long gone, and I am left with exhaustion, hunger, and questions.

I watch silently as Jax steps off his bike and he, likewise quiet and without a glance toward me, walks through the doorless entrance of the house. That's when I notice him favor his right leg and see a small stain of blood through the lower leg of his cargos.

Instinctively, I am concerned but hesitant as I follow him into the house. Looking around, I notice the house is a simple one-room cabin, cabinets barely in one piece, a caved-in fireplace at one end, and on the other is a metal bed frame with no mattress.

*No bathroom.* I suddenly realize.

But most of my hikes back home involved doing without the comforts of a bathroom. Still, it makes the reality set in a little more.

*I'm not in civilization anymore.*

I am now what they would probably refer to as 'a savage'. Which makes me wonder how many 'savages' there are out there.

"Are you alright?"

Jax's throaty voice behind me brings me out of my reverie. His voice is obviously much deeper than it used to be, but the concern I hear is the same as I remember.

"Yes, I am fine. Are *you* alright?" I ask pointedly, gesturing to his leg.

A sudden but brief grin flits across his face, and he goes a few paces to put his back to a wall, him facing the door, and sits down on the wood-planked floor. He had already removed his pack and now places it next to him, his rifle down alongside it, and stretches his injured leg out.

"You always did notice the little things about people. I guess that much hasn't changed," he remarks quietly, his glance only briefly meeting mine.

I have so many questions in line to ask him that I can't even decide on one, so I say nothing.

*Might as well do what you studied for,* a small voice speaks inside me.

Jax already has the med-kit out from his pack and his pants leg rolled up to reveal a blood-stained, haphazardly bandaged lower leg. Going over, I kneel beside his leg and reach my hand out for the kit, my eyes meeting his for a moment as he lifts his gaze.

"I can help."

There is a certain odd look of confidence in his face as he wordlessly hands it to me. Looking away, I open the case to see what I can work with. My hands are shaking, though, probably from part tension and mostly the hunger.

*I probably should eat first; I don't want to do more damage.*

"Would you happen to have a health bar I could have?" I ask somewhat sheepishly, realizing I have nothing and am relying on him for everything.

It feels disconcerting; I have had to rely on only myself for some time now.

He looks over to the pack and reaches into a side pouch, procuring one of the typical health bars distributed by the diet management department.

"I have one left. The rest is dried beef," he comments while handing the last bar over, adding with a small smile, "it also happens to be mint."

I cannot help but grin a little.

*He remembers my favorite.*

"We can share it," I offer, peeling the wrapper.

"Thanks. I'll wait until you're done, though." He nods to his leg.

"Okay…"

I hurriedly take a few bites, sitting back on my heels. I leave half left, rewrap it, and place it next to Jax.

"Were you shot?"

"Yes."

"Is the bullet still in there?"

"Yes."

"Did you try to take it out yet?"

"No."

"Are you feeling lightheaded or anything?"

"No"

The one-word answers are irritating me a little; I want to know more.

*Like how it happened.*

I guess I will have to dig later, but first I have to dig… *for a bullet.*

I swallow, suddenly nervous. I have stitched wounds before, but a bullet was not part of my hands-on practice. I was able to study for it, but bullet wounds in a town with no guns is highly unlikely.

Cleaning my hands with the sanitizer from the pack, I pull out what I think I need, including a Medic-issued windlass tourniquet just in case. As my fumbling fingers remove the soaked bandage, there is very little bleeding, fortunately, and I douse it with the cleaning fluid.

Hearing his breath hiss a little, I frown but don't look up from my task at hand.

"Sorry, should have warned you."

"It's ok," is his simple reply.

As I examine the wound, I give a hiss of my own as I realize it might need to be opened wider and that means it *will* bleed.

"Do what you need to do, you've got this."

It is as though he knows what I am thinking, *or maybe he has been through this before?* I can only assume this is something familiar to him. The confidence in his voice is directed at me, however, and I wonder how he can trust me this much when he has been away for so long.

Pushing my thoughts to the side, I force myself to concentrate only on this in front of me; a sort of tunnel vision focus that I sometimes get when extremely involved in something. The sounds of the creaking house, the steady wind through the trees, and the singing of morning birds all slowly fade. I can still hear my heart pounding in my ears, and I try to shut that out too. Applying the tourniquet first, I attempt to recreate the procedures in the videos to extract the bullet, reminding myself where veins and nerves are located.

*They made it look so easy,* I bemoan, a line of sweat trickling down the side of my face despite the coolness of the air around me.

I am vaguely aware of my patient tensing to battle the discomfort, but he is surprisingly quiet and keeps still. Finally, there is a tiny *clunk* as I manage to work the chunk of metal out, and it hits the floor. I breathe a sigh of relief at nearly the same time as I hear Jax exhale.

I look down at my bloodied hands and suddenly realize that I had forgotten to take out some zip-stitch sutures from the kit.

"Damnit," I mutter.

"Here."

I look up to see his hand extended toward me with three sutures in their sanitary casing.

"Thanks."

The zip-stitch works without a needle and thread. A super adhesive tape is applied on either side of the wound, and a zip strap attached to both sides is tightened until they click closed to bring the edges of the wound together. It's fast, it's easy, and most importantly less painful than the old-fashioned way it used to be done.

Three zip-stitches, and I am relatively satisfied with the effectiveness. Just to be sure, however, and because I suspect we will have to be on the move more than just the zip-stitches can handle, I wrap the injury with clean bandages as well.

After releasing the tourniquet, I look up and see that during the stitches and bandaging he has already eaten the rest of the health bar and is now taking a drink from a bottle of water.

"Nicely done," he comments simply, handing me the bottle of water and reaching forward to roll his pants leg back down.

I hadn't realized how parched I am, and I take a large swig of water before remembering that my hands are still red and sticky. Cleaning my hands first with the remaining sanitizer, I then clean the medic tools as best as I can before putting them away. I zip the case closed, and that's when I notice him watching me, something somber and almost sad in his expression.

"You're not the Lila I remember."

My brows dip in confusion, and I avert my gaze while shoving the kit back in the pack. "I don't think I've changed much."

"Yeah. You have. The Lila I knew would have been terrified to do this. I was always the one taking care of *you.*"

A rueful half-smile crosses my face, and I look him directly in the eyes, a twinge of condemnation unintentionally entering my tone; a trace of my suppressed anger threatens to surface.

"Well... You weren't there for me."

*Why did I say that? I know this isn't his fault. And honestly, it's a good thing that I became more independent, right? I don't even know what he has gone through.*

"I'm sorry," I murmur, lowering my head as I move the pack away and sit cross-legged beside him. "I didn't mean it that way, it's just been... frustrating."

I look back at him, hoping he isn't angry or hurt by my words as I push my own ire back down.

He sighs, leaning his head back against the wall for a moment to look to the ceiling, his lips moving soundlessly.

*Is he... praying?*

Looking at me once again, his countenance is strained, as though he is dealing with an internal struggle.

"No. You're right, I could have been there sooner. And deep down you know you meant what you said; you were always honest about your feelings. But in my defense, I was there for you when it most mattered, and by the Grace of God I am here for you now," he says this softly but firmly as he removes something folded from his jacket pocket and hands it to me.

"Please don't start preaching God to me..." I begin dryly as I unfold the paper.

My breath catches as I recognize the photo as the one that had been taken from my desk. The one of me and Jax as little kids; the smiles on our faces a small example of the untroubled life we once had.

"How...?"

I am bewildered, my brain not processing what he is trying to say with the photo, other than he must have taken it somehow or took it from someone. My thoughts race from one option to the next, and I finally peel my gaze from the photo in my hand.

"Were you there? Do you know Major Don Bachman, then?"

Without answering, he pushes himself to his feet and makes his way across the room to the kitchen section, only a slight limp as a tell-tale sign of his injury. He takes what looks to be a dark blue uniform from the cabinet and brings it over, dropping it onto my lap. Slumping down next to me, he sighs heavily and waits, his head against the wall.

Unfolding the clothes, I set aside the blood-stained slacks, obviously from when Jax was shot as the location is the same, and I examine the jacket. I see the multiple ribbons of a well decorated officer beside the left lapel and the ranking of major on the arm. I inhale sharply, my eyes resting on the name plate.

"You. *You* are Major Bachman. Wait. Did you approve my additional studies too?"

"Yes. You needed to be prepared for when I came for you. You'll need those skills where we are going."

It finally all makes sense, and suddenly I feel absolutely wretched and selfish for what I had said earlier.

"Jax..." I look over, and impulsively I reach a hand to grasp his. "I'm so sorry, I didn't know. You *were* there the entire time."

He squeezes my hand and smiles remorsefully. "Not the entire time. There are a lot of things I regret from the early days of my service."

Standing, he pulls me until I am on my feet and then releases my hand, reaching for his pack. I had half expected a hug, and I contemplate going for one; to feel secure in one of his embraces again. Part of me wants things to feel like they used to be with Jax, but they don't. I realize he is different and more reserved. I am different too, to be honest, and I leave the thought at that.

"But we can discuss that another time. We have to keep moving, Lila. We have at least three hours of travel."

"I have so many questions, though," I protest, "and besides, you should probably get some rest."

"I wish I could," he confesses, and I can see the weariness in his face. "But there is no time for that. The satellites come in-line with this area in another hour and they'll track us."

"Let me carry the pack, at least," I insist as I take the heavy bag, *heavier than I thought it would be*, and sling it over my shoulders. "Oomph, what the hell do you have in here, barbells?"

He gives a reserved smirk before heading for the bike, strapping his rifle across the front of himself. "Ammo tends to be heavy. You sure you've got it?"

"Yes," I reply with somewhat false confidence and follow him.

The pack is going to dig into my shoulders, but he is the one who has to drive, and I consider that to be the more grueling position to be in, especially with an extra passenger. He again hands me his helmet, and I put it on and settle in behind him on the bike, this time wrapping my arms around his waist. I can feel him take a deep breath in and then sigh before he starts the machine and speeds away cross-country, eastward.

*Where in the world are we going?*

And then a second thing dawns on me.

*In all legality we are married... I wonder how he feels about that. Or is it like what I tried with Gam, where it is just out of necessity? And honestly...how do I feel about this?*

With his steady breathing against my arms, I feel only a hint of the comfort I used to with him in the past; yes, I feel safe, but that is dissimilar. Back at the cabin I had seen the quiet intensity behind his eyes. The intensity is something different; something of determination. I sense that fortitude strongly emanating from him, and it is something I feel I should gain for myself.

*But how?*

# | 12 |

# Focused

She is right, he wasn't there for her, really, but he knows there had been no other way. It had taken him aback, though, when she grasped his hand; a reminder of younger days. Part of him wants to embrace that feeling, go right back to how it used to be and sweep her off her feet, but those days were before he knew who he was called to be.

He admits to himself that she has grown into an attractive woman, her long dark hair being one of his favorite features. Where once stood a gangly, sweet young girl, stands a tan, athletic woman, her once innocent dark eyes now a bright amber in the sunlight. What he sees in them, though, is anger hidden by a forced confidence. The other thing that makes him cautious is the resentment toward God he senses beneath her guardedness. Yet even with that, she is a catch for any man.

*But not for me,* he reflects in silence as he absently accelerates the ride, *her safety is part of a promise and an atonement for past sins. After this, the war against The Direction is first and foremost.*

*Keep me focused, Oh Lord.*

# | 13 |

# Arriving

An hour into our journey, the terrain becomes a lot rougher and our direction switches northward. I can see beneath the grass that there used to be a large road, bits of cracked and separated pavement still visible, but it is now a rough path broken up by trees, shrubs, and ground cover. The hover-vehicle breezes over the grasses, leaving little evidence of our travel.

Another hour in and the terrain has gradually increased in mountainous landscapes with an abundancy of pine trees, our course more northwest now. The growth is now so close that my knees nearly brush against leaves and twigs, and we are occasionally crowded against cliff faces.

"I wish I could go faster," Jax comments, weariness in his voice as he reduces our speed, glancing over his shoulder at me. "I'd rather not have us lose our legs on some of these trees, though."

"I can appreciate that," I retort with a grin, tucking my knees closer against the bike. "Where are we, by the way?"

"We're technically in the Oshana region."

Unexpectedly, to our right, the trees open up to a massive lake surrounded by pine-covered hills. The afternoon sun gleams across it and causes me to squint even with the helmet visor. Even at our measured pace, it passes by too quickly for me to enjoy it fully. Another moment, and I feel the bike decelerate as Jax pulls into a small path leading back south. He only goes a few hundred yards though, before he eases the vehicle into a brushy area.

"The rest is on foot," he confirms my guess as he glances at his watch.

I hand him the helmet, slide off the bike, and then tip back slightly as I am reminded of the weight of the pack. As a matter of pride, I glance and confirm Jax doesn't see as I shrug the pack more squarely onto my shoulders, grimacing. That's when I notice two other hoverbikes hidden beneath shrubbery right beside his.

*There must be other people...*

After covering his own bike with a camo cloth and branches, he turns as I am stamping the cramps out of my legs from the ride, giving me a scrutinizing glance up and down.

"I can take that now," he offers, nodding to the bulky load.

"Nope, I'm good."

"Lila, this is about speed, not pride. Drones will be in this area in less than an hour, and my scrambler is out of power. I've no doubt your strong, but now is not the time to prove it. We're already cutting it close."

I feel insulted at first, upset that he just assumes I am incapable, and then I feel inadequate because I know he is right. I reluctantly shrug the pack off and he takes it, shouldering it before briefly checking his rifle.

"What about your leg?" I challenge.

"I can handle that. You did a good patch job." He both shuts down my challenge and compliments me at the same time with a fleeting smile.

*Damnit.*

He walks ahead of me and leads the way at a quick pace. I watch his stride carefully, and he must be telling the truth because I can barely see a limp, so I look instead at the terrain around us.

Our path is relatively flat, but there are places on the sides where small cliffs shoot up and hills conceal much of the landscape beyond, not to mention the height of the pines along the trail are impressive to say the least.

Half an hour in, the temperature might be around fifty degrees Fahrenheit, but with my hoodie it feels like eighty at the pace we are keeping. Jax already stuffed his jacket into the backpack, and I wish I could take my outer layer off, but there is nothing but a sports bra beneath. Considering that, I am glad he has the backpack, although I can see his gait suffering from the fatigue now.

He stops and leans against a tree, tossing a partial bottle of water to me. I catch it and take a few gulps, trying not to finish the rest.

"Here, you need it more." I offer it back to him.

"I'm good, thanks. We'll be there soon anyway." He warily looks through the canopy of pines and into the clear skies as I finish the water.

"Like, how far?"

He glances around; I am guessing for landmarks and then looks at me. "Probably .7 miles."

"Please let me carry the pack. I assume you have been awake for well over 24 hours."

"Maybe I have. But it's less than a mile. Besides, you already look overheated in that sweater. I just needed a breather and we're good to go." His grimace says otherwise, and his jaw clenches as he shifts his weight off the tree.

I can't help but feel concern, despite wanting to chide him for possibly being a little prideful himself. "Jax, I got this. Yes, I agree, I wouldn't have made it the whole trek, but you're hurting and exhausted. I can take it the rest of the way."

He turns to head down the southbound path, but with a sigh he turns back and slips the pack off, handing it to me.

"Alright, fine."

I can't help but give a small triumphant smile, but I hide it quickly while shouldering the load. Leading the way again, he still has the limp, but his pace is steadier now. For me the pace is brutal with the increased weight. It's only for less than a mile, but I feel as though I am not nearly as strong as I thought I was. The final half mile is trudged in silence. Me because I can't speak beyond the heaving and him probably because he is listening for drones…

# | 14 |

# Drones

*She's tough, but maybe she needs to be humbled.*
*Then again, we all do.*

He can't help but smile a little as he hears her behind him, winded, but keeping the pace. His calf throbs, the pain shooting straight up his leg, but he ignores it and continues in silence, his hearing fixated on the sky and dreading the humming sound of the sentry drones.

*Just 200 hundred yards more.*

He can just barely see the cliff face through the thick trees. Even if he hears the drones, there is a chance they can dash and make it with the cover of the trees. Something tells him to fight harder through the fatigue and pain to quicken his pace, and he does.

*100 yards.*

And then comes the distant humming sound…

# | 15 |

# Into the Tunnels

"Run!" Jax suddenly yells, and I also hear the drone coming our way from the east. He tucks the stock of his rifle to his arm, holding it snug against himself as he breaks into a sprint. I try to keep on his heels, but I am slowly losing ground, my muscles threaten to seize, and my shoulders protest the weight.

A solid cliff face looms right before us through the trees and at first, I think we will run straight into it, but the gaping mouth of a cave swallows us instead. Jax and I keep going until we hit the shadows, then he stops and presses his back to the wall of the cave, sliding down to a sitting position and gasping for air.

I myself hurl the pack down and drop to my knees, my hands on the sandy floor of the cave. Heaving in a breath, I instinctively hold it as we hear the drone buzz overhead and leave, but both of us stare silently at the roof of the cave until the hum is no longer audible.

"That was too close," Jax groans. "We should have been here sooner."

I sit back on my heels, watching as he rests his head on the stone wall and closes his eyes. Forcing myself to my feet, I walk over and sit beside him.

"I'm sorry," I say simply.

I feel I have caused this, whether being too slow or taking too long to react.

"No, I took it too easy, I should have pushed the limits the whole trip."

"In other words, you were too careful because of me..."

"Maybe..." he admits, "but that's on me, not you. I should have trusted you to handle it."

"You also have your leg, you know," I remind him quietly.

A wry grin crosses his face, which is covered in sweat, but he doesn't open his eyes. "You know I've had worse. APA had to have mentioned that when you asked about me every single day."

My face flushes in embarrassment, realizing he must have seen my search logs from APA, and I protest. "I was pissed off someone I didn't know married me, and I wanted to know who he was."

"Every day?"

"It was a coping mechanism..." I mumble in reluctant admittance. "Besides, something told me one day it would be different.... And it was. That's how I knew something was happening."

"Something told you... maybe God?" He looks at me now, and even in the shadows of the cave I can see his green eyes clearly challenging me for a reply, as though testing me.

"I don't know..." I disclose, pulling my eyes away from his gaze. "But why would He care about that? He hasn't cared about anything before," I add morosely. "Maybe it's instinct."

"You don't believe that. We're still alive, isn't that enough proof of His care for us?"

My jaw clenches, and I finally spit it out. "I am angry at God for letting so many be taken away from me. It's not like I can flip a switch and believe that He actually cares for me just because I happen to survive. Besides, I've cursed Him so many times this past year. I don't think He wants to hear from me anymore, so why would He talk to me?"

I huff in indignation and get to my feet, moving away a few paces to grab the backpack and put it back on.

"Where to, now?" I ask, trying to change the subject.

Jax pushes himself to his feet, using the wall for support with a grimace.

"I'm sorry, I didn't mean to push." His voice is genuine but also tinged with discomfort. "We're actually here and being watched already."

He gestures toward a small black spot high up on the north wall, identifying a camera. "So, just a brief walk down the left tunnel."

He attempts to shift his weight to his right leg and hisses in discomfort.

Watching his pain, the anger I have for his 'preaching' subsides, and I feel ashamed of my defiance. Stepping swiftly over, I take his right arm and put it over my shoulder, offering support for his vulnerable side. He surprisingly doesn't protest, slings his rifle to his left shoulder, and uses the support, the extreme fatigue apparent on his ashen face.

"How long *have* you been awake?" I query, my right eyebrow raising as we slowly head down the left tunnel.

He raises his left hand and counts on his fingers, his head tilted down. "Possibly 35 hours. Give or take."

"Good grief, why?! Nevermind. I think I know the answer. I'm not worth killing yourself over."

"Every life is worth something," he quickly, though quietly, replies.

As we move deeper into the tunnel, motion-activated lights dimly illuminate our path, and I pause when I hear echoing steps ahead. My hand holding Jax's arm in place tenses with apprehension, and I stop my forward momentum.

"Don't worry, it's one of the crew," he assures.

The approaching footsteps come around the bend, and a familiar, baritone voice booms and echoes through the tunnel. "Jax, is that you? I hope that's who I think it is with you."

I look over and Jax's face, albeit weary, breaks into a sort of proud grin.

"Gam?!" I exclaim, not quite believing my ears.

None other than Gamar rounds the bend and his hulking presence is a sight for sore eyes. I have to remind myself that I am Jax's support right now, otherwise I would rush forward and embrace the towering man. Gam, however, rushes forward instead and takes over the support for Jax, his dark brows dipping in concern.

"What happened?"

"Too much to tell right now, other than the fact that Jax needs rest, and I need to make sure his stitches didn't break."

I am caught amid excitement for seeing Gam, puzzlement at how he is here, concern for Jax, and an odd sense of ease that leaves me more exhausted than relieved. Gam senses as always and with his free arm gives me a quick squeeze around my shoulders.

"I am so glad to see you here, Lila. Jax promised he'd bring you, and Jax always comes through with his promises. Let's get you to the main cavern."

"How are you here, though?" I ask as I follow at Gam's side.

I glance past him and see that Jax has a subtle smile of satisfaction. His silence is worrying, yet I guess it is to be expected with how long he has been awake.

"This man here arranged an 'accident' while I and the others were being transported north to the facility. His crew came and brought us here."

"Us?" My eyebrow lifts.

"Well… the four of us that survived," Gamar clarifies with slight sadness. "But we shall discuss that once we get settled."

Gam leads through a series of tunnels, until finally we arrive at a large, cavernous area, the ceiling twenty feet up and every area well lit. There is no one else here at the moment, and the silence is only disturbed by the echoing of our steps on the now-rocky surface.

Arranged on the sides are equipment boxes, computer towers with access screens, a massive battery bank, tables with papers and data tablets crowding them, and even what looks to be an eating area with a steel dining table, at least six chairs around it. The 'kitchen' seems to be made of stacked crates and a camp stove, but it looks functional enough.

Some of the stone walls have openings to other tunnels, although most are short to the point you can see where they dead-end. A few of the shorter tunnels look like they are set up as bedrooms or bunkrooms, canvas hanging on rods acting as privacy screens. A lot of the stoney walls seem cut, not by nature but perhaps long ago from mining activities.

"Do we have a medic area?" I hope Kassy made it with Gam, because she is hands down a far better, more experienced medic than I am.

"Just get me to my bunk," Jax tells Gam, dismissing my question. "I just need some rest."

"You're also most likely dehydrated." I give Gam a pointed glance, and he nods in knowing agreement.

"Then hand me a water and I'll go to bed," Jax argues.

"We have a medic corner over here." Gam nods to the right of the cooking area where a well-lit area is viewable in a large alcove; this area also has a privacy panel of canvas. "It has come into use many times, yet no one to properly use it for a while. That is until now."

Gam flashes a quick grin in my direction.

"Kassy didn't make it." I say it as more of an observation than a statement and the slight slump in Gam's broad shoulders confirms.

"Sadly no," is his only comment.

I know how much he loved his older sister, and I am slowly realizing how much everyone has lost, not just myself.

We get as far as the dining area, and Jax suddenly peels himself away from Gam.

"I'm good... Just need to get some water, and then I will go to my own quarters. No need to baby me."

He gestures to one of the shorter tunnels, yet I am dubious as he steadies himself against a nearby chair.

"I'll get you the Hydra-thlete. That should help, right, Lila?" Gam looks over his shoulder as he reaches into a crate and pulls out a bottle of electrolyte water, something I have used many times during guided hikes.

"Definitely," I nod as I unceremoniously drop the backpack from my shoulders to the ground and collapse into a chair, thankful to be off my feet.

Jax slumps into one of the chairs with a grunt and a heavy sigh, Gam hands him a bottle, and then hands one to me as well. Twisting the cap open, I drain half of mine before realizing Jax hasn't even managed to open his.

"Jax?"

I notice his coordination is off, or maybe it's his grip strength, as he fumbles with the cap, and the frustration slowly builds in his expression.

"Oh, we also have bathroom facilities over there," Gam points to the alcove right of the medic area, not noticing what I am focused on and continues.

"They just need to be emptied occasionally. Unfortunately, that's my job…"

I barely hear his words as I lean forward toward Jax, watching his eyes close.

"Jax, can you hear me??"

# | 16 |

# Collapse

Collapsing into the chair, the room swims around him. His leg feels like it is on fire, and his head is pounding. Their voices are muffled to him as his awareness flits in and out. Jax knows she is right, the dehydration and exhaustion are hitting him harder than he thought, but he is determined to push through.

*Just some water and then sleep...*

For most of the traveling the task at hand kept him on his feet, and now that he is where he needs to be, his whole focus has suddenly fallen apart.

*I can't even get this damned bottle open...*

Finally, he stops trying and closes his eyes for a moment, just trying to gather his bearings.

*Thank you, God, for bringing us back safely...*

For a moment Jax feels like he is falling, but it is oddly soothing, so he doesn't fight it.

## | 17 |

## Catching Up

"Gam, help me!"

I dive from my chair and catch Jax just before his head hits the stone, but his unconscious body weighs me down to the point I am kneeling on the floor, maintaining a hold on at least his upper half. I kick myself for not realizing how bad off Jax really is.

"I've got 'im."

Gam rushes over and with relative ease, lifts Jax from the ground.

"He needs an IV," I instinctively direct. "We have those, right?"

"Yes," Gam replies as he pushes past the canvas across the medic area.

The med-room is simple but seems to be well stocked. Four cots line the left side, a short, wheeled swivel stool near them, while the other wall has shelves filled with supplies. At the back is another steel table with a sink, although there is no faucet and the drain ends at a downward crevice in the rock, possibly drainage from bygone days when mining was done here.

In the center is a tall stool beside a steel table which could serve easily as an operating table.

*Hopefully I never have to use that for anyone.*

I grimace at the thought but push it aside as Gam sets Jax down on one of the cots, and I immediately locate the isotonic solution hanging neatly on the supply wall. This is something I was fortunately able to practice often back at Vouna recently, and it isn't long before I have the solution hanging beside the cot and a venous line in place on Jax's left arm.

"Gam, can you bring me cleaning solution and gauze? I might need zip-stitch, too."

"No problem." He nods and returns in a matter of seconds with the requested items, holding them until I need them.

With Gam as my assistant, although he never looks at the wound, I complete the re-stitching and rebandaging relatively quickly.

"Anything else I can do?" Gam asks as he helps clean my hands by pouring the sanitizer on them while I rub them over the sink.

"Do you guys have a diagnostic tablet?"

"No, that requires APA, and APA means we'd be connected to The Direction."

"Gotcha." I am reminded of how inadequate my skills are without APA's diagnostics system. "How about a trauma scanner?"

To my delight, Gam reaches a higher shelf and pulls down a tablet-like device about twelve inches by sixteen with a wrist cuff attached and hands it to me.

"We were not sure how to use it," he adds.

"No worries. This is one thing I *am* able to use pretty well, thankfully."

Turning the scanner on, I switch it to vitals and place the wrist cuff on Jax's right arm. I absently bite my lower lip as I change the settings a bit, holding it above Jax, and complete a full body scan. Setting the med-scanner on the table, I start flipping through the images produced by the device.

Gam is looking over my shoulder, enthralled.

"So that's what that does. I can see the muscles, bones, veins; it's so clear. What are you looking for?" His brow dips in concern. "He was only shot in the leg, right?"

"Yes, and the bullet is out of course. I just want to make sure there are no complications. His disorientation, unconsciousness, elevated heart rate, and low blood pressure could be hypovolemia, which is extreme dehydration, and we are treating that with the IV. There is also the lack of sleep, but I want to rule out blood clots. He was on that bike for hours and who knows how long before that. I don't even know long ago he was injured."

I don't look up as I go through the images, filtering it to display only the details that I want to see.

"This is tough without APA. How did people use to do this before digital assistants?" Even with the strange initial rush of feeling in my element, I am noticing how tired my body really is, and I rub a hand across my face.

"He's in good hands."

Gam places his large, warm hand on my shoulder, his eyes watching Jax for a moment. He looks at me and suddenly smiles.

"You need food. I will make you some, and some coffee. Make sure you finish this, though. I'm no good with IV's, so you'd have to give yourself one," he declares, taking a bottle of Hydra-thlete from a nearby shelf and setting it next to me on the table.

Without waiting for a response, he leaves the med-room.

I haven't realized how famished I am until he says "food", and almost in agreement my stomach growls. Swigging from the bottle he left, I ignore my hunger.

Gam's whistling while he cooks makes me hum along a little, and I slowly relax as I resume my examination of the scans, which fortunately goes faster once I find the feature in the device which efficiently analyzes and displays possible abnormalities on its own. It's not as good as APA, but it helps.

I am able to study each likely anomaly the program presents, and there is nothing that I can see to indicate problems, so I set the med-scan down with a heavy sigh.

*I am just overthinking things. Is it fear or precaution?*

"Done?" Gam's voice stirs me from my thoughts, and I turn to see him at the opening of the canvas with two plates of food.

*Omelets...*

"Yes."

I take one of the plates and quietly exit the med-room, pausing to take one more look at Jax.

Gam reaches over to a dial and turns the lights down a bit before leaving with me.

"And?" Gam gives me a demanding gaze.

"Oh gosh, I'm so sorry," I exclaim, "I didn't mean to leave you hanging. I was just…" I stop midsentence and answer his question. "He's going to be fine. The dehydration is the main concern, but if I keep the IV topped off it will pull him through. We just need to keep an eye out for infection; I don't know how long his injury was exposed."

"Good. Then we can sit and eat." He gestures to a chair across from him, and I sit as beckoned, a slight case of déjà vu going through my thoughts.

"This looks amazing, Gam."

"Don't compliment before you taste. Lately the only eggs and cheese come in freeze-dried form, so the consistency and flavor leaves something to be desired."

"You're just a food snob and a picky chef, Gam," I contradict and take a bite.

I quickly wash it down with a swig from my bottle. "But… you might be right this time."

He chuckles and takes a bite of his own omelet. Meanwhile, despite the off-putting texture, I finish mine in little time and sit back, closing my tired eyes.

"Gam…I'm so glad you're here," I finally break the silence, opening my eyes and giving him a smile.

His smile is warm but somewhat sad. "I wish it could have been all of us."

My smile fades a little and I nod. "I am so sorry about Kassy…"

He simply nods.

"Who else made it? Shouldn't they be here?"

"Jona, Jain, and Tess. They opted to go to one of the settlements out east, a lot safer than here. I chose to stay behind to help with the cause. Besides, they needed someone who could cook." His grin reminds me how strong his positivity has always been.

"The cause?" I know now that there are more out there, free, and they aren't savages, but what are they hoping to do? "What is the plan?"

"To bring light to the falsehoods of what The Direction has been trying to do and free everyone from their laws. Up until now, Jax has been a spy in the Defense Industry. He sent us the message this morning and updated us on his situation. He was able to copy some files onto a data chip, which might help convince more people to join us, but it cost him his cover."

Gam finishes his own omelet and grabs my plate, taking them both to a second faucet-less sink behind him. I yawn, exhausted, and think of asking for a place to sleep, but I have Jax to watch over and so many questions in my head right now that I don't think I can truly rest.

"How long has this cause been going on?"

"Oh, I am not sure. In this cave? At least three years, maybe more. They haven't been clear on that," he answers, sitting down while placing a cup of coffee in front of me.

I lean forward, elbows on the table as I wrap my fingers around the warm mug, smiling gratefully.

"Thanks. So, wait, who are 'they'?"

"Anytime. Oh, 'they' would be Jax, who leads this team, his second in command, Kain, then Gia, and the tech guy, Isaac. There were more before, but I'm not sure what happened, it was before I got here."

"Isaac…? I don't think I've heard that type of name since… since my dad read from the Bible," I ponder aloud, sipping my coffee.

"That's because he's from an eastern settlement where there is no discretion against religion. Which reminds me…" His grin widens as he reaches into the side pocket of his cargos and brings out what looks like a data tablet. "Isaac was able to get me a digital copy of the Bible."

I don't want to discourage him, despite not wanting to hear anything about religion, so I force a smile, taking another sip. "That's pretty awesome."

"You're too tired to fake excitement," Gam accurately accuses. "No worries, I won't read anything to you. But thank you for trying to be excited for my sake."

I can't help but chuckle. "Thank you, Gam..."

But I still want to change the subject. "So where are the other three?"

"Currently, Isaac and Gia are on a supply run, and I think Kain is up north on recon. Not sure when either will be back."

"So how do they get all this equipment and supplies?" I am fighting the inevitable sleep.

*So many questions to ask.*

"There are those south of here in Gamal who are secretly sympathetic to our cause, and they have clinics there that provide a lot of our medical supplies. Several farms there also provide produce, while we have a couple factories on our side. The main eastern settlement, which we call Vita Nova, provides our technology, including our power materials. They've been able to abscond a lot of the newer technology and integrate it with materials they find in ruined cities." After his long dialogue, he drains the rest of his coffee.

"I saw the battery bank, but there's so much equipment here, does that really power it all?" My attention peaks a little at all the new information, keeping me alert.

"Oh, that is courtesy of Isaac. He developed a system that uses solar panels underwater in the lake you passed. The reflection of the water prevents the drones from seeing them, and the water reduces heat from the panels so no massive heat signature for the satellites to detect, just a slightly warm lake."

"That sounds genius, although I admit anything involving electricity was not my strong suit in studies," I comment with a tired laugh, pushing myself to my feet.

"Checking on Jax?"

"Yeah, then I might try to catch a nap on one of the other cots, so I can be nearby just in case."

"Good idea, I am going to check communications and security. I'll check on you both in half an hour, I promise. If you need anything, just yell."

He smiles, his dark eyes glimmering as he walks over to me, wrapping me in a massive hug that swallows my entire upper body. I wrap my arms around his waist and let out a breath. For such a hulk of a man, he hugs like a giant teddy bear.

"Thank you," I mumble as I pull away.

"You needed it, Lila. Now, get some rest. I'm very glad you're safe," he adds with one more smile before walking over to the computer towers, taking a seat in front of the displays.

My heart is warmed by Gam's presence; his positivity is uplifting. I slip into the med-room, without turning the lights up, and quietly grab a new isotonic solution and replace the nearly empty one above Jax.

Wearily I crawl into the next cot, only giving a passing thought to the fact that I am still wearing the same grungy clothes I started this long day with. Facing Jax, I silently watch his chest move up and down steadily with his breathing.

*I should stay awake and keep watch... just in case...*

No longer able to keep my eyes open, my body disregards my thoughts and finally...

*Sleep.*

# | 18 |

# Settling In

*I miss this.*
I smile as Gam pours my coffee a second time. Unintentionally, I slept through the night. Gam says he looked in on me and Jax, and he didn't say he did anything else, but I noticed this morning that he had set up the final IV bag.

*He lied, he does know how to handle an IV*, I muse silently with a smirk.

"I think this is the most I have ever seen Jax sleep since I've been here," Gam comments as he munches on a piece of toast, sitting across from me. "And I mean combined sleep altogether," he adds in jest.

"He'll probably wake up soon, three liters of isotonic solution should be plenty, just make sure he gets an easy to digest breakfast. Don't let him stuff his face with anything too heavy."

"Yes doc," Gam nods.

Laughing, I shake my head. "Just a basic medic. Don't ask me to do open heart surgery just yet, Gam."

"Is that why I feel like I got hit by a bus? You tried open-heart surgery?"

I hear Jax's familiar voice, albeit a bit hoarse, from the opening of the med-room. I jump from my seat in surprise, a little too suddenly as half my coffee spills, and I look at him with a raised brow. I force myself to settle down while noticing that Jax carries the IV stand with him to the table.

"Ah, good, you didn't remove the IV."

"I'm smart enough to know not to disobey the medic's directive," he huffs in indignation. "Besides, I like feeling half-human, and if this gets me there, I'll use it."

He groans as he sits at the table beside Gam, who gives him a toothy grin.

"Good to see you awake, finally. Thought you died and went to Heaven, and I got jealous." Gam gets up. "Let me get you something to eat. Is toast suitable, Doc?"

"Yes," I reply, sitting back down in my chair and dabbing at the spilled coffee with a towel Gam tosses my way.

"No," Jax answers at the same time.

"If you have anything resembling fruit and yogurt, even if it needs rehydrating," I add, giving a challenging look at Jax, "that's good, too."

Jax's jaw clenches a little, and from his look I get the impression he is not used to people deciding things for him, but I am pretty sure there is subtle mirth in his eyes as well.

"I'm not a vegetarian; I live on dried meat products half the time."

"You did say something about wanting to feel half human, right?"

"Yes, but not at the expense of my diet being restricted." Jax eyes me, and I can't tell if he is serious or not.

I raise a brow. "I'm only asking that you eat light for one day."

Placing honey-toast in front of Jax, Gam's gaze shifts between the two of us, but he stays quiet. It is a full five seconds before Jax gives a slight, although tired, grin.

"Copy that, Doc."

I shake my head slightly, wondering if he is just testing me. "How are you feeling, anyway?"

"Better. Thank you." Jax gives me a sincere smile. "I may need to sleep the rest of the day though. But first...Gam, any news?"

He shifts his gaze to Gam, who returns to his seat.

"Isaac and Gia messaged. They should be returning in three days with fresh produce," Gam grins, and I assume it is because he is excited to make a meal with proper ingredients. "Kain just messaged and should be here tomorrow with new intel."

"Good, then Kain can process the data I got. I don't want to risk corrupting the chip with the transfer in case APA was able to plant a failsafe." Jax looks over at me. "My jacket is in the pack, if you can bring that? The data chip should be in one of the front pockets. I forget which one."

He rubs at his temples and leans back in his chair.

"Don't worry yourself about it, boss, there will be plenty of time for that," Gam insists, sipping his second coffee.

"Gam is right. I'll look. You should probably take it easy for now," I reassure.

Jax nods, watching me for a moment, and I reach under the table where I had pushed the pack yesterday. I pull out the jacket and search one pocket, then the next, finally removing a small square piece of plastic with a metal strip at one end.

"Is this it?" I hold it between my fingers.

"That's it, just put it over by the computers, on the center desk."

"Check the security notifications while your there, too, please," Gam adds.

"If I can even tell where those are," I comment as I head over to the computers.

"It's pretty obvious, anything tracking movement would be flashing with a yellow frame." Jax directs from his seat, sipping from a bottle of water that Gam hands him.

Stepping around to the other side of the desk to view the screens, I can see six different camera frames of the tunnels, none of them flashing.

*I guess that's good.*

Setting the chip down on the desk, I take one more moment to look over the screens and then walk back.

"All clear."

"Good. We do have a sound alarm set, but it malfunctioned this past week," Gam comments with a slight scowl. "I think I touched a button, and without Isaac we're a little short on tech help."

"I might not know much about electricity, but I am familiar with *some* computer programming, I might be able to help." I shrug, returning to my seat. "But how do you know it is malfunctioning; did you have unexpected visitors?"

"No," Jax begins, "well yes, but it was a wild dog."

"A BIG wild dog," Gam adds, a little nervously. "White and furry, but at least he didn't seem aggressive. Just walked in, looked around, took a package of dried beef, and left."

"Did you chase him off?" I raise a brow.

Not knowing Gam to be afraid of animals, I wonder why he seems nervous.

"Nope, he was fast asleep." Jax looks over at Gam, accusing lightheartedly. "We found out about it in the recordings when I wanted to know where my dried beef went."

Gam grins sheepishly and nods. "Yup, I broke the system and slept on the job." His face turns stern quickly. "But in all seriousness, that mistake could cost us. I'm sorry, Jax."

Jax shakes his head. "It was one time. Was it not working yesterday? I don't remember much about when we got back, so I can't recall."

Gam's brows dip. "Actually, I'm not sure. I hit dismiss as soon as I saw you two."

"It's possible you dismissed it before we reached the sound alarm. But Lila, you might as well check just in case. Gam knows the basics, so he can show you what he thinks he did; probably just an on/off. Just don't change anything major or put in any new passwords, or Isaac will have a fit." Jax finishes his toast. "In the meantime, I think I'll catch up on more sleep."

I go to stand and help him, but he holds up a hand with a small smile.

"Give me a little dignity, I promise I can make it."

Sitting back down, I resist the urge to follow him as he makes his way back to the med-room and returns to his cot. Gam grins, though, as I go over anyway and sneak a glance inside to make sure he is lying down. Satisfied, I turn and give Gam a shrug.

"Alright then," I change the focus, "is there a place I can call my bedroom? I think I could use some thinking time. You're the best company, Gam, I just have a lot to process."

"Yes, of course! I took care of that myself when I heard you were on your way," he beams happily, his dark eyes brightening with the cheer I missed so much. "Follow me."

I comply with his request, and he leads to a dead-end tunnel to the left of the kitchen. He draws back the canvas and turns the dial to a medium light setting, stepping back to allow me through. On the left corner is a simple cot, but it has been tidied up with grey sheets, a blanket, and a small pillow. To the right is a small desk with a chair, but what catches my eye are two photo frames, although at this angle I cannot see what they are.

I step in and am nervous to see, my heart somehow knowing. Sure enough, one is of my family: me as a little girl of 6, my older sister, and my parents, joyous smiles on their faces. The other is much smaller, but empty, and I know what it is for.

Wordlessly, with Gam silently watching from the canvas 'door', I take the folded photo from my sweatpants pocket and fumblingly open the back of the frame. I manage to place the photo in and secure the back, setting the now filled frame where it was.

"How...?" I whisper as Gam enters and in one step is at my side, his massive arm around me.

"I got Isaac to get the photo of your family from public records. He has a printer. And I knew the picture of you and Jax was special to you, and Jax promised he'd have it for you."

"Gam..." I am not exactly sobbing, not out of control, but the tears are slipping down, and I let Gam hold me firmly in a side hug as I stare at the photo of my family. "Thank you."

"You don't need to thank me, I just know how difficult it is to come to a strange place and not have anything."

And with those words I turn to him suddenly, realization slapping me in the face. "Gam, I have been so selfish. You've lost just as much, if not more, than I have. How are you so positive?"

I instantly regret asking, because I know the answer.

"I don't think I have to say anything," Gam replies, releasing me. "You know why. But here..." He places the tablet, the one that he showed me yesterday, on the desk that is now mine. "You don't have to touch it. No need to return it, I have a second one, so just leave it sit there if you want. I'll leave you to get some rest and quiet."

Before I can respond with anything, he slips through the thin 'wall' of privacy and I am left to sit with myself and contemplate. I sink onto my cot, and the first thing I notice is an extra foam mattress. Although it makes me feel thought-after, I again realize how little I have thought of others.

*Jax lost his family, too, and suffered who-knows-what, and I accused him of neglecting me. Gam lost his sister, and I expect him to be my support. What kind of friend am I?*

Staring at the photos, my gaze drifts to the tablet Gam left there, and I reach across, tentatively taking it into my hands. It flickers on at my touch and writing appears. I am guessing this is the last thing Gam viewed, Psalm 34:18, which is highlighted and reads: *"The Lord is near to the broken hearted and saves the crushed in spirit."*

*Saves? Since when did You save? My family, Jax's family, Gam's family...*

My angered, silent condemnation stops as I toss the Bible tablet back on my desk, throwing myself onto the cot. I lie there staring at the ceiling, the jaggedly hewn rock casting shadows in the lighting.

*Is God to blame when people don't even let Him have a say?* A quiet voice penetrates my moment of silent self-pity.

To be honest, it is a legitimate question, and I find myself sitting again, reaching for the tablet. I flip through the pages, recognizing so many of the versus my dad used to read, and I smile a little as I hear his voice in my head, reading them. It doesn't stop me from constantly arguing with God, however.

"For although they knew God, they neither glorified Him as God nor gave thanks to Him, but their thinking became futile and their foolish hearts were darkened. Claiming to be wise, they became fools..." I read aloud, but quietly.

"Really? So, because I take care of my problems myself, I'm a fool...?" I sigh with a frown and put the tablet back, more gently this time, though.

*...When people don't even let Him have a say...*

# | 19 |

# Alarms

Hearing muffled voices in one of the other 'rooms', I push the internal arguments to the side and bring myself to my feet. Glancing down, I scrunch my nose at the fact I am still wearing the sweats from yesterday, feeling the grime.

*And is that blood still on my sleeve?*

I ignore that as I exit my private area and track the voices to the med-room, checking my watch on the way.

*2pm?!*

Entering the medic area, I notice Gam holding an empty IV bag and Jax, sitting on the high stool with his arm on the table, points to the venous line still in his arm.

"I am just going to pull it out. I've done it before." His voice is kept low.

Gam shakes his head, keeping his voice equally quiet. "Wait for the doc. Pretty sure she's resting right now."

"I'm here now."

They both look over like two kids who got caught with their hand in a cookie jar, but Gam starts.

"I refuse to take it out, that part gives me the shivers," he vehemently declares.

"Gam, I know you don't like blood, but it's pretty simple," I assure. "Just have a swab ready to press down as you remove it."

"See?" Jax argues, gesturing a hand to me while looking at Gam. "Told you."

"Here, I'll show you." I walk over and grab a small sterile-sealed gauze on my way and some med-tape.

"Nope, uhuh, you guys have fun. I've got security cameras to watch." Gam throws his hands in the air and hurries from the room.

"Has he always had that fear or did this place do it to him?" Jax asks as I remove the gauze from the packaging and press it down on his arm.

"Always been that way. I had sports injuries plenty, like one time I had a cut in my scalp, and scalp wounds bleed like crazy. Poor guy passed out." I shake my head with a small smile as I slip the venous line out and hold the gauze firmly in place, using my free hand to work a strip of tape around to secure it. "There."

"Thanks," he nods, flexing his arm. "What kind of sport involves scalp wounds?"

"Horseback endurance riding, but I injured myself enough times I ended up being restricted. That was a few years back."

His brows lift in surprise. "You had a horse?"

"Nope, I didn't, but the program I was in provided one."

"But you know how to ride then," he muses, and I can almost see the wheels turning.

"Yes...so?"

"We need additional modes of transportation, and we have considered horses, but we need someone who knows what they're doing." He stands and places his hands on the table, and I absently note how well-built he is. "Think you could help?"

"I could try... provided I stay here."

He looks at me inquisitively. "What do you mean?"

"Gam says a couple of the others have moved on to the east, to one of the safer settlements?"

Jax nods and waits for me to continue, folding his arms now.

"Do I have a choice? To stay or go?"

His face seems to sober and he nods. "Yeah, we won't make you stay. Or go."

"Ok, good to know."

I bob my head, leaning my elbows on the table, waiting. I want to be asked, I don't know why it seems important, but I want to know if he actually wants me to stay.

"Of course, we really could use you," he finally adds, running a hand through his hair and then in turn rubbing his chin, scratching at the stubble with his gaze lowered. "I know you have Gam and my vote to stay. Just saying."

I nod. "Then I will stay. I'm probably more useful here... that and Gam would probably miss me."

A satisfied smile flashes across his face. "He definitely would. And we do sorely need a medic. You just wanted me to ask, didn't you," he says more as a statement, and I only answer with a smile.

"So, one thing we do need to clear up, though..."

"Uh oh... " Jax raises a brow and his smile disappears.

"It's nothing huge. I don't think... but this marriage thing..." I shrug my shoulders.

"Ah, don't worry about that, Isaac says he can easily remove those records. It's just words on a document." Jax shrugs it off with ease.

"Oh!" I am a little surprised it is that simple, and maybe a touch miffed at how Jax is so nonchalant about it. "Then that's settled I guess."

I push off the table and clear the gauze wrapper, dropping it in a trash bin.

"That *is* what you were asking for, right...?"

"I suppose, I just..." I don't have a chance to continue.

"Guys, he's back!" Gam's voice echoes through the cavern.

Jax glances at his watch. "Ah, proximity alarm, maybe it's Kain and he's early. What is it?" Jax inquires as we step into the main area.

"The massive dog; he was there," Gam gestures to one of the flashing screens, tapping it to clear the silent alarm. "And then gone. No sound alarm! I don't think I touched anything, I'm sorry." He looks at Jax apologetically.

Jax places a hand on Gam's shoulder. "It's alright, we'll figure it out."

He then looks to me, and I narrow my eyes at him but then sigh.

"I guess I could try to find out what the problem is, then. What do you think you did?" I ask as I lean forward.

Gam sighs and shakes his head, his muscular shoulders sagging slightly. "I just wanted the alarm to stop when the bats came through, about four days ago."

"Bats...?" I hadn't thought of those, and thinking of them makes me shudder, *I hate when they skim overhead*. Gam chuckles and smiles since he knows how I feel about bats.

"Since when do you hate bats?" Jax asks.

"Long story for another time," I mumble, dismissing the comment. "Show me where, Gam."

"Here," he touches the symbol for the control panel and points to the selection for security settings. "All I did was hit 'dismiss'... maybe a *few* times. All yours from here, though, I'm bad luck when it comes to computers obviously." He isn't upset about it, he just accepts his limitations and moves on, that's the contented guy he is. "Have fun. I'll be trying to make supper out of powdered zucchini."

He leaves the chair and saunters over to the kitchen, and I take his abandoned seat.

"Sounds good." I scrunch my nose at the thought of zucchini and then mumble to myself, "this should be simple."

Jax nods. "Good luck."

"Just gonna leave me here? Don't *you* know any of this??" I wave to the displays, watching Jax back away with his hands raised.

"Nope, I make decisions and start fights, not get involved in computers. You're the one who volunteered. Besides, I have to empty my pack and get the ammo I absconded put away."

"Fine," I heave a sigh. "Tell Gam he owes me coffee."

"Will do." Jax turns on his heel and grabs the pack from beside the table as I watch, and it surprises me how fast he has bounced back.

*Or he's feigning...*

"Gam, get the woman some coffee!" He hollers before crossing the room to an alcove opposite the kitchen, one I had noticed before which has a gate across the opening with a digital lock.

*Must be the weapons and ammo.*

"Yes sir," Gam replies, his voice booming across the cave.

I pull my gaze from their interaction and focus on the control screen, touching 'Security Settings'.

"Pretty simple," I talk to myself as I look over the options.

Each camera has a reset and an on/off selection. The power system itself has a shut down, but that has a password, as does the lock override for what Isaac has labeled as the *'Pew Pew Cave'*. I raise a brow, suddenly wondering what Isaac is like.

Finally, at the end of the list is a fire alarm with a simple on/off and a test option, and then the general alarm with the same options. The alarm is switched to off.

"Gam... this is so simple," I mumble to myself with a quiet chuckle, shaking my head.

I have been so engrossed that I do not notice the silent alarms flashing on the view-screens for the tunnel cameras.

"Who the hell are you, and what are you doing at the security system?!" A powerful, firm voice demands a reply, and I jump up from the chair, startled.

At the center, approaching from the main tunnel, a man about the height of Jax, similar build and dressed likewise, has a handgun pointed in my direction. His blue eyes are contrasted with his short dark hair, which is cut like Jax's.

"I SAID... who are you?" He booms again.

I instinctively raise my hands.

"I... I'm..." My mouth is suddenly dry; I have never had a gun pointed at me.

"Is that blood?" He must see the stains on my sleeves, and I feel myself turn ashen as he rushes forward, a look of murder on his face.

"Woah, woah, woah!" I hear Jax's voice and Gam's in unison, and I exhale, lowering my hands as they both come between me and what felt, for a moment, like my impending death.

"She's the girl I mentioned: Lila," Jax explains, placing a hand over the top of the man's gun and pushing it down.

He stares past them, at me, his icy eyes dubious. "And what was she doing at the security system?"

"I broke it," Gam confesses firmly, "and she knows more about computers than Jax and I."

"Broke it?" The man's dark eyebrows raise a bit, and I can see his expression relaxing, but I still don't move, almost holding my breath.

"Yeah, he keeps turning off the alarms," Jax confirms.

"That's easy," the man says, and to my dismay he pushes past them and walks in my direction.

I back out of his way and into the wall as he comes around the desk and touches the 'on' setting for the alarm. The alarm sounds a *ding* in confirmation.

*I was just about to do that,* I silently grumble.

He turns around and looks down at me, holstering his weapon. An unexpected smile spreads across his face and his blue eyes gleam.

"Pleasure to meet you, Lila, apologies for the scare. I'm Kain, by the way."

He extends a hand and I grasp it hesitantly. He grips firmly and grasps my shoulder with his other hand.

"Probably don't look so suspicious next time." With a mischievous wink, he releases me and turns back to Jax.

"Gam messaged that you got shot. You look fine to me."

And just like that, I have met Kain, Jax's second in command.

"Thanks to our new in-house medic." Jax gestures to me, and I give a sheepish grin.

"Ah, our new medic? I guess she decided to stay, then."

I could swear I see a glimmer of displeasure on Kain's face as he glances over, but he hides it quickly and well. Something makes me uneasy, and I keep silent, looking over to see Gam's reaction.

"Come on, I'll pour us all coffee." Gam seems at ease as he waves us all over for coffee.

Jax settles himself at the end of the table, and I wait to see where Kain sits. He takes a seat to Jax's right, so I take a seat to Jax's left. Gam brings the coffee and sits beside me. His calming presence puts me more at ease, and I feel comfortable enough to observe Kain while sipping my coffee. An attractive individual, he seems slightly older than Jax, his tanned skin and five-o-clock shadow giving him a roguish appeal.

"So, we have a chance to stop some of the shipments to the facility, this should put strain on the system. It might give us a chance to catch them off guard," Kain concludes something I must have missed while observing him.

"What about the possibility of disrupting APA?" Jax queries.

Kain glances over at Gam and me and then back to Jax. "I know you trust them, but they're still new, and this should be discussed privately once Isaac arrives. He'll have a better idea of the matter anyway."

He adds dismissively to us, "no offense."

Jax nods, giving a quick look over to me, something akin to doubt in his eyes, but I am not sure what the doubt is aimed at or who.

"At least you are here now and able to pull the information off the chip. Whenever you have the chance, it's over at the security desk."

"How about now?"

Kain stands, leaving his coffee behind, and heads over to the desk. Jax starts to get up to follow, but Kain shakes his head.

"Enjoy your coffee and rest; I'll let you know when it's ready."

Jax sits back down and leans his arms onto the table, his gaze on me. "Sorry for the alarming introduction, he tends to be overcautious and acts on instinct."

"It's alright, I probably did look a little suspicious," I confess uncertainly, raising my sleeve to indicate the blood stains.

"Ah, yes, I meant to get you new clothes. Gam, do we have anything her size?"

"Yes, actually we do, I just dug it out this morning, and it's not pink so Gia won't want it," Gam replies. "I'll get it for you after we eat supper."

I can't help but look over to Kain, watching as he intently focuses on a display, his fingers nimbly flying over the keys.

"I'm sorry...?" I turn my attention back to Gam, having missed what he said.

He chuckles and shakes his head. "I said I have new clothes for you. After dinner, though."

"Oh! Thank you." I give him a smile. "So, what is for dinner?"

Jax doesn't say anything, though his eyes shift from me, then to Kain, then back to me. I look at him questioningly, and he lowers his eyes to his coffee, taking a sip.

"Zucchini soup," Gam answers, drawing my focus back to him.

Both Jax and I stare at him, and I scrunch my nose.

"Hey, don't knock it 'til you try it," Gam defends. "Speaking of which, I have to add the rest of the spices and some powdered cream."

He sets his mug down and moves around the table to the cook stove.

"Damnit!" Kain's voice suddenly echoes, and I jump a little.

"What is it?" Jax questions, getting to his feet and striding over to Kain.

"It's corrupted."

"What?"

I watch from my seat as Jax's face grows tense.

"I know the transfer was good at the facility. This cost me my cover. It has to work. How do you think this happened?"

"Not here," Kain's answer is barely audible to me.

I continue to observe as Jax sighs and frustratedly tousles his own hair. Finally, he takes Kain by the arm to lead him to his own quarters, and they disappear behind the canvas, their voices low and muffled. I sigh and return to my coffee.

"Don't worry, Kain still doesn't trust me either," Gam gently reassures.

I nod and take a sip, giving a side glance to where the two men were.

*As attractive as he is, Kain is too intense for my liking...*

# | 20 |

# Suspicions

"So, why can't you just tell me out there?" Jax asks, his frustration apparent in his voice.

He had worked on his clearance for years, and it has finally paid off. But apparently it hasn't, according to Kain.

"Did anyone else come in contact with the chip other than you?" Kain's intent eyes almost demand a sure answer as he stares at Jax, his jaw tense.

Jax kicks at the stone floor and sighs, rubbing the back of his neck with his eyes closed, shaking his head.

"I don't think so. Heck, I didn't even try to extract the files because I didn't want to trip any failsafe."

"Are you SURE?" Kain prods.

Jax opens his eyes, staring at the floor for a moment.

*Lila.*

He doesn't say anything for a few long seconds until Kain grabs him by the arm. It irritates him when Kain gets this way, but he is good at what he does, so Jax usually gives him some leeway.

"Someone did, who was it?" He demands.

"Lila," Jax answers, shaking Kain's grasp from his arm. "But she only set them on the desk. That's all."

"Are you sure? She was there when I came in, she could have done anything."

"No. In that case why not accuse Gam?" Jax's defenses raise.

He knows she is angry and somewhat resentful, but she has always despised The Direction. At least according to Gam; that and Isaac's surveillance of her, which he refrains from mentioning for now.

Kain shakes his head. "Gam is computer illiterate, and we all know that. Unless he hid it for this long. In that case, that is some damn fine spying. My bet is on Lila."

"What if it was just a failsafe and you tripped it somehow?" Jax argues.

"I didn't trip a failsafe. The data had to be tampered with," Kain insists.

Shaking his head, Jax stares at the back wall of his room where a simple cross is hanging.

*There has to be another explanation...*

He finally turns to Kain. "Why would she do that? She was going to be taken to the facility for questioning if I didn't get there first."

"Maybe they got to her before and promised to let her go if she said yes to helping them."

"We can't jump to that conclusion, and I am pretty sure there was no previous contact," Jax continues to deny, a voice deep down telling him to hold to his conviction.

He has always found that following that instinct has led to the truth and sometimes even his safety, but Kain is persistent, and the doubt continues to aggravate him.

"Your most important data, the files that could have broken this mission wide open, are gone. I say it's worth jumping to conclusions." Kain sticks to his argument. "Don't let your infatuation with this girl cloud your judgment. Sure, I admit she's cute, but nothing worth getting us killed over."

"It's not an infatuation, Kain, it's a promise I made to her when she was young. And she will be valuable as a medic," Jax replies, trying to suppress the anger at the statement. "And while I value your opinion, you are stepping over the line."

"Sorry, just saying it as I see it."

Jax sighs and shakes his head. "Fine, we'll be more cautious around the BOTH of them. We can't entirely rule out Gam, even though I am convinced it is neither."

Kain throws up his hands, obviously not satisfied. "Fine. I'll play nice, but our mission discussions will be in private from now on. Keep in mind, I have been by your side for three solid years. You haven't known her for ten years now. A lot can change."

Kain is right, a lot might have changed and Jax knows that, and perhaps Isaac missed something in his investigation, but Jax's irritation rises again as his righthand man continues to challenge him.

"We have taken precautions and will continue to do so, I already said that. Do you still have the chip?" He puts out his hand expectedly.

"The data is gone, why does it matter?"

"Just give it to me," Jax commands, his patience worn paper thin.

Kain sighs and takes the chip from his pocket, slapping it into Jax's palm. "Not gonna do any good."

"We'll let Isaac decide that. Maybe by some miracle he can get something out of it. In the meantime, it'll be safest in my possession. Thanks for trying anyway. How about you get some rest, Kain? You get cranky when you're tired. Glad you're back safely, though."

Jax holds the curtain back, giving Kain a slap on the back. Despite his irritation, Jax knows he still has to acknowledge good work from his team.

Kain steps out but turns around, lowering his voice. "Be careful, Jax, there aren't many people we can trust these days."

He turns again and storms off to his own alcove.

Jax lets the curtain fall back in place and walks to his desk, grimacing as his leg protests his weight and in turn exhaling in relief as he sits in the chair. Turning the chip over in his fingers, he stares at it quietly, doubt and anger battling in his mind. Anger that he risked so much, and it has been all lost. Doubt because now he is questioning who he can trust.

Another frustration battles for his attention as well. The way Lila was watching Kain, and then Kain admitting he finds her attractive has him ill at ease, more than he expected. He knows Kain's moral compass in relationships is slightly flawed, and the man would easily get past his mistrust in the long run to pursue her, but he has no idea where Lila is in that way. Jax always discourages relationships in the team, it confuses things, especially in battle, and he has had arguments with Gia about this recently.

Taking a ring of keys from his pocket, he uses one to open a locked drawer in his desk and tosses the chip in.

*Just three days...Isaac can sort this chip thing out at least.*

Looking to his left, he stares at the cross on the wall.

*Please, show me who to trust... and the right decisions to make.*

# | 21 |

# Distrust

A lump in my throat forms as I see Kain exit Jax's room, and I can almost feel a judgmental glance from his frosty eyes. He pauses by the security system, swipes a few things on the screen, and then walks into the next alcove which I am guessing is his.

Gam is in the kitchen beside me, whistling cheerfully, unflappable man he is, and goes about making his zucchini soup. I barely hear him, however, as I debate whether or not to go to Jax and find out what that was all about. Instinct tells me it has everything to do with me, and despite what Gam says, I have the impression that Kain has it out for me specifically.

"Lila, please go tell Jax supper is ready," Gam requests, making my mind up for me.

Getting to my feet, I walk over and stand in front of the heavy curtain. "Knock knock?"

"Not right now," Jax's voice replies, sounding heavy and tired at the same time.

My chin dips to my chest. *What the hell did Kain say to him?*

It has something to do with the data chip, and I look over to the security system, noticing that the controls screen has the word 'LOCKED' on it now.

*Kain must have locked it.*

"Gam just said supper is ready," I murmur, shuffling my feet on the dusty stone below me.

I hear a heavy sigh. "Tell him I'll get some later."

"Alright..." I add, risking it, "is everything alright?"

"Just a lot on my mind..." He seems to hesitate before adding, "thank you, Lila."

"Anytime." I turn away and go back to the dining area.

Gam and I eat alone; the other two are a no-show. That is fine, though, because I am not sure I can be near Kain without asking why he keeps looking at me the way he does. It's perfectly fine here with just Gam and myself, our small talk uplifting, and honestly the soup isn't all that bad. It only lasts so long, however, as I am still disturbed and just want to excuse myself to go sleep it all away.

"Time for me to try some sleep. Maybe tomorrow will be better," I declare apologetically.

"Here," Gam delays me, reaching into a nearby crate and handing me a stack of folded clothes. "It's not much: the standard cargos and a shirt for day, sweats and t-shirt for night. I was able to find your size at least, and I can wash your own sweats and sweater tomorrow."

"Thanks Gam," I mumble distractedly, grasping the bundle of clothes. "Any chance we have anything resembling a shower?"

My tone is hopeful, but I know it is unlikely.

Gam places a pack of personal disinfectant wipes on top of my stack. "Best I can do."

A grin breaks through my melancholy expression. "Better than nothing. Thank you, Gam. See you in the morning."

"Goodnight, Lila, let me know if you need anything." His warm smile puts me a little more at ease, and I head for my alcove.

Dimming the lights, I clean up the best I can and change into the clean sweats and shirt. I lie down in my bed and fight to get to sleep, scowling in frustration as I can't help but overhear Kain and Jax in the later hours, talking in low voices as they get themselves something to eat.

*Is this another way to get me to be angry with you, God?*

The rest of the night is just as fitful, although I finally drift into an uneasy sleep as I listen to the distant *drip drip* of water somewhere in the tunnels.

# | 22 |

# Tension

I sit bolt upright, a little disoriented. For a moment my mind is seeing my bedroom back in the town, back in Vouna, with the picture window with the mountains… and the next moment my vision clears to a dimly lit recess in a rocky cavern. Finally, my recent memories kick in, and I remember where I am.

Donning my beige cargo pants and leaving on the grey t-shirt I slept in, I slip into my sneakers and push my way through my curtain into the main room. Jax is over in the weapons room, sitting at a table where it looks like he is disassembling and cleaning a rifle. Kain is nowhere to be seen, and I am fine with that.

The past couple days have been repeats of feeling gloom and mistrust since Kain arrived. The tension in the air is palpable. The only solace I have is in Gam's company, but it seems the silence from the two others is slowly getting to him as well, as he is exercising most of the time. The occasional reprieve for me is when he and I go for a jog between the drone surveillances.

Leaning back against the kitchen counter, my gaze scans the quiet room. I sip the coffee Gam left for me, watching him attack his pushups and weights with gusto, which are right beside the opening of the weapons area. I walk to him and sit on one of the benches, my glance flitting over to Jax as he studiously cleans the weapon before him. He looks serious, and I wonder if I will see him smile again.

"Where'd Kain go?" I ask Gam as he takes a breather from his reps.

Gam wipes the sweat from his brow with a towel and stretches his bulky shoulders. "I think he went for a jog."

I nod, taking another sip. "When are the others coming back, do you think?"

"Probably afternoon. It's only three hours from their last supply stop, which is the medical center in Gamal. Oh, before I forget, did you need some breakfast?"

"Nah, I grabbed a health bar."

His forehead scrunches and he shakes his head. "That's a terrible breakfast. Yeah, you get the nutrition, but where is the adventure?"

"You mean powdered egg and milk...?" I chide in jest. "Granted, you make it palatable, but some days I just don't feel eggs, anyway, you know that."

"I feel ya there," he admits, returning to his weights, talking between reps. "Don't worry...Gia knows...how to pick...good foods."

"I'll leave you to it, then, unless you need a spotter?"

"Not sure you could handle that. Maybe you should just join me in lifting some weights," he challenges in return. "Otherwise, you're not bothering me, so stay."

"Not my type of exercise..." I wave a hand dismissively, even though I know it would probably be good for my upper body strength.

*Or lack thereof.*

He answers with a grin, shaking his head again.

I stay seated near him, listening to his huffs as he curls a seventy-five pound dumbbell, also catching the sounds of metal against metal as Jax reassembles the rifle. My eyes are focused on the back of the security display, though, thinking through a few scenarios.

*Things are never truly deleted on those chips. Unless they get reconfigured.*

I muse silently, wishing I could be given a chance to check. According to Gam, however, Isaac is a genius and should already know every trick in the book.

"Earth to Lila." Gam waves his hand in front of my face, and I nearly drop my mug of coffee.

"What the heck!"

"You were a thousand miles away. I asked if you wanted to go for a jog before the drones come around."

"Oh, nah, I really don't feel like it."

"That's the best time to exercise, when you don't feel like it."

Jax suddenly intervenes, standing at the now-locked gate to the weapons and wiping grease marks from his fingers onto a towel.

I sit up a little straighter.

*Why do I suddenly feel guilty of something?*

It is like the possibility they think I did something makes me feel like I really did do something wrong.

"Oh, hey! Did you want some coffee?" I offer with a hesitant smile.

"Sure, that actually sounds pretty good right now." He actually gives a smile, and I jump to the task a little more eagerly than I mean to.

"Not like it's an emergency," Jax adds, and I feel a little happier hearing him in an almost cheerful mood.

"I'll take one as well, or actually I'll take my second," Gam chimes in, placing the weights back on their stands.

"You know, as the medic here, I probably should caution on the amount of caffeine we all consume."

Jax chuckles and Gam laughs.

The short moment of optimism doesn't last long, however, and I am just handing them their coffees when the alarm sounds.

Jax goes to the display and clears the signal, checking on the cameras.

"Kain is back. Thanks for the coffee, Lila."

He sips from the mug, his face somber again, and he returns to his room without another word.

Gam looks over at me, his eyes wordlessly saying *'sorry'*. I sigh and set my mug on the table.

"How about that run, Gam?"

He brightens up and gives a firm nod. "Right with you."

# | 23 |

# Stress

Retreating into his place, Jax lets out a sigh, settling at his desk and sipping the coffee she gave him. Picking up a reading tablet, he selects one of the many books Isaac had been able to acquire for him. One of his favorites being from an author from the 20$^{th}$ century, fictional work, dealing with espionage and wars.

Despite his interest in the novel, his focus is too erratic, and he tosses the tablet back on his desk.

"Jax, can I come in?" Kain's voice sounds urgent, but Jax's jaw clenches and he considers saying no.

"Yeah, come in."

Kain barely waits for the invitation and enters almost instantly.

"I saw our two guests leave down the opposite trail a few minutes ago. Should we really be allowing Gamar and Lila out on a jog without supervision?"

Jax sighs in exasperation. "Kain. It's not like they can take the hover-cycles; those are disabled unless someone has the data card on them."

"And what if they signal the drones?"

"Then we know not to trust them, and we evacuate." Jax rubs a hand over his eyes.

"And leave all this work as a simple loss?" Kain gestures to the main room.

"What work, Kain? What work?!"

Jax's temper flares, and he stands from his chair.

"The data we needed may be completely lost. Our only hope is that Isaac can get something out of it, otherwise we are just sitting here waiting for the next word from headquarters. Meanwhile, *they* are waiting to hear from *us* whether or not the information is viable!"

He hadn't realized how pent up he was, and now that he lets it out it feels better. He sits down again, dropping his forehead into his palm.

"Easy, Jax, I'm sorry…" Kain lowers his voice, raising his hands almost in defense. "I didn't mean to stress you. Maybe we shouldn't waste any more time on the chip and just close up and make our way to headquarters?"

Closing his eyes, Jax leans back in his chair. "Not yet… There's still a chance. And maybe we can go back in."

"Your cover is burned, Jax, you know that. And I've been there before, too, before you recruited me," Kain argues.

"Yes, you don't have to remind me, but we have someone who has never been seen in the facility before. We can create a cover."

"Gia's cover is already blown in the Eden region, there's too much of a chance someone in Oshana would recognize her."

"She's not our only possibility." Jax brings his eyes to meet Kain's intense gaze.

Kain is about to protest, but the proximity alarm goes off.

*Saved by the bell.* Jax instantly thinks, not even sure why he went down the path of nearly suggesting Isaac go undercover.

*The guy isn't made for undercover work.*

"Let's hope this is Isaac."

# | 24 |

# Out of Place

As invigorating as the run is through the forest trail, Gam and I realize the overhead surveillance is due in half an hour, and to me that is close enough to not risk any longer of a run. Walking the rest of the way in, we hear the security go off and in unison glance at each other. We don't need to say anything to know we are both planning on bracing ourselves for Kain's next 'interrogation'.

No sooner than we enter the main area, however, the alarm sounds again. Both of us look to Jax and Kain at the computers, and Jax's face breaks into a grin as he silences the sirens.

"It's Isaac and Gia! Backup, though," he directs the warning to me and Gam. "They are bringing the bikes with the hover-carts directly in."

We step aside just in time to avoid two hover-cycles pulling small flat trailers loaded with crates. A short but stocky woman hops off one, her hot-pink hair in frizzy spikes as she takes off her helmet.

"We come bearing gifts!" She declares loudly with her arms in the air.

"Gia!" Gam rushes forward and lifts her up in the air easily, swinging her around. "You're a sight for sore eyes; the best gift anyone can bring."

I can't help but raise a brow while noticing Jax look a little uneasy.

*Well, that is quite the greeting... No wonder he was so excited...*

Those brief musings stop as I watch the thinner figure in the pair get off and carefully place his helmet on the bike.

His hair is blonde and trimmed so short he almost looks bald, and although he is nearly as tall as Jax, he barely has any build. I half expect him to put on some glasses to complete the nerd appearance, but he instead makes an undistracted b-line for Jax and gives him a big hug. Jax seems to take this welcomingly, but I notice Kain looks uncomfortable, and I can't help but feel happy at that fact, though I am not sure why.

"Jax, I was worried there for a bit. I saw the chatter from The Direction, and you almost were a goner."

Isaac comments and then, as though he suddenly realizes there are other people here, he looks around. He singles me out first and grasps my hand before I realize what is happening.

"You're Lila. Goodness, I have heard so much about you!"

"Umm... hopefully only good things?" My eyes dart to Jax and he shrugs his shoulders.

Gia chimes in before I get an answer, Gam hovering over her almost protectively.

"Naw, Isaac just has a steel trap for a mind. He remembers every tiny comment and uses it against you ten years after. Hi, I'm Gia," she cheerfully introduces herself with a small wave of her hand.

"How about we get these things put away?"

Isaac interrupts and gestures to the crates they just brought, and swiftly everyone, even Kain, falls in place and starts dividing the procured supplies.

The next half hour is relatively and oddly relaxing, as we all work to stock the supplies where they go. I easily locate the medic crates and take them to the supply shelf in the med-room. Meanwhile, Gam is entirely in his element, gathering the fresh produce and placing them in a fridge which, according to him, has been empty for some time. Isaac gathers anything related to computers or the power grid and puts them where he wants. Technology is his domain, and he is hyper-focused now.

Despite the initial euphoria of being acknowledged and greeted, I feel somewhat out of place. From my supply wall in the med-room, I hear them banter about their current and previous journeys for supplies. While I never really fit in anywhere, to be honest, I feel more out of place in this moment as I hear beyond my canvas walls something that reminds me of a family. Even Kain is teasing and laughing, although Jax seems overall reserved.

Finished with my secluded stocking of supplies, I emerge in time for Gam's announcement, everyone already sitting around the table.

"So, because Gia brought back some fantastic ingredients, I will be making a meal of Chicken Cordon Bleu with garlic parmesan green beans and *fresh* mashed potatoes." He emphasizes with his fingers in a 'chef's kiss' motion.

"Cord on what?" Isaac questions dubiously.

I know exactly what Gam means because he has made it before for me, but I stay silent, taking a seat beside Gia.

Gia unexpectedly turns to me and smiles, her face friendly despite her muscular build, and she whispers, "glad you joined us. There has been way too much testosterone in this group for far too long."

She grins before turning her focus back on Gam.

The rest of the evening is a whirlwind, with me feeling like I am on the outskirts while they catch up on the past week's events, including explaining my arrival. As uneasy as it seems, the most unease I feel is the occasional glance from Kain. Even when the promised, *and delicious*, meal is before us, I catch his intense eyes in my direction more than a couple times.

*Just stop... What does he find wrong with me?*

Even Jax seems to be aware of this and eyes Kain occasionally. Nonetheless, I find myself smiling at the scene at the table, and I finish my meal. I lean back and take in the bits of conversations around me until it comes to a point that I just want some silence. Pushing quietly away from the table, I head for my own sanctuary, but Gam discreetly leaves the table and interjects.

"Are you alright, Lila?"

"Just a little out of place and tired. You made a fantastic meal; it made me feel at home... but this," I subtly gesture to the others at the table, "might take me a while to work into," I confess.

Gam gives a reassuring smile and a squeeze on one shoulder. "Give it some time, you'll be part of that too."

"Maybe. But for now, I think I'll go and read...something."

I conclude, looking past his shoulder to catch Jax's glance in our direction. And then Kain's, an inquisitive look on his face.

"See you in the morning then, Lila. Just remember... you *are* loved."

Gam reassures me before he turns, returning to the others, and I know what he is referring to. *God's love...* and I suddenly wish I feel it, then maybe I would not feel the need to be accepted by others.

*You're trying to fill an empty space with the wrong things...* The quiet voice catches me off guard.

I enter my little piece of sanctuary and find myself replying to the voice.

*I thought companionship is important. Prayer in numbers or something like that?*

Setting my lights down low, I grab the tablet at my desk and settle into my cot, not even bothering to change from my day clothes. Flipping absently through the pages as I have done the past couple days, I stop at Jeremiah.

*Now there's a man who was alone...*

"For surely I know the plans I have for you, says the Lord, plans for your welfare and not for harm, to give you a future with hope. Then when you call upon me and come and pray to me, I will hear you. When you search for me, you will find me; if you seek me with all your heart, I will let you find me, says the Lord..." I mumble the words to myself.

Releasing a sigh, I let the tablet drop to my chest and stare silently at the rocky ceiling.

*If I seek with all my heart...My heart is too exhausted for that right now.*

I close my eyes, the sound of voices in the other room slowly fading as I drift into sleep.

# | 25 |

# Isaac's Stuff

Gam and I are the first awake. He hands me a cup of coffee, and I really do wonder if I drink too much caffeine. I sit cross-legged in the chair opposite him at the table, cupping my hands around the steaming mug. Even though the heaters are working steadily, the chilly drafts from the cold morning air still break through.

"I never thought to ask, do you have your own cave section? I only counted four private ones and one with multiple cots."

"Gia gets the single one. Isaac and I bunk in the same section," Gam replies. "Isaac said Kain used to be in with him at first, but they argued too much."

"That's an understatement," Isaac, somehow walking quiet as a mouse, unexpectedly adds while standing at the end of the table.

"Do you like giving me a heart attack, Isaac??" Gam exclaims, a hand to his large chest.

Isaac grins and walks around to the freshly brewed pot of coffee, pouring himself a mug. "Nah, but the look on your face is always the best. Besides, it's a way I can get back at you for snoring."

He sips from his mug, and instead of sitting with us he walks over to his computer stations.

"I don't snore..." Gam mumbles, and I let out a snort. "Wait, I do?"

I shrug, going to the previous subject. "Does *anyone* get along with Kain?"

"He's actually a charming guy." Gam chuckles at my statement. "He just doesn't appreciate Isaac's faith and pesters him about praying in the evenings."

I nod, about to add something, but Isaac's voice raises in uncharacteristic anger.

"Kain Leon Weaver! What did you do to my system?!"

My brows jump, and both Gam and I stare over at Isaac, surprised at how loud he can yell.

"What's the problem, Isaac?" Jax emerges, a data tablet in his hand, seeming like he has been awake for some time now.

At the same moment and already looking like she can take on the day with her grin, Gia shows up in grey sweats and a pink sweater.

"Isaac's starting off the day happy, I see."

Kain, looking half asleep and disheveled, comes out yawning.

"Kain here put a password on my system. MY system!" Isaac fumes.

"Settle down," Kain grumbles as he types in the password and walks away.

"No," Isaac continues, "I told you it doesn't need one. I have everything that needs to be locked, locked, with MY code, and that's good enough."

"I was worried about our new *friends* messing with the security," Kain replies as though Gam and I are not present, and I can't help but glare at his back while he pours his coffee.

As though sensing the aggravation, he turns around and gives me a mock smile, snidely adding, "no offense, of course."

Gam cranks his head around and gives Kain a stern look, almost making him take a step back.

*You don't mess with a guy as big as Gam.*

"Not necessary. There is nothing in the unlocked part of the system that they can harm. I have fail safes everywhere."

Isaac argues as he reviews all his settings, not even bothering to look up at his target of anger.

"What about Gam shutting off the audio alarm system?" Kain challenges.

"Both Jax and I receive alerts on our watches whenever it's silenced. Sometimes silence is better, so any intruder is less likely to be prepared for us."

"Like you'd be able to hurt a fly," Gia interjects, prodding him in the side.

"You know what I mean, less prepared for *you* guys."

"Well, there is the fact that my watch didn't alert when that dog showed up and ate my dried beef," Jax adds.

"What dog?" Isaac raises a brow, taking his gaze away from his display.

"The dog that caught me off guard," comments Gam from his seat at the table. "By the way, can I get one of those watches? I was holding down the fort while everyone was gone, and it might have come in handy."

"Only have two…but you do have a point, anyone left alone should have one," Isaac admits. "And there is a chance the dog was too low to trip the secondary sensors."

"See? If the system were locked, then Gam wouldn't have turned it off, and the alarm would have been on for him in case of a real intruder," Kain argues as he walks over toward Isaac.

"No." Isaac's eyes shoot a glare at Kain. "You don't mess with my system. Plain and simple."

"Then yell at Jax for letting a possible SPY look into the alarm problem."

"Lila is not a spy," Jax steps up close to Kain, his grey-green eyes darkening in defiance. "Isaac has tracked The Direction's surveillance on her for quite some time now."

Hearing this, my eyes widen a little, and I can't help but feel that my privacy has been violated. I almost say something but remind myself that I always figured The Direction was watching, it just hits closer to home when my suspicions are confirmed.

Kain stops suddenly, taking a small step back. "What? Why didn't you tell me?"

"Need to know, Kain, and it was my private mission anyway. Besides, you're partly right about still being cautious."

*So, I am a mission now?*

I am a little dizzy with all the new information, but I force it down with a swig of coffee, watching things unfold. I don't see Gam reaching across the table, but I feel his hand as he gently squeezes my arm for a moment.

*I guess technically he was spied on too...*

I give him a quick, thankful smile.

"I knew about it," Gia confesses.

"That's because you're nosey, Gia, and always watching over my shoulder," Isaac snorts. "But back to the fact that you still let Lila mess with my settings?"

He folds his arms at Jax.

"It was necessary. I made a call and figured you wouldn't mind her just looking it over," Jax defends himself, folding his own arms.

"Well... she did take some college courses on programming. But next time, ask me! And no huge changes. Like passwords."

He glares again at Kain before continuing to scold Jax.

"It's why I created our private messaging system. It's not like you outrank me. I am technically a private contractor, and I hope still your friend, so please respect that." Isaac waves his hand dismissively. "Now, back to what I really wanted to tackle this morning. Where is the chip?"

"Fine," Jax complies, stepping away to his room and returning with the chip. "And yes, you are still my friend."

Isaac grins widely, his jovial manner almost instantly returning. Gia, her expression having been tense for a while as though she were preparing to knock someone out, suddenly brightens with a pleased smile.

Kain had remained silent since hearing about the surveillance, but he still keeps a terse expression, watching as Jax hands over the chip to Isaac.

"I do still think we should review this privately," he suggests.

Jax also looks about ready to throw punches at this point, but Gam stands, rolling his shoulders back in a stretch.

"It's all good, I was going to go read outside anyway."

"Yeah, I'll be in the med-room. There are some things I wanted to reorganize to my preference." I stand and make my way to my said destination, abandoning my coffee.

Gam leaves quickly once Isaac turns off the auditory alarm, and I slip into the med-room, quietly organizing the medical supplies and only feeling slight guilt as I try to listen in on their conversation.

*Curiosity killed the cat...* A little saying my mom had often repeated hits my memory.

# | 26 |

# Chips and Hope

Isaac moves over to his diagnostic system at the next desk and sits down. Kain goes behind him and leans back against the rock-hewn wall, folding his arms. Jax lets out a sigh and plants a palm on the corner of the desk, taking weight off his leg.

"I'm gonna be over there," Gia points over to the weights. "NOT being a geek. Just holler if you need something carried or punched."

Isaac grins. "I'd rather you not punch my computer, so we're all good for now."

"Can we get this over with?" Jax interrupts but then shakes his head at himself, "I'm sorry, I don't mean to be terse. I'm just anxious to see what happened, and if you can recover anything."

Nodding, Isaac becomes a little more serious. "I know, if we can get something out of this, we might be able to gain some ground against this organization."

He clicks the chip into a port on the side of one of the computers, tapping on the screen and typing on his keypad, his brows furrowed in concentration.

Jax glances over to Kain, noticing that the man is almost holding his breath. Kain catches the glance and unfolds his arms, propping a foot against the wall behind him.

"Hey, I'm sorry, Jax, I was just worried," he lowers his voice, trying not to distract Isaac.

"It's alright, just try to remember that we are all on the same side here and to trust me when I say I've got your back, alright? We've always had each other's backs."

Jax keeps his voice low as well, and he forces a small smile. Kain has been a thorn in his side the past few days about trusting too easily, but he is still grateful for the pitbull the man is when it comes to fighting.

"That's strange..." Isaac suddenly blurts before swiveling his chair to face Jax. "You got this chip clean and fresh from the facility, right? And used the override code I gave you?"

"Yes, why?" Jax confirms.

He had grabbed it straight from the supply station, knowing the system would most likely have rejected any other data chip, and he had carefully followed Isaac's protocol to retrieve the data.

"Because it has been wiped. I mean totally wiped."

"Well yeah, we know that," Kain pipes in.

"No, you don't get it," Isaac replies, not meaning to be rude but saying it as a matter of fact. "When you erase data on a chip, the data is technically still there, and on a fresh chip it is highly likely to retrieve fragmented data and rebuild it, accessing all the files that were deleted."

"And...?" Prods Jax, still not quite understanding what the lanky computer specialist is trying to relay.

"Well, this chip has been reformatted, meaning returned to factory settings, which wipes everything completely."

"Well, that's what we figured, so is there a way you can tell who did it?"

Kain almost demands, and Jax grows tense, sensing what Kain is about to suggest... again.

"If you are asking if it was Lila, I can confidently say no. I reviewed the cameras from my tablet before I went to bed last night, and she was not there long enough. The chip remained right on the desk until you tried to pull the data, Kain."

"What if the footage were deleted?"

*Drop the bone, you darn pitbull,* Jax groans inwardly.

"No," Isaac almost looks offended. "The footage can only be accessed with my password. Not even Jax gets to touch that stuff; it's a totally separate system."

He adds, "besides, these chips do not allow reformatting unless someone has a high security clearance, and I don't mean ours. I mean really high Defense level. Like Colonel or General ranking."

"You mean someone in the Defense Industry somehow wiped the chip?" Jax queries, wondering how it is possible.

"Was it wiped at the facility?" Kain questions.

"Yes, Jax, and no, Kain." Isaac shakes his head. "The data log that was left behind says it was reset on Wednesday, right when Kain tried to access it. Now, unless Kain is a General of the Defense…" Jax glances over with a raised brow in amusement as Kain snorts, suppressing a laugh while Isaac continues. "…then my guess is that while Jax was retrieving data, APA somehow, against her usual protocol, implanted a failsafe with a high-end security clearance to reset the chip when it's plugged into a computer that does not have The Direction registration."

"That means we would never have been able to access the files anyway," Jax says as more of a statement than a question.

He lowers his head, his hopes for the success of this mission feeling as though they are being beaten down with one blow after another.

"Not exactly," Isaac remarks ruefully, pointing to the computer he is currently using. "I have this baby here to mimic the registration, and if my guess about APA is correct, there is a chance if we had used this, we would have successfully extracted the files. Not a guarantee, though, so don't go punching Kain right now."

Jax's jaw tightens, and he tries to take Isaac's words to heart right now, because at this moment he wishes he could put the blame on Kain, but that would be poor leadership.

"I was the one who asked him," he admits, shaking his head.

"But." He turns to Kain, holding his gaze steadily. "You do owe Lila an apology, I think."

Kain nods, ducking his head, not unlike a scolded dog. "I'll do that as soon as..."

A *ding* from Isaac's display draws their attention, and both of Isaac's eyebrows shoot up.

"Now this is even stranger..." he mumbles.

"Don't leave us hanging," Jax comments.

"Right... well according to my scanning software, the wipe didn't completely work and there is a portion of a file remaining. Now granted this looks so badly scrambled I am not sure my program can retrieve much, and it will take some time for it to restore some of the data to readable quality."

With that glimmer of hope, Jax stands a little straighter. "You mean we might actually have something?"

"That would be crazy," Kain murmurs.

"Yes. Well. It's a long shot but give my program an hour and we'll find out then."

"I hate waiting, but we can have some coffee in the meantime..." Jax moves away from the desk. "And let's get Lila and Gam back in here. It's time to make amends."

"I'll go get Gam!" Gia's voice comes to life across the room; obviously she has been listening the entire time, and she sprints toward the tunnel.

"I'll go get Lila," Kain offers.

Jax holds up a hand, an unanticipated protective instinct stirring in his subconscious as he stops Kain. "Pretty sure she's a bit nervous around you right now. I'll go get her. You'll get your chance to make peace."

Kain sighs and nods his head. Although usually stern and unflappable, he seems nervous.

"Yeah, I just really owe her that apology, and I'm rushing it, I guess. I want to get it over with."

"Understandable. You'll have time," Jax reassures, though a little surprised at how on edge Kain seems about the apology.

He suddenly wonders if it has something to do with Kain's attraction to Lila and he makes a mental note.

"Knock knock," he says in a low voice, standing by the med-room and raising an eyebrow as he hears multiple bottles hitting the floor.

## | 27 |

## Apologies and Data

Even though I have been listening the entire time, and I know I am finally in the clear, I am nervous.

*Probably because I have been listening and eavesdropping is a spy thing.*

When I hear Jax's 'knock knock', I drop about a dozen bottles of sanitizing solution.

"Come in," I answer as I crouch to pick up the scattered containers, shaking my head at myself.

Jax looks mildly amused and comes over to help me pick things up.

"Yeah, I figured you'd be listening," he comments with a grin.

"Ahh, yes, maybe I was. I'm glad I didn't have to say it without you knowing," I admit sheepishly.

"It's all good. It's not like these canvas 'walls' have much sound protection. You leaving the room was to appease Kain. And… well, I guess you know how that all turned out."

I watch as he stands and notice a grimace.

"How is your leg?"

"It's fine," he dismissively comments, continuing with what I am assuming he really came in to say. "I am sorry, Lila, that I didn't defend you as I could have. Isaac has been sure of you being free from any connection to The Direction for some time now. The whole data chip thing just had me frustrated, and I started to doubt everything."

"I understand. Pretty sure I would be frustrated, too... but I will only forgive you if you do one favor for me." I look at him steadily, my tone serious.

"That depends on the favor," Jax replies cautiously.

"Let me check your leg. I want to be sure you're not hiding an infection from me."

"That's all?"

He seems relieved, and suddenly a mischievous side of me wishes I had demanded more, like coffee waiting for me every morning for a week or something. Gam takes care of that anyway, though. Jax obliges, and after I check and confirm it is only slightly swollen, I hand him anti-inflammatory medication.

"Twice a day, no more than that though."

"Yes, doc," he replies, heading for the main area. "Oh, and we..."

"Are all having coffee. Yes, I heard that, too. Mine is probably cold though." I confess.

"Damn, I thought *I* had good hearing," he mutters as he and I head out to join the others.

"You need to lift weights, Isaac." I can hear Gam's laugh, and then I see him giving Isaac a tight side hug.

Isaac looks as though his thin frame is being crushed and he yelps. "Gam, I'm going to ask you to please try not to crush me."

"That was only five percent of my strength; any less and it would be a tickle," Gam argues but lets go anyway, putting his arm around Gia instead.

Gia's short frame looks so small compared to Gam. I almost laugh but subdue it to a quiet chuckle. I notice Jax give them a dubious look, and I wonder if he doesn't approve of their relationship.

"Here."

All of the sudden Kain is right in front of me, a fresh mug of coffee in his extended hand. The look in his blue eyes is nervous, but he conceals it with a rather fetching smile as I take the mug.

"Thanks…" I raise the mug to my lips but stop for a moment, not able to help my next words, spoken in jest of course. "It's not poisoned, is it?"

He seems a little flabbergasted and glances at Jax.

"Roll with it," Jax advises, and it makes me smile knowing *he* at least catches my humor.

"Umm…no. I was just trying to apologize."

Kain almost stumbles over his words, and I wonder if I am seeing the real side of him, not just a macho façade.

"I understand, Kain. I'm new here, something awful happens to your mission, and one plus one always equals two. It's only reasonable to suspect me."

I think he is surprised at how readily I accept the situation, and he numbly takes a full ten seconds to reply.

"Well… then we're all good? Maybe start fresh?" Then the charming side of him kicks in, and he extends his hand with a wide grin. "Hi, I'm Kain, Jax's right hand man."

"Hi, I'm Lila, the strange woman Jax dragged back to the cave."

I grin as I accept his hand. What I don't let him see is how leery I still am, like something engrained won't let go. With a quick side glance, I notice Jax watching as he sips his coffee, a mixed look of pleased and perplexed on his face.

*I wonder why?*

The atmosphere is so much better than in prior days, like a heavy fog lifts from the whole group. It changes quickly for me, though, as I hear a computer give a *ding,* and Isaac dashes over to his setup while the rest continue their discussions on food, hover-bike issues, and the terribly uncomfortable bunks. My eyes are watching Isaac, and I feel apprehension.

"Think we need the medic over here!"

Isaac's voice carries across the room, and everyone turns their attention to him at his computer station. Without thought, I set my coffee down and head over.

"What is it?"

I am only vaguely aware of four other sets of footsteps behind me.

"We got a portion of the file," Isaac almost breathlessly exclaims. "But I have no clue what all this means. It's like some science gobbledygook."

"Isaac, I'm a medic, not a scientist."

"More scientifically inclined than I am."

I move around the desk and lean in to look at the display, and I instantly recognize some text from a medication, or maybe immunization trial, and my eyes narrow as I try to decipher the terms.

"What do we have?" Jax moves around and stands beside me.

Kain hovers behind the both of us, staying back against the wall. Meanwhile, Gia and Gam take up an area on the other side of Isaac as I briefly read over what Isaac has uncovered, only saying bits and pieces aloud while I try to interpret things in my head.

**Investigative Trial Title:** Long Term Effects of A combined mRNA/HDCSs vaccine, developed by Pharma-Solutions and DWP against VHFsSARS-S41 with a mixture of the original strain of VHFsSARS-S41 and S.42 and S.53 lineages of the sigma variant of VHFsSARS-S41.

**Internal Reference Number:** 9145DWP

**Ethics Ref:** 205184DP

**DWP Case ID:** 9145DWP

**Date of Investigation Report:** 03-25-2045

**Chief Investigator:** REDACTED

**Lead Investigators:** REDACTED

**Sponsor:** REDACTED in cooperation with the Center for Health Control

**Overview:** First level analysis. Investigative teams for the PharmaS2041, a combined mRNA/HDCSs vaccine, developed by Pharma-Solutions and DWP to counter the VHFsSARS-S41 pandemic, is running trials to analyse and isolate cause and effect. ...<datacorruption>... Genomic materials stored in the form of DNA are decoded into mRNA through transcription, and mRNA in turn serves as the template to produce the protein through translation. Key steps throughout these processes are under the control of multiple ...<datacorruption>... Rigorous regulation is not only important for the prevention of the generation of aberrant proteins, especially truncated proteins, but also avoids the accumulation of unprocessed RNAs, which can ...<datacorruption>... PharmaS2041 failed to undergo sufficient human trials and analyzation during development/production and was expedited for distribution in attempt to outmaneuver spontaneous mutation in VHFsSARS-S41. Research identified aberrant proteins and the malfunction of mRNA as a causation in an increased number of termination of fetuses during otherwise healthy gestation. Following continued distribution of PharmaS2041, unanticipated high rates of infertility were investigated and testing on infertile subjects indicate a relation to affected DNA strands from the experimental balance of mRNA and HDCSs from fetal cells for expedited activation of immunity. Analysis on defects in fetuses also indicates...<datacorruption>...<endfile>

"Pandemic, vaccine with mRNA and HDCSs... bunch of explanation on how it should work. Clinical trials skipped, rushed into the public because of a pandemic... umm... vaccine, inoculation, the first round causes drastic numbers of fetus terminations... umm, basically miscarriages." I read ahead a few lines, some of the terminology confusing me.

"High numbers of infertility. Numbers were more than they anticipated? I would need to grab a medical manual for half of this, but I guess the gist of what I gather..."

It suddenly dawns on me what I have been reading. My mouth goes dry, and I stand straight, dumbfounded.

"What?" Jax queries, "is it something we can use?"

"Ah..."

I hesitate, not even sure what I am reading is accurate. "According to this, a company called the Pharma-Solutions and DWP created an inoculation for a viral pandemic and gave it out to the public for quick immunity before trials were complete. Miscarriage numbers peaked, and for whatever years this study covers, fertility plummeted, resulting in..."

"The depletion of the population," Gia murmurs, finishing my sentence.

"What is DWP?" Jax wonders aloud.

"I don't know, but according to this, this is how the population depletion started," I reply. "Maybe not the information against The Direction that you wanted, but it's a start."

"Maybe headquarters can use this with some of the other information our other teams have gotten," Gia conjectures.

Isaac shakes his head. "Not sure this will be enough to do much. There are also names redacted as you can see, so we can't use any of that, although that might not even help with how long ago this study took place. Best we can use is case ID to get someone back in the facility and grab that. It should include all the studies."

Jax nods and gives Isaac's shoulder a firm grip.

"Good job, anyway. This sheds some light on some history at least. More than the nothing we thought we had. Send it to headquarters and we'll wait to see what they say."

"Yes sir."

"And thank you, Lila. We would have had our faces in medical manuals for hours." Jax nods in acknowledgement.

"Anytime. Although I'm pretty sure I fumbled through most of it."

I suddenly realize how silent Kain has been, and looking over my shoulder to the wall, I notice he is gone.

"Where'd Kain go off to?"

At that moment both Jax's and Isaac's wrist devices sound a subdued alarm. Jax points to a camera display to the right of us, and Kain is jogging out of the tunnel.

"He blows off steam by running when something makes him angry. He's probably still kicking himself for the data chip," Jax explains.

I nod and feel a hint of regret. I haven't given thought to how awful Kain must feel for the unintentional erasing of the data chip. It makes me see his behavior in a different light.

"Done, sent, finished, along with the status report you wrote, Jax," Isaac confirms.

"Thank you. Hopefully we'll get word back to help us figure out our next step."

"I have a question," I raise a hand.

"Yes?" Isaac and Jax ask in unison.

"For Isaac…" I clarify.

"Go right ahead." Isaac swivels his chair to face me. "Ask anything. Well, almost anything."

"How are you able to transfer data? I thought The Direction had control over all satellite communications."

"Not all," Isaac grins proudly. "There is one collection of satellites, once known as Nightlight. Some enterprising individual long ago wanted a network for everyone without the influence of government. Vita Nova has been able to access some of these still-functioning satellites and heavily encrypt them for our use only. We can only do basic communication right now, but we are working on getting audio devices and satellite images connected. No luck yet, but one day…"

"Impressive, and pretty awesome."

"Well, I still think this little success calls for a celebration," Gam intervenes. "It is Sunday, after all."

"It's Sunday?" Jax exclaims, looking at his wrist. "Good grief, it is! Then we should all take the rest of the day off. Not that we have much to do yet anyway, at least until headquarters gets back to us."

"What do you have in mind, Gam?" Gia asks, looking up at the giant beside her. "I can help."

"Steak, potatoes, wild asparagus, and flan. I'd make cookies, but we still don't have an oven."

"You're going to use up all our stuff all at once," Isaac protests.

Gam shakes his head with a grin. "With only a fridge and no freezer, it only stays good for so long anyway; might was well use it while it's fresh. I'd rather not dry all the good stuff."

"Fair enough. But Gia and I worked hard to get that stuff, so we better get the largest portion!"

Gia nods in agreement with Isaac's demand.

# | 28 |

# History

I walk away and allow them to continue their banter, returning to my coffee at the table, though it is now cold for the second time. Wrinkling my nose at it, I set it back down. Jax comes up beside me and grabs the mug, dumps it in the sink, and proceeds to pour a fresh one.

"There. No need to suffer cold coffee." He hands the steaming mug to me.

"Thanks." I smile appreciatively, watching as he pours a new one for himself as well.

I open my mouth to say something else, but Gam and Gia are soon in the kitchen, and they go about preparing the highly anticipated lunch, practically chasing Jax out of their way. Isaac remains over at his computers, typing and swiping at screens intently. I sit down at the table, and Jax sits opposite me, leaning forward as though expecting me to say something.

"What?"

"You looked like you were about to ask me something before Gam and Gia came whirling in," he responds.

"Ah, yes, you have always been good at reading faces." I grin slightly. "I was just going to say, since you guys all pretty much know all about me through Isaac's hacking skills..." I give him a pointed glance, and his expression seems almost apologetic.

"Ask away." He waves a hand and leans back in his chair.

"How did you get involved in all this?"

"Oh, that is a long story…" He sighs, ruffling a hand through his hair, his gaze dropping to the table. "I'll try to make it short."

"Short or long, I've got nowhere else to be," I encourage.

"Where to begin… So, I was around seventeen years old when they took me and my siblings. I still don't know where they are." He flinches a little at that statement before he continues. "I was immediately drafted into the Defense Industry, and I used it as a coping mechanism, officially changing my name so I wouldn't have to think about my family. I excelled in my studies, proved to be loyal to The Direction's work, and received some of the medals you saw before."

He pauses, and I don't press him for more yet, waiting as he takes a deep breath.

"I was sent with a team to a far north area where they picked up signs of a gathering society, small, but it was growing. We arrived there to find a small rundown town centered around this beautiful, ancient, stone church. As the people were all being collected, I went into this church, which the group had started to repair, and there was an old man there who called himself a priest. He said his name was Father Sebastian."

I raise a brow, recognizing the word priest as something referred to in the Bible, but I say nothing.

"He said something about being sent from the east, and I was confused at that time because I had been told all along, just like you, that civilization didn't exist that way. I thought he was crazy at first, but there was this immense peace and conviction around him. I don't know why, but the entire week we were there to clean up and remove evidence of people, I never told anyone he was there, and I would go back to him and speak with him.

"My team ended up being stationed there as a halfway point to try to find out where the people had come from. I continued to keep Father Sebastian hidden, giving him food, learning more about his faith and people eastward, and that he originally came from across the ocean as a missionary, from a place called the Vatican. I was intrigued." He stops suddenly, his thumbs rubbing against the sides of his mug.

"What happened to him?"

I instantly regret prodding as a sudden look of sadness washes over Jax. He passes a hand over his face as though trying to wipe it away and he does, his expression passive again.

"There was a group of armed people who came into the town to try to find out where the others were taken. I was shot, and Father Sebastian pulled me to safety. Thinking he was one of the attackers, my men shot him..."

Jax tilts his head down, staring into his coffee, and I get the impression he doesn't share this very often.

"I'm sorry...You don't have to keep going..."

"No, it's alright. He's the reason I changed. The reason I found out what morals were, what faith was, and who God is. I know you don't really like talking about that."

"It's alright, I'll eventually get used to it."

I assure him, even though I am surprised at how devoted Jax seems, and it makes me uneasy as all I do is argue with God. Meanwhile, Jax trusts Him completely.

*It seems mismatched.*

He resumes his account.

"The resistance was stronger than our small squad could handle. I was the only one to escape, but barely, and when I got back, I lied, telling Defense that the church was destroyed. After I recovered, I took some leave time and returned to that church, in plain clothes, and there were only a handful of people holding it as an outpost. That's when I met Isaac and another priest, a student of Father Sebastian, Father Malachi. Fortunately, they had already known of my falsified report to Defense, so they didn't shoot me on the spot. Father Malachi has a good instinct for people as well, and he convinced them to let me stay. That's when I learned about the resistance and Vita Nova."

"So, the church area, is that Vita Nova?" Gam asks as he sits in the chair to my left, Gia at the stove keeping an eye on the flan.

"I didn't think I'd get an audience." Jax laughs a little but continues, clearing his throat and shaking his head. "No, it's not. But I returned to the Defense Industry at the end of my leave, secretly maintaining contact with Isaac, and that's when he recruited me into the militant resistance and gave me the location of this base here. So that means…"

He counts on his fingers.

"Four years in the Defense service, met Isaac, then after three years in the resistance I met Kain, who was already voicing doubts about The Direction and was able to provide us with some vital information about drone schedules and satellite access codes, allowing Isaac to track when they were about to pass over."

I do the math quickly in my head.

"And that's when he was recruited, about three years ago? Is that why he had to leave, because he got the information?"

"Yup. And haven't regretted it since," Kain suddenly adds from behind me.

I turn my head to see as he sits himself to the right of me, making me tense slightly.

"Welcome back," Jax nods. "Feel any better?"

"A bit. Sorry about that." He glances over at me with a quick smile before nodding to Jax. "Needed the air. Keep going. I don't want to deprive Lila of a good story." His face breaks into a grin, and I find myself a little more at ease.

"I'm almost done." Jax waves a hand dismissively. "A year after Kain joined us, I was able to take a trip back with Isaac to meet where our orders actually come from."

"You've all, other than Gam, been to Vita Nova?" I ask, leaning forward.

"Sadly no," Gia pitches in. "Only Isaac, who is from there, and Jax know where it is and what it looks like."

"And they're not sharing," Kain comments ruefully. "Probably better than this cave."

Jax chuckles softly.

"Not gonna say. Made a promise, and Isaac would kill me."

"You bet I would!" Isaac's chipper voice sounds from behind his screens, and his blonde head pops from the side so he can see Gam. "When is this fancy meal? I'm hungry!"

"You're like a child," Gam comments with a hearty laugh as he gets to his feet. "Everything is ready. Just need to fry the steaks last so they are good and hot still when served. If everyone is ready to eat?"

An "Anytime!" comes from me, a hearty "Yes!" from Jax, and a cheery "Of course!" from Gia. Kain sounds an "Aye aye!", and a "Well, duh!" comes from Isaac.

It isn't long before the Sunday feast is set on the table, and everyone sits, about ready to dig in, when Jax raises a hand.

"I would like to say a prayer before the meal, something Father Malachi taught me. I feel it is only fitting to be thankful when we thought all was lost. You guys don't have to follow along, of course."

"I'm in," Gam replies with a nod, glancing at Gia, and although she seems hesitant, she too nods, as does Isaac.

My jaw tenses a little, but I give a slight shrug when Jax looks to me for approval, something of hope in his eyes. My hands stay on my lap, though, as Jax, Gam, Isaac, and Gia fold theirs.

"Bless us, oh Lord, and these Thy gifts which we are about to..."

Jax begins the prayer, and I somewhat tune it out. I glance to my right where Kain is sitting and notice he doesn't fold his hands either, his eyes lowered to his plate.

*I see I am not the only one not amicable with God these days...*

I don't feel connected with him through it as I expect, more so perturbed, even though I do not know why.

"...Amen." Jax ends the prayer.

"I could get used to this." Isaac grins, piling his plate high.

Other than the awkwardness of the prayer, I finally feel at ease at this table, both conversing and being conversed with, learning more about each of them, and by far this is the closest I have felt to a family meal, probably since I was fifteen.

*I could get used to* this...

# | 29 |

# Fitting In

Five months and barely any word from Vita Nova, just a cryptic "Hold tight", and then "New information. Maintain silent status while waiting". The latest message had something to do with having a lead on a leak in their ranks, but still the closing "Maintain silent status".

I have since learned that there are other groups stationed in the Oshana region not far from The Direction facility. Our assumption is that they have been able to gather information, and headquarters is trying to piece everything together.

*A waiting game for us.*

While simple routine has been my life in the past, even I feel like a fish stuck in a bowl, not being able to do anything but sleep, eat, exercise, repeat. Alright, so maybe we do more than that. Reading has been a good addition, and Isaac keeps us supplied with plenty of material, whether it be novels or, for me, medical study materials.

Granted, there have been the occasional injuries for me to act as medic. Gam with a few burns, Jax sliced his hand open while repairing one of the underwater solar panels at the lake, Isaac with some sprains because he tried to jog with Gia, and Gia…well, Gia doesn't seem to get injured ever.

Kain got an injury on his arm from one of his knives. Only because he was trying to teach me how to use and throw them, and I inadvertently hit him. *And then myself...* On the same day, I sliced my finger open on the same knife. No injuries were ever very serious, but enough to remind me that I am still the medic.

I *have* gotten better with knives, thanks to Kain, who has been particularly attentive to helping me learn. He himself is proficient to the point his knife throwing is about as accurate as Jax's shooting at close range.

I learned that Jax is good with any weapon, but excellent with rifles and decent with handguns, and he has helped me learn the basics. Can I disassemble weapons like he can and name the parts? No. He gets frustrated when I continue to fumble during practice, but I remind him that I am the one he wants if he gets shot. I will argue that I am a decent shot, at least.

Gia has been pretty fun to be around, even if she is occasionally short-tempered. She has been teaching me self-defense moves, showing me ways I can use my small stature to overpower larger attackers. That is where she uses Gam as an example and smiles proudly when I am able to use one of her moves to immobilize him. Which doesn't happen often, since he is stronger than the average man.

In exchange, I have been teaching Gia about being a backup medic. I figure if anything happens where I am not available, Gia has the strongest stomach for blood and should know a few basics. Cleaning and stitching wounds, administering an IV for either isotonic or blood transfusion, and a couple emergency procedures that might commonly be needed on a battlefield.

Gam has taught me some skills in the kitchen; but I honestly like to leave that to him. Isaac and Jax have gone on a few supply runs, only for four-day spurts as we only needed the basics like cooking fuel and fresh foods, but each time felt like eternity.

Those times were the quietest, since Gia and Gam commonly spent their time together. Kain was at least surprisingly decent company, inviting me out on jogs and sharing the latest jokes he got from whatever reading material Isaac gave him. As flirtatious as he is, though, *and attractive*, I still can't be perfectly at ease around him.

Both Kain and Jax have taught me just enough on driving the hover-cycles that I can probably use them without dying. I honestly don't trust my skills with them yet, and I wish we had horses, but stealing horses from a riding facility is the opposite of staying silent so that hasn't happened yet.

One thing I have come to realize, after growing up in a town with mostly girls, sometimes the testosterone in this cave is overwhelming, and I have to go for a run solo. I would run with Gia, but she is barely girl herself despite her love of everything pink.

Even with that, I find myself enjoying their company more and more. The comfort of the routine is deceiving, though, and I have to remind myself that one of these days it will change.

*And I feel it will be soon.*

Even Jax and Kain seem to sense it; they seem on edge this week. Isaac is also constantly checking his computer for updates.

Then it happens...

# | 30 |

# Someone Has To

Sipping coffee, I do my usual visual scan of the main area. Isaac and Jax are over by the computers, speaking in quiet tones. Gam is working weights with Gia, and Kain sits at the other end of the table, absently flipping a knife. He catches my glance and gives a quick grin, his blue eyes glinting with some sort of mischief. Being used to his occasional antics, I roll my eyes and return to my coffee.

"We've got an update!"

Jax suddenly announces, and I look over, silently musing again how he looks good with a sandy-red beard, which he has allowed to grow for the past months. Inwardly, I debate whether he looks better cleanshaven or with facial hair, but I push that aside as the rest of the crew leaves their spots to move toward him and Isaac, and I follow suit.

"Headquarters has identified multiple files that they need, to complete their research into the organization's motives and operations. They need one more operative to enter the facility and access the files. This is a high-risk operation."

"So, is one of the other teams running this operation, then?" Gia asks with a raised brow, and I notice that her hand is held by Gam's.

"No. One of the teams has been compromised and eliminated," Jax replies soberly.

"Church location," he adds, and I feel a pang of sympathy, noting the repressed anger in Jax's eyes as he keeps a confident expression.

"Should we tell them about the other?" Isaac mumbles quietly up at Jax from his desk chair.

"Well, I guess we should now that you said it aloud," Jax replies with slight irritation before clarifying. "The second team has had to pull back due to increased surveillance in the area. They're trying to get to a backup base. The others are occupied with other assignments, so they'd have to wait."

"That leaves…us?" Kain questions, his tone dubious as he continues. "I'm burned, you're burned, who here is ready for that type of operation?"

"No need to remind me, Kain. Headquarters says we can wait for backup, as we are the best location for an operation like that. That may take two more months. Meanwhile, we are losing ground. Isaac is noticing an increased security which might limit his ability to create covers. So, if we wait two months, we might be locked out completely."

"Then one of us has to do it," Gam's usually boisterous voice is almost a whisper as I notice him squeeze Gia's hand, also noticing a brief look of what could be disapproval on Jax's face.

"Isaac is out of the question," Jax makes that clear. "He is irreplaceable at the computer and for communications."

"I could…" Gia tentatively volunteers.

Both Jax and Kain give her a doubtful glance, and Isaac is the one who speaks.

"With your cover being burned in Eden, Gia, it's too risky, I wouldn't recommend that."

*Do it…*

An inside voice I have heard before. I step back slightly, my heart picking up pace and my hands suddenly sweating.

*What? Why?*

I know the answer. Jax and Kain have been there. Isaac is crucial here. I would never forgive myself if Gam were harmed. He and Gia are connected at the hip, and I couldn't watch Gam go through that loss if Gia took that risk. There is no reason I can't, other than lack of experience, but experience is only gained by doing.

"We have to wait for more manpower; that's the best we can do. Isaac will try to keep up with the changing protocols put in place and ho-...."

"I'll do it."

Jax stares at me, and I can't tell if he is perplexed, doubtful, or proud. It is as though all those expressions meld into one until he gathers his composure before anyone else notices.

"It's the best option. I have a face that is not easily recognized or noticed, I have never been to the facility, and..." I pause, not sure if there is anything else that can help me win my case. "And I have the best tech support."

I nod to Isaac.

Isaac himself looks a little surprised, but he gives me a firm nod.

"You know you do. And I think I have the perfect cover for you."

Jax moves around from the desk and comes over to me, gently grasping my arm and pulling me to the side before lowering his face closer to mine with genuine concern.

"Are you sure? This is dangerous. Probably more so than what I did. Whatever false identity Isaac plants could go wrong, and APA might pick up on it." He keeps his voice quiet.

"I'm sure." I try to steady my voice when I am honestly terrified.

There is some exhilaration, but I am still out of my element here and that makes it frightening as well.

Jax looks unwillingly resigned and nods, releasing his hold on my arm.

"I guess..." He continues, addressing the others. "Lila is going in. Isaac, prepare a cover and help Lila build a background story. We should put this in play ASAP. And because she is still a little rough on the hover-bike, I'll get her there and back."

"I'll do that," Kain offers. "You'll be needed here, Jax, and you know I'm the better getaway driver."

He tries to put a little humor in the situation with a slight grin.

Jax nods slowly, even though he looks dubious. "Alright, good point. Kain will drive. Gia, get her armed up and prepped as much as you can. Find her a fitting outfit for whatever cover Isaac can come up with. Operation should be ready for activation in..." He checks his watch. "Seventy-two hours."

I suddenly feel like I am alone in the middle of the room. Jax silently retreats into his own room after giving the orders, Isaac focuses intently on his task with Gia moving to his side to see what she needs to do to prepare me, and Gam passes by and gives my shoulder a quick squeeze, but I barely feel it.

Kain gives me a wink and a whispered, "don't worry, I gotcha, girl."

He goes over to grab a leftover from the fridge, seemingly unphased.

"I need to go for a run," I manage to spit out, first checking my watch to verify I would be clear of drones. "Hit the alarm, Isaac?"

He gives me a quick thumbs up, and I head down the tunnel, breaking into a run by the time I get to the forest trail. I don't stop until I can barely breath, my sides aching as I fall to my knees, gasping.

*What the hell am I getting myself into??*

# | 31 |

# Last Supper

Since my moment of insanity when I initially offered to go undercover, I haven't regained my sanity. Instead, I have slowly felt more confident, pushing the apprehension down to a quiet simmer. The past two days have been spent preparing my cover and working with Gia and Gam on additional hand-to-hand combat, since my cover is medical, and I will not be able to bring any weapons with me.

I hover over Isaac's shoulder as he asks me to proof read his creations.

"That one," I point to one of the abbreviations, "Psy.D. means I'm a psychologist, and that won't work."

"I wanted you to be impressive with the additional credits." He shrugs.

"A simple MD and DBMS will get me what I need. I can skate by with some basic terms when it comes to those, but I can't speak that head shrink lingo."

"Fine, I'll delete it. Usually those with high clearance have at least five things in their credentials. Two is the lowest, so you'll probably be ignored if you need anything, because you're below them."

"All the better," I argue. "Skating by without being noticed is fine by me."

"True," Isaac admits.

"I had a question, by the way." I don't wait for Isaac's response. "Why can't you pull the files from here if you have your override code?"

"Oh, that's simple. All important files, especially on research and governing notes, are kept in a closed system, only accessible at the location. APA really only has the power to lock the system down; no direct contact with files."

"Ah, makes sense." I nod as I continue to look over the ID; I look so different with glasses in the photo, and I scrunch my nose. "Any other way you can track me other than those glasses? I look odd."

"You look cute," Kain comments from the other side of the desk, giving one of his teasing grins as he cuts an apple with his knife.

I roll my eyes and shake my head. "Your opinion is useless."

Kain snorts a laugh and walks back to the kitchen. "Respect your getaway driver."

The comment makes me laugh a little, and it somewhat lifts the heavy, serious mood I keep feeling. Nevertheless, the simmering apprehension is still there, and it always requires me to mindfully push it back down.

"Can't risk anything else." Isaac ignores the banter. "The glasses also break up your appearance and reduce the risk of APA picking up on any familiar features."

"I thought you were able to wipe my previous identity?" I raise a brow, a slight lump in my throat.

"Yes…" The computer genius hesitates. "I can't guarantee there isn't a backup system that APA might access if she suspects anything."

"I guess…" I release a sigh.

"Also, with your glasses, if you hear three beeps, that is me warning you that APA's system has flagged you. I can monitor all that from here, but my ability to alter the program is limited."

"And then what do I do?"

"Run like hell," Gia adds, emerging from the armory with a bundle of clothes and a white lab coat in her hand.

"Not sure that will help me either," I bemoan. "Is that my disguise?"

"Yes, most of it, but Gam has food for you, first." She nods toward the kitchen.

"I'm not so sure I can eat." I grimace as my stomach, albeit empty, is twisting at the thought of food.

"You have to try," Gam recommends, placing plates of chicken and rice at the table. "We'll even eat with you... well most of us."

He glances over to Jax's room. I glance over, too. Jax has been avoiding me for the most part. I am not sure if he is mad at me or just worried. He has helped with the cover and gone over route plans with Kain, but I wish he were around more.

*I could use a little additional confidence from his presence.*

I walk over to the table with everyone, and the food does smell good. I know I need something, so I convince myself to eat at least most of the meal. Even though the table-talk is a little subdued, I take solace in the fact that they are trying to be as normal as possible for our last meal.

The last supper in the Bible flits through my thoughts...

*This better not be the last one.*

# | 32 |

# Keepsakes

Jax can hear the others talking, trying to keep things light during their meal.

*I can't pretend like that today.*

He shakes his head a little. He has barely even been able to speak with Lila lately.

During their meal, he sits at his desk, staring absently at the surface and unable to decide if he is overly worried, angry, or both, and it bothers him that he can't control himself this time.

*I made a promise to save her, and by her choice she is going back into the belly of the beast. Am I free from that promise?*

He doesn't think so, and the guilt of letting her do this is eating at him. Knowing he should accept her decision, however, and knowing this is their best chance, there is nothing more that he can do for now. He lowers his face into his hands, battling his desire to forbid her from attempting the deadly mission.

"She has no experience," he mumbles aloud. "I never send my people in this ill-prepared."

*She'll need as much help as she can get, then...* The quiet voice chimes in, and an idea comes to mind.

Taking his keys out of his pocket, he unlocks his desk drawer and reaches in, removing a small box. He flips the lid open and pulls out something about three inches long: a simple metal crucifix he had gotten from Father Sebastian. He never really knew what to do with it until now.

Going to shut the box, he pauses, touching a simple union band that sits at the bottom. A small smile pulls at the corners of his mouth, but he forces it away and closes the box, placing it back in the drawer.

*Don't get involved, Jax...* He tells himself.

## | 33 |

## Time to Go

"How does the override code work?" I ask Isaac quietly as I wait for Gia to bring the rest of my gear.

"It was put in place a while back by a good friend of mine, my mentor, who was involved in programming APA's base codes. He pretty much designed her. He buried it in the data and APA *has* to obey it, although it only applies to locks, schedules, identities, and viewing The Directions chatter, otherwise we would have had APA shutdown long ago." Isaac shrugs. "It is vital to our operations, though, and as long as it is kept secret, it should stay hidden indefinitely. Someone would have to know the code and find it in APA's central system."

I nod a little. "Couldn't your friend, having access to the base code, shut down APA himself?"

Isaac's face somehow seems a little sadder. "He barely managed to escape with his life, and that was before my time. He pretty much taught me everything I know about APA, but he passed away a couple years ago."

"I'm so sorry, Isaac."

"It's alright. He lived a good life, and Jax pulled me through that loss long ago. Still stings a bit, but having a good friend like him makes the difference," he comments with a small smile.

"These are standard issue boots, but I was able to get ones with steel-toe just in case you need to kick a shin." Gia interjects and sets a pair of grey mid-calf boots on the floor in front of me.

*Only Gia would think of that.*

I realize they look exactly like Defense Industry boots, just grey. "I would think a scientist would be wearing shoes, not boots?"

Gia shakes her head. "Easier to mass produce one type for the entire facility. Which leads me to the next thing. You get to wear cargo combat pants still! They just have to be grey. Beige is Defense, grey is Science department. Same with the shirt. Boring grey. Although, it does have a cool style; at least scientists have some taste." She scrunches her nose and hands me both the pants and shirt.

I grin a little and take the clothes. "Well, at least that's good news. I'm not one for vibrant colors anyway. No offense to you, Gia."

"Offence taken." She gives me a mock scowl, then adds in a more serious tone. "Now, let's get a move on here."

"Yes, let's see what Dr. Katee Ren looks like," Gam comments, standing next to Gia by Isaac's computer space.

Kain is sitting on the corner of one of the desks, already dressed and armed to the teeth with his favorite knife, side arm, and an AR, with several spare mags on his molle vest. At his back is a well-stocked backpack, med-kit included. Even though it is unlikely anyone will see him, he still opts for everything to be standard issue from the Defense Industry.

Ducking into my private space, I change into the grey apparel and slip the boots on, lacing them up. I put on the glasses Isaac gave me and step over next to my desk. There is a mirror there, courtesy of Gam, and I look myself up and down.

Gia is right, the shirt is different than that of those in Defense. Sleeveless, it is almost like a wrap: one layer goes over the other and velcros in place off-center. It has the option of a high collar that velcros around the neck, or it folds down into lapels. I choose the high collar; it feels more modest to me and seems nerdier.

"Knock knock."

I hear Jax's voice, and for some reason it makes me more nervous. "Come in."

Jax steps in, and the first thing I notice is that his eyes no longer seem to have the frustration from before, a more resigned light to them. I allow myself to relax.

"It's a good look," he comments, his tone as genial as I have heard it in three days.

"I feel ridiculous and extremely nervous," I confess in a low voice as I stare at my reflection.

"That's to be expected before a dangerous mission," he replies knowingly.

*...dangerous mission...*

"Hey, Lila..." He hesitates. "First, I'm sorry I have been avoiding you. I had made a promise to keep you safe, and I thought that letting you do this was breaking that promise."

"A promise to whom?" I raise a brow.

"It doesn't matter..." He shakes his head. "We can talk about that when you get back."

*When I get back...* This is the optimism I have been waiting to hear directly from him, and I find myself smiling a little.

"Even though I think this is crazy, and I don't like putting you at risk," he continues. "I can't let you go without telling you how gutsy you are. You've come such a far way from the young woman who preferred the comfort of routine. I..." He stops himself, and I almost wish he would continue, his voice in its confident tone is calming, but he seems reluctant.

"Thank you..." I peel my gaze from my own reflection and notice he is looking down at something in his palm.

"I know you probably don't want anything to do with this, but if you could, please humor me and just take this with you. Father Sebastian gave this to me, and I think you need it more." His tone is sincere as he extends his hand, and I recognize a familiar image, similar to what my dad used to carry.

*A crucifix?* I am hesitant, but Jax's face is hopeful and the gentleness of it reminds me of when we were younger.

"Alright..."

I accept the item and note how worn the edges are, as though someone has handled it constantly, to the point the metal edges are slightly sharp. I decide that my back buttoned pocket is the best place, and I put it there.

Jax seems relieved, and he gives a faint smile before he puts on a poised expression. "Let's go finish your prep. You need to be on the trail within a half hour to avoid the drones."

And just like that, the gentle Jax is shielded by the leader Jax. Which I honestly don't mind right now because I will take the confidence boost any way I can get it. My stomach is in knots, and I am almost regretting the meal. We step out to see the rest of the crew patiently waiting.

*Well, mostly patient.*

Gia rushes forward and holds out the last item in my disguise: the lab coat. I slip it on and Isaac hands me a small tablet and a clearance card with a photo of me, wearing the glasses. Clipping the card on my lab coat, I stash the tablet in a zipper pocket of my pants.

"That tablet has your documents of transfer," Isaac reiterates what we have gone over already, but I appreciate the repetitiveness. "You are from the Gamal region, the eastern research facility. Your transfer documents need to be swiped over to the desk. After that, you will go into file 105 in the tablet, and those are the instructions for locating and extracting the files.

"Your clearance should allow you to do this without APA challenging you. Wish I could have done that for Jax before, but I hadn't been able to go deep enough into the system until now, and the inside help from the Gamal facility has been vital. I gave you my override code, too, just in case you need to hack any locks with your tablet if anything happens to your ID. You memorized that.

"We have no comms ability yet, but if you need to message me, use the tablet, piggyback it to their signal booster but only for a couple minutes at a time, and short, non-detailed messages in case APA grabs it. That's all I got, Lila."

"Got it." I nod, every bit of me tied in knots by now, but these people, this team... they are counting on me, and I am ready.

*At least I think I am.*

Kain is at the entrance of the main area, looking eager to leave. The rest of them stand frozen for a moment.

"Come on, guys, this isn't a funeral, they'll be back by evening," Jax suddenly breaks the silence. "Let's get going!"

A grin spreads across almost every face at the encouragement, and after a few quick goodbyes, Kain and I start jogging toward the hover bikes at the end of the trail. We reach there, and I climb behind Kain on the vehicle, yet as we begin heading north a sudden feeling of underlying dread hits me.

*Something is wrong...*

| 34 |

# Dogs and Danger

Two hours into the ride, we have been making good progress, even with the slower pace in the trail sections that have more overgrowth. The travel has helped me settle myself, and I spend most of the time repeating all the details in my head. There is still a feeling that something is wrong, but I chalk it up to my nerves.

"I calculate we have about five minutes before we park the ride and walk," Kain comments as we slow to a crawl alongside a cliff edge. "I'll get you close enough you can slip into the lot from the woods."

"Sounds like a plan," I acknowledge, tucking my knees in to avoid a branch.

I continue my mental preparation, especially Isaac's override code, which is terribly long. For a moment, I recall his words when he first shared it on day one of preparations.

*"Don't share this with anyone, Lila. I can't stress how important this is. This code has gotten me almost everywhere in the system, and no one has picked up on it. If you get caught, pray they don't get that code from you, because then I'm blind. That means no help for you, either."*

Grimacing now, I hate to think what would be done to me if I did get captured. I try to push it out of my thoughts as Kain picks up speed, the trail widening enough. As we round a righthand bend, however, suddenly in front of us is a massive white dog.

"Shit!" Kain mutters, and the bike fishtails when he veers off to the side, the rear clipping a tree.

This sends the bike spinning, throwing the both of us free, and then it slides sideways, slamming into a tree. I find myself sliding along the trail, rolling the last few feet. Slightly disoriented, I struggle to my feet, thankful for the helmet as I take it off.

"Kain?" I look around, slight panic gripping my throat.

"Here."

I hear his muffled voice, and I exhale with relief as he climbs out of a bush and yanks his helmet off.

"Damnit, I shoulda hit the stupid thing!" He shakes his head, going over to the vehicle.

"That might've ended up worse; he was huge!"

"Probably right." He nods as he pulls the bike up and tries to start it, shaking his head.

"Does this mean we are walking the rest of the way?" I add in a disappointed tone as I walk over and see the entire side of the hover vehicle smashed in. "At least that wasn't our legs."

I try to throw in a positive.

Kain gives the bike a firm kick, muttering swear words as he throws his helmet down as well. Without another word, he starts walking down the path, and I fall in beside him.

He finally sighs. "Fortunately, we don't have far. I can secure us a new bike at the facility. It shouldn't take much."

*I hope.*

Walking for another ten minutes in silence, we are about to take a lefthand turn when I suddenly hear voices. I reactively grab Kain's arm.

"What?"

"Shhh…."

I pull him into the woods, off the path, and we sneak forward until we can see through the brush. Up ahead, right where we would have driven in at full speed, a squad of Defense guards have a barricade across the path.

"I guess the dog saved us," I whisper.

Kain does not look all too pleased, a scowl making him look honestly frightening, and something in his eyes gives me pause. He shifts the rifle to his left hand and reaches to the holster at his right leg.

"Damnit. I think I lost my handgun in the crash. I was going to hand that to you."

"I'm not looking to kill them anyway, that might send alarms," I oppose. "Isaac and I studied the aerials; I know a different route."

I head directly west through the woods, looking around for landmarks. Glancing back, I notice Kain seems hesitant, but he soon follows. It isn't long before we come on another path going south to north. The remnants of asphalt and a short cliff face to our left confirm that this is the road.

"This dead ends two-hundred yards from the southwest corner of the facility." I keep my voice low, just in case, and Kain nods, his jaw tense.

We pick up the pace, jogging in complete silence, and I feel as though I lose a year of my life each time I hear something in the trees or brush. Kain seems relatively at ease, even though he looks miserable.

*He really hates it when plans are messed up...*

"Hold up," I whisper, slightly out of breath.

The trail has ended for a hundred yards already, and just through the trees we can make out the outline of a large building, so we slow to a walk.

I suck in a breath, and suddenly my palms are sweaty as we close the distance until we are just at the edge of the woods. The entrance is visible fifty yards across a parking lot crowded with hover-cycles, med-buses, and Defense Industry biodiesel trucks as well as some propane-powered vehicles. Although the building is moderately large, it is not as big as I was expecting, but I remember the floorplans Isaac had and saw how massive the underground part of it is.

"This will be easy to take one of these vehicles," Kain comments quietly, a grin finally showing as he gives me a wink. "I'll see you in one hour. Tops. Good luck, Lila."

I nod and swallow the growing lump in my throat, straightening my lab coat and making sure I don't have any dirt smudges. Slipping out of the trees and in through a few vehicles, I pause behind a large truck and take in a deep, steadying breath before exhaling slowly.

Finally, I step from behind the vehicle and walk as though I have just arrived in it, trying to make my strides long and purposeful as I cover the distance between the back of the parking lot and the doors to the facility.

According to Jax and Isaac, there will be two guards right inside the door. The door will unlock with my card, and the guards will verify the photo. After that, I need to stop at the front desk.

"Dr. Katee Ren, Dr. Katee Ren..." I quietly repeat to myself until I reach the doors.

My fingers shake as I tap the card to the reader, and I hear the lock *click*.

"This is it..."

I grasp the handle and pull. Stepping through, I am immediately faced by two guards, one a woman and the other a man nearly the size of Gam. The woman guard looks down at my ID and then at my face, nodding.

"Welcome, Dr. Ren." She steps back, as does the massive guard.

I simply nod, not sure if I can trust my voice yet, but it gives me an air of snobbery, too, and that benefits my cover. Approaching the front desk, I take the tablet out of my pants pocket, thankful it was unharmed by the earlier crash.

"And you are?" A testy looking middle-aged woman with short black hair raises a brow.

"Dr. Katee Ren. I'm here to gather research on..."

"Transfer documents, please," she tartly interrupts, holding up her own tablet.

Steadying my hands, I lift my tablet and select the necessary files, swiping them across my screen toward her. A 'Transfer Complete' message briefly shows on my screen, and I look up at the woman.

"Ah. East Gamal Research Facility. I see. How's the weather there these days?"

"Too rainy. I hate it," I dryly reply, suddenly glad that Isaac and I had looked up weather and other news from that area.

The receptionist snickers and nods. "Can't blame you there. I heard the floods are bad. Anyway, welcome. You've been sent a map of the facility on your tablet."

Her attention goes back to her desk, and just like that I have full access to the facility. I am glad she isn't looking now, because I feel the color drain from my face.

*Now the hard part...*

| 35 |

# Pestering Isaac

"How is she doing?" Jax hovers over Isaac.

"She was registered and accepted. You know, you don't have to keep asking. I already have Gam asking every two minutes." Isaac sighs as he steadily watches his monitors, the data reports coming in from the facility constantly.

"Everything going alright?" Gam asks, wiping the sweat from his face as he walks over from the weights area.

"See???" Isaac mutters. "Yes, Gam, so far so good."

"What about cameras? Can we see those?" Gia pipes in.

"You guys are impossible..." Isaac again mumbles under his breath before answering. "Pretty sure I did mention that system is locked tighter than my own personal computer and that's saying something. Despite literally years of trying, the cameras are out of reach."

"Oh!" He adds. "She's accessed the elevator and is on her way down. Her glasses just updated. That signal might get sketchy as she gets to the lower levels, and I can't risk piggybacking onto APA's signal extender. It might trace us."

"Sublevel 10...?" Jax asks, somewhat apprehensively.

Isaac simply nods, giving Jax a quick knowing glance.

"Keep us updated. I'll stop asking," Gia promises. "I can't stand here looking at the screens. Mind helping me wipe down the weights, Gam?"

Gam nods, and the two of them head to the weight section. Jax watches them for a moment, wondering if he should speak with Gia again about her and Gam, but decides it can wait for another time.

"Any update from Kain?" Jax continues to stay near Isaac, sitting in the second desk chair.

"He said they ran into vehicle issues. He's currently trying to acquire a new ride."

"He already wrecked a bike?" Jax frowns. "That was the clearest path."

"I don't know." Isaac gives his mandatory shrug. "Something about a dog."

*A dog??*

Jax shakes his head, puzzled, and leans back in the chair. Ever since those two left, he hasn't been able to shake the feeling that things are not going to go well, and that he is missing crucial information. In all these years of being undercover, his gut instinct has never been wrong, and he is not happy about that right now.

*Please God... let it be wrong this once...*

# | 36 |

# Elevators

"How many subfloors are there??" I suddenly mumble aloud, not meaning to as I stare at the buttons in the elevator before tapping my clearance card and pressing Sublevel 10.

Another woman in the elevator grins a little and points to the button that says Sublevel 19.

"That many."

"Oh, I'm sorry, this is my first time here," I blurt out, my cheeks flushing.

I rub my hands together absently, trying to avoid any shaking.

"It's ok, the first time is overwhelming." Her pleasant smile is almost relaxing, and I notice she is pregnant and pretty far along.

"Congratulations." I nod to her stomach, wincing as I wonder if that was weird to do.

"Thanks." She grins. "My husband and I are pretty excited and scared. It's our first. Are you married?"

I really want this elevator to move faster; the more questions, the more risk I have of messing up, but she seems sweet. "Uh… yes."

"No union band?" She queries, looking at my hands.

"Oh… I wear that on a chain around my neck. With my line of work sometimes rings get in the way." I shrug, thankful to say something truthful.

"Ah, that makes sense. Well, this is my stop," she comments as the doors open on Sublevel 5.

"Nice to meet you." I nod.

"You too, Dr. Ren."

After she leaves and the doors slide shut, I sigh and close my eyes, leaning against the back wall.

"Stop talking..." I tell myself quietly, fidgeting with the ring beneath my shirt, the conversation reminding me of it.

Finally, I arrive at my floor, and I stare ahead at a long hall with glass walled rooms lining either side. Jax had described this to me, so I know I must be in the right place, but he had been here when everyone had finished for the day. Right now, each room has at least two people wearing lab coats, intently focused on their work.

I try not to look in any of the rooms, keeping my pace purposeful and even, and I quickly reach the end of the hall. Using my access card, I open the door to the computer room and am immediately hit by the overwhelming sound of the cooling units.

Pushing the annoyance out of my thoughts, I sit at one of the computers and grab the chip Isaac had given me. He had cleaned it and made sure it was given a new internal identification number, identical to an unused one in storage. This saves me precious time, as I do not have to go find a new chip.

"Hello, Dr. Katee Ren," APA's cheerful voice chimes in. "What can I do for you?"

"I need all these following files on this chip," I reply as I put the chip in the port. "Case number 9145DWP, and all files between 0250 and 1005."

"Very well. You have the clearance, please proceed. Unfortunately, I cannot retrieve those files for you, as I am restricted from linking to the file system. If you need instructions, however, I can help with that."

"Thank you, APA," I mumble dismissively as I start searching the files and transfer them to the data chip.

The case files are easy enough to find, and they transfer to the data chip.

"Would you please clarify why these files are needed?" APA interrupts again.

*What? This wasn't part of the process...*

"Excuse me?"

"A new protocol is in place where an explanation for the use of files is necessary."

"Ah..." I swallow and try to delay as I wait for the 755 other files to move over.

*The case file...the virus.*

"I need the research on VHFsSARS-S41. There are possible cases in Gamal region, and we need to verify. We can't afford a pandemic when we are just starting to make progress."

There is a small pause, and I hold my breath.

"Thank you, Dr. Ren. Have these illnesses been reported?"

"We are keeping it in-house to prevent unnecessary panic. If these genomes match those of the virus we are dealing with, we will file the report."

"Very well. I will keep a record of our conversation in case you are questioned."

"Thank you." I fight my building anger, trying not to let the disdain for APA enter my voice.

The files complete their transfer, and I remove the chip, grasping it firmly in my fist as I exit the room. I exhale slowly, forcing myself to slow my pace when I want so badly to run for the elevator and get out.

I slip into my ride to the surface and touch the button for the main floor.

*So close... just this unbearably long ride.*

My heart finally begins to slow as the floor numbers tick closer to ground level. The elevator sounds a *ding,* and I let out a sigh. My heart drops to my stomach, however, when the doors slide open to reveal two guards blocking my exit.

"Dr. Ren, please follow us." It is definitely a demand and not a request.

"Um, is something wrong?"

"This way please." One leads and the other steps in behind me, and I follow them down a hall, opposite the way I want to go.

I feel the chip pressing against my palm, and I know I have to put it somewhere.

*Not anywhere on me.*

My mind is racing, and my heart is pounding in my ears as I see a second elevator ahead, noticing a large potted plant beside the door. While we wait for the elevator, I move slightly to lean against the wall, close to the plant, and as subtly as I can, I drop the chip into the soil.

*Just in time...*

The doors open, and the officer behind me nudges the butt of their rifle into my back, urging me in. I am sweating and trying to control my breathing when I see the one in front of me press the only button available: Sublevel 20.

*20?*

That level wasn't in the blueprints Isaac showed me, and I feel there is a reason, and it is probably not good. Closing my eyes, I try to measure my breathing. Somehow, I know this is going to test my limits.

*Don't give them Isaac's code...*

# | 37 |

# Sublevel 20

"Uh... What the hell." Isaac's blonde brows pinch together, his blue eyes squinting as he stares at the tracker display.

"What?" Jax sits forward suddenly.

*Isaac rarely talks like that... how bad is it?*

Both Gam and Gia stop their debate about what exercises are better when they hear Isaac, and they quietly approach.

"Umm..." Isaac types a few reset commands to verify and then sits back in his chair, as though in defeat. "She got to Sublevel 10... and then ground level."

"That's good, right?" Gia asks tensely, her fists resting on the desk as she leans forward.

"Yes..." Isaac hesitates.

"Just say it." Jax knows, *more like feels*, he won't like what he is going to hear.

"Her signal went to the rear elevator, the one that goes straight to Sublevel 20," he replies in a quiet tone. "Why would she go there? I didn't even show her the other blueprints that had it marked as an empty level."

Jax's face takes on a darkened look, and his beard-covered jaw tightens.

"Jax?" Gam looks intently at Jax, stepping closer, not imposingly but more imploring. "What is it you know that we don't?"

Jax takes a few moments to regain his composure before answering. "That's where detainment and the interrogation rooms are."

Their faces all take a downcast appearance and only perk up when Jax's tablet gives a *ding*. They look to him hopefully. His face only grows more stern, though, and he swallows, setting his tablet back down slowly.

"Kain confirms it… Lila's cover has been blown. Kain is going to sit tight for now and stay in that area. Security is heightened, and he's going radio silent."

*For once I wish my gut feelings would be wrong…*

| 38 |

# Water and Shock

They have taken my ID, they searched for weapons, they confiscated my glasses, they know my real name, and they even took the union band from my neck. My tablet sits on a small table in a corner still, because they continue to ask me for the password. Not even APA has broken the code.

*Isaac, you're a genius.* I muse with some satisfaction.

I don't really know how long it has been, maybe days, or it just feels like days. There are no windows or any indication of time in this concrete room. There is one single door in front of me with an access card lock, and the small table with my tablet. My arms and legs are tie-strapped to a single, locked down, steel chair in the center of the room. To my left is an observation window where I occasionally get to see groups of onlookers, probably waiting for information.

Hunger has since gone to a dull ache, and I barely get any water, just enough to keep my voice functional to answer questions.

*Or not answer them, because so far, I am not.*

Of course, the occasional events of something they call waterboarding allows me to swallow some water, *between the feeling of drowning.* Sitting here in the silence, my heartrate increases again as I apprehensively think about what they have done so far. What they refer to as waterboarding has, regrettably, had me pass out a few times.

The process? They unlock my chair, tilt me backwards to the floor, lay a cloth over my face so I cannot see, and then the water gets dispersed. They pour it slowly over my covered face, until I feel my nostrils and throat fill with water, burning like fire, and I reach the verge of inhaling half of it. Sometimes I pass out, other times I come to the point of vomiting bile, and they flip the chair to the side, so I don't suffocate for real. I have lost count of how many times they have done this.

The absolute silence is torture enough, especially when the only thing I hear at times is when they are approaching the door, and their voices pounding my head with questions. The lights in here are terribly bright as well, and I find myself just squeezing my eyes shut, trying to gain a moment of dark and peace. Lamentably I have had no access to a bathroom either, and am loathe to admit this chair has been my only commode.

I shudder, and my eyes fly open when I hear footsteps coming down the hall outside the door. Fighting my bonds, the straps dig into my wrists, but they only give the slightest fraction to allow me to shift my hands closer to my side. Not enough to slip my hands out. I quickly stop moving as I hear the lock disengage.

My usual tormentor, a short statured thin man with dark hair and beady eyes enters. He had at first politely introduced himself as Hilam before things got brutal. I sigh and lower my gaze to the floor.

"More water? Good...I'm thirsty."

I am not sure where this defiance comes from, but it pushes away some of my fear, and I clench my jaw, waiting for the questions that will follow.

"You know, Lila..."

He stands in front of me, his tone deceptively gentle, and that's when I notice a baton-type device in his hand with prongs at the end. I grimace, because he has used this a couple times before.

"You could take our offer and be transferred to a new town; live a good life there as a Medic. Just give us the password to your tablet." Hilam points at the table with his baton. "And also the override code."

"What override code?" I hold his gaze, feigning ignorance as best as I can like I have each and every time.

"We know you have a computer expert in your group, and we know he gave you an override code that is being used on our system." His tone isn't so friendly now, and I hear more steps approaching in the hall.

"Says who?"

A smarmy grin spreads across his face. "Says your friend in the other room. Kain... is his name? He doesn't handle torture as well as you would think."

My face must betray my dismay as the little man lets out a laugh and shakes his head.

"What did you do to him?"

I grit my teeth, fighting again at my restraints. I want so badly to get my hands on this man, but an officer enters the room, his muscle, and proceeds to tighten the tie-straps further.

"Just tell us what we need to know, and then you can both be free." He taps the baton against his other hand.

"I'd rather die." I would spit at him, but my mouth is dry.

*Why?? You could have at least let Kain get away.* My routine during these sessions has also been to argue with God.

I don't have much time to argue any more as Hilam thrusts the baton into my side, and I am overwhelmed by a wave of electricity that freezes my breathing, my mind, and almost feels like my heart is being stopped. My muscles seize, and my body involuntarily tries to fold itself over to battle the pain, but my arms are strapped so tightly to the back of the chair that it only causes more pain.

Finally, it ends and I gasp, shutting my eyes tightly as the light in the room seems to be intensified by the shock.

"No..." I mutter, shaking my head, and the process repeats a few times, my torturer's muscle man frequently making sure my bindings remain tight.

In an attempt to shut out the all-consuming pain, I force myself back into my mind and my argument with God.

*All Powerful and You can't stop this? Why can't You just get me out of here? Or let me die...*

*My God, my God, why have you forsaken me?*

The plea in my head, not my own, suddenly slaps me in the face, and I recall these words used by Jesus himself during his suffering on the cross, *where He died for our transgressions.* Suddenly, my mind leaves this concrete room. I am that little girl again on my dad's lap, listening to him read from the Bible, his soothing voice washing over me. I had just had a bad day; a boy in the town punched me for standing up for another girl, and I was feeling sorry for myself.

*"...For it is better to suffer for doing right, if that should be God's will, than for doing wrong. For Christ also died for sins once for all, the righteous for the unrighteous, that He may bring us to God, being put to death in the flesh but made alive in the spirit..." I am proud of you, Lila, for standing up for the innocent. Don't ever begrudge the suffering you receive for good you have done. Christ Himself died for us...*

A sudden rush of cold water takes me out of my moment of peace. I must have passed out, but I am wide awake now, dripping wet. First thing I notice is that my right side feels as though it is on fire. The officer in the room is holding a now-empty bucket, and Hilam lets out a heavy, purposeful sigh.

"Let's try something else..." He nods to his help, and the officer sets the bucket down and takes out his sidearm, pointing it toward my head. "Give us what we want, or...well, I guess I don't need to say or else. You get the picture."

I stare silently at the floor, watching the water spread. Squeezing my eyes shut, I shake my head and wait for whatever is next.

*Maybe peace...? Forgive me for being so bitter...*

The man suddenly breaks the silence.

"I have a better idea. Officer Marc," he speaks at the officer, and I open my eyes and look up to see him smile eerily. "Go kill the other detainee."

"Yes, sir," Officer Marc replies and leaves the room.

"No!" A try to throw myself forward at the diminutive man, but the chair holds tight, still locked in place.

Hilam's smile continues, and as he leaves, he holds the door open until the sound of a gun firing echoes down the concrete hall. Letting the door close, the lock clicks in place, and I am left in complete silence again. My heart feels as though it has dropped into my stomach, and a sick feeling takes over the hunger and thirst.

*God, what have I done?*

# | 39 |

# Traitor in the Ranks

"This is day four. Do we have anything at all?"

Jax hovers over Isaac for the millionth time. He rubs at his clean-shaven chin, having cut the beard this morning.

"No. Not since yesterday when the facility issued the notice that Dr. Katee Ren is actually Lila Collins."

"That didn't surprise me. Kain is still laying low. He says the security has brought in dogs and more manpower, so rescue is slim."

"That's bad news." Isaac grimaces. "Good news, though, I figured out how to create a malfunction in all the cameras. I might not be able to get in to view them, but I am able to shut the power down to them. Just in case she finds a way to break free, they can't track her."

"Good job." Jax nods approvingly.

"And that is the other good news. It lets me know I am still able to use my override code, which means she still hasn't given them anything," Isaac confirms, then adds, "or she's..."

"Don't say it. We're not giving up. I will gear up, and once we hear back from headquarters, we can see if I can meet up with Kain and we'll go from there."

Jax leaves the desk and heads for the armory. He refuses to entertain the idea that Lila might have been killed. He wants to think he would feel this reaction with any of them, but this hits a little harder than he likes.

"Speaking of headquarters." Isaac's brows raise as his screen notifies him of an urgent message, and he selects it.

"Jax..."

Stopping in his tracks, Jax looks over and instantly doesn't like the look on Isaac's face. He goes back to the desks, coming to stand next to his friend. Nothing prepares him for what he sees on the screen, though, and his face goes ashen and then flushes with anger.

**Priority Notice**: Infiltrator identified. Markers found in data deletion confirmed to be the code of Colonel Kai Demal. Identification photo acquired this morning from an inside source at the facility, photo attached. Base compromised. Immediately secure the individual and proceed to secondary base.

"Where are Gia and Gam?" Jax's voice is low as he fights to keep the anger and dismay from coming through.

"On their way back from an evening jog." Isaac's voice is quiet as well, disbelief in his tone.

"Good...Armor up, Isaac."

Isaac nods numbly, immediately going to the weapons alcove. Jax's hands ball into fists as he battles the feeling of utter betrayal.

# | 40 |

# Judas Kiss

*Beside restful waters he leads me...water...*

I must have fallen asleep finally, despite the lights, but I suddenly feel the impact of a boot on my already-burnt side, and I slam sideways, chair and all, into the concrete. With the seat unbolted from the floor, I wince and gasp as my left shoulder is pinned between the floor and the chair, which bears my full weight.

"Wake up, sleepy head. Can't have you resting on the job."

I hear the all too familiar voice of Officer Marc.

Clenching my jaw, I blink, trying to force my vision to focus through the searing lights. Everything is still blurry at first, but I notice through the glass that I have an audience, *I think Hilam*. The officer in the room with me yanks my chair back into place.

"Hello, Lila."

My name is said by a different familiar voice, and I feel a kiss on my cheek that seems all wrong somehow.

Officer Marc kicks me down again before I can gather my senses.

"Are you awake yet?"

"Yes..." I hiss an answer, the whole room sideways again but finally clear to me.

That's when I see him standing there.

*Judas...*

Kain gives me a harrowing grin and a wink before he steps out of the room, joining Hilam in the observation room. They seem to exchange a few words and then some laughter, but I can't hear them through the thick glass. Anger seeps in and numbs the pain as Officer Marc sets the chair upright and again kicks me over.

This time I am able to use my knees to roll forward, pressing my forehead down against the cold concrete for the smallest respite. Yet only for a little before he pulls me up again, repeating a few more times.

"That's good enough. We'll let her have the night to think things over. We can't have her die on us just yet." The familiar nasally voice of the short oppressor echoes through the speakers.

Officer Marc complies, righting my chair and bolting it back to the floor.

"I'll be back, honey," the Defense Officer sneers.

I watch as both men leave the observation room, and in turn the officer leaves my prison. The lights suddenly go out, and I am left in absolutely darkness, my breathing the only sound.

"My God, my God, why have you forsaken me..." I whisper the words, licking my dry lips as I close my eyes, even though it is dark either way.

I resign myself to a rough sleep in this chair. Any sleep is welcome at this point, but an image of a crucifix, a cross with Jesus's body, flashes through my memory, and a sudden realization hits me.

*They never searched my back pocket!*

With renewed determination, I fight against the bonds at my wrists. My fingertips are already touching the button of the pocket, but I can't get much farther.

I don't know how long it takes, my sense of time is destroyed, but I finally have enough freedom in my one hand to undo the button and grasp the metal object. Working the sharp edges upward against the tie-strap of my more mobile hand, I flinch as I nick my own skin a few times before the bond is cut.

This gives me more freedom to cut my other wrist free, but it is a difficult task to reach my upper arms which are also strapped firmly to the chair. Finally, with both arms free, it is a simple task to free my legs, although all this is done by feel in the pitch-black room.

I try to stand, but my legs are so cramped from being bound so long that they give way at first. Crawling across the floor, I feel around until I reach the table in the corner, pulling myself to my feet and forcing my legs to stabilize. Grabbing the tablet, it activates, and the low glow of the screen illuminates the room somewhat.

Before I type in the password, I press my ear to the door, listening intently to be sure no one is approaching. I unlock the device and note the time: 20:12. Pulling up the control panel for the facility, I type in the memorized override code, and I hear a *click* indicating a small victory.

Cautiously, I crack open the door the slightest bit and notice the hall is dimly lit. At the same time I realize there might be cameras out there, so I shut the door and sit down with my back to it for a moment, trying to figure out how I am supposed to avoid them.

*Isaac...*

I select the piggyback option Isaac had added, typing a quick message, and click send. I count the time in my head carefully.

A message comes in reply. *"Cameras down. All clear."*

I then quickly disconnect from the signal booster.

Exhaling in relief, I open the door once again and quietly step into the hall, retracing the steps the guards had taken to get me here. I duck into a storage closet, though, when I hear voices ahead, and wait until they pass. Carefully, I continue my path, anxious to be out of this facility. I reach to my chest instinctively, forgetting that they took the ring, and I grimace.

*I'm never going to get that back, am I...*

# | 41 |

# Packing

"How come none of us suspected Kain as the mole?" Gam's normally calm voice booms in incredulity as he throws food and bottles of Hydra-thlete into a crate. "We sent Lila into a trap."

"Unfortunately, yes," Jax admits but keeps his manner calm.

Gia is over at the armory, angrily shoving ammo into a duffle bag, and she pauses to look up. "Let me after him, Jax."

"We can't play our hand yet, Gia. There is no reason to think he knows we're on to him. He's still updating me, which I don't know if I trust those updates, but at least he's still communicating. He says he'll be back in a few hours."

Isaac nods, sitting in his desk chair and looking somewhat odd with a molle vest on and a sidearm at his hip. "The order from headquarters is clear: we capture him and retreat to secondary base. Kain has never been there, so it won't be compromised."

"And what about Lila?" Gam voices what they are all thinking.

Jax lowers his head, staring at the floor. "I still want to go get her, but I can't risk any of you guys. This is on me."

"We've still got your back, boss, don't make us walk away right now," Gia pleads, a fire in her eyes.

"I can't..." Jax begins.

"Hey!" Isaac suddenly shouts, cutting him off as he leans forward.

"What?" They all ask in unison.

"My override code was just used on a door on Sublevel 20," he exclaims, pointing to his display. "And now there's a message from the tablet I gave Lila."

"This could be them, though. They could have gotten the code and are testing it," Jax cautions, he himself trying not to let his hopes get too high.

"The message reads... 'Help. Escaping. Cameras?' She's asking about the cameras." Isaac furiously types out a message and clicks send.

"We need to go help her," Gam implores, and Jax looks at him, trying to fight his own impulse to just rush out and assist in the escape.

"We need to stay here. When Kain returns, we need to make sure he won't hurt anyone else. I have no doubt he is responsible for the destruction of the other two bases. Getting Kain out of the way is the best way we can help Lila right now," Jax argues, trying to convince himself as much as the rest of them. "Plus, we can't be sure it's actually her. I think it is best we continue to pack what we can and be ready to move out."

Each one in turn realizes the possibility of that fact and the importance of being ready to leave, but their expressions sadden as they continue gathering essential supplies. Jax takes a moment, however, to go into Lila's room and retrieve the photos, pausing to look down at the one of the two of them.

*God, be with her in her time of need...*

## | 42 |

# Freedom

It has taken painstakingly long to work my way to where my tablet shows a set of stairs while avoiding the nightwatch, but each time, miraculously, I have a way to duck out of view. I have even been able to secure fresh pants, a health bar which I ate quickly, and a bottle of water from a locker room. But unfortunately, I was unable to unlock any weaponry as those require physical keys.

*Not even a knife...*

Heading up the twenty flights of stairs, I absently touch the back pocket of the clean pants, feeling the cross shape through the fabric, my other hand grasping the railing as I half pull myself upward. I am exhausted, still hungry, and my side still burns and aches, reminding me of what I am escaping.

There is surprisingly not a soul on the stairs, and I make it to ground level. I don't open the door to the hall, however, as I slide to the floor and try to catch my breath. Taking this moment, I type in a message on my tablet. *"Watch out for Kain, he turned me in."* But a thought crosses my mind, and I quickly delete it.

*Kain might be there already, and what if he reads it? What if they don't believe me? Plus, the more I connect to the signal booster, the more I risk APA catching on.*

That sudden thought humbles me, and I begin to wonder if they *would* believe me. Kain and Jax have worked together for over three years. I have been with them for barely half a year, and despite Jax and

Isaac vouching for me, how can that compare to years of friendship and no proof of my claim?

Knowing it is something I will have to face later, I mentally push it aside and move over to listen at the door as I have done with every door so far. I am satisfied with the silence and slip into the dimly lit hall. I make my way to the elevator, releasing a satisfied sigh as I locate the chip still in the potted plant, and I place it in my side zipper pocket of my pants.

*I still have to make it out of here...and there is no back door.*

I hope the guards at the door haven't seen my face before, as I plan to act as though I am a frantic scientist who saw 'the prisoner' running down a hall. In the back of my mind is the thought that my escape has already been discovered, and my heartrate increases in trepidation.

Avoiding rushing around the corner to the lobby area, I peek around instead and am relieved to see there currently is no receptionist. Oddly, however, the front door is open, and out in the moonlit night I catch a glimpse of two guards a few paces away, their back to the door as they face a dog that is barking incessantly.

"Get outta here, mutt!" The one guard yells. "Shut up already!"

"Every damn night for the last three days, barking straight at the door," the other guard complains. "Why don't we just shoot it?"

"Because I like dogs."

"Well, I don't like this one!"

I don't wait another second, and I dash as quietly as I can for the door, turning left away from the guards and directly toward the woods. I don't even look back, but I hear the dog still barking. It is only once I am in the woods that I realize that it looks like the same dog that caused Kain to crash.

*Did it follow us here??*

At the thought of Kain, though, my mind returns to apprehension and the need to put distance between me and the facility. Despite my side and legs protesting, I break into a jog. The farther I get, the more relief I feel, and the exhaustion slowly wins over the adrenaline.

Finding a heavily brushy area, I crawl between a few bushes and allow myself a breather. The ground is cold and slightly damp, but it feels like a hug to me compared to the chair in the concrete room. I shudder at the memory. Trying to push the thoughts away, I turn my tablet on to the lowest setting and select one file, thankful that Isaac snuck it on without asking me. After a bit of reading, I manage to drift to sleep.

# | 43 |

# Let It Be Her

"Everything is pretty much packed, at least anything we can take." Gia comes over to Isaac, who is transferring the data from the computers to a portable drive.

"I'm leaving this one running until last minute." Isaac gestures to one last display. Other than the cameras, the rest are dark. "I want to keep an eye out for messages and the facility logs."

"Anything new?" Gam asks as he loads the last items onto one of the hovercarts Jax drove in.

"No. The last thing my code was used for was to open a locker room."

"Nothing for the front door?" Jax adds to the query, hoping for more, but something tells him this is a waiting game.

"No, but one of the cards from the guards was used. That could mean anything. There was one thing." Isaac hesitates.

"What is it?" Jax looks up from where he is loading dufflebags onto the second hover cart, his expression still unchanged as he maintains his composure.

"So, I didn't tell her, but I put the Bible on her tablet. It was just accessed five minutes ago."

"Could be anyone, but we can hope it is her. In the meantime, let's eat and keep an eye out for Kain."

*Please let it be her.*

## | 44 |

# Late Start

Without realizing it, I slept through most of the night and started the rest of my journey at six in the morning. It makes me nervous because I get the feeling they have started the search long ago. Even though my body is still exhausted, and the health bar earlier is gone from my system, I keep pushing myself to keep a steady pace.

*Maybe I can locate some edible plants on the way.*

*Ten more hours of hiking...*

# | 45 |

# Making the Call

Glancing at his watch, Jax's eyebrows furrow, and he shakes his head. "Kain should have been here. It's well past midnight."

"Yeah, 3am to be exact," Isaac mutters irritably. "I could have been sleeping."

Almost in answer, a *ding* sounds from Jax's tablet and everyone watches with bated breath.

"He says something came up. He has to stay low still."

"Ah ha!" Isaac declares unexpectedly, making them all jump a little. "The facility just issued a notice, and I think I know why Kain has to 'stay low'," he adds, moving his fingers in quotation marks.

"Spit it out." Gam narrows his eyes; even his patience is tested.

"Lila is marked as escaped and they're sending a search party," Isaac discloses.

Jax stands silent for a moment, ruffling his own hair before he looks to each of them, their eyes steadily staring at him, waiting. All their faces tell him they want to go find her, and that makes his decision easier.

"Whoever needs it, get a quick nap. We leave to find both Kain and Lila at zero five-hundred."

## | 46 |

# Kain and God

Avoiding most of the main paths, I rely on the topographical map in my tablet. I stop to listen and am thankful that so far, I have only had to take cover due to one drone. The trees themselves are dense enough, I doubt they can see very clearly anyway, but I don't want to take any chances.

I have been traveling most of the day so far, my water now gone. My stomach gave up grumbling about hunger, replacing it with a headache, but at least my side is now down to a dull ache. Stopping at a relatively steep decline, I stare down at the creek at the bottom; the one I want to follow back home.

*Home.*

"Finally, only an hour left to walk," I mumble to myself, slipping the tablet back into my pants pocket and preparing to carefully descend.

"Well, I'm glad I caught you here, Lila. It would be a mess if I had to do this back at the cave. Not sure how I would be able to explain that one."

Kain's confident voice sends a chill down my spine, and I turn slowly to see him only twenty paces away, his AR shouldered and aimed at me. I consider stepping backward and letting myself tumble down the hill, but I know how quick Kain can be. I would be a sitting duck if I didn't recover from the fall fast enough, so I stay where I am.

"How did you find me?"

"You forgot about the satellites that pass over every twelve hours." He jerks his head upward to the sky.

"Damnit," I mutter under my breath.

"You know, Lila, if you had just accepted their offer back there and got placed in a new town, this wouldn't be happening. This is going to be tough to explain but doable: poor little Lila panics, tells them where the base is, and now they have to abandon everything. Unfortunately, she was also killed."

He gives a mockingly sad face, dipping his gaze to his sights, and I can see him squeezing the trigger.

*Please make it quick...*

I shut my eyes, waiting, but instead of the loud *bang* and a bullet hitting me, I hear a subtle *pop*, and nothing happens.

"What the hell," Kain mutters, going to clear his chamber to rack another round.

I take this opportunity to rush forward, knowing my best chance is to knock him off his feet before he can recover focus. He is too quick, though, and uses the butt of the gun, driving it into my stomach, and I stumble back, gasping as I hit the ground.

I roll away a few times to try to put a little space between us, and I struggle to my feet just in time to see him pull the trigger again. This time there is the expected *boom* but combined somehow with an awful sound of metal cracking.

*And I am still standing, un-shot.*

*Squib load...*

I remember something Jax described to me before, when teaching me about guns; when a round doesn't have enough power for the bullet to clear the barrel. And then you better not try to put another round through like Kain just did. I see the barrel of his rifle peeled like a banana, completely destroyed, and it is lucky for him it did not explode closer to his hands.

*Not lucky for me...*

Kain releases a string of swear words and hurls the gun to the side. He is still without a handgun at least. He drops his backpack and promptly takes out his knife: a straight dagger-style fighting blade. I grimace, trying to steady myself and step back. Right now, I am no match against any well rested, uninjured man, let alone Kain with a knife.

"Kain, you're Jax's friend, he'd die for you, why are you going down this path?" I raise my hands, wondering if maybe there is a way to reason with him.

"Oh, Lila," he retorts condescendingly. "As smart as you seem to be at times, you sure can be pretty unimaginative. The Direction is setting me up quite well: all expenses paid, a woman of my choosing, three if I want! All I need is to find and bring down Vita Nova and destroy any information collected against The Direction. I get my early retirement, a life of ease, no clutter, no living in caves, no dehydrated meals, and no YOU."

"Why do you hate me so much?" I ask, surprised by his vehemency.

"Because you gave Jax hope, you keep giving him hope, and he focuses too well when he has that." His words confuse me a little.

"Just let me go, then, and I'll take them up on that offer to live in a new town. It's a better choice than dying, that's for sure." I throw in a slight laugh, selling the lie as convincingly as possible, but the light in his icy blue eyes isn't changing.

"You told them that you'd rather die than return to that life, so what makes me think you changed your mind so easily?" He is asking with a sly grin while advancing a few paces. "Besides, you forget, I was there watching them interrogate you, and you didn't give an inch."

Stepping back a bit and sideways to avoid colliding with a tree, I give him a shrug. "People sometimes have a change of heart when faced with reality. I'm obviously at the end of the line here."

His smirk is now turning to a scowl while retorting, "I don't buy it."

*Fight or run, fight or run?*

Standing there, I realize either bet is going to end in a hand-to-hand combat, so I might as well face it now while I still have some energy left. Knife in his right hand, I flinch when Kain surges forward and runs me against a tree with his left hand. Bringing my left arm and blocking his knife-strike, I slam my other fist right beneath his ribs. This buys me just enough time to push away from the tree.

I smash my steel toe boot into his shin, *thank you, Gia...* my left hand grabbing his wielding wrist. Finally acting on a bit of my training from Gia, I twist, ducking beneath his arm so my back is against his chest, and thrust my weight into him. Combining that with a pull on his arm, not to mention my short stature compared to his tall frame, I roll him over me, his back on the ground.

He is too quick, though, and before I realize, his free hand is pulling me over with him, his grip firmly on my arm. Keeping my back locked against him helps me avoid the thrust of the knife or any harsh blows while we struggle on the ground, but he quickly turns the tables and pushes me away, sending me rolling a few times. Unfortunately, I end my roll on my back, and he is instantly over me.

*Adrenaline, fight or flight instinct,* that's all I feel, that's the only thing filling my thoughts until...

*God help me!*

I have never cried to God before, mostly argued with Him, accused Him, but never begged for help, but right now seems like a perfect time to start. I hope He will have pity on my prior obstinance and deliver me from the wrath of this madman who is about ready to slice my throat.

Maybe it's my imagination, but suddenly I feel like I have gone beyond fear and am feeling a rush of inner strength.

*Or is it Heavenly grace?* I have a tiny glimpse of a memory, the times my Dad would speak of the power of God through people, though the recollection is fleeting.

Slamming my forehead into the bridge of Kain's nose is enough to break his focus, and with strength I didn't know I had, I force him over and roll him, regrettably with me, down the steep embankment. The sky and ground are mixing, disorienting the both of us as we each struggle for a solid hold against each other until finally we break free.

We are at the bottom, and the distance between us now is just enough to allow me time to struggle to my feet.

An odd pain in my left shoulder gives me pause, and I notice the knife straight through, jammed between my scapula joint and clavicle. Somehow during the tumble, he had managed to get in a strike.

"Aah! Damn it!" The cry escapes my lips without thought when Kain grabs my shirt from behind, and he pushes me back to the ground, grabbing my braid to hold me there.

*No wonder Gia has her hair cut short,* the notion ruefully comes to mind.

"Not so stubborn now, are we?" His remark is burning, but nothing compared to the burning pain I feel as he pulls the knife from my shoulder with deliberate slowness.

A gush of warmth swells from my shoulder, coursing its way down my arm, and seeping across the chest of my shirt. I have been injured before, I have even been crushed by a horse, but this is different. Yes, the interrogation was bad, but this is different. I know enough about injuries to know this will be life threatening if it has nicked the axillary artery, but there is no way to tell right now while he holds me.

I feel helpless as my attacker methodically searches my pockets and finally finds the data chip. I don't even try to fight; I have no leverage.

*Just wait for the moment...* a quiet voice says.

"This is all too easy..." Kain gloats. "With you gone and the mission a failure, they'll be forced to retreat to Vita Nova, and I will be with them. I'll locate their base and finish my job, all thanks to you."

*They will all die. Each one of them will be found and killed. The mission will fail. The Direction will succeed in the slaughter of the innocent. It's now or never..* I hear the voice in my head again, so far away but powerful, and not my own.

Suddenly, something I learned long ago, something I briefly read again recently, is being repeated in my own voice.

"Our Father, who is in Heaven, Hallowed be Thy name..." I don't know if I am getting all the words right, but I feel like it is altering something, and a warm strength seeps into my own soul, covering over any lingering fear. "Thy Kingdom come, Your will be done..."

Kain is staring at me in confusion, making him stand straight and step back, letting go of my hair. His right arm extends with the blood-stained knife firmly grasped, pointing at me.

"What the hell is that?"

"On earth as it is in Heaven..."

"Heaven?! Is this some lame God thing? I thought you hated that stuff. Honey, let me remind you, there is no God, only power and wealth, and I intend to have both. And when I'm done with you, for you that's it, there is no Heaven. Only regret and then the black of nothingness."

I watch his expression grow darker and darker with each word, anger and spit coming from his mouth in vile hate. It is like something deep within his soul is crawling to the surface, and it dismays me that someone can be that hateful and somehow hide it for so long. At the word 'nothingness', his arms spread wide in a gesture.

*Now!*

Surging to my feet, I hurl myself forward, aiming my good shoulder low into his midsection. Both of us hit the ground, and the impact causes his knife to fly who-knows-where, and I quickly roll to my feet while he is down and stunned.

Without thought, my foot flies to his side, the steel-toe enough to knock the wind out of him. This only allows me a moment, though, to gather my surroundings, trying to locate the missing blade. *Too little, too late.* Getting to his feet and gathering himself, Kain deftly removes a knife from the side of his boot.

*Oh, I've never seen that one. How many does he have?!*

I remain at a severe disadvantage, wounded and *still* unarmed. I square off at him and wait for the attack. In his rage, he rushes too fast, and I am able to dodge the first strike, causing him to stumble, but he recovers quickly. The years of combat and his overall physique can still outweigh my current newfound will to survive. I know this all too well as I wheel around to meet the oncoming force of his towering frame.

The hill we had previously rolled down is at my back, the forest surrounds us, and the creek running southeast is about twelve paces behind Kain; there is no escape. Uphill is not an option. I already feel the energy slowly fading as I heave air in and out, my shoulder injury making itself known by a lack of mobility in my arm.

There is no time to make a decision, other than what instinct provides, as he closes the distance and sideways strikes at my throat. I duck and block with my right arm. The weight of his strike pushes me down to the point I nearly lose my footing as I brace my forearm against his forearm, the knife inches from my neck.

Quickly, before I lose more leverage, I release the pressure and throw myself to my side, rolling a few times, closer to the creek. This movement disturbs his balance once more, the knife impacts the ground where I was, and I have time to jump to my feet and start running.

*I need the distance between us.*

Instead of pursuing, however, as soon as I am to my feet he throws his small boot-blade, and I feel it sink into my back with that same burning sensation. I know that he was aiming for my heart, and by the grace of God, even with Kain's precise knife-throwing ability, it hits a few inches low and to the left. The impact is no less shocking, though, and I stumble forward and trip, landing facedown into the creek I am trying to cross.

Sputtering and struggling to my hands and knees, I blindly grope for a rock, a stick, anything underneath the babbling waters. I have nothing, my fingers are not working, not grasping, and I gasp as I feel a boot on my back pushing me down back into the waters as the short but lethal knife is yanked out.

There is no following stab as expected, no slicing, just more weight on my back as he uses his free hand and pushes me deeper into the water.

*Waterboarding...*

Panicking, I try to hold my breath for as long as I can, the oxygen in my lungs dwindling, hastened by my futile struggle against the weight on me. Despite the front and center hysteria, in the back of my mind I feel an immense grief and anger, not for me, but for what will happen to everyone now.

*This is it... God, I am sorry. I tried. It's up to You. Save them. Please.*

Unexpectedly, a profound sense of peace washes over me, and I close my eyes and stop struggling.

*This is it.*

The sounds around me are muffled by the water, my consciousness gradually drifting, yet I think for a moment that I hear a deep growl, not from a human but a wild animal. The arm and boot that are holding me down suddenly release.

# | 47 |

# Guardian Angel

I don't waste a moment before lifting myself, gasping, first to my hands, then my knees, and finally, unsteadily to my feet. The fog in my mind slowly clears, and I turn around to see a massive dog, *or maybe a white fluffy wolf,* with its front paws planted on the back of a motionless Kain, who is face down in the creek.

For the moment I am frozen as the large white dog raises his bright eyes and stares at me, tongue lolling and jaws parted as though in a smile.

*I have seen this dog before.*

He was the one who caused the wreck with the bike, subsequently preventing us from driving into an ambush. And then recently, when I was escaping the facility, he stood there barking at the guards and distracting them.

*And could this be the same dog Gam kept seeing in the caves?*

Seeing him this close, however, gives me pause, even though I feel he would never harm me. He seems to sense this and steps off the still-motionless Kain, goes to the embankment, and sits, watching studiously.

Rapidly the adrenaline I was surviving on begins to drain from me, and I am slowly becoming aware of pain in both my shoulder and back. The fact that I am still standing, though, means another miracle: the knife to the shoulder *must* have missed the axillary artery.

Hissing at the discomfort, I cautiously move toward my attacker and tentatively reach to feel his pulse at his neck. Feeling nothing indicating signs of life, I struggle to roll him over and am taken aback by the wide-eyed look of shock on his face. I remind myself there is no pulse, and that is when I see the handle of his own knife, the blade fully buried just left of his sternum.

Relief and exhaustion consume me as I stumble to where the dog sits, and without even thinking, I sit down on his left and wrap my arm around him, burying my face in the fur of his neck. I lose track of time as I just sit there sobbing on the shoulder of this unknown rescuer. This Godsend.

*Yes. The God who has kept me alive...The crucifix, the empty stairwell, the dog, the squib load, and the dog again...That had to be You! I am so sorry for my doubt.*

Finally, the light in the sky is dimming. I assume it to be about 19:30, and I am aware of how much I need to look after my own injuries. Even though it has slowed, the blood from my left shoulder has already soaked my vest-shirt and mostly covers my arm. I can't see my back injury, but I reach my good hand around to feel and am agreeably surprised at the minimal blood.

*Perhaps because the blade is so thin and relatively short.*

"Hurts like hell, though," I absently comment aloud, and my new companion whimpers in response, batting at my leg with a paw as he looks up at me.

Not even sure where the strength is coming from, but with help from my friend, I struggle up the hill to where Kain had dropped his backpack. I know he has... *had*... a med kit, and that is my first goal.

Before long, I have my shoulder mostly patched and decide to leave my back to someone who can reach it better.

"Back at base, of course." I find myself speaking again out loud to the furry companion by my side.

He tilts his head at me and again whimpers, as though concerned. I am beginning to wonder if he knows something I do not, and I become a little leerier and more watchful of my surroundings despite my exhaustion.

*Maybe Kain has backup on the way.*

"I think it's safe to message Isaac now," I murmur, taking the tablet from my pocket.

"Ah, well, that's not good."

I grimace as I look down at a smashed screen. It doesn't respond to me touching the fractured display, and I drop it into the backpack.

"I guess it's just us."

The dog pants in reply.

Shivering, I grab Kain's jacket from the pack. I am loath to wear something of his, but the temperature is already dropping and the blood I lost already decreases my ability to maintain heat, especially with my soaked clothes.

I struggle to slip my injured limb into one arm and grimace as the added weight of the fabric rubs against both my injuries as well as the burn on my side. Fortunately, it being several sizes larger than I wear makes it easier to tug over both shoulders. After digging out a health bar, I sling the backpack onto my good shoulder and tentatively navigate down the hill I had climbed. This time I am not so keen on rolling.

*I need to get that data chip back.*

Standing by the bank, I am immobile for a moment, staring at the body in the water. I shiver as the past hour flashes through my thoughts in bits and pieces.

"Our Father, who *art* in Heaven…" I suddenly murmur, trying to remember the rest of the words.

The dog pants loudly beside me and gives a quick bark as if approvingly.

Finally, braving the dead eyes of someone who once was a teammate, I step into the icy water and dig into his pockets for the data chip. It takes some time, as I have no clue which pocket he had put it in. With cargo pants and a molle vest, there are many to search. I finally locate the chip and place it back in my right zipper pocket of my pants.

There is one more thing I need: a weapon. I look around for as long as I can afford in the dying light for the larger knife that had been thrown during the fight, but to my disappointment, I cannot find where it has gone.

*That leaves one option.*

Returning to the body, and with a scowl, I remove the knife from his chest and wash it right there in the creek, drying it on the jacket, *Kain's jacket*, before slipping it into my own boot.

Turning to go, I am stopped as the dog, *I should give him a name*, plants himself in front of me and whimpers, staring at the body. Something beyond me compels me to turn back to Kain's motionless body, grab onto the drag-handle of his molle vest, and try to drag him up onto the bank.

Only managing to get his upper half out of the water, I call it good enough as I wheeze and grimace, a shot of pain traveling through my left lung. My grasp releases suddenly from the drag-handle, and I land on my butt. Sitting there for a moment, I reach over and close Kain's eyes, somberly reflecting.

"May God have mercy on his soul."

I find myself surprised by these words today which keep escaping without me truly understanding, yet they give me a certain peace, and with resolve I push myself to my feet and head southeast, following the creek.

"Only an hour hike, doggo," I comment as I take a small bite of the bar and offer a piece to my dog who is padding steadily by my side.

*My dog... or maybe my guardian angel?*

# | 48 |

# Keep Praying

"I'm wondering if we should have stayed at base. This is just too much territory to cover for the four of us, and it is already 16:47." Gia grouchily comments, shifting her AR to her other side and looking at her watch. "Not to mention the number of surveillance drones and the satellite we have barely dodged."

"And my drones need a recharge," Isaac adds, tapping at his data pad. "Last I looked, chatter at the facility hasn't mentioned a re-capture, but for some reason they did scale back their men."

"It's possible they're letting Kain handle this one to keep it quieter. That might be a good thing for Lila." Gia theorizes but shakes her head a little in realization. "If she doesn't know about Kain, she might have messaged and met with him already."

Gam nods thoughtfully. "Or she may also be taking a longer route to avoid bringing them to us. Especially if she doesn't know the base is already compromised."

Jax stands at the edge of a cliff, glassing as far as he can with his binoculars, listening to them as he prays at the same time. Turning around, he nods somberly.

"We'll head back and get the bikes from where we left them at the creek. Then we go double-check the base. We're pretty far North already, so there is a likely chance we've narrowly missed one or the other. Kain is radio silent. That might mean he's still searching, and that means he hasn't met with Lila. Or let's hope not."

"But," he adds, his expression tense, and it pains him to say this. "If neither of them arrive by nightfall, we need to head east. I can't risk your lives anymore."

They nod soberly in agreement and gather their packs, cautiously heading southward, even though it feels like defeat. For two hours they go into autopilot as they hike, only pausing once to avoid drones. No words are exchanged as they all feel the weight of the situation.

Suddenly Jax stops, and they all hear it as well. "Gunfire. Pretty sure south of here. Just once."

"And pretty far," Gia adds.

"Let's double time!" Jax commands, and they pick up their pace.

This is the first time they have had any direction to go on, and a glimmer of hope sparks and gives speed to their steps. Even with the new optimism, though, Jax feels a sense of urgency and foreboding.

*Pray...*

"Our Father, Who art in Heaven..." he begins in a quiet whisper while they run through the woods.

# | 49 |

# Lungs

Thirty minutes into my walk, and I know I am in trouble. Each breath sets my left side on fire, and the pain grows, the rest of my body shivering. I have to stop every fifty yards and try to recover. Even then, my heartrate remains elevated; borderline thready. Looking down at my hands, the paleness and the blue-tinge to the fingertips completes the symptoms and tells me everything I need to know.

*Tension Pneumothorax, or maybe Hemopneumothorax...*

The knife wound in my back has most likely caused a collapsed lung and possible internal bleeding. Wheezing, I sit down again and close my eyes, leaning my head back against a tree. I hear the whimper of my furred companion and feel his wet nose inspecting the side of my face.

"I know, boy..." Forcing my eyes open, I know I shouldn't fall asleep, and I start searching Kain's backpack instead.

If I find something like a straw or IV needle, I will consider giving myself a needle decompression to drain the air and possibly blood from my chest cavity, releasing the pressure on my lung. That has its own risks, though, with how shaky my hands are now. A slight sense of panic starts to grip me, and I squeeze my eyes shut, trying to calm myself.

*God, I think I need a little help... I know You saved me back there for a reason. Think you could do it again?*

I hear a small yip and a whimper, and I open my eyes, watching as the dog bounces up and down, looking to me and then looking toward our destination.

"I can't," I force a reply, my chest tightening with the effort, my body leaden.

Not taking no for an answer, the canine jogs over and grabs my jacket sleeve, tugging at it. I finally struggle to my feet, using him for support, and force myself to continue following the creek. After fifty more yards, I can barely focus, and even though it is still evening twilight, a different kind of darkness is creeping in, starting at my peripheral vision.

The dog yelps and stops at a clump of bushes, but once I force myself to focus, heaving in a painful breath, I realize they are actually four hover-bikes covered in a camo cloth.

"You smart dog…" I gasp out.

Then my legs give out and my vision fades the rest of the way, completely black. My hearing is muffled, as though someone is covering my ears, but I can hear the dog's deep, echoing bark, before my consciousness fades.

# | 50 |

# Catching Up

The four of them follow the creek, keeping up a quick pace but slow enough to keep an eye on the tracks before them in the dying light. They had found Kain's body and spots of blood alongside the creek. That's where they also saw and started to follow a set of size 8 boot prints, and oddly enough dog tracks as well.

"Looks like she stayed by the creek. She might even be back at the base by now," Gia comments.

"I doubt it." Jax's voice is tinged with concern despite his efforts, and something tells him it was her blood back over by Kain. "Her stride looks to have shortened and slowed considerably. She could very well be shot or stabbed."

"Or both," Isaac adds, and Jax gives him a slight glare.

"We should pick up the pace again," Jax urges. "We're quite close to the bikes anyway; she may have seen them and taken one."

Suddenly, a deep, persistent bark echoes from the direction they are headed.

"That sounds like it *is* by the bikes," Gam exclaims, and they all take off at a run.

| 51 |

# Family and Safety

My head hurts, and my mouth is dry, but the first thing I feel is that I can actually breathe better.

*And I am warmer.*

It still burns a bit to inhale, and my shoulder and back ache, but my heartrate seems more normal. Hesitantly, I open my eyes and once they adjust, I notice that the light flickering on the rock ceiling reminds me of a campfire.

Only my eyes move at first, my body still feeling weighed down, but I am able to see above me that someone has hung an IV bag on a climbing peg in the rock. It isn't clear, like isotonic fluids, but red, and feels warm as it enters my vein.

"Finished our one bag of isotonic and just put on the blood. Make sure you drink plenty of Hydra-thlete." I recognize Gia's firm voice.

"Yes, ma'am. Going to have to call you doc pretty soon," Jax's voice replies.

Hearing their voices surrounds me with a feeling of safety. I try to speak, but I am still in a state between sleeping and waking, and it takes some time for the sounds and sights to register. Part of me wonders if this is a dream or a hallucination from blood loss or lack of oxygen.

Suddenly, a large black nose surrounded by white fur snuffles over my face, whimpering.

"Hey you…" I finally manage to whisper hoarsely, recognizing the face of my canine rescuer.

"Lila?!" Three voices, Gia, Jax, and Isaac, exclaim in unison, and their faces filter into view on my left as the dog pulls away.

"Don't ask me to get up."

I groan as I turn my head, receiving a wave of pain in my shoulder, but it allows me a better view of them. I notice a small campfire behind them.

"The opposite," Gia sternly replies. "*Don't* move. I have a needle catheter in your chest in case we need to remove more air. But the patch job on your back should prevent that necessity. If you take it easy."

She raises a brow, almost daring me to argue.

"No problem. I don't want to move. Where's Gam?" My voice is still barely above a whisper, but I suddenly realize his dark face is missing from the group, and a pang of worry hits me.

"Oh, he had to step out because of all the blood stuff going on." Isaac grins, obviously taking delight at Gam's expense.

"He tried to stay and help," Jax adds.

I notice his beard is gone, and I am too tired to decide if I like it or not.

"But once Gia heard you and I are the same blood type and started using me as a walking blood bank," he gestures to a bandage on his arm, "it was too much for him."

It is getting difficult to keep my eyes open, and I reluctantly let them close for a moment, feeling as though I could sleep for weeks.

"Lila?" Jax places his hand on my arm.

"Just… tired. I have to tell you…" I force it out, trying to hang onto consciousness. "Kain…"

"We know," Jax interjects, his voice quieting. "He betrayed us all."

Eyes still closed, I notice Gia slip the familiar cuff from the trauma scanner on my wrist, and I am assuming she is checking my vitals. I hear her voice, low in consideration of me.

"She'll be fine tonight. Just tired like she said, and who knows if she has really slept much the past week? Fluid in her lungs, I'm guessing waterboarding, and the burn on her side, electrical shock..."

I vaguely feel Jax's hand gently squeeze my arm as I drift into a welcomed sleep.

*Thank you, God, for this new family and safety...*

# | 52 |

# Assurances

The cave they are in now is north of their usual base, down in a deep draw. It is a much smaller cave, but enough space to fit the four hover-bikes with the two bike trailers in the back and for them to sleep and move around a little. Branches and a camo cloth cover the front to block anyone outside from seeing light during the dark hours.

After everyone took turns sleeping or keeping watch through the night, Gam is up early preparing coffee. He hands one cup to Jax and then one to Isaac, who is tapping at his data pad, his brows knit together.

"They found Kain's, I mean Colonel Kai's body, and my cameras back at base show they raided and destroyed whatever was left. The longer we stay, the greater the risk we get caught."

"I agree. When can we move out?" Jax directs his question to Gia.

"That's what I'm not sure about," Gia admits, shaking her head. "I think give her two days? You're the actual medic, Lila. Will you be alright by then to hang onto a hover bike?"

Lila goes to reply, grimacing as Gia helps her sit upright with a rolled mat against the cave wall, but Jax gives a low chuckle and shakes his head.

"She'd probably try to tell us she's fine to move, even if she isn't, so if *you* think two days, we'll wait two days."

"I *can* answer for myself, Jax." Lila raises a brow, her voice still on the raspy side. "One day is good enough."

"Are you sure?" Jax asks dubiously, sipping his coffee while watching her expression.

He notes the look of defiance on her face but catches a hint of doubt too, and by now he knows she would sacrifice her health for their safety. It reminds him of himself, but he would rather she not make herself a martyr.

"Stop drinking coffee at me," she grumbles in response. "Gia won't give me any."

"You're the one who told me dehydration and caffeine don't mix well." Gia sips her own coffee but turns away when Lila shoots her a glare.

"Two days, then," Jax comments decisively.

Lila releases a sigh in defeat then laughs a little, although at that she grabs her side with her good hand, grimacing. The large, white dog who has never left her side sits up and whimpers, nudging at her leg with his nose.

"I'm good…just hurts to laugh. And breathe. And move. And… fine. Two days."

Gam goes over and hands her a bottle of electrolytes, concern on his face as he lowers his large frame to a crouch beside her.

"You sure you don't need three days?"

"No. We can't risk it. You guys can always tie me to…" She pauses, a shadow over her countenance, and Jax watches as she absently rubs at the deep marks on her wrists from the tie-straps.

"On second thought, please don't," she adds in a quieter voice.

Jax stares down into his coffee, wincing as he realizes her thoughts are back at the facility; back at Sublevel 20. He can't help but feel guilty for trusting Kain all this time and nearly costing Lila her life. What should have been his job, protecting her, he gave to the enemy.

"It's not your fault, Jax."

Lila's quiet voice breaks through his ponderings, and he looks up, not realizing his expression was that readable. Something in her amber eyes is different, though.

*There's no more anger…*

"She's right," Isaac agrees. "It's not your fault. Kain tricked us all. He was obviously planted as a mole from the beginning, and he took his time building that trust. And we all trusted him."

Gia simply nods.

Gam shrugs. "Yeah, he was a jerk sometimes, but I never would have imagined he could be that evil. And I thought I was a good judge of character."

"Thanks, guys." Jax nods slightly, moved by their compassion.

The guilt still lingers, though, and he feels he needs to personally apologize to Lila soon. He watches her lean her head back against the stone, her eyes closing and her lips moving silently.

*Is she...praying?*

# | 53 |

# Small Victories

It is good to be able to sit up and interact with them, albeit painful still. Gia had to cut my shirt when they first found me, so I am mildly self-conscious, wearing only a black sports bra and my cargos. She did a wonderful job on the stitches at my shoulder, but the collarbone she said is fractured will have to heal on its own.

Even with the peacefulness of being with them, I am hit with a sudden gripping feeling in my chest as flashes of the past few days intrude on my thoughts.

*It was my comment about being tied...*

My fingers trace where the tie-straps dug in. I manage to stay long enough to tell Jax it is not his fault, and I vaguely hear each of the others reiterate my sentiment.

As things around me drift away, my heart pounds in my ears, and I can almost see the searing light and smell the concrete. I hear the scraping of metal as a chair is tipped back. A burning in my lungs has me hold my breath, and I close my eyes.

*This too shall pass... calm my heart, Lord. You are my Refuge, my Stronghold, the Rock in whom I trust... Our Father...*

After some time, I feel a heavy paw on my lap, then the dogs head, and slowly I pull myself back to reality, entwining my fingers in the long white fur. Opening my eyes, I am finally back in the dimly lit cave, the smell of coffee, earth, and dog grounding me.

I look over to my right to the back of the cave, where Gia and Gam are debating over breakfast, and Isaac is taking stock of his equipment.

*When did they go over there?*

A glance to my left has me meeting Jax's gaze, a perturbed look on his face. I suddenly wonder how long he has been watching and how long I was 'gone'. I shift my gaze to the dog's head in my lap, my fingers still buried in the fur. I feel Jax's presence as he slides down against the cavern wall to sit at my left, and I don't know why I never noticed it before, but something from him almost smells like pine.

"You just went there, didn't you." His voice is low and a statement more than a question.

"Yeah… for how long was I…?" I distractedly pet the dog's fur, stealing a quick glance to see Jax lean forward on his knees.

"At least five minutes. The others didn't notice."

"Good…Please don't tell them."

It seems embarrassing to me. I can handle the wounds of others without a flinch, but a simple memory shuts me down.

"Don't keep it all to yourself, though, it only makes it worse. If you ever need to talk, Lil', I'm here."

Something in his voice tells me he has probably been through this before. The old familiar nickname makes me smile a little, and I rest my head back again.

"I'll keep that in mind…"

"I do have a question…" He hesitates before continuing, and I feel apprehensive at first. "Were you praying?"

A grin pulls at my lips slightly as I embarrassingly realize he caught me, and I turn my head against the stone to look at him, noticing a hopeful glint in his eyes.

"Maybe I was…"

A smile lightens up his face, and it relaxes me to see him not so worried.

"God is the only reason I am still alive. He gave me hope. He was my strength when I had none left…" I clear my throat as the awareness hits me again that I should be dead, but for the Grace of God. "And this dog; pretty sure God sent him."

The dog's tail thumps on the dirt as though in response.

"You'll have to share the dog's story when the others are done debating which health bar to eat for breakfast." He comments with a slight grin as he reaches over and ruffles the dog's ear. "But in all seriousness… I am glad you and God are on speaking terms now."

"Me too," I admit.

"Keep using that to get through the tough times."

Again, he seems to speak from experience, and I simply nod. He hesitates about something again, looking down at the ground for a moment.

"Spit it out," I persuade quietly, closing my eyes for a moment, my energy not lasting as long as I hoped.

"I just wanted to let you know… how sorry I am that you went through that. I should have been there with you or not let you go. You risked your life for nothing, and if you hadn't made it…"

I suddenly realize they don't know I actually have the chip, and my eyes fly open, a little more oomph in me left to spend.

"Jax!" I exclaim, interrupting him, and he looks mildly alarmed at my outburst. "First of all, I meant it when I said it's not your fault. Part of me believes it had to happen this way."

He looks at me thoughtfully for a moment, his sage-green eyes solemn. "You said first of all…What is second?"

Reaching into the right side pocket of my pants, I take out the chip and hold it in the air. "Not for nothing…For all the files we need."

His expression goes from confusion, to disbelief, and then astonishment.

"You got it?! You got it! Guys, Isaac, she got it!" He takes the chip and jumps to his feet. "Isaac, let's see what we have and get it sent to headquarters."

The excitement is tangible as the other two rush over while Isaac quickly grabs the chip and one of his data pads. Everyone waits with bated breath, standing around Isaac. Even the dog has left my side and bounces in place near them, feeling the anticipation. I struggle to lean forward from the wall and grimace, wishing I could get to my feet and be there.

"They're all there. Everything," Isaac confirms in an almost dazed voice, looking at me. "How?"

"Long story..."

"That she can tell another time," Gia directs, and I give her a thankful smile.

"And now it is sent." Isaac grins about as wide as I have ever seen from him. "We'll wait to hear back if it is enough."

A chorus of cheers and hugs fills the small cave, though they try to keep the sound subdued just in case. I suddenly find myself surrounded, the dog returning to my side as well, but thankfully they don't hug me just yet.

*I'll collect on that when I recover...*

"You did it, Lila." Gia grins, and Gam beams proudly.

"GOD did it." I correct, and I receive nods of agreement and a couple '*amens*'.

"This calls for a celebration," Gam declares, going over to the supplies with Gia. "I might have a few ingredients up my sleeve for a better meal than health bars."

Isaac goes back to his security tablet. "This calls for me to check on the trail cameras I have in place nearby to make sure our brief ruckus hasn't attracted unwanted attention."

"This calls for a nap," I comment with a tired grin as Jax quietly sits back down next to me, a smile still stretched across his face.

I cringe in discomfort as I shift to lie down but sigh with relief once I relax, letting my eyes close finally.

"Hey, Lil'," Jax's quiet voice delays my slumber.

"Hmmm?"

I am faintly aware of a blanket being placed over me and the weight of a dog's head on my leg. The words are barely audible.

"I'm glad you're still here with me."

# | 54 |

# Moving On

Leaning against the wall of the cave, I fasten the black sleeveless shirt Gia has given me, almost wishing I didn't have it as it abrades my stitches and the burn marks at my side.

"And the last thing I remember is Yeti barking, and that's when you guys found me."

I finish the story of the dog, only briefly going over the encounter with Kain, just enough to tell Yeti's part in the story. I am not exactly ready to recall things in their entirety.

Isaac gives a low whistle from where he is helping Gam strap some of the supplies to the bike trailer. "So, this is the dog that scared Gam and ate Jax's dried beef."

Gam gives him a punch on the arm. "I wasn't scared. He surprised me."

"Anyway." Gia rolls her eyes at the two. "Lila, why did you name him Yeti?"

As though sensing he is a hot topic, the dog lifts his massive head off the floor, his tongue lolling.

"My dad had this myths and legends book, with something about a large hairy snowbeast named Yeti. Around here I think it was Bigfoot, back when there used to be tribes of what they called Native Americans."

"Until the government probably wiped them out with the inoculations," Isaac snorts morosely, struggling to get a crate back on one of the trailers.

"Here, let me help you," I offer, moving forward, but Gia puts a hand out.

"Nope, not gonna happen. You're first on your feet this morning, so no way you're lifting anything."

"I'm just tired. My lung is going to be fine," I argue.

"Not according to the trauma scanner. Your lung isn't even fully expanded yet. That, and I heard you coughing last night." Jax backs up Gia's statement as he helps Isaac secure the final cart.

"Everyone is against me this morning. I wasn't even allowed to pour my own coffee." I send a glare to Gam.

"Five pounds, Lila. That's what the medical documents say. That pot was at least eight," Gam defends himself.

Yeti sits beside me, his shoulder all the way to my hip, and I find myself using him for support despite my protests. They are right, I am nowhere near recovered, but I feel useless as I watch them wrap up the impromptu camp.

"It's the perfect day to leave," Isaac comments, securing the last of his tablets. "Defense just finished combing the western borders. That means this area is next."

"And what about the detour stop I asked you to look into?" Jax queries.

"The Advanced Medic Facility on the east border of Gamal?" Isaac's words pique my interest, and I stand a little straighter. "No go. They got shut down shortly after Lila escaped."

"Probably another handiwork of Kain's," Jax muses with distain.

"Wait, I thought we had to get to the backup base first, why are we interested in the medic facility?" I ask.

"You," Gia replies as she throws her backpack on.

"I'm fine." Their concern is touching, but I really am convinced I *will* be fine.

"I wanted a second opinion." Jax nods slightly to Gia. "No offense to you."

"None taken, I wanted it too, but I guess Kain ruins one more thing from the grave."

"This means we'll be tight on supplies." My own brows furrow, as I know that the facility of which they speak is, *or was*, the one we always got our medical supplies from.

Isaac shakes his head a little. "We'll be good for a while. Bear Base is fully stocked."

"Bear Base? The one we are headed to?" I raise a brow.

"Yup," Gia confirms. "We didn't name it, though. Usually we just go Base 1, Base 2, stuff like that."

"Who named it?" Gam is curious now.

"Nik." Jax mentions, and I notice him shake his head in amusement.

I tilt my head a little in puzzlement, and Yeti seems to mimic my movements, tilting his own. "Who's Nik?"

"Pretty much the caretaker, but he likes code names for the bases," Isaac explains dismissively as he throws his own pack on. "Alright, hate to say it, but I think it's time."

Jax nods and looks at me. "Ready?"

"As I'll ever be." I put the helmet on that he hands me, and it allows me to hide a look of discomfort as I prepare for what I know will be a painful five-hour drive.

| 55 |

# Making Progress

Jax grins a little as he watches Yeti perched on the supplies trailer pulled by Gam, the dog's tongue hanging out in delight as the wind throws his ears back. The journey through the wooded hills was tedious and took longer than anticipated as the trailers, even though narrow and designed for tight paths, took a little more cautious maneuvering.

Gia drives the second bike with the trailer and supplies, while Isaac rides solo. Lila is behind Jax, and he can tell when the jarring motions begin to take a toll on her as she situates her right arm around him for support instead of the rails.

After passing through the southern outskirts of an abandoned city, the terrain opens up to treeless wide prairies of tall grasses. Fortunately for her, this promises a smoother ride for a short period. This is not so fortunate for security, however.

Though it is unlikely for drones to travel out this far, Isaac theorizes the chance of the surveilled range being extended is likely, due to the captured information. For this reason, they take turns activating Isaac's custom designed scramblers on each bike.

Things could become sketchy, though, as they approach the timeframe for the satellites. Fortuitously, or more likely strategically planned, they reach a landscape that offers several opportunities to hide against buttes and deeply grooved, dry riverbeds.

The last few miles are rougher than expected due to washouts from recent rains, and Jax almost wishes the clouds are still present as the sun beats down. The temperature swings in these areas are drastic.

*Perfect timing for a rest,* he considers as he notices Lila pressing her helmet into his back for respite.

Isaac selects a butte with an almost cave-like overhang and pulls his bike as far in as he can. Each of them follows suit, Jax last. He waits for Lila to move and get off first, and she does so, taking her helmet off.

"You alright?" He inquires, noticing her pallor.

"I will be," She quietly replies and sits in the alcove next to Yeti, the faithful dog sniffing at her face before lying beside her.

"Alright, our hour of patience starts… now." Isaac marks on his watch before swigging from a bottle of water.

Gam tosses bottles to Gia and Jax, but hands one to Lila, sitting himself beside her. "How're you doing, doc?"

"It's a little tougher than I thought it would be," she confesses, resting her head back and closing her eyes.

"Just another hour and a half of travel," Jax assures, saying a quick prayer in his head that it will go quickly.

"Oh!" Isaac exclaims, reading something on his tablet.

"Come on, Isaac, share with the class," Gia prods.

"We will have company at Bear Base in four weeks, from Vita Nova."

Jax's brow raises. "What kind of company?"

"Like… the General."

"Who's the General?" Lila tentatively inquires, her eyes still closed.

"Pretty much our boss. Although I've never met him. He usually stays in Vita Nova," Gia comments. "I wonder why he's meeting with us?"

"Wonder no longer," Isaac quips. "He wants to update us in person and plan our next move against The Direction."

Jax lowers his gaze, a hint of a smile on his face. "Finally, progress."

After years of gaining allies, recruiting inside sources, and obtaining access to the systems, they are finally going to make a dent.

"Did you let Nik know? He likes to have notice way ahead when dignitaries are involved." He mentions to Isaac while watching Lila trying to catch some sleep with her head on the dog.

Jax's protective side doesn't want to let her out of his sights, meanwhile his guarded side silently cautions him, and he looks away.

"Will do." Isaac nods and taps at his tablet.

# | 56 |

# Rough Travels

Hanging on with one arm has been harder than I expected, and part of me wishes I could just sleep during the trip. Gam had asked about using one of the trailers, but Isaac says they are maxed out with their weight limit, and our supplies are at a minimum already.

Next best option is sleep during this hour reprieve, and I try to find a comfortable position, my head on Yeti. It seems I have just barely fallen asleep, the voices of my companions drifting away, when Gam nudges my right shoulder.

"Sorry to wake you, but it's time to get going."

I can't help but groan as I force myself to my feet, every part of me feeling stiff and sore. Jax gives me an almost apologetic glance while handing me the helmet, and just like that, we are on our way again.

As we travel, the scenery changes and helps distract me. We pass the occasional deteriorated road, but our path is mostly straight across grass until we dip into a valley covered in ancient trees. Most of them are decrepit and fallen, leaving a gnarled mess for us to navigate. I find the appearance oddly appealing, though, like we just entered some mythical story.

My reverie is disrupted as Jax's bike clips a fallen tree, and the jarring motion has me instinctively use both arms to stay on.

"Damnit," I mutter through gritted teeth when a wave of pain hits me.

"I'm sorry, do we need to stop?" Jax asks, slowing the vehicle.

I probably should, suspecting I ripped my stitches, but we are late already.

"No... I'm alright. Keep going." The strain in my voice belies my statement, but either the wind or the helmet muffles it enough that he doesn't notice and picks up speed again.

The pain dulls to an ache, and I return my attention to the landscape, which again changes as we cross a dilapidated bridge over a wide, shallow river. It opens again to grassy hills until we turn in a more southeasterly direction. That is when my breath is taken in a good way.

*Very different from what I knew in the Eden region.*

This is an area once known as The Badlands; the vast emptiness is beautiful and deceptively welcoming. I find myself looking up at tall buttes, the multiple layers of different earth types telling stories of floods and erosion. The tops are oddly flat, and most of them have tall, brown grasses as the cold nights have removed their color. The sky itself seems to go on forever.

*God, what a beautiful creation! How could one doubt Your existence with all this...* I think briefly of Kain's denial of God's existence and wince a little, remembering the vehemence.

With the smoother terrain, our speed picks up, and for a short stint I notice we are on a road, *or what used to be one*. The grasses and twiggy shrubbery have broken through the pavement and time has shifted pieces apart from each other.

Just as suddenly as it began, it ends, and we are back in rolling plains with dying grasses. I can't help but smile a little as we pass through a large herd of wild horses, and they scatter, their thundering hooves bringing a more pleasant memory from my past. I can almost smell them.

Yeti barks from his position behind Gam, looking like he might try and jump off to chase them. Fortunately, he stays and turns his head to look at me, tongue hanging out in a wide doggish grin.

Finally, and just in time, because even my good arm is beyond sore, we slow as we enter an area that reminds me a lot of the hills around our former base. Trees crowd our paths, and I hold tight to Jax as he and the others weave through coulees and smaller draws. Crossing a creek, we ease up one more narrow gorge, and everyone stops before leaving the cover of trees.

Ahead of us, nestled in the grasses of a wider tree-bordered draw is an odd formed-brick structure. The face of it is visible, but the rest of it seems to be buried in the hill. Recesses that look like former windows are pitch black, and the only entrance is a single solid wood door.

"Well, that's different," I comment as I get off the bike and remove my helmet.

I can't say I am excited to step into a concrete box, *again*, but a loud voice distracts me from my misgivings.

"You guys made it!!"

A boisterous, cheerful man with glasses, the height of Jax and nearly the build of Gam, comes running out the door toward us. He first grabs Jax in a crushing embrace, then Gia, lifting her off her feet, and then Isaac. Yeti is exuberantly running circles around the group.

"You must be Gam."

The cheery man extends a hand and sizes up Gam, grinning in approval before dragging him into a hug. Gam is a little taken aback but laughs uncertainly and returns a quick hug.

"And you. You must be Lila!" He turns with the biggest of smiles, and to my dismay, grabs me up.

"Nik, don't!!" Both Gia and Jax protest too late.

# | 57 |

# Truthful

"Lila, I'm so sorry." The boisterous man, who is apparently Nik, apologizes profusely as he hands me a clean cloth, and I press it over the broken stitches on my shoulder.

Sitting *on* a beautiful solid wood table in the brightly lit interior of Bear Base, my feet dangling, I flinch at the pressure on my collarbone and shake my head.

"It's fine. Pretty sure things broke open during the trip anyway."

"No, it's not fine," argues Gia irately, her temper showing as she returns from a hallway in the back of the open-concept dining and living room, new gauze and zip-stitches in hand. "Didn't you tell him *anything*, Isaac?"

"I might have failed to mention a few things," Isaac confesses, smiling sheepishly as he carries his equipment to another room.

Gia gives him a glare while she helps me replace the zip-stitches and tapes the gauze over. Glancing to the living room, I note that Yeti has already made himself at home on a round rug.

The bear hug had sent me to my knees, wheezing and fighting a new wave of discomfort in my shoulder and lung. Before I could protest, Gam had grabbed me up and taken me in, setting me on the table. He has since left for the kitchen to avoid the sight of blood. I look down now and notice the drips of red on the beautiful wood.

"Sorry about your table, Nik."

"It's seen worse. I've butchered deer on it before." Nik grins. "Besides, it's *our* table."

"Here, I found this, too." Gia pulls a sling from her pocket and helps adjust it to my left arm.

Jax is ominously silent when he returns from the bikes with the familiar medical device and hands it to Gia before stepping back, his arms folded.

"I'm fine, I just had to catch my breath." I insist but then add with a sigh, knowing she won't relent. "Fine, if it will make you happy."

"Yes, it will." She grins a little and activates the scanner.

"I'll be back. I need to make sure Gam doesn't break my kitchen…I mean our kitchen." Nik excuses himself.

"Alright, I'll let you look it over because you're the doc, just promise you'll be honest with us," Gia asserts.

"I promise." I nod with a small smile.

"Good."

I notice Jax give her a pointed look, and she hands me the pad.

"Umm…I'm… going to help Isaac and yell at him some more." She grins impishly and heads for Isaac's data room, where I assume he is hiding while unpacking.

I remain seated, facing the front door, and flip through the images. Jax leans himself to the right of me against the table, folding his arms again as he stares at the door, *or more like through*. I can almost hear the wheels turning in his mind, and I have a feeling that he is not happy with something I did.

*Or didn't do…*

"What's wrong?" I ask quietly, my eyes still perusing the data, mostly to avoid his eyes.

By habit I try to fidget with the ring that is not around my neck anymore, and I grimace at its absence. He takes a deep breath, and I prepare to be chewed out.

"Was it back at the trees and river that the stitches broke?"

"I suspect so." I bite my lip.

"Why didn't you let me stop, then?"

"I didn't think it would bleed much, and we were already running late."

"Lil'..." He pauses and moves to stand in front of me, waiting until I look up at him. "I need you to do something."

"What...?" I see an earnest look in his eyes, his jaw tensing the slightest, and I suddenly feel guilty for withholding things.

"Please don't be a martyr. At least not with me."

"I don't like weighing people down," I remonstrate, glancing away.

I can't help but meet his gaze again, however, as he leans closer and places his hands on the table at either side of me. His grey-green eyes are serious, almost troubled.

"Lil', you have never, and will never, be a burden to me. No one here is a burden to anyone. We hold each other up. Can you please be truthful with me from now on?"

"Okay, I promise." I agree in a murmur, and I see his face relaxing as he holds my gaze for a long moment.

"Good..." He moves back.

"I'm sorry, Jax," I add when he sits next to me on the table.

"You don't need to be sorry..." His tone is calm, and he smiles a little, lightly bumping my right shoulder with his arm. "I know how independent you have had to be, but you don't have to go it alone anymore. Now, what's the prognosis?"

He indicates the forgotten medical tablet on my lap, and I quickly recall what I had been doing. I raise a brow at his back-to-business attitude, and I try to fulfill my promise, clearing my throat.

*I'm not used to referring to myself as I would a patient.*

"Umm... The left lung is mostly reinflated... There's some inflammation, but fluid is mostly gone at least."

"Is inflammation normal for collapsed lungs?"

"Umm..." I hesitate and look over, though his gaze is on the images on the display. "It's in both lungs. Nothing to do with the injury. This is from before that."

*I don't want to say it directly.*

*Help me get over that, God, please.*

"Oh." He looks at me and frowns in realization. "Is that something to worry about?"

"I'll know more in a few days. Most of the time several days of rest and anti-inflammatories takes care of it."

"Any other risks?"

"You're really testing my promise here, aren't you?" I accusatorily raise a brow and receive an almost sly smile in return.

"Well?"

I set the tablet down on the table behind me and shake my head slightly. "Very minimal that I know. It could lead to infection, which is treatable."

He nods slowly. "Well, now that we're here, you can take it easy. And I mean to the point of laziness. I insist."

"And I intend to do that, as soon as Gam makes us something proper to eat." I have been exhausted the entire time but now realize how hungry I am too.

"How about you go relax on the couch, and I'll make sure Nik and Gam aren't fighting over what to make." Jax smiles as he hops off the table, turning to face me. "Need help?"

I open my mouth to say no, but then I look at my arm in the sling and my feet dangling nearly two feet off the floor. Looking up again, I narrow my eyes at him.

"Is this another test on my pride? It's Gam's fault I'm up here."

Jax's genuine laugh catches me off guard, and I suddenly realize how much I miss his laugh, and honestly the sound of laughter in general. Without a reply he steps over, takes my hand, and places my right arm over his shoulders, supporting me as I slide off the table.

"Thank you."

"Anytime, Lil'."

# | 58 |

# Sleep Well, Lil'

There was a moment as he was leaning close to her that Jax had a fleeting thought of how attractive her eyes are, and he had stayed too long, watching them. Pushing the thought back, he reminds himself there is no room for attraction. This team relies on stability, and they are just now starting to gain ground in this conflict against The Direction. Besides, he can see that the trauma she has gone through has definitely changed her, and he doesn't know how much and if it's for good or bad. It could go one way or the other. He will support her if she needs it, but that will be all.

*When she needs it...*

After leaving Lila in the dining-living room, Jax finds Gam and Nik in the kitchen, sharing future meal ideas while they make beef stir-fry on the Biogas stove. Nik has a green thumb, so he often has fresh vegetables on hand, and the abundant game in the area, including wild cattle, makes it easy for him to provide meat.

Isaac has finished setting his equipment up in the data room, and Gia gives up harassing him. She instead sits on the counter, eating an apple while listening to the two cooks swap recipes.

"Looks like dinner will be in..."

Jax walks back to the living room and begins to relay the timing to Lila, but he notices she is sound sleep on the large couch. Yeti has made himself at home on the couch as well, right beside her legs.

Looking around, Jax finds a blanket and covers her, avoiding covering the dog. Yeti's eyes follow him closely.

"I'm not hurting her, doggo," he assures quietly, scratching the white companion behind the ear. "Thanks for taking care of her, by the way."

Yeti huffs softly in reply.

*And thank You, God, for saving her.*

Jax smiles gently down at the two before stepping away, just in time to see the others carry plates, cups, utensils, and a large wok of food, setting them on the table.

"She joining us?" Nik asks, pouring mint iced tea into each cup.

"Nah, I think I'll leave her sleep." Jax shakes his head.

"Oh! Should we eat this at the kitchen table then? You know how loud Nik gets." Gia grins, and Nik shakes a fist at her.

"You get loud too, Gia," Nik chides. "But yes, we'll take it into the kitchen."

They gather all the settings and food again, carrying them back to the kitchen quietly. Jax glances back before leaving the two rooms.

"Sleep well, Lil'." He lowers the lights and leaves to join the others.

| 59 |

# Struggles and Comradery

Nik tells me this place is a geothermal masterpiece. Using the earth's heat and a thick brick-formed concrete structure, the building can maintain a comfortable temperature all year round with very little additional heat needed. His guess is that it is over a hundred years old but still in amazing condition. They have since added and upgraded different features.

The front of the place faces west, and only half of the west wall is exposed to the outside; the rest is buried. Entering the door, the dining table, Nik's pride and joy, is first, and the space is open to the large living room to the left.

To the right is the arched opening to the kitchen. Straight ahead on the east wall is a door for the bathroom, and to the left of that is the data room, which is also Isaac's room. He seems to prefer to sleep near his equipment.

At the north far corner of the living room is a long hall. I have been given the first room to the right, as it is across from the entrance of the medic room. The next door on the right is Jax's room, and after that is a second bathroom.

One more door at the north end of the hall is the door to the armory and supplies. The hall then opens up on the west to an exercise area, and that is where the final three rooms are accessed: Gia's room, Nik's room, and the bunk room where Gam stays. All throughout is an imprinted concrete floor with a generous number of rugs to cut down on the echo.

Even though the only windows are two one-way privacy windows in the living room and one in the kitchen, the lighting is decent with the help of numerous fixtures. That, and the screeded walls painted white hide the fact that each room is essentially a concrete box.

*Which that thought occasionally gives me unease.*

Any heat needed is provided through in-floor heating with a concealed outdoor wood-burning boiler which uses a freshwater scrubber to prevent smoke emissions. The boiler also provides hot water, something I have definitely missed!

Much like the last base, the power is generated by solar arrays submerged in a nearby lake. Energy is converted via inverters and stored for night needs in battery banks in a hidden cellar beside the lake.

The well is tapped into an aquifer, and the water is drinkable, eliminating our need for bottled water or filtration. My favorite part? The bathrooms. Functioning toilets and running water. Being able to wash with hot running water has been a definite plus. The first time was rough, though.

I hadn't realized how awful my hair had been matted with a combination of sweat, dirt, leaves, and blood, and it took some time to get it cleaned and combed. Especially since I couldn't bring myself to put my head under the showering water, *and I still can't*. I tell myself that it is better not to get water on my bandages anyway.

*Don't lie to yourself...talk to Jax.*

I push aside the tiny voice. Despite my promise to Jax when we first arrived, I still don't like to bother him. He has been pretty busy writing reports, helping Isaac with upgrading trail cameras in the area, and helping Nik cut dead trees for winter boiler fuel.

The physical problem I consider to be the biggest is not being able to put my clothes on normally. Even though it has been three weeks since we arrived, the broken collarbone and the extent of the muscle damage limits my mobility.

"Hey, Gia?" I call from the northern bathroom with a frustrated sigh.

I have spent the past five minutes trying to fasten my undergarment with one hand.

"On my way!" Gia cheerily calls from the exercise area.

So far, she has helped each day, and it has become routine.

"I told you, call right away, I'm happy to help." She smiles widely, and I notice her spiked hot-pink hair is slowly losing its dye and dark blonde shows through.

"I know, but one of these days I will master the one-handed fasten," I insist.

She laughs, and after helping with the fastener, immediately starts braiding my hair. It is something she insists on doing every time, but this time she doesn't even ask.

"Coffee is ready, Nik made fresh bread, and Isaac has some news," she updates me as she grabs a grey zippered vest shirt, helping me with that as well, and finally puts the sling back on.

"You're like a mom." I laugh a little, but my lungs protest with a few coughs.

"I'm not *that* old looking, am I?" She fakes a horrified expression but at the cough gives me an insistent look. "Still with the cough?"

"It is getting better, I promise," I dismiss. "I definitely appreciate this, by the way."

"Nah, it's OK. I think I just miss my sister; this reminds me of helping her when she was a kid," Gia confesses.

"The one out east? Meg?"

She nods in reply and opens the bathroom door, stepping aside to let me out first. Yeti is sitting right in front, waiting, his eager eyes glinting at me.

"Has anyone let you out yet or have you ruined another rug?"

"I let him out," Gia confirms. "He kept licking my face when I was lifting; left me no option."

"Thanks. At least he's learning quickly. I think Nik wasn't too happy about his rug." I grimace a little, remembering how upset he had been.

Walking down the hall with Yeti following, I can hear laughter in the kitchen, and a smile finds its way across my face. The past several uneventful days have put everyone at ease, and they all have shown a new side of themselves. More smiles, more laughter, and sharing stories. There is also the fact that progress against The Direction has lightened everyone's spirits.

*I wish it worked that way for me...*

Every day still feels like a battle for peace in my mind, but prayer helps, and I can at least smile as I see the harmony and cheerfulness of the others. After the first flashback at the small cave, things were just in a haze the first week here, and I was simply too tired.

Two weeks ago is when the anxiety started to ramp up. Reading medical documents on post-traumatic stress, I have tried ways to ground myself during the worst moments, but it is not that simple. Some days are better than others, though.

"Good morning." The four men seated at another wood table to the left of the kitchen entry greet me and Gia in unison as we step in.

"I haven't decided if it is good yet." Gia smirks and sits herself next to Gam.

"Maybe if someone gets me some coffee," she adds, elbowing Gam, who gives her a quick kiss on the cheek.

Jax has already gotten up and walks over, just as I do, to where the coffee is keeping warm on the stove. He grabs a mug, offering it handle-first to my right hand, and I hold it as he pours the coffee.

"Thanks."

"Anytime, Lil'."

My smile widens, and I don't even have to force it like usual; this morning feels different.

*Maybe the news Isaac has to share is good...*

I notice there is a certain glint in Jax's eyes, and I know he wants to say something.

"What…?" I raise a brow, taking a sip of my coffee.

"Nothing… just… your smile. It's not forced this morning." Smiling down at me, he gives a nonchalant shrug.

*This guy can read me better than I can read myself…*

I stare at him for a moment, taken aback. I didn't think the struggle affected my outward appearance that much, and without thinking, honesty comes out when I reply.

"I guess somehow this morning I don't feel like I need to pretend it's a good morning."

"Good." Jax nods with a certain look of satisfaction and without another word, returns to the table.

I follow and by habit sit beside him. Isaac is already fidgeting and amped up, eager to share his latest findings. Nik has the sliced bread and a homemade jam available at the center of the table, but nobody gets a bite in before our in-house computer genius starts speaking.

"So, I was up pretty much most of the night…" He begins.

"Hence you making a mess of my counter making snacks?" Nik snickers.

"Shush. Yes. Necessary. I was on a roll!" Isaac waves a hand dismissively.

"And how much coffee did you have?" Gia actually looks a little concerned.

"Too much caffeine might not be good for you," I add to the harassment.

"Take your own advice." He retorts with unusual tartness, but I know he is just jesting.

"How about we let the poor man continue, he's about ready to explode." Gam is the voice of reason, and everyone obliges.

"Thank you." Isaac sighs and continues. "So, I have been monitoring the satellites that The Direction uses, and in the past few days several of them have gone offline. A few of them from a meteor shower and others I was able to hack and cause malfunctions, triggering self-destructs."

There is a brief chorus of cheers and enthused table pounding with grins all around. Jax gives Isaac a grip on the shoulder.

"Nicely done, man. And thanks be to God!"

Isaac holds up a hand. "I'm getting to the best part... Our area here is now clear of any satellite observation, and so is Vita Nova. And very soon, the entire region of Gamal."

Everyone pauses for a moment before the realization hits.

"No more risk of detection...?" Jax voices first, almost in disbelief.

"Nope... And here's the odd kicker: they continue to lose satellites hourly." Isaac seems more puzzled than happy, but perhaps that is his nature: to him if there is something unknown, it is something that needs to be solved. "A massive solar storm rendered many inoperable, but the largest casualty now is the ones that are pushed out of orbit by the same storm, one-by-one either drifting in space or burning up in the atmosphere. There should be a pretty lightshow tonight in the sky."

"But why would that be puzzling?" Nik leans back in his chair. "I've heard of solar storms doing that before."

"Because," Isaac leans forward, tablet still in his hand. "Our own satellites have barely been affected. Signals got a little messed up for a bit, and that's why I was sorting through data all night, but we have lost only two out of the forty-some satellites in our repertoire. I haven't been able to figure out if they have more shielding or what. Not even my technical director back at Vita Nova has a clue, just a best guess."

"Can we rejoice in the victory and not focus on the mystery for a moment?" Gam gets up to get the pot of coffee and proceeds to refill everyone's mugs, despite a glare from Gia. "Sometimes the miracles just need to be acknowledged, not understood."

"I can sort of agree with that," Isaac concedes. "But when multiple unknowns happen, it's just...odd."

"What do you mean?" My brow knits, curious as to why he is so perturbed despite the good news he just delivered.

"According to an inside source, the flairs caused a geomagnetic storm that just disconnected and threw thousands of drones into collision courses, rendering them useless. They don't have enough production ability to replace them for several months."

"Well, that's a good thing! And a storm that size explains the amazing northern lights last night." I nod.

"When were you outside?" Jax raises a brow, detouring from the conversation.

"Probably one in the morning..." I reply and shrug, dismissing Jax's inquisitive gaze.

"Ahem..." Isaac brings our focus back. "As I was saying... This is strange because their drone system has a safety shutdown and shielding process when they sense an approaching geomagnetic surge. Somehow, APA miscalculated, and the storm was stronger than anticipated. The drones never received a safety-shutdown notice."

"Was anything at the facility affected? And how about our power grid and devices here?"

"Ah, excellent question, Gam. First of all, the facility is pretty much built as a faraday cage, so unfortunately, they're all fine. For us, this building was shielded with copper, so everything in here is safe. I have a satellite dish outside which I have wired into here, but I made sure to have that covered during the peak of the storm. Lastly, our power grid is mostly protected. A couple of things may need replacing, but I'll know more later. I just wish I could figure out how our satellites are still functioning."

"Isaac, buddy..." Jax leans forward and looks intently at him. "I know you hate not knowing, and that makes you excellent at what you do, but I think Gam is right. Sometimes celebrating the miracles is more important than fretting over the mysteries. I trust you will figure it out in the long run, but today, let's enjoy this flood of good news!"

Isaac's face slowly breaks into a grin, and he places his tablet down. "You're right... My eyes are hurting anyway, so I guess it's time for a break."

"That's the spirit!" Nik exuberantly cheers. "And now is the time to bring out my newest brew!"

"As in… alcoholic beverage?" Gia's face brightens.

## | 60 |

## Libations

"Uh oh." Jax shakes his head with a chuckle, knowing how loud and crazy Gia and Nik can get. "This could be really good, or really bad. But I say we've earned some time to kick back and celebrate."

Nik had already left the room before Jax agreed and emerges from a walk-in cellar in the corner of the kitchen, carrying a massive plastic barrel, setting it on the table. "Gam, you're the tallest here, grab those glasses above the sink over there, please."

"Gladly!" Gam easily reaches the glassware and hands them to Gia, who is waiting at his side.

*They're practically tied at the hip,* Jax ponders with a bit of trepidation.

It is something he has spoken about again with her, cautioning against getting so involved with a team member with the war going on, but part of him is happy to see Gia connect with someone so well. He realizes she hasn't lost her temper nearly as much as she used to before Gam, and that was her argument for the relationship, so he conceded. Her connection with the team in general *has* improved.

"Isaac, take a break from your obsession." Nik is working on opening the barrel and pesters as he notices Isaac going for his tablet again, and him barking orders pulls Jax from his thoughts. "Go grab me the longest ladle by the stove."

"Ahhh fine." Isaac grins and does so.

Nik ladles the amber liquid into the glassware and hands them out. Jax receives one and goes to pass it to Lila. To his surprise she declines, even though it seems like she would rather take it.

Lila shakes her head slightly. "Wish I could, but I'll stick to a mug of coffee, water, and Hydra-thlete."

"How come?" He notices her hesitate and look at the others around the table, although they are preoccupied with complimenting Nik on his craft.

"I might have prescribed myself a few things that don't mix well with alcohol."

*Anti-depressants...?*

Jax's forehead creases, slight worry seeping in. He wants to ask, but he sees apprehension growing on her expression, and another idea comes to mind.

"I won't ask now... on one condition."

"And that is...?" She seems dubious.

"If you go outside again in the middle of the night, let me come with you."

Lila looks a little surprised but deflects. "I don't want to wake you."

"I'm awake a lot around that time, so I will probably be reading," he persists.

"If you're worried about me being alone out there, I do bring Yeti." She nods toward the ball of fluff in the east corner of the kitchen as he gnaws on a bone given to him by Nik. "And a handgun."

Jax can't help but be amused by her stubborn hesitation, but he has one more card to play, and it isn't a lie either. "Maybe I'd like the company."

"Alright," she obliges finally, although giving him an unconvinced look.

He wonders if she intended to agree all along and was just making him work for it.

"Thank you... and cheers!" He clinks his glass against her coffee mug and turns back to his team.

It makes him contented to see them happy again. Jax takes a sip of Nik's ale, his eyebrows lifting, and he raises his glass to Nik who is still standing over the barrel.

"Now THIS is one of your best so far! I really hope you have more than one barrel, because we'll probably need it."

"I have four." Nik grins deviously, and Jax second-guesses his decision to allow everyone to let loose.

## | 61 |

# PTSD

In the course of the celebratory day, I come to find out that Gia and Nik are almost equally loud when inebriated. Another discovery is that Nik is married, but his wife is currently visiting Vita Nova and will be travelling back with the General. Which leads to another thing I learn: Isaac's dad is the General, and fittingly so, as the General's name is Abram Miles. I assume naming his son Isaac was purposeful.

Ever since being with the group, I have always known Isaac to be talkative but add a few ales, and it is almost too much. Fortunately, Nik and Isaac are a good match for back-and-forth swapping of jokes, and they entertain each other quite well.

I have never seen Gam drink until now, and I am not sure I see too much difference from the times he has too much caffeine. Just a bit more laughing and the occasional random song, and he does have the voice for it! Which leads to him begging Isaac to bring out a karaoke program the tech had created a few months ago during the down time.

The party has since moved to the living room, and despite an offering of a fresh steak from lunch, Yeti has left me, opting for the quieter outside. I ponder stepping out myself, but Jax reappears from the kitchen, handing me a bottle of Hydra-thlete as he sits to the right of me on the couch.

I notice he has only had one glass of ale so far. "No ale for you? Just because I'm not drinking doesn't mean you don't have to."

"Well, it's no fun being the only sober one." He grins, then adds teasingly. "So, thank you for staying sober with me while I play security detail for these fools."

I suddenly realize he is half serious. In the festive moment, I hadn't thought of the need for at least one of us to be completely sober for the sake of safety. We are still technically on a battlefront of sorts.

"Oh…I hadn't thought of that. And I guess I wouldn't be much use even when sober."

"I think you'd hold your own pretty well," he reassures. "I notice you are always carrying your side arm lately; that's forethought right there."

*Or a twitch…* I just shrug.

Ever since the recent events, I have never wanted to be without my handgun.

"What song should I sing, Lila?" Gam asks with a grin from across the room.

I raise a brow and realize I haven't seen him this enthused for a while. He is always cheerful by default, but I believe the ale is finally getting to him.

"How about that really old one you like about horses drinking beer and men drinking whiskey or something?"

"Coming right up." Gam promises.

My eyes are on Isaac trying to show Gam how to use the karaoke setup, but I glance over to catch Jax smiling as he watches the others.

"Good to see them this happy, isn't it?"

"It's been a rough few years," he admits, the smile fading slightly. "We've lost a lot of friends together, seen each other through some rough stuff, and we always made sure we kept each other's spirits up. Whether it be stupid jokes, funny stories, or the most powerful: praying together. Being so hotheaded, Gia was always a little reluctant with that until Gam came along. Part of me wonders how I ever ignored Kain's hesitation, though."

I flinch at the name, and unwanted recollections filter into my thoughts, but I notice him frown as well.

"He pretended very well, Jax."

"Yeah… I know."

Jax's smile returns a little, and I wish the full smile would come back. Seeing it somehow makes me feel less weighed down.

"Were you and he ever involved in those months?" He suddenly asks and it catches me by surprise.

"Why would you think that?" I try to read his expression but it is passive.

"He flirted a lot."

"And that's all it was, and all one-sided." I release a sigh and pinch the bridge of my nose, suddenly feeling stressed by the subject matter.

*Judas kiss…*

I fight against the memory, but it is like whatever evil spirit Kain carried is fighting back.

"I'm sorry, Lila, I only ask because I want to understand what you're dealing with after all that."

Jax looks over, and I read slight regret in his eyes. I know he is honest and means well, but the topic is testing my resolve.

"He always made me uneasy from the very beginning, Jax," I confide.

He smiles slightly over at me. "You're a good judge of character then, Lila, better than I."

"I doubt that. Even if that were true, I could use more than that. The one thing I wish I had was your confidence. You're a good leader; I couldn't make the hard decisions you do."

Unexpectedly, he takes the bottle out of my hand and sniffs it. "Nope, not beer. Do electrolytes make people drunk?"

I yank the container back and send him a glare. "Just take the compliment, dammit."

He grins but replies seriously, "I would love to take the credit, thank you, but as confident as you think I am, some days I am scared shitless. Credit all goes to God."

I go to reply, but Isaac flops down to my left and loudly announces, "alright, hush, first karaoke of the day! Gam and Gia."

The suddenness of Isaac's movement and voice has me jump a little, making me unexpectedly nervous, and what I have been fighting in my mind becomes front and center. I feel like I am about to lose the control I thought I had over it, and I lean forward, trying to slow my breathing.

*Pray...*

Everyone seems to be unaware of my disquiet as they are focused on the festiveness but not Jax. I am vaguely aware of him watching me, yet even that is fading as I can feel reality slipping away.

*I have to go, I can't let them see...*

*Pray...* The prompt comes again.

"Our Father, Who art in Heaven..."

I gain enough focus to get to my feet and head down the hall, though the walls seem to stretch and turn into somewhere else. Assuming I have found the door to the med-room, I enter the dimly lit space. I don't stop to turn the light up or even close the door, though, I just find the far side of the room by feel and slide to the floor with my back to the screeded surface.

"Hallowed be Thy name..."

My lungs seize as I try to pray. I shut my eyes, and I can't fight anymore: the searing light, the dead silence, the smell of concrete, and now I am waiting for the footsteps.

*I don't want to be back here, please God...*I plead silently.

"Thy Kingdom come, Thy will be done, on earth as it is in Heaven." Someone else's voice takes over the prayer, cutting through the silence, and I feel a large hand enveloping mine.

"Lil', if you can still hear me, squeeze my hand."

Jax's voice is in the concrete room with me. I can feel his hand, and I try to grip it, but when I look down all I see is concrete, a chair, and my arms strapped. I squeeze my eyes shut again, but the light still comes through. There is the scraping sound of metal as the chair drags across the concrete and then the feeling of falling backward.

*Here comes the cloth and the water... I can't breathe.*

"Lil', you have to breathe... Trust me. Take a deep breath. Focus on my hand." His patient voice, though muffled as the water spills over my ears, calms the pounding in my head.

*Breathe*...I don't want to, but I take a deep breath and somehow, it is not water.

*Focus...*

I focus on the warmth in my hand. Gradually, while I focus on this, I hear Jax more clearly as he quietly prays, and a hint of pine breaks through the smell of concrete.

I don't know how long it has been or how long it takes as I feel each sense of reality slowly return. Finally, daring to open my eyes, I see the dimly lit med-room before me; no more searing light. I become aware that my face is wet, but not with the water, just tears. It takes me a long moment to realize, though, that the pine smell is Jax sitting against the wall at my right side, his hand holding firmly to mine, and I use it to ground myself the rest of the way.

"Welcome back, Lil'," he speaks quietly.

Jax doesn't move, doesn't rush me, he just waits.

"How long was I gone?"

"It doesn't matter, you're back now."

"How long..." I want to know; I hate not being in control of my own time, and it has happened too often lately.

He hesitates, glancing down as he squeezes my hand gently. "About half an hour, maybe more."

It dawns on me that Jax had to have been here the entire time, patiently waiting, but I am unable to say anything else.

"Would you like me to bring Yeti in from outside for you?" Jax offers quietly.

I nod numbly, and he gets up, pausing at the doorway to look at me with an expression of concern, *and perhaps guilt*. I wonder if he thinks him speaking about Kain is what caused this.

*He wouldn't be entirely wrong...*

| 62 |

# Stars and Confessions

Jax quietly watches four inebriated individuals cheer every time the night sky is graced with a 'shooting star'. The karaoke went on for some time, followed by a raid of the kitchen, and then at about midnight everyone decided to watch The Direction's satellites fall from orbit.

Shortly after he brought Yeti in from outside for Lila, she had excused herself to her own room. He feels bad for questioning her about Kain, but he had wanted to know if there is any remorse there that she is dealing with. Regrettably, he realizes he probably should have avoided the topic as it pushed her over the edge, and he means to apologize when he sees her next. He also intends to be more cautious and observant, knowing by experience what she is going through.

Standing with his arms folded, sidearm at his hip, Jax smiles as another streak in the sky brings another cheer. The five of them are standing just outside of Bear Base, the night air cold but not quite freezing, typical of an early October in this area. He had grabbed his jacket, though, because he intends to be out for a while.

"Well, that should be most of them." Isaac calculates, a large grin on his flushed face. "Don't know about you guys, but I think I need some sleep."

"Thanks for making sure we didn't do anything stupid." Gia smirks as she walks past Jax, giving him a punch in the arm a little harder than she means to.

"I've got your back, Gia." He grins and rubs at his own arm.

*That's gonna leave a mark...*

The other three give Jax either a fist bump or a high five, each entering the building. Looking over his shoulder, he watches the door close. Slowly the sound of laughter fades, and he is left alone in the starlit night, the crickets chirping and the trees stirring in a gentle wind.

He stands silently for some time, staring into the night sky with his hands in the pockets of his cargo pants. Without looking at his watch, he guesses it is about zero one hundred. Part of him hopes she sleeps through the night, but he plans on waiting either way. In the meantime, there are things he needs to discuss.

"Hey up there... Kind of wanted to start by saying thank You. This is a huge step forward and gives everyone a glimmer of hope. I pray for the souls of our loved ones, and all those who fought beside us against this tyranny. I ask forgiveness again for the wrongs I have done, especially before I knew You. Help us continue our fight with humility, wisdom, and Your strength. I also ask that You take care of Father Sebastian up there..."

He takes a moment to pray individually for each Isaac, Gia, Gam, and Nik. "Help me to lead them wisely and support them."

Jax pauses, lowering his head down before looking to the sky again. "I have another huge favor to ask...and I know I ask a lot of them, but..." Hesitating, he takes a quick glance behind him at the closed door before continuing. "Lila is just getting to know You again, and You know what she is going through. And I think I messed up tonight. Please, tell me how I can help her like Father Malachi helped me."

*Rejoice in hope, endure in affliction, persevere in prayer...be patient.*

"Easier said than done..." Jax smiles contritely.

He spends the rest of the time in silence, watching the stars shift in the heavens.

*Peace...*

One more streak across the sky catches his attention, and he feels a small rush of liberation, knowing it gives them another chink in the armor of the enemy.

"The Lord shall cause thy enemies, that rise up against thee, to fall down before thy face: one way shall they come out against thee, and seven ways shall they flee before thee…"

"The Lord will send forth a blessing upon thy storehouses, and upon all the works of thy hands…"

Jax is startled as Lila's voice behind him continues the scripture, followed by a brief fit of coughing, which is something he has noticed is persisting lately. He turns to face her as she walks toward him.

"I didn't realize you knew scripture that well."

He sees she is still wearing her normal clothes, with her arm in the sling, her sidearm at her hip, and her braid somewhat messy. The only change is a blanket around her shoulders for the cold air. He wonders if she even slept. A white, furry streak charging up the hill behind her lets him know Yeti is taking this chance to explore the area.

"I would always read the Bible Gam gave me, but being able to talk with God at that time was a different story…" She admits with a somber smile before looking up to the stars.

"Get any sleep?"

She answers with a one-shoulder shrug. "A little. It was a busy day; I'm surprised you're still awake."

"I had to wait and apologize to you for earlier."

Lila seems confused at first, but then she shakes her head. "It's not your fault. My mind was already there."

He is not sure if that is better or worse, but she quickly changes the subject.

"That can't be the only reason you're out here." She calls him out.

"I had a few things to talk to God about." Jax turns back to face west and sits in the grass.

Lila sits beside him. "Any answers?"

He looks over and watches her subdued expression as her eyes skim over the stars. "Sort of... Lately I've heard you coughing still. Everything alright with that?"

"It's mild. Nothing some anti-biotics, pain relievers, and anti-inflammatories won't fix in a few days." She looks over, and there is honesty in her eyes.

He relaxes a bit. "So that's why no drinking."

She nods and gives a small laugh. "I really wanted to. Everyone was having such a fantastic time. I mean, it was fun anyway, but I guess I wasn't feeling it as much as I wish I could. A drink would have been nice, might've helped..."

Even though he is happy to hear her honesty, he flinches a little and shakes his head, suddenly realizing it might have been a bad idea had she accepted the drink.

"Drinking doesn't help what you are going through, and sometimes it makes it worse."

"I know..." Her voice drops down to a murmur, her troubled eyes back to the stars. "It's just wishful thinking, Jax, wishful thinking..."

Jax perceives that without the others around, he is finally hearing the raw, honest Lila. He realizes regrettably he has been too busy to give her time to approach him without the others and wonders if that added to her instability today.

"I'm here now, if you need to talk... but I won't push if you don't want to."

Lila stays silent for a while, to the point Jax thinks she is opting to not talk at all, but she finally looks at him and in the dim light he can see the dismay in her eyes. He is hit with a sudden pang of sorrow for her, and a hint of anger at anyone who took part in what happened back at the facility.

*Although I have my suspicions as to who.*

"I have to leave the door open in my room; I can't sleep with a closed door... The silence at night is unbearable. I keep waiting for footsteps down a concrete hall, and it's so much worse when there are actual footsteps late at night...That's why I come out here."

She stares through the trees below them, and he lets her continue, not interrupting, even when the pauses are long.

"I can't put my face under the shower head; even using a washcloth is difficult. I avoided going out the last time it rained... I tried one time, and I nearly lost it, but Yeti pulled me back. Metal scraping, the smell of concrete in the cellar. The lights when someone sets them too high. I end up losing bits of time, and tonight... I just..." She cuts off her sentence. "Praying helps, Yeti helps... You being around helps...The others don't know, but you see it." She looks at Jax with a slight smile.

"You're not alone, Lil', we're here for you. I'm here for you." He reassures, wishing there is more he could say.

"Jax...?" He hears a tightness in her voice.

"Yes?"

"Isaac says I need to give a full account to General Miles of what happened, from the start of the mission to the time you guys found me..." He watches as she looks away and visibly swallows. "Is that true?"

"Unfortunately, Isaac is right," he confirms apologetically, wanting there to be another way. "You could try writing it down..."

"Can I just tell you, to see if I can make it through? But not tonight... maybe tomorrow night." She squeezes her eyes shut, forcing a slow breath.

"We can do that. We can even record it, so you don't have to tell the General directly."

Jax waits quietly, listening to her inhale slowly, then exhale.

"Jax?"

"Hmm?"

"Will you stay with me again?" Her voice is uncertain, her eyes still closed.

"I'll stay here as long as you need." He moves closer until his arm is against her shoulder, so she knows he is still there, silently praying as he does so.

*...defend us in the day of battle, be our protection against the wickedness and snares of the devil...*

Yeti appears from the early morning shadows as though from thin air and sits at the other side of Lila.

*May God rebuke him we humbly pray...*

# | 63 |

# Pulling Things Together

Today the General will arrive, and Nik is all in a tizzy making sure everything is perfect and polished. It occurs to me it isn't the General he is trying to impress, but rather his wife, and I can't help but smile at that thought.

The past week has been rough to say the least, but I had spent a couple hours each night with Jax outside, slowly, bit by bit, going through the details of my time at the facility and the encounter with Kain. He had recorded everything and promises to remove the times of incoherence.

*And the times where there is only his voice, praying for me or calmly trying to bring me back to reality.*

There is an odd feeling of shame at how many times I fell apart, but Jax assures me constantly that post-traumatic stress has no partiality, sometimes making the strongest feel like the weakest. I am relieved, however, that I will not have to go through this in front of General Miles.

Isaac has been frustrated, as the day after the success of the satellites, he discovered that the geomagnetic storm had destroyed the hovercycles. Trying to repair them has been his focus the entire week. The good news is he found out in time to put in a request to Vita Nova. We now have a handful of diesel, biofuel, and propane vehicles arriving with the General. Fuel limitations will be difficult in the long run, though.

Gam and Nik are discussing meals in the kitchen, while Isaac has unfortunately moved the hoverbikes into the living room and is still fretting over them. Gia, at my request, has taken Yeti out for a run. The massive dog has been so pent up, and I am still not ready for heavy exercise. Lastly, Jax is probably editing the audio as promised.

The apprehension combined with excitement is palpable and a little more than I can handle right now, so I quickly pour a mug of coffee and head for my med-room. I plan on passing the time by removing my sling, stitches, and trying mild range of motion exercises. After that, hopefully just relax and read some scripture, or some interesting writings Isaac stumbled on recently from someone named Augustine of Hippo.

Taking my data tablet, I select an instrumental music list Jax had asked Isaac to find for me, which helps fill the silence at times. Jax has also regulated the lighting throughout the base to only max out at a level I could tolerate, somehow doing this without letting the others know why.

There is a certain comfort in his concern and attentiveness in the little things like that. Looking over at one of the counters, I smile at the two photos he had made sure to bring from the cave in Oshana.

Other than my beige cargo pants and sidearm, I am down to my go-to black sports bra, the sling off and zip-stitches removed from at least the front of the through-wound, albeit uncomfortably as the adhesive is still pretty strong. I haven't braided my hair today for once, and it keeps getting in my way. Ignoring that, I go through the range of motions, and things are pretty stable, other than uncomfortable numbness from my elbow to my fingertips. I take the med-scanner off the shelf.

"Well, that's gonna be fun," I mutter under my breath, sitting on one of two tall swivel stools.

Looking up, I suddenly realize Jax is leaning against the doorframe.

"Everything alright?" He pushes off the doorframe and comes to lean against the steel table instead.

I reach over to the tablet and pause the music

"All fine. Just annoying rehab stuff. Ah shit," I mumble, grabbing for my shirt next to the tablet.

"Lil', you forget... I was in Defense. That's modest compared to locker room attire," he calmly reminds me.

I open my mouth to argue at first but realize I could use his help. "In that case, would you mind removing the stitches at my back?"

"I can do that," he nods.

"So," I begin to ask, flinching a little as the stitch-tape pulls at my skin. "When the General comes, is there any formality or anything? Only thing I've seen were the occasional parades, uniforms, saluting, all that from the Defense."

"Not really. We are mostly informal. Those of us recruited from the Defense end up out of habit saluting with the usual 'yes sir' and 'no sir'. You don't have to worry about any of that. Even in the Defense, Medics have more leeway." He finishes removing the zip-stitches and leans back against the table in front of me again, continuing. "There is some hierarchy, but there are so few of us that we don't have a very stable military structure. Rebels, I guess you could call us"

"How many?" I stretch my shoulder a little, my nose scrunching at the tightness of the still-healing muscles.

"I would estimate about seventy with combat experience, mostly stationed in the various bases, and that includes you." He nods to me, folding his arms across his chest.

I look at him doubtfully. "I wouldn't consider it combat experience."

"Don't sell yourself short, Lil'." He shakes his head, and I do not continue to argue.

"Fine..." I stand and go to put the scanner away on one of the shelves. "Where do you stand in the line of hierarchy, then? I'm assuming pretty high, considering General Miles wants to directly update us, unless it's an excuse to visit his son."

"Nope, unfortunately we are one of only a handful of field units left with bases close enough to Oshana. We are the second unit to be updated personally, hence why it took so long."

"Oh... how many were there before?" I brace myself for the answer, slipping my shirt back on, pressing together the Velcro closure, and then pulling my loose hair out from under.

"Not sure. Isaac thinks ten at one time. That's not counting the ones still operational in Eden and Gamal of course. We lost the two recently, so possibly only six now."

"Do you know if the bases were just compromised and they survived like we did?"

The expression on his face is both hopeful and worried. "I'm not sure. I hope to find out more once the General arrives, which should be soon. You ready?"

"Do I have to be in the same room when he's listening to the audio?" I don't know why I didn't think to ask before, but now I am uneasy.

"No." His smile is reassuring. "I've gotcha covered there."

"Then yes...I'm ready." I nod. "Oh, and thanks for the help with the zip-stitches by the way."

He is about to reply when a loud string of swear words comes from the other room, surprisingly from Isaac and no doubt because of his bike problem. I grimace as it is followed by a crash and metal scraping across the concrete.

Jax reaches over and turns the music back on with my tablet, tapping the volume up slightly.

"I'll go see what's going on." He gives me a quick smile as he leaves the med-room.

Sitting on the stool, I pull up one of the books in my tablet, humming slightly to the music.

*"What grace is meant to do is to help good people, not to escape their sufferings, but to bear them with a stout heart, with a fortitude that finds its strength in faith.."*

# | 64 |

# Keeping Things Together

Jax walks into the living room to see the usually cheery Isaac kicking at one of the hovercycles. In all their years of knowing each other, Jax has rarely seen him this upset.

"You alright here, Isaac?"

"No, not at all, they're destroyed. What is my dad going to think? I should have brought them in during the storm." Isaac sighs and flops down on the couch, which is pushed against a far wall to make room for the vehicles.

Sitting next to Isaac, Jax shakes his head, resting his forearms on his knees.

"He'll understand that you can't think of everything. We've all been through a lot, and he knows that."

"You *have* met my dad, right?" A slight grin crosses Isaac's face as his visible anger slowly subsides.

"Yes, but wouldn't you think that the fact that we got the data needed weigh in your favor? Besides… He would be a broken man if he lost you, too, and you know it. He's probably thankful that you made it here, and a few pieces of replaceable equipment isn't going to overshadow that."

Isaac leans forward onto his knees, nodding somberly. "I know you're right…But to be honest, and I guess the thing that is really getting to me, is this will be the first time I've seen him since Mom died. She was always the one who could help him calm down when things got to be too much. I have no clue how he is now, and I don't mean just as a dad, but a leader, too. Is he stable enough? Is he taking care of himself? Maybe I worry too much about him, but I didn't want the loss of these machines to be an addition to the strain."

"I think, even with the little communication we have had, he still seems solid as a leader. Maybe sadder as a person, but that's to be expected. He's got good people surrounding him at Vita Nova, looking out for him." Jax reassuringly grips Isaac's shoulder.

Isaac's eyes glint a little, but he sniffs and nods, slapping his own knees. "You're right. I think I just let it get to me. Even with the losses, we're gaining a lot of ground fast, with satellites, the data Lila was able to get, and everything by the Grace of God. That should be enough to cheer the General up, too."

"That's the Isaac I know and love."

Jax grins, relieved to see his friend come around quickly. Of course, he usually does, but everyone has a breaking point, and Jax considers it his job to make sure no one reaches that. Through the years, that has become more difficult, though.

"Would you mind helping me get these things out of here? He should at least have a place to sit without tripping over bike parts."

"You bet...We'll get Gam and Nik to help, too." Jax gets up from the couch, heading down the hall to where he last heard Gam and Nik in the exercise room.

Pausing at the med-room door, he looks through the partial opening and sees again what he noticed when he was in there: Lila's hair, uncharacteristically unbraided. He considers fleetingly how much he likes it that way but instinctively brushes the thought aside. Her quiet humming, however, reaches him and he smiles a little.

"May the Lord give strength to His people. May the Lord bless His people with peace." He murmurs the Psalm quietly as he continues down the hall.

# | 65 |

# Losses

Isaac gives us plenty of warning ahead of time when his camera five miles out to the east picks up the images of a small convoy of beige and green vehicles. This camera is at the point that the paths narrow to only allow smaller vehicles, and that is also where Gia has been waiting for them as an escort. I stand beside Isaac and watch on his tablet as a few of the larger vehicles are parked and covered with camo cloth.

"Is the path that way wide enough for the UTV's they're using?" I inquire, remembering how narrow the paths were for our drive in.

"Should be decent," Nik answers, standing behind me and watching as well, probably hoping to get a glimpse of his wife. "The east path is a bit easier to navigate."

"They'll have to take it slow, though, so we should see them in about twenty minutes," Isaac confirms.

I nod silently and wipe my sweaty palms against my cargos. I am not even sure how many are expected, but I am hoping for my nerves' sake only a few. As solitary as I was before all this, I am not exactly solitary now so much as I prefer the company of those I know well.

We're standing in the dining area when Gam pops his head around the kitchen opening with a bright smile. "Anyone want some peach muffins? I love having a real oven again."

Isaac doesn't look up as he switches to one of the closer cameras on the trail. "Nik will take one, of course, probably two. He never says no to food."

"That is true!" Nik grins, putting his hands on his hips and puffing his chest out. "I need to watch my girlish figure, for my wife."

"How about you, Lila?"

"I'm too nervous to eat," I decline.

"You're too skinny to not eat," Gam argues, bringing over two muffins and handing one to Nik.

"You always say that." The muffin does smell delicious, but my stomach tightens at the thought of eating anything.

"This time it's true." He gives me a more serious look, and I know he is not wrong.

"That's because of the healing process; it takes a lot of calories. Don't worry, I'll stress eat once I meet our guests," I assure him with a slight grin.

"Fine, I'll eat this one," he concedes and takes a massive bite, pretty much half the muffin.

Yeti suddenly shows up from the other side of the couch and plants himself almost on top of Gam's feet, looking up pleadingly. With a hearty laugh, Gam gives away the other half and rubs Yeti's head.

*Fifteen minutes... Where's Jax?*

While the others have themselves planted in the dining/living area, debating how Nik will greet his wife, I excuse myself to the kitchen to grab a glass of water.

Walking to the west wall of the kitchen where the sink is, I fill a glass and take a sip, staring out the tinted window. The smell of the peach muffins fills the entire kitchen, and I look over to the left where there are at least two dozen.

"You should try one."

I nearly jump out of my skin and whirl around. Jax is sitting at the far end of the table in the kitchen, near the east wall, a tablet in his hand.

"What the heck... I didn't even see you there."

His brow raises as he shrugs his shoulders. "You never looked. But I *am* sorry for startling you."

"It's alright, I'm not very perceptive right now." I give my own shrug and lean back against the sink counter. "What are you doing hiding in a corner?"

Jax looks hesitant, glancing at the tablet in his hand. His expression is guarded, but I see the tension in his jaw and know it is something negative.

"It's ok if you can't share details." I walk over to sit kitty-corner from him. "But is something wrong?"

A slight smile breaks through the tension, and he leans forward onto the table. "You're obviously perceptive enough to read me."

"Sometimes." I watch as he stares at the display for a moment.

He heaves a sigh and sets his tablet down.

"General Miles sent a report ahead so I could be read into some of what he'll be going over." He pauses, and I flinch as I see the tension return. "I'm not sure I want the others to hear this yet, especially Nik. He is so excited to see his wife again, and I don't want to dampen that."

It stings to see him troubled. I know he is the backbone of this small group, and it takes its toll. Heaven knows he has been going above and beyond to help me through my difficulties. Yet seeing him visibly showing the burden means whatever he read must hit home a little harder.

"Would it help to get it off your chest? You could tell me," I offer, resting my forearms on the table.

Jax rubs at his chin, staring at the table before raising his gaze to me. "You're honestly the last person I would want to burden with depressing news."

"Honestly? I would rather hear it now than test my anxiety waiting until I do hear it."

He gives a tense laugh, and he nods. "Touché. It is probably better you hear it now, then. The report describes the extent of the damage and loss. There was a second Defense officer planted in another base on the Gamal/Eden border, a woman named Quin. Communications between her and the other infiltrator…"

"Kain." I interject with a grimace, and Jax nods.

I realize that he is probably avoiding the name for my sake.

"Yes. Those communications were found on Quin, and she was taken into custody. That's how Kain was discovered. But not before you were captured and he was able to relay not only his own findings and every base he knew, but also every base she knew. Every medical clinic supporting us and their base was identified as well." He pauses and looks down at his hands folded together on the table.

My heart slowly drops to my stomach, somehow knowing the next part, and I take a sip of water, my throat suddenly dry. I slide the glass over to his hands, and he silently takes a drink before continuing.

"The destruction of the other two bases were just the start. Only two survivors from those, and it was only done to push us to retreat to Vita Nova, where Kain would have completed his assignment. That was until they found the body and knew their mission was scrubbed. Then the purging of the remaining bases, all but two, was initiated. We lost twenty-seven men and women that we know of, and possibly six others were captured. That's not counting how many supporters were killed at the clinics." He rubs his hands over his face, his elbows on the table. "A few of the remaining survivors have to run solo until there's no risk of them being tracked to headquarters."

"Jax, I'm so sorry…"

Then a thought hits me. If I had taken time to at least hide Kain's body it probably would have killed me, but he wouldn't have been found so soon.

*Would that have saved everyone?*

Or if Jax and the others had taken care of the body instead of rushing to find me. It is as though Jax reads my thoughts, or maybe just the stricken look on my face as he holds my gaze with sincerity.

"Before you even think it, Lil', even if we buried him, costing precious time, it wouldn't have saved them. Believe me, I thought that myself at first. But information shows that Kain had to confirm your death and his rejoining with us, and without that by a certain time, The Direction would have done exactly what they did."

Although I am relieved that is not a guilt I have to carry, the thought that we escaped and survived while twenty-seven others were slaughtered is a humbling thought.

*Why are we special?*

"Did you know many of them?"

His downcast expression tells me yes without him saying. I am not sure if I could handle that many losses, and I wonder if he really can either in the long run.

"Several. Many of them have families in Vita Nova." Jax's hands clench together, the muscles in his arms tense, and I can almost feel the anger building.

"And the ones who were captured? Do we know where they were taken?" I look down and find my own hands clenching together, and I can guess the answer to that one.

"They are held in a secure location in Gamal right now, but they are scheduled for transport to the facility in Oshana," he quietly replies.

I can feel his eyes on me, and I look up. "We can't let them get there, Jax. Someone has to save them."

"I know. I'm sure the General has a plan."

Despite his assurance, the trepidation is written all over his face. He knew what happened to detainees there, even before me. And now we both know there are six of our people probably going to go through that if they aren't rescued. We both stare at the table in silence.

"Two minutes, guys!"

I glance over as Isaac calls into the room, breaking the quiet, and ducks right back out. Looking back at Jax, I watch him slowly pull himself back together. He suddenly reminds me of me, *at least the recent me*, trying to put on a good face.

"I guess we better be in there." He exhales as he stands.

"Jax?"

"Yes, Lil'?" His voice is calmer, and his expression is steady, although he looks at me with concern. "Are you alright?"

*Still worrying about others...*

"I was going to ask you the same thing."

"I'll be fine." He gives a tentative smile as he turns to walk away.

I stand and reach out, grasping his arm before he leaves. He seems taken aback and looks at me questioningly.

"I'm going to say something a wise man once said to me... If you ever need to talk, I'm here." I give him a smile.

Reaching over with his other hand, he lays it on mine and nods slightly. "I'll keep that in mind."

He pulls away and heads for the archway to the dining room but pauses, looking back.

"Thank you, Lil'."

"Anytime, Jax."

# | 66 |

# The General

He had been worried the news, particularly about the prisoners, would test her resolve and push her to the edge, but he was ready to help bring her back. What Jax hadn't expected was to have her offer solace to *him* when she saw how distraught he was over the report.

*Two are better than one, because they have a good reward for their toil. For if they fall, one will lift up the other...*

He nods to himself at the scripture passage and looks around him at the ready faces outside the front door, awaiting their guests.

Father Malachi was always his confidant when circumstances allowed, but it has been quite some time since Jax has been able to contact him. And now after hearing about the devastation of the outposts, he wonders if Father Malachi was one of the casualties, and that thought only adds to his disquiet.

Only Isaac has been a close enough friend to confide in otherwise, but even then, he can't remember the last time he did so. Admittedly, he confides in God when he is stressed or frustrated but acknowledges that sometimes one needs more. For them, however, Jax's door is always open.

Jax takes a deep breath as two UTVs pull up with a total of seven people. One is Gia, four are plainclothes, and two are armed and fully geared-up escorts. Out of habit he stands at attention. Lila stands to the left of him, although a step back, Isaac to his right, Gam after him, and Nik is already running over to one of the vehicles.

He can't help but smile as Nik scoops a petite woman with long dark hair and glasses right out of the vehicle and spins her around, giving her a sound kiss.

"Fae!"

Nik's wife laughs and clings to her husband. "Obviously someone missed me."

Jax turns his attention to the first UTV, where a man his height with salt and pepper hair, just a bit longer than a high and tight, climbs out. Although not particularly toned, he is not fat either and carries himself with confidence. He wears the common beige cargo pants, a sidearm, and a dark leather jacket over a beige button-down shirt.

"Sir." Jax reaches a hand out.

"Jax." General Miles gives his hand a firm shake with a smile that makes crinkles at the corners of his blue eyes as he pats Jax's arm with his other hand with a look of both sadness and determination. "Good to see you in one piece, still."

The General's smile widens as he gives Isaac a firm but quick hug, holding his son's shoulders in his hands for a moment before stepping back. "Isaac."

Isaac's face is one huge smile, and he seems happy enough with the simple gesture and seeing his dad's smile. "Hey Dad, glad you made it."

As Isaac introduces General Miles to Gam, Jax suddenly notices a familiar face beside Nik and Fae: a man in a long black garment with white at the collar. His hair is short and dark, his chin boasting a long black beard with grey streaks, and his cheerful brown eyes sport a pair of dark rimmed glasses.

"Father Malachi?!"

The sight of his former mentor makes him grin. Now knowing he is alive is an immense relief, so much to the point that he is almost fighting tears, but he manages to keep his composure.

"The one and only. Good to see you, Jax." Father Malachi, a few inches shorter than he, embraces Jax and holds onto him for a solid few seconds. "I have been praying for you nonstop. And for you."

He turns to face Lila.

Her brows go up in question as she shakes the priest's hand. "How? I mean, then again, I am guessing Jax told you."

"Yes, he did mention you, and then one day God told me you needed prayer, and I've been praying for you ever since." Father Malachi smiles as though this is a perfectly normal thing to say.

Jax chuckles as Lila looks even more confused. "You'll get used to that. Father Malachi pretty much has a direct line."

"We all do, Jax," the priest gently reminds. "Sometimes we just turn it off."

"This must be Lila." General Miles steps over.

"Yes, sir." Lila extends her hand, and Jax can hear the nervousness in her voice.

The General takes her hand, and there is a serious but kind expression on his face. "Call me Bram for now. I hear we have you to thank for the vital information."

"It was a team effort," she gestures to the others.

"With you taking the brunt of the damage," Bram corrects, his head tilting a little as he assesses the woman in front of him, and Jax knows he is trying to read her character; something the General commonly does. "How has your recovery been?"

"My shoulder still hurts but otherwise healing fine." She gives a slight smile, shifting uncomfortably under the scrutiny.

"Mhmm." Bram looks to Jax, as though trying to pull answers from his expression, and finally nods. "Right then. This is Professor Marie Hann."

From behind him steps a woman in her forties: tall, trim, and with long brown hair in a simple braid. She has a formidable presence; her bright eyes are intense and purposeful, her demeanor confident. Jax instantly gets the impression that if she were to start an argument, she would win it.

"Hello." She takes time to shake each of their hands, repeating their names as she does so.

"She is our lead historian and is here to help describe what we are dealing with. She and a few others, your wife included," Bram nods to Nik who is possessively holding the tiny Fae in both his large arms, "have put together a rough, true, history of what happen from the 21$^{st}$ century until now. But we'll discuss that once we get settled. I could use a drink."

With a definitive nod, General Abram Miles walks into Bear Base, followed by everyone but the two guards who stay outside the door.

# | 67 |

# The Truth

The General seems both kind and intense at the same time, and I feel like I need to watch my every move around him. Not that it is a bad thing. It reminds me of Jax in a way, as in I get the impression nothing gets past him. It is no less unnerving, though.

Other than Father Malachi, who has excused himself to pray in another room for the success of our briefing, everyone is sitting at the dining room table. Oddly enough, Yeti sits right by Bram at the head of the table. Jax sits at the other end, and I am in a seat near him. I raise a brow at Nik, who has his wife on his lap, barely letting her go even when he had gotten coffee for everyone.

I had been briefly introduced to Fae, and she is a sweet woman, almost reminding me of a female Gam, without the massive build and with a much quieter voice. She and Nik haven't seen each other for nearly six months, so I guess it is not surprising that he won't let go of her.

General Miles had brought a bottle of bourbon with him, and he now pours a small amount for each of us, passing the glasses down. Prior to this sit-down, he reviewed my audio report in private with Jax, so at least that part is over. Professor Marie has four different data tablets in front of her and has been scrolling through digital paperwork. Each time someone different speaks, however, she raises her eyes, intently identifying the speaker.

I swirl the glass absently, watching the honey-colored liquid move, but I haven't taken a sip. I have also tuned out most of the general updates from our side, but when it came to the report on the multiple destroyed bases and lives lost, I paid attention, not to the news itself, but to the others. There were varied responses: anger, sadness, and horror.

They are a lot more somber now, and one glance at Jax tells me he is feeling the dejection of the others more than they probably realize. His head is tilted down, and he stares at his folded hands on the table, not even touching the glass with the bourbon.

"Now with those major updates out of the way," General Miles concludes, "I turn the discussion over to Marie's control."

He gestures to her. Professor Marie squares her shoulders and clears her throat, her eyes looking at each in turn.

"Alright, so I will try to keep this short. This took a lot of research over the years. Our one breakthrough was connecting with the Nightlight system; it stored a lot of helpful information which we were eventually able to confirm and add far more to with the data Lila brought. What some of you may have heard in The Direction history is that in the mid-21$^{st}$ century a devastating illness struck the entire world, reducing the population by half."

"Holy shit, I didn't realize it was that much," Nik exclaims.

"This virus," the Professor continues, a stylus in her hand, which she points each time she emphasizes, "was labeled VHFsSARS-S41."

I lean forward a little, recognizing the acronyms from the document Isaac had managed to unscramble, and since that time I had researched more into the viruses.

"Lila would know what that means."

She gives me a pointed look, and I instantly know she wants my interaction. I suddenly want to hide under the table, but I swallow and nod.

"Viral Hemorrhagic Fever somehow combined with a Severe Acute Respiratory Syndrome," I reply, then add as I am given a confused look by most. "Basically, the patient bleeds and coughs to death.

Hemorrhagic causes damage to blood vessels. The respiratory one attacks the lungs. Arguably each one is bad enough on their own, but with this double one the Hemorrhagic Fever causes bleeding in the already stressed lungs, and most patients drown in their own blood."

There is silence at the table, and I wonder if I was a little too graphic. Isaac finally gives a low whistle.

"Well, that would suck."

"Correct. And an understatement, Isaac." Marie keeps going. "The problem is that this virus was not natural. It was designed. It was created to decrease the elderly and those with compromised immune systems before moving on to general population."

"Who the heck would do such a thing?" Gam chimes in.

"The Directive of World Population; that's the DWP on the documents. And just as it sounds, they were in charge of research on population control. Based out of what is now known as Oshana, this company created the virus to reduce population."

"But I thought the inoculations were created for that."

"Yes, Isaac, that was the next step. They made the virus devastating enough to cause panic, and then a dual-vaccine was rushed into production to save lives, or so they claimed. They used human stem cells, taken from fetuses..."

"Babies," I interject before I can stop myself, but she nods, fortunately not upset with my interruption.

"Correct. They developed one part of the vaccine with these for the VHFs part of the virus and then combined it with an mRNA vaccine against the SARS. mRNA stands for Messenger RNA. It pretty much tells your DNA how to make specific proteins to trigger the body's immune system against the virus. What they had also done was introduce another command in the mRNA. This one ended up causing mass miscarriages and sterilizations around the world."

No one says anything, but most of us are leaning forward, waiting for the next horrific twist in this story which is our true history.

*So much different than what my classes had taught.*

"Unfortunately, the DWP realized too late that it was not only successful in further depletion of the population but caused subsequent cases of birth defects and disabilities as well as the next generation being influenced. They were able to identify a gene altered by the vaccine which was introduced into the DNA of children that *were* successfully born, causing further complications.

"They then put together a plan to allow the population to continue to plummet. By the first part of the 22nd century, population in what was known here as the states was reduced from a whopping 340 million to barely two million."

Marie pauses to take a sip of her bourbon.

"Sorry, repeating this gets grueling and makes me sick to my stomach," she confesses.

Bram nods, leaning back in his chair. "Take your time, Professor."

"Nope, we need to be back on the road, so we should finish this. Now where was I." She glances at her tablets. "Ah, yes. So, with the population that low, the governments and industries, as you already all know, were demolished. Now in steps this research company called The Direction, pretty much a redo of DWP, offering a safe haven to all those who are willing to take part in their effort to restore population with healthy DNA.

"That entire time, they had been studying the human genome and realized that a small number of certain Christian sects had refused the vaccines because they involved fetal stem cells. These lines were the *only* ones free of the negative genetic mark. The effort to get them involved with the Safe Haven project, however, ended up being more difficult as these same people believed in building and supporting their own communities, governed only by their church.

"So, one private community at a time, they slaughtered the adults and took the children until they had the number of subjects they needed. They cut off communications with all other countries to avoid any influence, wrote their own history, and eliminated religion. APA was designed and put in place to regulate all this. They still needed produce and industry, though, so they accepted a certain number of 'defects' as they called them, to work in Gamal."

She stops there for a moment and looks around at the stunned expressions. "We all knew this organization was doing something devious, but this all is horrifying to me as well, and it doesn't stop. Because elderly and non-workers, or anyone with disabilities, would be a drain on resources, they were promptly removed. Yes, as in killed," she answers everyone's questioning eyes.

"Even 'miscarriages' were arranged for those with clean DNA if they noticed any abnormalities in the baby. Children identified as having autism? Not allowed. They even occasionally culled, and still cull, those in Gamal if they go over their 'acceptable' level of 'tainted' population." She emphasizes with her fingers as quotation marks.

"This is where it gets tricky. They were still having difficulty maintaining 'pure' DNA, but of course we all know things happen in nature that cause defects, unavoidable even without the vaccine's impact. This is where the surrogates come in. Only the healthiest pairings were chosen, and those children were raised strictly for The Direction, most of them used for Defense and the rest as scientists and the brains behind the plans. They have even tampered with the DNA in utero to 'fix' issues. Which doesn't always work out so well."

"What happens to the surrogates after they are...used?" I finally cut in, because it is something I have always wondered.

Perhaps the women have jobs they continue, but somehow, I don't think the actual answer will surprise me.

"They are disposed of...killed. And not all of the women taken to be surrogates make the cut, either, and are murdered. Just like the elderly, the mentally disabled, and anyone who is permanently disabled by injuries. Or anyone who questions their methods for that matter." Marie answers with a strained voice, her stern face softened with a look of grief as she pinches the bridge of her nose.

"Ah, yes, one more thing, which was more recent in this twisted history. Because they wanted to have an excuse to collect women for experimental surrogacy, they put an additive in the foods provided to the towns to affect the balance of X versus Y chromosome-bearing sperm in men, resulting in a reduced level of Y, meaning fewer males were born."

I notice Nik, a constant snacker, with one of the standard health bars half-eaten, and at this he stares at it a moment and slowly puts it down on the table. It would make me laugh if this topic weren't so serious and depressing.

"This led to most women being unable to marry, hence being put into the surrogacy program without anyone suspecting anything was amiss. This was all a long game. An extremely evil long game."

There is absolute silence. The only sound is Yeti panting and a few of those around the table sipping from their bourbon. Bram doesn't push anyone or rush the process; he just sits there sipping from his own glass. Something in his eyes makes it seem as though he has seen the horrors himself, but he hides it well in a calm deportment.

"That… gives a lot to chew on." Gam is the first brave soul to comment. "I always knew it was wrong, a lot of us did. Something deep down said it was. But this is worse than I thought."

Everyone solemnly nods in agreement, and General Miles clears his throat and leans forward onto the table.

"Now for our plans."

| 68 |

# The Next Mission

At the corner of my vision, I see that Jax leans forward too. I know this is the part he has been waiting for, and me as well. This quick history lesson has stirred an anger I haven't felt in a while, and I want to do something to help work against this evil.

"In the long run, we want to try to connect to all the Nightlight satellites. This might give us a chance to see if there is anyone else in the world trying to reach out; see where they stand and if they can give us assistance. Isaac and a couple others back in Vita Nova are working on that. Our immediate concern is our captured men and women."

"What is the plan?" Jax jumps into the topic immediately.

The General holds up a hand and then taps his fingertips onto the table, looking straight at Jax.

"I know how much this hits home for you, Jax. You of all people know exactly what goes on in the facility and on the interrogation level, as does Lila." He gives a knowing look to me, causing my gaze to drop, and I stash my hands on my lap under the table as my fingers fidget in discomfort. "That is why you can't be part of that rescue."

I can see Jax wants to argue, his jaw tense, but I know he won't question General Miles' decision in front of the others.

*But why him of all people?*

I suddenly wonder if Jax was ever part of interrogations; it never dawned on me until now, but I force the uneasy thought to the side.

"I have a team ready to be mobile in four hours, led by Regie. You know how capable she is. They are from the other remaining secure base. With the satellites being down and the drones in limited quantity, they will have the best chance now since they can move immediately. They will ambush the transport and rescue them that way. You all need a little more recovery time, which is why I am giving you an assignment you can move on in two weeks."

"And that is?" Isaac inquires.

"Remember the facility down in Gamal in the center of that abandoned city you identified in The Direction communications?" Bram continues after Isaac nods. "That is their main surrogate center. You are going to free those women, gather data, and destroy their setup. They have a Defense turnover and supplies arriving in fourteen days which gives a security gap you can get in on, so it is time sensitive. We have additional blueprints and details on the mission that will be sent to you now."

He nods to Marie, and she taps her tablet a few times before swiping it toward Isaac's tablet.

Jax still doesn't seem pleased with being cut off from the other mission, but he nods slowly. "I'm down with that. I've seen how they treat those women. Where will they go when we get them out?"

"To a new base in far east Gamal. There is an off-grid home there who has been taking in runaways, and they have agreed to bring the women in and support them until they are stable."

"How many are there?" Gia finally speaks, and I think the newly discovered history had her stricken silent until now.

"We estimate about twenty-five," Marie answers.

"Why so few?" I am puzzled, *there have to be more*. "Is there another surrogate facility?"

She shakes her head and looks down in what I can only assume is sorrow. "They've recently gotten more selective in their DNA. Something about the 'god gene', but we don't have enough information on that. We just know that most women don't even make it to the facility."

"I think I need to leave the table, I'm sorry." Fae suddenly looks ill, which I can understand, and she pulls from her husband and heads for the kitchen.

"That should conclude our meeting anyway." The General nods and stands. "If there are any further questions, Marie here can answer."

"Jax," he adds. "I'll need another moment of your time. Will you join us please, Lila?"

My brow knits as I stand from the table. His request seems more like an order, even though it is in the form of a question. I can't help but feel nervous, wondering what this is about.

# | 69 |

# Questioning

Bram leads the way to the med-room and steps to the side to allow Jax and Lila through, Yeti at their heels. He closes the door, and Jax notices Lila flinch a little. She composes herself, though, and stands next to him at one side of the steel table in the center of the room while General Miles stands on the other side, his arms folded. Yeti settles himself at Lila's feet.

"Jax, I know you wanted to go on the rescue mission, and I know you were going to brace me about it after the meeting, so here's your chance."

"I just think that we know the region best." Jax considers arguing his point; he wanted to be in on the rescue, maybe as a form of reparation, but the General is right. "However, I respect your decision, sir, and you're right. This team needs more time to recover."

"Good." Bram lowers his arms and sets his hands on the table. "You're a wise man, Jax, which is why I am going to ask you to be honest with me with this next question. Both of you, be honest with me."

Jax nods. "Yes, sir."

"Alright," Lila tentatively answers, shoving her hands into her pockets.

The tension is visible on her face, like she knows what he is going to ask.

The General's eyes are stern but sincere as he holds Jax's gaze. "In your opinion, is Lila stable enough to still be an asset to your team?

And before you answer, let me add to that. Is it fair to *her* to keep her in the field? We can bring her back with us to Vita Nova to recuperate fully, and I don't just mean physically. She has more than earned that."

Jax suddenly realizes he has not thought of that and looks down, his lips tight as he contemplates what Bram just said. Lila has become so integral to their daily routines that he wasn't considering that her struggles might change those dynamics. That, and the option to have her safe in Vita Nova was not something that was on the table until now, and now that it is, he has to consider what's best for everyone.

*What's best for Lila...*

"No, I'm not leaving." Lila's voice cuts his thoughts short before he can answer.

Jax looks over to see determination on her face, something that he has noticed more as of late.

"They'll need a medic."

Bram eyes her almost challengingly, testing her resolve. "We have an available medic and can have him in place within a week. Gia can cover for you until then."

Jax watches Lila look down as she seems to struggle inwardly, her fortitude seeming to waver for a moment before she looks up. Her eyes glint with unshed tears and she clears her throat, her voice low.

"Sir... I trust everyone here. I know them. There is no place for me in Vita Nova, no person that I would know, and my skills are better served here."

The General's expression softens, but he doesn't relent. "We would have work for you, and I believe a young woman you knew from Vouna, Tess, recently moved there from another settlement."

Although he is conflicted himself, wanting her to stay but also wanting her to be safe, Jax contributes to the discussion.

"You could come back after some time, Lila. You'd be safe there. You'll have a chance to recover."

She looks at him as though he betrayed her, and he inwardly flinches.

"I don't need to be safe, Jax, I need to do what I feel God is calling me to do."

He is surprised by her unexpected fervor and encouraged. This is a Lila he isn't familiar with, and he is realizing how much her faith has grown.

*She's going to be alright...*

Lila steels her expression and faces Bram, who is studying the both of them.

"I no longer know Tess. That was when I was a different person." She turns her eyes again to Jax, almost pleadingly. "And I know God has a plan for us all here, and that's what keeps me going every day. This is where God wants me to be. If I walk away from that, I know I will lose the battle."

Jax understands she means her own internal battle and watches as she faces General Miles one more time.

"Please don't make me leave. This is where I belong."

Bram takes in a deep breath and folds his arms, something of approval in his expression, though he guards it carefully. "At this point it is not up to me. Jax, this goes to the first question. Will having Lila stay with the team be a liability? Will it put anyone else's life at risk?"

"No. She's right. She belongs here with us."

Jax doesn't even hesitate. After seeing Lila's conviction, he has no doubt that this is how it is supposed to be, and he wants that kind of steadfastness at his side in any battle. He looks over and meets her appreciative gaze, her expression that of relief.

"Good, then that's settled. Now, if you excuse me, I need to catch up with my son before we leave." The General's face relaxes as he shakes both their hands and then promptly walks out of the med-room without another word.

Jax hears Lila exhale as though she has been holding her breath the entire time.

"I think I might drink that bourbon now."

She braces her hands against the edge of the table, her head bowed.

"You and me both." Jax admits, running a hand through his own hair. "Probably not a good idea, though."

"I'm not talking the whole bottle, Jax."

She gives him a light punch in the arm before heading for the door and he grins a little. Pausing in the door frame, she looks back at him hopefully.

"Coming?"

She looks tired, and he notes that she also looks too thin, but in this moment she seems content, and he smiles at that. "Fine, one glass, but only if you try one of those muffins as well."

"Deal."

| 70 |

# Deals

The entire day has been grueling, the toughest moment emotionally being when the General questions my ability to stay here. I have often asked myself this same thing the past few weeks, whether I am going to cost them their lives at some point. Yet in that moment I recognized that there is nowhere else I should be. I am at peace with my decision.

Shortly after, the General and Professor Marie left with the two armed escorts. He had briefly given all of us encouraging praise for our efforts before parting. And of course, Fae and Nik were barely seen for the rest of the day, leaving for a walk and only showing up for supper.

To Jax's delight, and honestly mine because he is a calming presence, Father Malachi has been assigned to stay with us as our in-house counselor. I want to ask him why he dresses so oddly, though.

We also now have one biodiesel truck identical to those used by Defense, two propane-fueled UTVs, and five biodiesel dirt bikes with enough fuel to cover basic use and our future assignment.

*Zero one hundred...* I flinch as I wake like clockwork after the usual onslaught of dreams. *Nightmares.*

Walking quietly through the darkened living room, followed by my furry companion, I tug on a jacket and slip outside, silently shutting the door behind me. I deeply inhale the cold night air and release it slowly, watching as my breath drifts in the breeze. Yeti jumps at the small cloud, trying to catch it, but he quickly loses interest and pads off to check the trees.

Some clouds obscure half the stars, but a half-moon cuts through enough to give the wooded canyon land an ethereal blue glow. Only the bravest of crickets are making sounds in this cold night, and I focus on those until I am lost in thought, the recent history lesson at the forefront.

A slight yip from Yeti toward the front door brings my attention back, and I turn to see Jax stepping out of the house, pulling a denim jacket over his shoulders.

"Hey there, I thought you'd be sleeping through the night," I comment, but one look at his face is all I need to know he has barely slept.

"Not so lucky." He shrugs with a faint smile.

"Rough night?"

He nods and sits in the grass to my right. I follow suit and sit beside him, like we have done every night this past week. Except this time, fortunately, I don't have to relive things.

"I'm glad you are staying, Lil'." His low voice cuts through the silence, and I direct my gaze to him as he continues, his eyes focused on the moonlit terrain. "Just promise you'll let me know if it ever becomes too much for you."

"Only if you promise likewise," I challenge.

"Deal."

| 71 |

# Acquisition

I hadn't realized how heavy all the gear is for someone in the Defense. The cargos are the same, but the molle vest I have over a standard issue Defense jacket shirt carries multiple magazines for my rifle and handgun. What also adds to that weight is the bullet proof plates Jax requests that we all use.

At my feet is a fully stocked med-pack, but if I have to carry that, I estimate I will be carrying around seventy-five pounds, counting my weapons. The additional two weeks of recovery has barely gotten me in shape enough, so I hope I don't have to run with the pack.

I am slightly envious of Jax sitting to the right of me in our supply truck, since he has no additional gear other than a sidearm and a knife. He is wearing his own Defense dress uniform, nameplate removed. The stain and damage to the pantleg had been mended by Fae. I catch myself studying him, and I have to admit he cuts a striking figure in uniform, but he looks irritated at the fact he has to wear it again as he tugs at his collar.

Nik sits at my left in the cab of the truck, driving, while Gam, Isaac, and Gia are in the back with the supply crates. Usually, Isaac stays behind, but the plan requires a few technical processes, so he will be staying in the truck while speaking with us through our comms. Fae and Father Malachi remain at Bear Base, and I smile slightly as I think back to the priest saying a blessing over us and the vehicle as we were leaving.

"Alright, let's briefly go over the plan again." Jax turns on his comms device so the three in the back can hear as well. "Once we intercept their actual supply truck and incapacitate the unit, we take their name badges and the Major's nameplate; he's there as an inspector. Isaac swaps the photos on the ID cards and Gia grabs their truck.

"Isaac will be updating the surrogate facility's system by a remote proximity hack, saying they have to evacuate the women. The surrogates go in our truck, and the staff evacuate in their own med-bus with instructions to head for their secure bunker to the west. Isaac says it is minimally staffed, and only two guards, which should be easy enough to handle.

"After they leave, Gam stays with Isaac and the women for security while Lila, Nik, and Gia go with me into the facility. I go with Lila as she secures any data and medical supplies we need, meanwhile Gia and Nik place the explosives. Then we get out. Fast. Let's make this as successful a mission as Regie and her team had. Everyone copy?"

"Copy that," I and the four others respond.

The news of the successfully rescued detainees has been a boost to morale and has us almost amped for this undertaking. I am still nervous, though. Combat gloves soak up the sweat from my palms, and even though the air is a crisp forty-some degrees outside, I feel a bead of sweat trickling down from under the side of the Defense cap.

"You good?" Jax asks with the comms off.

I nod and can see the edginess on his face as well. "You?"

"Yeah, I hate this uniform, though. Comes with too many ghosts." He comments quietly, his brows furrowing as he stares at the open plains going past us which gradually change to slopes and small buttes.

I haven't heard Jax mention much about his past and what he used to do in the Defense. I still wonder how involved he was with Sublevel 20, but I have never asked. Now is not the time, though, when I notice Jax sit a little straighter.

"Here it is." He points and tells the others as we approach a well-maintained road going north to south. "Ready up!"

We drive to one section of the highway that has a couple small buttes on either side, just over a hill in the road, and Nik parks on the right shoulder, facing south. Everyone but Isaac hops out. Other than Jax, we are identically geared up, sidearms at our leg and rifles slung in front of us.

Jax nods, and wordlessly, Nik and Gam unbolt one of the tires, jack up the truck, and toss the loosened tire on the ground. They then scramble, along with Gia, to either side of the road, concealing themselves in the outcroppings. Rifle across the front of me, I stand next to Jax on the road beside the truck and double check to be sure the five syringes are in one of the vest pockets.

"How are we timewise, Isaac?" Jax inquires via comms.

"Perfect. We should see them over the hill within five minutes," Isaac confirms.

"Almighty and eternal God, protect us on this assignment. Protect us with the shield of your strength, and keep us safe from all evil and harm," Jax murmurs quietly.

"Amen," I reply, and he gives me a quick, albeit reserved, smile.

"Here we go..." He takes in a deep breath once we see a truck identical to ours crest the hill, and he steps out onto the road, waving his arms.

Remaining beside the truck, I click the safety off on my rifle and try to slow my breathing and steady my shaky hands. The afternoon sun glints on the windshield of the slowing truck, and I am glad for my sunglasses, not just for the light but to hide the uneasiness.

"Hey!" Jax's voice does not show a hint of nerves, and I wonder how he does it. "Glad you guys came by. I'm a little shorthanded here, and my comms went down."

He gestures to our truck.

Two Defense guards in similar gear to mine step out of the cab along with an officer, a Major like Jax used to be, in dress uniform.

"Where's your name plate, Major?" The man pauses and suddenly goes to reach for his sidearm.

"I wouldn't do that," Jax warns, his own weapon already in hand. "I have marksmen on either side. Lay down your weapons and kick them over here."

I shoulder my AR and train my sights on the other two, my finger hovering over the trigger guard. Each complies with Jax's instructions, while at the same time Nik silently hops from a butte and goes to the back of their truck, bringing two more Defense guards out and disarming them as well.

"You're Major Bachman. I thought you were dead," the uniformed officer comments, and I see Jax flinch at the name.

Jax doesn't reply but instead removes their ear pieces and tosses them in a small faraday box Isaac had given him. "To the back of the truck."

I follow behind, rifle still at ready as all five reach the back of their own truck. Nik removes the name badges and the officer's nameplate in addition to all of their ID cards.

"Are you going to kill us, now?" The officer scowls.

"No, today is your lucky day. You get a free pass, so make good use of it," Jax dryly replies and nods to me.

I let my rifle hang on the single-point sling and reach for the syringes, injecting the contents into each of the five. "Twenty seconds."

"In! Now!" Jax orders, and they climb into the back of the truck.

Within the twenty seconds, they are unconscious. Gia and Gam move out from their cover as Nik climbs into the back to zip-tie the ankles and wrists of our detainees. We all choose a name badge and ID card, Jax taking the name plate of the Major, and Isaac hops out to rapidly print our images onto the access cards. Gia climbs into the cab of the Defense vehicle, while Gam puts the tire back on our truck, and we are quickly back on the road.

It happens so fast I am only now processing the fact that the first part of the mission went smoothly, *disquietingly so*. Even though it is a good feeling, I know this is only the beginning. I look at my hands and they have finally stopped shaking, but within the hour will be the next phase.

"Good job, Lil'," Jax quietly comments, while I watch the landscape passing by as it opens again to wide prairies.

"I was terrified. Not sure how good that is."

"You still did exactly what was needed," he assures, though he guardedly watches my expression.

"Yeah, did you see the look on their faces? They never saw it coming," Nik interjects with a grin.

"Job isn't done yet." Jax calmly reminds us, and I nod, woefully aware of this.

# | 72 |

# Out of Time

As the miles tick down, Jax feels more uncomfortable, his gut warning him of something insidious. He clenches his jaw and fights through it; there is no turning back at this point without a solid reason. Catching Lila's glance, he knows she sees the apprehension, and it again surprises him how good she has gotten at reading him.

"What's wrong?" Lila is leaning toward him a little, keeping her voice low.

"Nothing," Jax replies at first, then acknowledges he can't ignore his instincts and keep her in the dark. "Just a feeling that we're missing something."

"Should we let the others know?"

"Know what?" Nik looks over at Jax, his usually cheerful face tense. "Is this one of your gut feelings, Jax? I don't like those."

Jax nods slightly and addresses the others over comms. "Stay frosty, guys. I've got an odd feeling about this but nothing to go on. What do you have so far, Isaac?"

"We're clear so far, and I've been within range for a few minutes now. Even after the satellite loss, the organization still has signal towers for communication, but I have cut off the surrogate facility's connection to them. To them, we are now 'The Direction', so I sent the falsified orders for evacuation, and they are prepping the women now. I also instructed them that we will handle the data-wipe, which will allow us to take it intact when we get there."

"Good. How long do we have before APA notices their lines are disabled?" Jax questions.

"She notices already but won't notify anyone for fifteen minutes from now. The only Defense backup they have is two hours out, so that leaves *us* about two hours once we get there. Plenty of time."

Jax nods, his jaw relaxing a little, and he hears Nik exhale in relief.

"It's probably just because you haven't gone undercover for some time, boss." Nik shrugs. "Nerves get the best of us sometimes."

"This is closer to a raid than undercover," Jax argues but nods a little. "But you could be right."

He notices Lila's worried look as she stares straight ahead, yet she doesn't say anything. The feeling does not go away, and he hopes he doesn't regret pushing it back down.

"Alright, everyone, ETA ten minutes. Isaac, go through the layout of the facility one more time."

"As always with these places, single door entry. So, we have the main level: the front half is living quarters for the women. Straight down the main hall at the end is the medical room, and that's where all the supplies are.

"The access to the basement is there by the doors to the med-room, door and stairwell to the left. Their security room is opposite that, but you won't have to worry about that once the place is destroyed. At the bottom of the steps the hall immediately turns left and then takes another left. The second to last door is the data room; all the rest are research labs. Once the staff is gone, I can remotely unlock all the doors, so you won't have to worry about that. Our only difficulty is going to be comms: it's their typical faraday building, but I should be able to piggyback our comms onto their booster, it might just take a few minutes."

"How many women will they have ready?"

"Thirty-two. More than we expected, because they received a new group recently," Isaac confirms.

"Good job, Isaac, let us know if anything changes. Comms stay open now."

Jax watches as the scenery changes to include scatterings of trees and finally dilapidated buildings. They come to a single intersection with another maintained road going east/west, while across the way is a low steel building with dark one-way windows. The adrenaline begins to kick in, and Jax shifts in his seat in anticipation.

"Action time, everyone." He glances to see Nik steel his expression, meanwhile Lila tightly grips her rifle as she seems to put herself through a slow breathing exercise.

The building is within a large, fenced yard, but the gate is wide open to the small parking lot in front of the single door where thirty-two identically dressed women are standing with packed bags, waiting. Off to the side are four women in lab coats, six other various staff, and two male Defense guards, all waiting without any sign of being alerted to the coup.

*This is promising...*

Jax relaxes just slightly, as Nik pulls in and turns around, backing up to the waiting women. They all look apprehensive, a few of them several months pregnant, but they are all depressingly compliant as though their spirits have already been broken. It hits him again just how sinister The Direction continues to be, and he frowns.

They wait until Gia pulls in with her truck, and she parks it off to the side, farther from the guards. That is when Jax hops out, followed by Lila and Nik. Nik shoulders his pack as does Gia, though Gia stays by her truck for the moment.

"Alright, in we go, ladies!"

Nik puts on a sour face and nudges the first one with the barrel of his AR. Jax knows he hates doing this, but it is a good act, and the women hurriedly climb into the waiting truck where Gam helps them up from inside.

"What's this about, Major?" A young lab attendant approaches with a tablet in her hands. "Communications never explained anything."

"Need to know. Just know that your lives are at stake, so if you would please all get in your med-bus." Jax's face takes on a serious expression as he points at the parked bus near the door.

"Sergeant, get these people out of here, now! You are to drive them immediately to the safety bunker west of here." Jax barks an order at one of the guards.

Lila is right beside him with her rifle at low-ready, and he catches her raise a brow at his authoritative manner.

"Yes sir!"

The guards give a sharp salute and practically herd the group with their rifles. A few of them grumble swear words under their breath, but they all eventually file into the bus. The two armed men hop into the driver and passenger seats and pull out of the lot, picking up speed and taking a westerly direction down the highway.

Jax waits with a held breath until the vehicle disappears over the hill.

"Alright. Nik, Gia, clear the place first. I don't want to risk letting our guard down." He knows very well this could still be a trap.

"Yes sir," they both reply and slip through the door, rifles at high-ready.

"I'll grab the duffle bags for the supplies," Lila comments, her voice unexpectedly steady.

Jax watches as she removes and sets her rifle in the truck before retrieving two empty supply bags. Isaac in the meantime hops out from the truck full of women and jogs over to the other truck, heading to remove its tracking device as planned.

*Another vehicle in our collection...*

Jax allows himself a little positivity, but the nagging feeling still persists, and he eyes his surroundings.

"All clear," Gia and Nik call through the open comms.

"Alright then. Gam, stay with the women, Isaac is your backup. Nik, Gia, start with the incendiary devices in the basement. Lila, first supplies, then data. Let's go."

"Yes sir," comes the unified reply, and Jax smirks a little in satisfaction.

Lila has to jog to keep up with his hurried stride, and he slows a bit, reminding himself that she has the weight of the molle vest and plates. They reach the med-room in short time, and Lila wordlessly starts filling the bags. One filled, she hands it to him as he silently stands watch, listening to the comms while Gia and Nik confirm locations of each set explosive. Isaac pitches in once when he confirms that the second truck is ready.

"I'm gonna need a third bag." Lila comments without stopping, continuing to fill the second bag. "This is a lot of items we'll be needing once the new bases are established."

"I'll go get it. You should be good here with Gia and Nik in the building."

"Alright," she answers, and he hears slight trepidation, but she gives him a firm nod.

Jax shoulders the first filled bag, sprinting down the hall and out to the truck, tossing the supplies in. The women waiting there jump a little, but Gam reassures them everything is fine. Grabbing another empty duffle bag, Jax grimaces and his heartrate spikes when he hears Isaac.

"Shit, shit, shit. Jax, we have a problem." Isaac is standing by the side of the truck, tapping at his tablet, and Jax frowns at the ashen expression on his face.

"What."

"There is a Defense officer nearby that APA signaled, and she notified him of a possible breach here at the facility." Isaac swallows, and Jax can see his hands visibly shaking.

*Isaac shouldn't be out here...*

"How far?"

"Thirty minutes, maybe more, maybe less. I can't track whatever he is driving."

"Probably a hover bike," Jax comments through gritted teeth. "Alright, get in the back. Now."

"Gia, Nik, assuming you heard that, are you nearly done? Lila, just bring the second bag out; we'll have to leave it at that." Jax addresses the others as Isaac hops in the back with Gam and the women.

"Copy that," comes Lila's reply.

"We're only halfway done, just finished the lower level, heading to the upper," Gia answers.

Lila hurries out, tosses the bag in, and then turns to go back, but he grabs her arm gently to stop her.

"We need to go."

"We need to get that data," Lila challenges, a tense but determined look in her eyes.

He ponders a moment, every fiber in his being telling him they should go now, but she is right. The more information they have on what they are doing to these women, the better they can help them.

"Alright, let's go."

As he follows her back down the hall, he instructs the rest of them through the comms. "Nik, get out now and take the truck. First, toss my gear and Lila's gear in the other truck, then get those women out of here. Gam and Isaac will be with you. Take a straight route across country. It's going to be bumpy, so tell the women to hold tight. You need to put as much distance between you all and here. Gia, finish up with the devices and get the other truck ready to roll. Dump the unconscious captives in the brush."

Several tense 'yes sirs' sound through the comms, and Jax knows Nik doesn't waste time as he hears him exit one of the upper rooms and run down the hall behind them, starting the truck. Lila skips steps going down into the lower level and turns left, breaking into a run down the brightly lit hall, and he jogs beside her. The damp smell of concrete hits his nose, and Jax frowns at a brief recollection of another place like this.

"We're on route," Isaac confirms over comms, but it is getting staticky. "I have the explosives on an outside long range signal device. Message me on your tablet when you're clear, and I'll send the signal. One last thing. Once I reach a certain distance, my lockdown on communications to The Direction will drop. I recommend you shut your comms off within five minutes or APA might be able to tap into them from the signal booster. Boot up the comms again once the facility is destroyed."

"Copy that. And Godspeed. What's your status, Gia?"

"Nearly done. Still all clear up here."

"Copy. If you see anyone, do not engage, stay hidden and the first chance you get, you drive out of here."

"But, Jax..."

"That's an order, Gia. Gam would kill me if anything happened to you," he adds more mildly, although not liking to use her bond with Gam to sway her loyalty.

*Relationships with teammates muddle the battlefield...*

"Yes, sir..."

Gia is pissed, he can tell, but he can deal with that later. His goal right now is their safety.

"Alright, shut down the comms."

"Copy that."

He turns his off, and Lila deftly hands hers over so he can put them in the faraday box, which he places in his pocket.

Jax stands at the doorway, watching down the hall once he and Lila reach the door to the data room, a small concrete space with a few computer towers. She quickly slides into a chair, starting the transfer of all files to a portable drive, her fingers perceptibly trembling.

"This could take some time, how long do we have?" She asks, strain growing in her voice, and he knows she is struggling being in this place.

*Keep strong, Lil'...*

"I say five minutes, then we take whatever we get. Are you good here, Lil'? I'm going to be at the stairwell so I can hear upstairs." He is reluctant to leave her, but she looks at him and nods firmly, still nervous, but resolute.

"I'm good."

"Remember. Five minutes." He waits for her nod and jogs down the hall, rounding the first bend.

Nearly at the turn for the stairs, his hackles suddenly raise, and he has the feeling he should have his sidearm in hand despite Gia recently calling all-clear. Jax goes to reach for it as he approaches the stairs.

*Too late...*

A quick, uniformed, elbow comes flying at his face from around the corner and hits him hard enough to cause him to stumble back against the wall, his vision blurring and head throbbing.

| 73 |

# Major Marc

"Well, if it isn't my good buddy, Major Don Bachman." Major Marc, now apparently Lieutenant Colonel Marc, gloats as he shoves the stunned Jax down the hall and removes his sidearm. "I saw you on the security cameras upstairs, and I thought it was my birthday. I saw your girl, too. She's next. Backup is on its way, so they will take care of your other soldier upstairs."

Jax's focus slowly returns, and he watches Marc remove the mag from the handgun, toss it one way, empty the chamber, then remove the slide, tossing it the other way. Finally, he tosses the last piece behind him. Jax pushes himself to his feet and backs up, farther down the hall. He stops when Marc removes his own sidearm, steps closer, and takes firing stance.

"Looks like you moved up the ranks." Jax comments tartly as he fights the throbbing in his vision.

"Yup, and with you as my detainee, or more likely in a body bag, too risky to have you alive, I will probably be recommended for full blown Colonel." Marc shrugs a shoulder.

"We used to be friends. I was even over at your family's place for dinner several times," Jax argues while adrenaline pushes the rest of the pain away, hoping that somehow Marc could be reasoned with.

Yet he knows in his soul that Marc has always been corrupt, always took pleasure in the worst assignments, and always enjoyed interrogations a little too much. That is what happens when The Direction raises you from childhood for Defense. He often wondered if Marc was assigned to Lila, and that still makes him livid.

"That meant nothing to me when I flagged you as high risk when you kept playing favorites with that girl." Marc continues to chide.

Jax waits, hoping for a moment to make a move, as they are only a couple paces from each other.

*Praying for that moment...please.*

Almost in answer, there is the sound of a biodiesel truck firing up outside.

*Gia...*

This distracts Marc and causes him to turn, just briefly, but it is enough. Jax hurls his whole weight into Marc and drives him into the concrete floor, the weapon flying out of his hand and sliding across the floor toward the stairs.

Jax tries to reach the gun, but Marc grabs him by his uniform belt and drags him farther away, slamming his elbow down into his lower back. Gasping at the blow, Jax rolls from his grip and scrambles to his feet, taking out his Kbar in a reverse-knife grip instead.

Marc does likewise, squaring off with a grin. "You know I'm the better fighter."

"I seem to remember we were pretty well matched. I'll take my chances."

Jax readies himself, raising his left arm to guard. One thing is for certain, he is not letting this man past him and down the hall.

*Hurry up, Lil'...*

Marc makes the first move and strikes for his clavicle, his other hand grabbing Jax's knife-bearing wrist. Blocking, with his forearm bracing and pushing against the striking arm, Jax twists his wrist from Marc's grip and strikes for the underarm, but Marc grabs and pins his arm, redirecting his own leftward strike for Jax's throat.

Jax lets out a hiss as he angles his left arm to guard his neck, and the blade slices through the uniform fabric and down his forearm. He grabs his attacker's wielding wrist and ducks down, twisting and turning to free his knife-hand, using the momentum to drive his elbow into Marc's chest, while at the same time aiming for under his arm again.

Marc jumps back a bit, barely avoiding the blade, and catches his wind before diving back into the attack. They parry a few more strikes, wearing at each other's endurance, and both turning out to be well matched.

Striking for Jax's stomach, Marc also grabs Jax's wrist as he in turn back-hand stabs for Marc's thigh. Jax grabs the wielding wrist as well, and they wrestle for the upper hand, arms crossed and locked against each other. The dull ache in Jax's arm is barely noticeable to him, but it effects the strength of his grip, and he knows he will lose it soon.

Jax slams his forehead into his opponent's nose, sending him back a step, and he breaks free just in time to have Marc plant a solid kick against his stomach. He staggers back, going down on one knee and heaving to catch his breath.

"Give it up, Jax."

Marc steps back a bit toward the stairs, and Jax regrettably realizes that in their struggle, they have moved that much closer to the firearm and it is now at Marc's feet. His former Defense partner quickly drops his knife and picks up his weapon, adopting shooting stance again.

"I told you I was always the better fighter. Now, drop the knife, hands behind your head."

Jax's heart pounds heavily in his ears, and he settles his other knee down on the concrete, dropping the knife and placing his hands behind his head, locking his fingers.

*I've done all I can, God, please protect them...*

"I never did get to tell you," Marc begins, and Jax is reminded of how much the man loves to gloat, only postponing the end result. "I had a great time helping wipe out all your bases. And I will *personally* see to it that your girl gets the best room on Sublevel 20."

Anger simmers in Jax's veins, but he knows in this position he can do nothing.

*Delay him...just a little more time.*

"Not if she kills you first."

Marc seems amused by this. "I'm pretty sure she won't see me coming after she finds your body. Besides, I've already called the calvary. I can close her off down here until they swarm this area. I prefer to handle her myself, though. Goodbye, Jax."

Marc tips his head to his iron sights, and Jax knows there is nothing more he can do to delay. Closing his eyes, he forces himself to breathe slowly, silently praying for forgiveness, for peace, for the safety of his unit: his friends.

*For Lila.*

Suddenly, four shots sound out in the concrete hall, and the deafening ringing in his ears tells him he is surprisingly still alive. His eyes fly open, and in front of him in a crumpled, lifeless heap is Marc, four gaping wounds to the chest.

*Lil'...*

Jax clambers to his feet and spins around. Down at the corner where the hall turns, stands Lila, firearm still raised in her hand, looking as though she sees a ghost.

"Lila." He reaches her in a few strides, placing his hand over her weapon and pushing it down to her side.

"Lil'?" Jax grabs her shoulders, looking into her distant eyes, and he wonders if her mind is even there with him. "Lila. We have to move, now!!"

*If I have to carry you, I will...*

Jax presses his hands on either side of her face when he sees her eyes squeeze shut, lowering his voice, calming himself as much as her, and knowing they need to leave quickly.

"Lil', are you with me?"

# | 74 |

# Fighting Through

I slow my breathing down, trying to focus on the feel of the fabric on my sleeve. Anything other than the lights, the concrete, and the cramped room. Finally, the display *dings* to indicate a completed transfer, and I disconnect the portable drive, slipping it into my pants pocket.

Exiting the room, I hear voices, the words muffled but echoing enough down the concrete walls that I can distinguish Jax's voice. The other voice takes a moment to recognize, but when I do it hits me as though I have been kicked.

*In the side.*

*Officer Marc.*

I finally remember his name, or at least what they called him. I hadn't even been able to recall it when I was telling Jax about my time at the facility, but now it is as clear as day. Suddenly I wish Yeti were with me.

To me it seems the hall squeezes in, and I press my back against the wall, trying to control my breathing, the bright lights slowly seeming to get brighter.

*No... if he's here, that might mean Jax is in trouble.*

I can't let this get him killed. If I lose him, I am afraid I will truly lose myself. He means more to me than I think even he realizes.

I force myself off the concrete and quietly move closer to the turn in the walls, staying against the inner wall until I am right at the corner, and I stop. Shakely, I remove my sidearm, settling my hands into the proper position I have practiced so many times since joining the team.

*Muscle memory... Rely on it.* A small voice reminds me.

"I had a great time helping wipe out all your bases. And I will *personally* see to it that your girl gets the best room on Sublevel 20." I hear Officer Marc's condescending tone, just around the corner.

And I hear it again in my memories.

*"I'll be back, honey."*

Pressing myself against the wall again, I squeeze my eyes shut, my heartrate climbing. I fight to be cognizant again, but I want to be far away from here right now.

*Pray...*

There it is again. That tiny voice that got me through it all in the first place.

"Not if she kills you first," Jax's confident voice reaches through to my besieged mind.

*God, I can't. I am not strong enough for this...*

*But He said to me, "My Grace is sufficient for you, for My power is made perfect in weakness."*

The voice inside me repeating that sacred scripture mostly brings me back. I am reminded again that I can't do much on my own lately, let alone save a life.

*Or take a life...*

*The Lord is my strength and my shield; in Him my heart trusts, so I am helped...*

I take a deep breath.

"Goodbye, Jax." The familiar voice burns into my head, but my eyes snap open, and I slip around the corner and raise my sidearm.

In a matter of split seconds, I see Jax kneeling on the floor with his hands behind his head, his back to me. Then Officer Marc past him, with that smug smile, until he raises his eyes to look at me, and the smile leaves.

*It's a target...Just like you've practiced countless times. Don't hit Jax...*

The sound of the gunfire fills the concrete hall, and my ears are overwhelmed by the ringing. The walls press in, my vision clouding, and it seems there is nothing but me and the hall, the smell of gunpowder mixing with damp concrete. Vaguely, I feel a hand over mine, pushing the weapon down, then hands on my shoulders.

"Lila?" Jax's voice is so far away. "Lila. We have to move, now!!"

I close my eyes, pushing out the thought of Officer Marc's face. Something warm holds my own face, breaking through, and I hear Jax's voice more clearly as I focus on the faint smell of pine.

"Lil', are you with me?"

"Y-yes..." I nod, and open my eyes, the hall finally coming into focus.

Jax looks down at me with relief and removes his hands from my face.

"We need to go, Lil'." He is calm but insistent, and I numbly nod, holstering my sidearm.

He leads the way, only pausing to grab and holster Officer Marc's sidearm. Stepping past the fallen body, I turn my face away. I am still feeling numb; in a haze. As we step outside, the second truck is right in front of us, facing away and ready to leave.

"Get in, damn it!!" Gia yells, hanging out the side of the window. "Whatever took you so long??"

Jax leaps up, climbing over the tailgate, and reaches with his right hand to help me up. We are barely in when Gia tears out of the lot and accelerates across the grassy hills. I slump into the back on the floor against the strapped down supply crates and watch as the facility behind us gets smaller.

After tapping something into his data pad, Jax looks out at the shrinking building and waits. I wait, too, and watch as billows of flame and smoke wipe out the sin against humanity. Finally, I am hearing everything a little clearer: the biodiesel engine, the tires tearing across the ground, and Jax exhaling.

I don't feel relief though. I feel grateful to be alive, grateful Jax is alive, but I also sense a foreboding. I begin to wonder if it is just a new symptom of my unhinged self, but I feel a need to be prepared.

Searching around, I locate my med-pack and my rifle stashed under one of the side seats and scoot over to kneel beside them. Between the jarring bumps of the ride, I place the single-point sling around my right shoulder and neck and settle the rifle across the front of me. Looking over to the other side, I wonder if Jax feels the threat as well, since he removes his uniform jacket and tosses it to the side while pulling his gear out from under one of the other seats.

"Your arm."

I nod to the long, bloodied gash down his left forearm, regrettably realizing I haven't even asked him if he is alright or injured. Even though it is not life threatening, it would certainly make it hard to use his arm.

"It'll be fine." He dismisses it and grabs a combat jacket.

"You'll be able to use it better if you let me wrap it at least," I argue, pulling my med-bag over to him.

"If you can do it quickly. I've a feeling we don't have much time." Jax's eyes keep darting to the retracting scenery behind us, and my suspicions are confirmed.

*If he feels it too, it's not just paranoia...*

Working against the bounces from the rough terrain, procedural memory takes over as I clean and zip-stitch his arm. Meanwhile, Jax uses his free hand to remove our comms from the small box and reactivate them. While my fingers are working on applying a gauze wrap, I barely notice as he reaches over and puts one of the devices back in my left ear for me.

"Nice job." He nods appreciatively and flexes his fingers before quickly slipping on and zipping up the combat jacket.

He taps the comms on while fastening his molle vest in place. "Gia, you have your comms on?"

"Yes sir," comes a sharp reply. "I heard the hovercycle come in but never saw anyone. Whoever it was, they were like a ghost. What the hell happened?"

"Story for another time. Turn north and pick up the pace. I think we're being followed, and I don't want to lead them to the others."

Jax says this as he looks at me with an oddly calm, matter-of-fact expression. I wordlessly nod in agreement and shift my attention to our own dust clouds behind us, trying to see beyond them.

"Copy that," Gia replies, and the truck turns sharply left, throwing me off balance.

Jax quickly grabs me by the vest before I go over, and we settle into the side seats to hold on as the vehicle skips over uneven terrain.

"You would be right, Jax," Isaac's voice crackles in with an uneasy tone. "We're free and clear out here at least but just caught chatter that they are tracking you somehow, and they are pissed and determined."

"Keep your course, Nik, we'll draw them away."

"Yes, sir."

"Isaac, you did remove the tracker, right?" Jax also watches behind us as he deftly slings his rifle to the front of his chest.

"I'm offended you asked that. But yes, I did."

"What if Officer Marc put something in here before he came into the surrogate center, just in case?" I instinctively suggest, and Jax suddenly turns to me, an unexpectedly surprised look on his face, but he doesn't say anything.

"Who? What the heck happened back there? Never mind, tell me later. Use a scrambler. It will unfortunately knock out the comms, but it's your best shot," Isaac advises.

"Copy," Jax replies, his eyes still questioningly on me, then adds to the others. "Be safe, we'll contact you when we can. Gia, take us to the buttes. You know where."

"Copy that. Gia out."

Jax takes out a small handheld scrambler from his vest and flips it on. The comms squeal and then go dead, confirming the efficacy, and we are now radio silent.

"Lil'." He pauses, and my baffled expression seems to perturb him more, but he asks calmly. "How do you know his name? His nameplate only had his last name, and I have never mentioned him before."

"He was at the facility, one of my interrogators. The others called him Officer Marc. I didn't remember until I heard his voice today." My attention is so hypervigilant at the moment, watching behind us, waiting to hear other vehicles, and my hands gripping my rifle, that the reply comes unusually easy.

I catch Jax's grimace and a brief look of anger, but he seems as focused as I am on our surroundings, though the engine and tires drown out most sounds. Sitting close side by side is the only way we can hear each other.

"He was also my partner in the Defense; we ran assignments together. Don't feel bad about shooting him, though, he is...*was* a sick individual."

"I got that impression," I retort, my finger fidgeting with the safety on my weapon.

His glance is apologetic.

"Thank you for saving my life back there, by the way," he adds.

"That was all God...but you're welcome."

# | 75 |

# Secrets

When she mentions Marc by name, Jax knows his suspicions are confirmed, but he asks anyway. As he tells her briefly about being Defense partners with her interrogator, he holds back the rest. The fact that years ago, he himself used to be head of interrogations...*torture*... and that he trained Marc.

He contemplates telling her, but he doesn't know what that would do, or if she would even trust him anymore. And right now, he needs her by his side, stable, for whatever they are going to run into next.

# | 76 |

# Road Blocks

It is a grueling drive, with no way to relax, and it keeps us on edge the entire time. My legs are starting to ache from bracing against the more frequent turns and jolts, and the landscape left behind us shows that we are entering trees and hills. I would love to be in the cab with Gia right now, but distance is vital, so we don't stop.

We suddenly slow down, and I wonder if the paths are tightening, but Jax's apprehensive face and the subtle click of his safety argues otherwise. He seems as though he is trying to listen to something when an odd *whizz* sound startles me.

"We've got company!" We can barely hear Gia's yell from the cab.

"Get down!" Jax orders, pushing me to the floor, just as bullets impact and tear through the weaker sections of the truck.

"Brace yourself. Gia's gonna do something crazy," Jax adds when three thumps sound from Gia's fist at the wall of the cab, and he grabs one of the floor straps with one hand and my vest's drag-handle with the other. I in turn grab a floor strap, my rifle uncomfortably digging into my side beneath me.

The truck suddenly accelerates, and there is a horrifying sound of metal slamming into metal, the impact jarring and tossing us. The engine revs and pushes forward, though a little slower than I like.

"Get ready!" Jax gets to one knee and raises his AR, aiming through the open back of the truck, above the low tailgate.

Instinctively I do the same, and no sooner do I switch my safety off, a crushed blockade comes into view with a dozen Defense scrambling to their feet. Jax picks a couple off on the right; either killing or disabling, there is no way I can tell. Fleetingly I wonder if they have families.

I don't know if it is temporary hearing loss from the sounds or my heartbeat drowning everything out, but I can't even hear the gunfire from either side. And thankfully I cannot hear the sickening sound of bullets whizzing by anymore. Autopilot kicks in, and I find myself taking out two others. One thing I do notice is a moment when Jax seems like he is thrown back, but he gets to his kneeling firing stance again, and we focus on the last of the combatants.

More crunching of metal, but not as jarring, and we finally begin to accelerate away. I notice that Gia has taken out a few hovercycles.

*Nicely done, Gia...*

The distance grows, and I finally lower my rifle after a hundred yards of hills and trees, trying to breathe more slowly while the adrenaline continues its course. The path flattens out as though we have hit an overgrown road bed, and the pace increases. Neither of us leave our ready-position, though.

"Thank God that is over, but keep alert, there could be more." Jax hisses, lowering his rifle, and I instantly pick up on the discomfort in his voice.

"Are you hit?" I don't move from my spot, but I look over, eyeing him for any signs of blood.

"The plate caught it. Pretty sure my ribs aren't going to be too happy, but I'll be fine. I'm not bleeding," he insists with a slight smile, which quickly vanishes when he looks at me. "But you are."

"What?"

With the haste of a seasoned field medic, or because he has done this before, Jax lets his rifle rest across him as he grabs the edges of my front plate carrier and forcefully pulls me off my knee, pushing until I am sitting on the floor against the crates. Wordlessly, he grabs the med-bag.

I am about to tell him I feel fine, but I look down and see the cargos of my right thigh completely soaked in red.

"Oh…"

# | 77 |

# Not Done Yet

After a couple more hours of driving, they leave the truck behind with the scrambler in it. He knows that once the scrambler dies, Defense can track it there and that should give them time. Jax supports Lila as they hike, trying to get far enough from the vehicle and scrambler to enable their comms. He had at first tried to carry her and her med-pack, but she noticed his discomfort as his ribs protested the additional weight. That is when she insisted on walking.

"It's a through and through, and it didn't hit the femoral. Jax did a decent job, so you don't need to check it, Gia." Lila insists as Gia supports her other side.

"All I did was apply the combat tourniquet and follow your instructions with the stitches," he argues. "How's your arm, Gia?"

Back at the truck, Lila had removed a bullet and zip-stitched Gia's upper arm. She now flexes her fingers, testing her mobility.

"Good. Barely feel any pain."

"Good thing the bullet proof glass held up as long as it did." Jax comments, humbly realizing how close the three of them came to dying today.

*Twice.*

"Do you think they had families?" Lila suddenly comments with a disconcerted look, and having had those thoughts before, he understands she is talking about the people they had to fire upon.

"Don't go there, Lila," he replies quietly.

"Been there too, Lila," Gia adds. "It had to be done."

The exhaustion is felt all around as the comms finally activate, and they find a semi-sheltered alcove among the buttes. Jax lets go as Lila pulls away from them and drops the med-pack from her shoulders, balancing her weight on her left leg. Jax and Gia dump their packs as well, and they all sit against the sandy rock, leaving their rifles slung to the front of them.

"Isaac, you there?" Jax taps the comms on, while Gia passes a water bottle to Lila, and Lila in turn passes it to him.

"Man, it's good to hear your voice, Jax!"

Jax spends the next few minutes confirming that the women have been taken to the safehouse and Isaac and the others are now on their way back to Bear Base without a hitch. He then messages Bear Base via his data tablet.

"Looks like Father Malachi is going to pick us up in a UTV in a little over an hour." He exhales with a grimace and shifts to reduce the pressure of his plate carrier on his ribs.

"You should have Lila check that. Even with a plate, your ribs could be in your lungs, and pow, no more breathing," Gia bluntly comments as she chews on a piece of dried beef.

"I'm glad you're not the lead medic, Gia, you have terrible bedside manners." Jax shakes his head.

"She isn't wrong, though," Lila adds, and he meets her concerned gaze.

Resting his head against the natural wall behind him he smiles a little. "I'll be fine until we get back to base. I'd rather not take my gear off until then. I promise I'll let you know if I have trouble breathing, and I promise I'll let you check when we get there."

"You better." She challenges before resting her head against the sandstone and closing her eyes.

Jax notices she still has a grip on her rifle, her finger laying over the trigger guard. One glance down at his own weapon shows the same for him, and part of him wonders if he will ever know a time when he won't have to be wary like this. The other part wonders if he would ever be comfortable in a normal life. He endures a certain sadness, witnessing Lila slowly adopt the same cautious behavior: always prepared, always ready for battle. After today, though, he suspects she will always have his back in a fight, and that gives him comfort.

"I hope the hour goes by quick. It's getting kind of cold," Gia comments, her arms folded over her rifle, and Jax nods in acknowledgment.

It dawns on him how Gia doesn't even hold the same level of vigilance anymore, and Jax isn't sure if that has something to do with Gam, or maybe she is reaching her limit. Making a mental note to speak with her about that, he stares across the dusty lands.

There seems to be a concentrated cloud of the dust which grabs his attention. It has been a particularly dry year, so dust devils are pretty common, but his instinct claims otherwise.

"Jax, do you read me?" Isaac's voice comes over the comms.

All three of them pull their heads from the stone wall, and Jax taps his earpiece.

"Copy. Everything alright?"

"Did you disable the scrambler?"

"No. It's still with the truck and should have enough power for a few more hours, giving us time to be gone by the time they arrive." Jax replies as he watches the dust in the distance, his brows furrowing.

"Well, somehow they've got a pin on you again," his friend regrettably informs him, concern in his voice.

"Marc's weapon…?" Lila suddenly suggests, and he looks down at the sidearm in his holster in dismay.

"Shit. Isaac, does the Direction have trackers on guns now?"

"Not really. The only ones they started to track recently are the sidearms of high-clearance officers."

Jax takes the handgun out quickly and releases the mag, unchambers the round, and removes the slide.

"How do I take it out and destroy it?"

"How the heck do you have…? Never mind. Remove the slide; it's an iridescent green sticker on the inside of the slide. Melting it should do the trick. And then get out of there."

Gia and Lila are already on their feet and shouldering their packs while he removes the sticker. He takes a lighter from one of his vest pouches and melts the device before reassembling the sidearm and putting it back in the holster.

"Tell Father Malachi to cancel his trip. And Isaac… say a prayer for us."

"Copy that. Isaac out."

He stands with a grim expression, flinching. "At least we know we can drive the truck now."

Lila is leaning into Gia, and Jax grabs her other side so they can begin a hasty trek back to the truck.

"You're going to have to take a long route, Gia," he directs. "We head south east, overshoot, and then come around and arrive on the east entrance to our canyon. This will let us be sure we aren't followed, and hopefully before dark."

"Yes sir."

# | 78 |

# Homebound

"Gia..." Jax begins. Lila is asleep between them in the cab of the truck, her head on his shoulder as he keeps her from being jostled by the rough terrain.

"Don't even say it, Jax. You couldn't have known the gun was being tracked." The stocky woman shakes her head as she focuses on the westerly path, predicting what he was going to say.

The light is quickly fading, but she doesn't turn the headlamps on yet. Although they have managed to lose their pursuers back in the buttes, they still remain on high alert while they come down the home stretch.

He shakes his head as well, grimacing at the uncomfortable jolting. "It still almost cost you guys your lives."

"And I said it's not your fault. It's what we signed up for. Besides, I disobeyed your order, otherwise I would have been free and clear." Gia gives a quirky grin.

"There is that." Jax laughs a little then grunts as his chest protests.

"You alright over there, boss?"

"I'll be fine. How are you holding up?"

"Excited to get back home." She smiles.

"To Gam?" Even though he still doesn't fully approve, Jax likes to rib her about Gam.

"Shut up." Her smile vanishes.

He smiles a little, glad to see her spirited attitude is still there; it lets him know his team is still solid.

*I hope...*

"Just get us home, Gia."

"Yes, sir."

# | 79 |

# Concerned

"Lila, please just get off your feet for a minute," Fae pleads, following me with a cup of tea and one of the cookies she baked today.

She kind of reminds me of Yeti, who is also following closely by my heel. For a tiny woman barely reaching my shoulder height, she is a force to be reckoned with when it comes to caring for people.

"I slept plenty on the way here, and then some," I argue, actually regretting that I slept.

It left Gia driving the entire time and Jax as the only backup.

*I should have been on alert...* But the exhaustion had been overwhelming.

"She needs to keep moving. This is what she feels called to do."

Father Malachi calmly mentions, and he hands me the trauma-scanner I was about to reach for. He has his usual black outfit on and holds a string of what looks like beads in one hand.

"Well, she's going to bust her stitches and bleed all over the floor," Fae argues.

"Thank you, Father... I'm fine, Fae, I already put new ones on when I changed this morning." I protest as I limp out of the med-room, scanner in one hand, crutch under the other arm, and Yeti eyeing me as though he is judging.

To my dismay, I had woken up on one of the couches where Gam had placed me when we arrived at dark. Meanwhile, Fae informs me that Jax and Gia had passed out on the rugs on the floor from exhaustion and probably relief, still in their gear, but they retired to their own rooms before I woke. Father Malachi had stayed awake, watching over us and praying.

"I promise, after I make sure Jax is alright." I pause, leaning against the wall for a breather, and smile at her a little.

"Fine." She sighs in frustration. "I'll help my husband in the kitchen, and hopefully *everyone* will be *resting* at the table for breakfast in half an hour. And no coffee. You all drink too much caffeine."

She gives me a raised brow in challenge, and I watch the petite woman walk down the hall. Amusingly, Yeti bounces after her instead of staying, possibly because he understands there is food involved. I have to admit, in the short time I have known Fae, her persistent kindness continues to grow on me.

"Would you like some help at least, Lila?" Father Malachi asks calmly, his eyes behind his glasses twinkling with what seems to be a permanent joy.

"Aren't you tired? I'm pretty sure Fae mentioned you stayed up all night to watch and pray over us. Thank you for that, by the way." I watch as his bearded smile broadens, and he gives me additional support under the arm that carries the scanner.

"There is always enough strength for me, through the Lord, to help those in need. Besides, I have rested plenty while praying the entire time all of you were battling evil."

We stop at Jax's door, and I lean against the wall again, taking a moment to look at the priest inquisitively, wishing I had his resolve.

"Father Malachi, I know you've seen a lot of horrors, you've seen friends die... How do you find peace?"

"I know death is not the end. You know this as well, I can see that." His face takes on a calm, reassuring expression. "Lila, don't mistake your struggles with trauma as a lack of peace. What you need to go through is different, and you are taking the right steps with prayer and seeking counsel."

I flinch a little, because it feels as though he can see straight through to my soul, especially since the only thing I have mentioned before is being interested in seeking advice from him. That was only in passing, though.

"It's alright, Lila, whenever you are comfortable. I will continue to pray for you. When I first knew him, Jax took some time as well to come to me."

"So, he *did* go through something similar?" Part of me feels guilty for asking, and he gives me an almost gently scolding look.

"That's for you to ask him, and for him to share or not share. Speaking of Jax, I believe he just finished morning prayers." Father Malachi turns to the door and knocks firmly.

*How does he know?*

Jax comes to the door, and I notice he has changed into clean cargos, but he must have been in the process of getting a new shirt when the priest knocked, because he is not wearing one now. I glance away at first. It would not have gotten to me in the past, but my increasing affection for him in general has its impact now.

*Stop it, Lila, you've seen shirtless men before.*

I scold myself as I feel my face flush a little before I draw my attention to the results of the bullet's impact on the plate. The bruising is on the whole left and center section of his ribs, with most of the damage in the vicinity of the heart, and it hits me that without the armor plates, he would have been killed instantly.

"Good morning, brother." Father Malachi greets him warmly, giving him a quick, careful embrace, and I catch the grimace of discomfort on Jax's face before he subdues it. "The good doctor is here to check on you, so don't grumble, and let her do her job."

"I'll leave you to it and see you at breakfast." The priest gives me a slight nod, and he smiles before he turns to walk toward the kitchen, singing quietly in some other language. "Tantum Ergo, sacramentum…veneremur cernui…"

Still leaning against the wall by the door, I raise a brow as I watch him leave, and then I turn to see Jax eyeing me skeptically.

"What are you doing on your feet?"

"My job." I gesture to the device in my hands. "And you promised."

He seems a little distracted but sighs and ruffles his hand through his hair. Reaching into his room, he grabs a clean combat jacket from the back of a chair and steps into the hall.

"Do you need help?" He asks and offers his arm, watching as I try to wrestle the crutch back into place.

"I'm fine."

"You're stubborn," he comments with a frown.

"And you don't need the additional weight," I contest as we reach the med-room, and I sit with a relieved groan on one of the stools, stretching my leg out straight.

"Let me decide that next time." His tone is gently imploring.

"I'm sorry." I drop my gaze and occupy myself with turning the scanner on, selecting my settings.

"It's alright. I guess I would do the same," Jax confesses.

"That looks painful." I comment while I examine the bruising, quickly changing the subject.

He drags the other stool over to me and sits with a grimace as I start the scan. "Yes, but I've had worse. Will we miss breakfast with this?"

"Nope, the scan is already done. I just need to wait for them to process while I listen to your lungs and heart. And yeah, it looks like you've had worse."

I refer to other various scarring on his toned torso, and he gives a small shrug. I get to my feet next to him and press a stethoscope to his chest to listen to his breathing, and then to his heart.

"It's been a long war. You're racking up quite the number as well." Jax's tone isn't chiding or teasing, just matter of fact, and he catches my arm to steady me as I get back to the stool.

"Thanks. Don't we make quite the pair, then?" I smile a little ruefully while I review the images.

He gets oddly quiet after my statement. I wonder if I should have avoided saying that, since I know how he feels about relationships in the team. I have heard him argue with Gia before, about her and Gam. I have little time to ponder anymore though, as I flinch at some of the results and set aside the med-scanner, suddenly feeling uncomfortable.

"What is it?" Jax's eyes try to read my expression while he goes to put on his jacket shirt.

"Well, no lung damage. Three cracked ribs which, with some ice and rest, pain relievers, and no insane activity, will heal just fine." I disconnect a portable monitor bracelet from the medical device and hand it to him.

"What is this for?"

"You have a myocardial contusion, which is a bruise on the heart. It's minor, but I should monitor your heartrate and pattern for the next week or so, just in case."

I look at him apologetically, and to my surprise he nods without protest and puts the wrist band on, tucking it beneath his sleeve, as though this is nothing serious.

*To me it is, though.*

As strong as Jax is, as invincible as I would like to think he is, I am humbly reminded by the recent close calls that I could still lose him one day.

"Lil'." He leans forward. "I'm going to be fine. I'm in good hands. Just do me one favor?"

I raise a brow. "And that is?"

"Don't tell the others. I can only handle one person worrying over me." He smiles a little.

"Alright." I never said I was worried about him, but he must see it.

"Now, how about we get breakfast?"

He stands and offers me his arm for support, and this time I accept, using the crutch on the other side. I am not sure if I want to go to breakfast right now, though.

There is a reason I have been hiding in the med-room this morning.

# | 80 |

# Hiding Things

He isn't going to let Lila know it bothers him, but what she told him about his heart sounds serious. The thought of being taken out of the war right now has him perturbed, but Jax pushes that aside to the place with countless other unwanted thoughts.

Looking over at Lila, who is holding his arm for support, he notices she seems a little tense as they walk toward the noise of banter in the kitchen. He assumes that is why she has been in the med-room most of the morning, and guesses she is fighting that feeling of being on edge after a battle, something he has done many times before. Jax stops, and she looks up at him questioningly.

"You don't have to go in."

There is a look of gratitude in her eyes.

*And something else.*

"There you two are." Father Malachi's cheery voice comes from the archway before she can answer, and on a tray, he carries three plates of food. "I was wondering if you two would join me outside for a quiet breakfast."

Without waiting for an answer, and being followed by Yeti, he makes for the door.

Jax smiles. *He always knows...*

# | 81 |

# Chink in the Armor

Jax sits at the head of the dining table and waits for Isaac to return with the monitor and camera. In the past two weeks, Isaac and a few programmers in Vita Nova have been able to upgrade the satellite connections to be able to support video conferencing. Now, headquarters wants to update them on the information found on the data they pulled from the surrogate facility and give them a new assignment.

Father Malachi sits to his right, sipping a cup of tea, and Lila is to the left. Jax muses on the past week as he watches Lila fidget with the crucifix he had given her, Yeti's head on her lap. Their in-house counselor had sat with him and Lila the times they couldn't sleep, offering advice, and sometimes simply praying.

Jax has come to realize that spending time with Lila has helped him as well, to the point he prefers her company when he is stressed, especially now with how much closer she has become with God. Otherwise, the exhaustion from the last assignment has everyone in a relatively quiet routine.

Gia sits beside the priest, and Gam sits beside her, holding her hand beneath the table. Jax furrows his brows as he wonders what they have been discussing during their daily walks with Father Malachi this past week. He has his suspicions that it is about marriage, but he will let them share when they are ready. Then he has to decide if that will affect the team dynamics negatively, but something tells him that Gia is about ready to throw in the towel anyway.

Nik brings a collection of cured meats, another one of his culinary specialties, to the table and sits beside Fae, who is next to Lila. Fae is trying to describe the ocean to Lila, but Jax tunes out that and other conversations at the table. He absently rubs at his wrist where the monitor used to be. He is happy to be mostly in the clear, although with instructions to take things easy for at least another week. Jax only admitted to Father Malachi that it had him nervous, not about death so much as about being incapacitated and unable to take part in the fight.

*"You are a child of God first, relying on God and trusting in His plans for your life even beyond the battlefield. Being able to fight or not does not define your worth. The value of all life is the very thing you have been fighting for. Keep this scripture in mind, my brother: 'Are not five sparrows sold for two pennies? And not one of them is forgotten before God. Why, even the hairs on your head are all numbered. Fear not; you are of more value than many sparrows.'"*

Jax thinks back to Father Malachi's words, and it makes him ponder what he *would* do in life if this war were to finally end. Since the age of seventeen, he has only been a soldier; being a civilian is a foreign concept.

He is brought into the present moment when he hears the priest ask about Lila's crucifix.

"Is that the one from Father Sebastian?"

"Yes, Jax gave it to me." She nods a little. "Pretty much saved my life."

Father Melachi smiles warmly. "One of countless times Christ has saved someone by His death on the cross."

"Alright, everything is ready. He'll see us, we'll see him, and he'll hear us as well."

Isaac's appearance with a display and camera quiets the conversations, and everyone waits as he sets them up at the end of the table opposite of Jax. He taps a few things into his tablet and swipes toward the monitor, casting the video over.

"Good morning." The image of General Miles appears, and he is sitting at a table beside Professor Marie Hann.

"Good morning, General," everyone greets in unison.

"First, I know I did this in message already, but I wanted to congratulate you on a successful mission the other week. We received more information from the data than expected."

"Thank you, sir, the teamwork was on point." Jax replies with a firm nod, his hands folded in front of him on the table.

"That's why we'll be needing you all again, but first I'll have Professor Marie update you on the latest data."

The General gives a firm nod to the woman beside him, and she looks up with the same intense eyes they remember from the first meeting.

"Good morning." She nods, her voice firm, and she doesn't wait for a reply before continuing. "I am sure you remember me briefly mentioning The Direction has been more strict with their DNA selection, and the data you sent from the surrogate facility has clarified more on the 'god gene' project.

"There was once a theory that a certain gene was responsible for the belief in a higher being. The Direction has taken it to the next step, though, and they are trying to find a way to alter it in their population. Now, there really is no 'god gene', but something called VMAT2, which transports things like dopamine, serotonin, adrenaline, etcetera, for storage and release.

"The organization theorizes that parts of its function contribute to mystical sensations, like feeling the presence of God or a connection to a larger universe. They have been trying to find a way to play with its function for a while now, trying to control emotions. They've picked up their effort recently, though." And here she pauses, looking over to the General.

"Why is that?" Lila asks first, her expression curious.

General Miles continues the conversation, clearing his throat. "That's where the news of The Direction's latest struggles comes into play. They have been having a difficult time since more people are starting to question things, and there has been an uptick in believers in various religions. Despite the efforts to knuckle down on contraband, like Bibles and other books, people keep getting their hands on them.

"Towns in Eden are in upheaval. They only have four towns remaining without conflict, and the rest they either let go or have Defense units in place to keep them in check. Gamal is also in disorder, and that reason I will let Isaac explain."

Isaac's face breaks into an excited grin, and Jax wonders how long he has been holding this bit of news quiet.

*I'll have to talk to him about keeping secrets.*

"First off, Gamal has been at odds with The Direction for some time now. Not blatantly, but them being 'discards' has always left a sour taste to them. But anywho… Last week, I and a few of my colleagues were able to distribute the true history to all the databases in the homes and factories. Knowing the truth has led to full blown riots, factories shutting down, and deliveries of products being held back."

Jax looks around, and he knows that each one of them, even Lila, wants to throw in a cheer for this. Most of them have smiles spread across their faces as they nod to each other in approval of the news. Father Malachi smiles in an almost knowing way. Jax himself leans forward with a reserved smile, waiting for what he knows comes next. Glancing over, he notices Lila doing the same, her expression eager.

"Can you do that data thing to the Eden homes as well?" Nik interjects.

Isaac shakes his head. "Sadly no, their security is extremely tight still. That would take breaking APA, and I can't do that from here."

"And that's where our next mission comes into play." The General's expression on the screen is almost that of excitement as he leans forward onto the table. "With the Defense strung out with all the chaos, they have left APA's programming base at the center of Eden with very little security. We are going to disable APA and all security systems The Direction has."

Everyone now leans forward, and Jax can almost feel their mix of apprehension, disbelief, and eagerness. He himself didn't see this one coming; it is a goal they have always wanted to reach, and each time it seemed impossible, but now it is a reality. His smile broadens, even though his mind automatically wonders what this might cost.

"When, and who is involved?" Jax's hands clench and unclench together a few times.

"I have two teams already at the location for scouting purposes, but as long as you are recovered and ready, you will be the team to infiltrate the base in three weeks. Lila, do you believe you and Jax will be recovered enough for this mission?"

She gives a firm nod, her voice confident. "Yes, sir."

General Miles' glance rests questioningly on Jax, who leans back in his chair and gives a firm nod as well.

"Good. Details will be transferred." They watch as the General nods to Professor Marie beside him, and she starts tapping on her tablet. "You will be escorting Isaac into the central system, and there he will deactivate APA."

Jax tenses suddenly while he looks over to Isaac, who does not look surprised, but still looks apprehensive. He knows the man doesn't handle field work very well, and the last one had him pretty severely shaken up.

"Wait. You know as well as I, sir, that Isaac stays at base for a reason. Is this something he can talk Lila through remotely?"

His peripheral vision catches Lila nodding in agreement, but he keeps his focus on the display as the General shakes his head, a certain look of regret fleetingly breaking through his confidence. Seeing the look, Jax realizes that Bram doesn't want his son in battle either.

"Isaac himself says there is no other way," General Miles confirms.

Isaac clears his throat and looks down at his tablet for a moment before looking at Jax.

"It's too complex, and you know already, Jax, that I am the most familiar with APA. I'll be fine. I've got a good team to watch my back." He gestures to those at the table.

Jax wants to argue, but he knows Isaac is right.

Bram clears his throat, breaking the moment of quiet. "Now, if you will all please leave the room, I need a word with Jax and Father Malachi."

Jax watches everyone in turn say goodbye to General Miles, and he smiles a little as they surround Isaac while going into the kitchen, flooding him with various questions and words of reassurance. He glances over to Father Malachi still seated beside him. The bearded priest gives him an encouraging smile.

# | 82 |

# Second in Command

"Now, I have a matter that I need you to decide on, Jax." Bram leans forward again, as does Jax. "I know we haven't had much of a military structure, but as serious as this has gotten, we have been building that structure. Which leads me to ask that you please select a second-in-command. It's not typically necessary for small units, but this is different, and you will be commanding larger units soon. I know you've had unofficial ones before, but I need to know who to put in charge if anything happens to you. I know other than Isaac, Gia has been with you the longest."

Jax folds his hands, and his jaw tenses. "I already asked Gia shortly after the incident with Kain, but she flat out refused. She says she prefers taking orders and letting others make decisions."

The General nods. "What about Nik?"

Father Malachi interjects, pressing his glasses back up his nose. "I would honestly not recommend Nik. He only handles pressure if someone else is taking lead. When he takes lead, he often does so in anger or frustration. I do not say this disparagingly about him, he is a good man, but he has his limits."

"That's alright, Father, I already made my decision." Jax nods and sits back again, folding his arms across his chest. He knows this is the right decision, *although she might disagree at first*. "Lila will be my second-in-command."

General Miles looks a little taken aback and tilts his head a little, narrowing his eyes in challenge. "Can she handle that sort of pressure?"

"Lila has shown she can take charge as a medic and make quick decisions. She has my back one hundred percent of the time as well. I have confidence she'll fill the role just fine."

"I believe Jax is right." Father Malachi nods in agreement, and Jax gives him a grateful smile.

"Alright, confirm that with her first, then get back to me. Oh, and Jax." Bram's expression goes serious, yet almost sad, and he lowers his voice. "Take care of my son, and remind him I'm proud of him."

"Yes sir." Jax nods and inwardly flinches when he realizes the immense weight that puts on him.

The screen goes black, and Father Malachi stands and pats him on the shoulder. "It will be fine, my brother. I am going to my noonday prayers. Be sure to save a sandwich for me."

"Will do."

Jax nods and pushes himself to his feet, watching the priest walk down the hall humming. Heading for the kitchen, he leans against the alcove, arms folded, and smiles slightly as he watches everyone centering around Isaac. Lila seems to sense his presence, and she looks over with a smile. A pang of unease hits him, though, as he wonders how all this will unfold.

*Be strong and of good courage, do not fear or be in dread of them; for it is the Lord your God who goes before you; He will not fail you or forsake you.*

| 83 |

# Midnight Thoughts

*Zero one hundred hours...*
This time I just lay in my bed, going over the past three weeks since we got word on our new mission and Isaac's involvement. There is a certain apprehension, a concern from everyone over Isaac being in such an involved assignment, and the pressure to be prepared has occupied everyone.

We have all run drills countless times, learning more about close quarter combat, like 'slicing the pie': pretty much a way of avoiding dying when going around enemy corners. Jax's spare time has been spent helping Isaac brush up on tactics and self-defense. Mine has been spent getting strength back in my leg and accepting the fact that if anything happens to Jax, somehow, he believes I can take over. Oddly, the focus on the next mission has kept me grounded as I go through daily reviews of our plans.

There have been very few nights I have needed to leave my room when I wake up. I mostly pray and read scripture. I sought out Father Malachi once during a particularly difficult moment, but I have avoided troubling Jax with much, even though I like the time spent with him. I know he has enough worries with Isaac.

Mentally I go over our plans again; it is a constant presence in my thoughts. The weather in late November can be difficult, but thanks to additional Nightlight satellites added to our collection, we, *or I should say Vita Nova*, has been able to monitor storms. Our timeframe is mostly lined up well with the weather.

To my surprise, I learned that APA's data base is only thirty miles west of my small hometown of Vouna, out in The Wilds where I had hiked so many times. I also learned, with some sadness, that the town is now abandoned due to riots. Part of me wonders where everyone is. There is no way The Direction has room for them as detainees.

*Were they killed? Did they run to some safe haven somewhere?*

These thoughts suddenly hit me, and I close my eyes, not in sleep but in apprehension as I quietly pray.

*Please, may they be safe...*

Suddenly a gentle knock on my door, which is left cracked open out of habit, pulls me from my restless reverie, and I push myself out of bed. In a sense of needing to be prepared, I had already changed into insulated cargos and a Defense issued jacket shirt. Even my boots are on and my sidearm is in the holster.

I pull the door open wider, and Jax stands there with a heavier jacket in his hand, already wearing one himself. I assume he has slept just about as much as I have, possibly less. Wordlessly, not wanting to wake anyone else, I take the jacket and pull it on, following him to the front door. Yeti, however, is quite awake and follows at our heels.

Stepping out into the brisk November night, I notice flakes of snow floating through the air, illuminated by a moon that struggles to cut through the clouds. A thin blanket of snow already covers the ground. Yeti dashes past us, chasing and jumping at flakes, his hot breath coming out in clouds as he huffs at his escaping quarry.

"I know you still don't like going out in the rain, but I figured you wouldn't mind snow." Jax watches the dog with a somewhat sullen expression.

"That's true," I reply quietly, watching the white specks slowly descend and land in Jax's hair.

It is strangely quiet tonight as the falling snow seems to absorb every sound, and I find myself reflecting on how much I miss the night outings alone with him. As much as it has helped having Father

Malachi around, I am most comfortable when it is just Jax. I get the impression Jax feels likewise about me, and I wonder if it is more than that for him but he is just suppressing it because of his rule.

*Like I am...*

"I'm worried, Lil'." Jax finally breaks the silence, standing with his hands in his jacket pockets and staring into the night. "I've spoken with Isaac countless times, and he says he's alright, but this still isn't alright to me. I've known him for over seven years. He and Father Malachi are the reason I'm here, doing what I'm meant to do."

I let the silence take over, suspecting he has more to say.

"I don't know if all of us are going to come back, and I don't want to face the loss of anyone here. Each time it just weighs heavier."

"Do you go through this with every mission or just this one?" I ask not only for him but myself, because I feel the same apprehension, and I wonder if this is how it will be every time.

His eyes meet mine for a moment, and there is an uncertainty I have seen before, but he always hides it well with the others.

"Every mission. Every time. I know they think I'm this confident leader who has it all together, but like you, I still struggle. They need the confidence and stability, and that alone comes from God, through me, but I don't always feel that."

Pushing my hands into my jacket pockets, I look to the sky as the clouds begin to gradually disperse, allowing the moonlight to slowly brighten the canyon.

"Have you reached your limit, yet?"

"I'm not sure there is one for me. I don't know what else I would do other than this," he confides quietly. "Maybe if I had walked away years ago."

I look down at my feet for a moment, then to him again with a slight smile. "I, for one, am selfishly glad you didn't."

Jax's eyes brighten with a smile as he looks over. "I think I needed to hear that. Thank you, Lil'."

*I love that smile...*

"Anytime, Jax."

| 84 |

# A Walk in the Park

The majority of the drive so far has been spent in mostly silence. Due to snow and ice, we have had to drive south and catch the maintained highway heading southwest across Gamal, which has us all on edge. Fortunately, we have only crossed paths with two other Defense units in identical trucks going the opposite direction. The increased anarchy throughout Gamal works in our favor, and no one stops to question us.

Nik drives, while the rest of us are in the side seats in the back, a canvas flap secured at the opening to block out the biting wind and a propane heater to give us a little warmth. Even with that, it is still cold in here. I notice that Jax looks more comfortable on this assignment without his old uniform. Instead, he wears the usual Defense gear, including a molle vest with plates.

We all wear identical gear, with an addition of combat helmets and balaclavas, courtesy of some suppliers in Gamal in exchange for communication devices *not* connected to The Direction. One of the weapons manufacturers have even begun to distribute firearms and ammo to private militias against the organization. This led to General Miles beginning negotiations with the groups, offering to support their efforts.

Isaac has informed us that the data center is beneath a Defense headquarters in The Wilds, within a fenced area I had often passed by during hikes.

*An odd coincidence... or God prepared me even then?*

There is no road directly there; it is only reached either on foot or dirt bike.

*Or horseback, which I would have preferred.*

Another disturbing bit of information given to us from the reconnaissance teams is the fact that, due to the minimal amount of Defense available, they have placed fragmentation mines in the wooded terrain around the center. One of the recon teams, led by a Sergeant Hann, has marked most of these on a map, but they can't guarantee every one of them has been accounted for.

*I wonder if the Sergeant is related to Professor Marie...*

"Alright, let's go over this again." Jax pulls the face portion of his balaclava down so he can speak more clearly, tapping comms on so Nik can hear. "It is currently 01:35. We're nearly at our first stop. From there we walk. Lila knows these paths like the back of her hand, so she takes point. We have a route selected where the mines have been identified; we can avoid those. We'll be relying on moonlight for vision, though, so let's be extra cautious.

"Isaac will shut down their booster and cameras, so APA won't be alerted, but she might alert another facility if Isaac doesn't shut her down within half an hour. We have to move fast. There are two guards at the gate and approximately ten in the base, but that number is unsure. Nik and Gia are the best shots; they will take the hill above the gate and take out the guards once I, Lila, Gam, and Isaac are in place. That's where they will remain to keep us informed and give cover fire if anything goes wrong.

"We *have* to clear the base. We can't risk any word getting out, or our route out will be a shit storm. That's why we acquired suppressors this time. We use tie-straps and sedatives for those who comply. I'm not expecting that, though. Be prepared for strong resistance. This is their brains they're guarding. We get Isaac to APA's center and keep guard. Lila will help him if he needs it.

"Isaac says the job should take him ten minutes tops, but let's be prepared for hiccups in case they've placed additional protocols he has to sort through. Then we leave, head north to recon's temporary base, and wait for headquarters to confirm our next move onto Oshana facility to shut that down for good. Copy?"

"Yes, sir," everyone replies in unison, and the apprehension mixed with preparedness is evident in how we all lean forward a little.

I tighten my gloved hand around the grip of my rifle and nod. It all sounds so straightforward, but nothing about this is a walk in the park.

*Or the woods...*

My other hand tangles in the hair of Yeti's fur. I had an odd feeling he needed to come with us, and Jax readily agreed, probably assuming I need the dog for support.

*It is more than that, though.*

That small voice told me I need to bring him, and I know by now to listen.

"Isaac, go over the layout again," Jax instructs.

"Yes. Ok," Isaac begins, and I can hear the nervousness in his tone. "So, it's a very simple layout, fortunately. The front room is open space, pretty much a lounge area. Through two doors on the left is the mess hall and kitchen, and to the right is an open hall leading to the sleeping quarters; one room for the commanding officer and then the larger one is the bunk area. After that is the locker room slash bathroom. At the end of that hall is the elevator, which is unfortunately the only way to get to APA's center, which *will* have guards in there. It's a single room filled with computer towers, cooling units, and somewhere in there will be the access monitor. Do NOT shoot any of the equipment; it won't destroy everything, but it will alert APA. And do NOT throw any grenades, not even shock grenades, into the data room, that WILL disrupt things and cause a lockdown. That's it."

"Copy that." We all nod.

Before I am even mentally prepared, we come to a stop and all hop out into the cold night, stepping into three inches of snow cover. We are at the edge of a heavily wooded forest in an area very familiar to me. The Wilds have always been a beautiful place, but tonight it seems eerily silent, and the light layer of snow combined with moonlight make it seem almost like a dimly lit day.

Jax pulls the balaclava back over the lower half of his face and nods to me. "Ready?"

I nod silently, and despite the nervousness, I start down the trail almost on autopilot, with Yeti right at my heels and the others right behind. I occasionally glance at the tablet in my left hand to remind me where the mines are.

"Even though I walk through the valley of the shadow of death…" I whisper under my breath, and I hear Jax behind me quietly following the Psalm.

# | 85 |

# So Much for Stealth

Lila moves in front of him as though she knows every rock and tree in the path, only pausing to signal behind her in an indication that they need to go around a trip mine. Jax wishes recon could have stayed to offer additional support, but they had to move ahead to prepare the next site. And of course, this task requires more stealth.

At one point they pause by an incline, and Lila nods to Jax. He in turn points to Gia and Nik. Without a sound other than the snow crunching beneath their feet, they nod and climb the hill. Jax watches in puzzlement as Yeti begins to follow Nik up the incline instead of staying with Lila.

She does not seem surprised by this though, and Jax, Gam, and Isaac follow while Lila slows and winds her way to the right, until they come to a chain link fence. They follow that until two security lights become visible ahead. The lights illuminate the area facing east, coming from a small gate beside a watchtower which houses two visible guards.

Jax forces his breath to slow, tapping Lila's shoulder as a signal, and she steps back to guard the rear, letting him take lead. Glancing behind him, he sees Isaac give a thumbs up to indicate the shutdown of the cameras and signal booster.

"Gia, Nik, you're a go," he quietly speaks in the comms, readying his rifle with the safety off.

The two guards fall, and a split second later he hears the muffled gunfire. Waving the others to follow, they move to the locked gate. Jax watches as Isaac's fingers fly across his tablet, and a *click* indicates the lock disables. Isaac resumes his place behind Jax and in front of Gam and Lila.

Pushing through the gate, they break into a jog while lowering their profile, Jax leading the way through the wooded uphill path. He signals to stop and goes to his knee when they come to a wide clearing. Lila stays a few paces back, watching the path behind, while Isaac and Gam go down on one knee as well.

In front of them is a mostly unassuming single story log chalet with four east facing windows and a single door in the front. It reminds Jax a little of their own Bear Base, because the rear of it is imbedded into the side of the hill behind. The inside is lit, and they can see three fully geared and armed Defense guards sitting at a table, conversing. He grimaces a little at the fact that, according to specs, the windows are bullet proof.

*This is where it gets tricky.* He thinks grimly.

"Door unlocked," Isaac quietly confirms and then slips behind a tree, his rifle at ready.

He will be staying and guarding the path until they clear the building. Without a word, Jax, Gam, and Lila move forward, the snow crunching beneath their boots as they rush to the door. Gam goes to one side of the door and Lila to the other. Jax goes to one knee again a few paces away where the light doesn't reach, rifle at high-ready and sites trained at the door.

He looks to Gam on the right, noting that the large man's gloved fingers are shaking, but he gives a firm nod. Jax switches his glance to Lila on the left; her face is covered as all theirs are, but her eyes are resolute, her hands steady, and she gives him a nod. He returns a nod, focusing on the door again, and she reaches across to the handle.

Throwing the door open, she ducks back, and the three combatants inside leap to their feet. Jax takes one down and then the other before they even have a chance to raise their rifles. The third hesitates in confusion, baffled by the identical equipment they wear, which ends up being his downfall as Jax places the third precise shot.

Despite the suppressors, the sound still carries through the building, and Jax hears the shouting of an officer barking orders.

*So much for stealth...* He bemoans, even though he already assumed it would go this way.

Without hesitation, Lila lifts her rifle from her position beside the door and lines her sights up with the hall across the front room. Jax jumps to his feet and takes up a position behind her, just in time to see her take out two armed enemies coming around the bend.

*Damn, she's getting good at this...* He doesn't have time to decide if that is a good thing.

Ducking beneath her rifle, while Gam watches the kitchen from the doorway, Jax rushes in and to the west side of the room. Pressing himself against the wall, he approaches the hallway to the sound of rushing footsteps, a stun grenade in his hand.

"Flashbang!" Lila warns when something is thrown around the corner.

Gunfire from the hall and her tells him that more are coming around as he shields his eyes with his arm while the Defense stun grenade goes off, the sound disorienting him temporarily.

*Shit...*

# | 86 |

# The Brains

I duck away from the door as the flashbang goes off and then quickly return to my post. Gam isn't so lucky, and he rubs at his eyes, staying behind cover until he regains his sight.

*Jax...*

I barely notice when bullets hit and splinter the wood of the doorframe beside me, returning fire until the half-dressed Defense officer goes down. I know there are more, but they stay back in the hall out of sight. Jax is against the wall, ten paces away from the hallway, and he looks like he is struggling to regain his balance and focus.

"Gam, cover me."

Gam, mostly recovered, rushes to my side of the door. I run across, grabbing Jax by his vest to push him against the wall behind me, and I face the hallway until he is stabilized, taking down one enemy as they round the bend.

Jax gives me a tap on the shoulder, and I let him take lead again. With practiced expertise, Jax approaches the hall and tosses his own stun grenade. After it takes effect, he rounds the corner, goes to his knee, and fires.

Without really realizing what I am doing, probably procedural memory from our countless practice rounds, I join in a high/low position right behind him while Gam covers our rear. In the next moment, five more half-dressed combatants, disoriented by the grenade, are brought down in the gunfire. We stay this way at the corner for a few seconds until we are sure no one else is coming from the three doorways down the left wall of the hallway.

One by one we clear each room, verifying no one remains, and wordlessly we move to clear the mess hall and kitchen as well. Satisfied that the upper floor is clear, we head back down the hall to the elevator, and I avoid looking down at the lifeless bodies when we step over them. Jax turns and looks me over as though verifying I am not hit, and instinctively I do the same to him.

"Gam, post at the hall here. Isaac, come on in, it's time to head downstairs," Jax confirms over the comms, pulling his mask down.

"You good?" He asks me directly, and I nod, not quite trusting my voice as I continue to eye our surroundings, impulsively staying vigilant.

Gam is at the corner just when Isaac jogs in and down the hall. He looks a little more relaxed as he taps on his tablet and unlocks the elevator. The doors slide open, and Jax and I step in. Meanwhile, Isaac stays behind and waits with Gam.

"Remember, it will be guarded. At least two of them," Jax reminds me quietly. "There's a chance they wear ear protection for the cooling fans, so they might not have heard the gunfire. Don't bet on it, though. They will be careful with their shots. I'll slice the pie first. Then you. Keep them guessing."

"Shit, I wish we could use a grenade," he mutters under his breath.

I nod as I step to one side of the elevator doors, and he steps to the other, pressing the button for the lower level. Despite adrenaline already spiking the entire time, it feels like a second wave hits, my heart pounding in my ears. No sooner do the doors slide open than the expected guards open fire and riddle the back of the elevator with a few holes before they cease, most likely preserving ammo and waiting for us.

Jax is the first to carefully move his rifle out and with keen aim, despite the guards firing upon him, he takes one shot and ducks back in.

"One more," he mouths, holding up one finger, also making a gesture indicating the last one is to the right.

I nod, knowing it is my turn, and I go to a low position. Taking in a deep breath, I ease my rifle around, the sound of the coolant fans almost deafening. I quickly take in the layout of the room, looking down rows of computer towers that fill the large space.

A guard leans out from one of the right towers, and expecting his target to be to his left, his reaction is delayed enough to allow me a shot, which hits him in the plate carrier and throws him back. Jax steps out and follows up with a second, dispatching the guard before he can get back up. It startles me a little at how calm Jax was with the follow-up, but he and I continue to clear the room.

Because comms is blocked down here, we head back upstairs and inform Isaac that it is time. After confirming with Gia and Nik that everything is still all clear outside the perimeter, Jax and I go back down with Isaac.

It is unnervingly calm while we wait for him to complete his work, and I focus studiously on the elevator doors. I shift my weight from one foot to the other, grimacing, only now noticing the fatigue in my right leg. The amount of time larger muscles take to heal is sometimes aggravating.

Jax stands beside me, and I notice him getting restless as well. He glances to Isaac at the monitor, then to the elevator, and then to me.

"Almost ten minutes. I don't like being blind to what's going on upstairs. You good here?"

I am about to answer, but Isaac speaks, his voice almost unbelieving as he sits back in the chair.

"It's done…"

"What?" Both Jax and I are hesitant to think positively, yet the surprise is still there.

"It's done." Isaac gets up, and there is a look of relief on his face, although his hands still shake as he swipes things on his tablet. "I even have my own program in place. We have full access to all security. All facilities. The Direction is officially flying completely blind."

There is a numbing feeling, almost like this is too good to be true, but Jax taps my arm to get my attention back and nods.

"Then let's go." He heads for the elevator.

Still avoiding looking at the fallen bodies of the Defense unit, I silently follow. It doesn't take us long to be outside and heading down the path, retracing our steps while Jax contacts Gia and Nik.

"Nik. Gia. Work your way back to the truck. APA is down, and we're good to go."

"Holy shit," Gia's voice comes across comms in a quiet whisper followed by a "yes sir."

I know we are all feeling it now, the desire to shout a cheer, but we are not safe yet. Jax leads the way, and I bring up the rear. At a jog, we leave through the gate, then he allows me the lead, and I wind through the trees the way we had come, the moon still lighting the way.

*200 yards and we're clear...*

Yeti's bark sounds strongly about fifty yards ahead of us and stops me in my tracks. My blood runs cold as the next sound is that of an explosion, a sharp yelp from the dog, and then Gia's voice down the path as well as on the open comms.

"Nik!"

"Man down! Nik is down!" Gia's voice comes over the comms again.

"On my way, Gia," I reply, clenching my jaw as I break off at a run, slinging my rifle to the side so I can focus on traction and balance.

At one point the trail hits a sharp decline, and I turn sideways to skid down, being sure to aim for the verified clear part of the path down below. These trails in all types of weather are so familiar to me that it is like second nature to spot changes. I see them to my right before I even stop skidding, and the dread I am feeling is proven.

Gia is kneeling over Nik, her hands pressing into his side and covered in blood. The snow all around is scattered with the spray, and right at Nik's side is Yeti, breathing shakily as he lays flat on his side, his fur streaked with dark liquid.

*God, please let Nik still be alive... Tell me what to do.*

# | 87 |

## Vouna Clinic

Jax can feel the blood drain from his face at the familiar sound of a fragmentation explosive being triggered, followed by Gia's voice on the comms. Lila reacts instantly, and he follows closely as she retraces their steps at a run, skidding sideways down a steeper section of a slippery snow-covered decline. She doesn't miss a mark, however, and aims for the proven part of the trail.

He notices other skid marks to the right of them and grimly realizes Nik must have missed the mark. They come to Gia at the bottom, kneeling over a motionless Nik. Lila is at their side in an instant, lowering her mask and yanking her gloves off, checking the fallen man.

"Nik slipped. Yeti was already at the bottom, like he knew, and he jumped up, trying to push Nik back. I think Nik would be gone now otherwise. How bad is it, Lila? I used my clotting pads on his side, but I haven't had a chance to check elsewhere."

Gia is talking a mile a minute, tears streaming down her face, and this is the most shaken Jax has ever seen her.

He holds his breath as he waits for Lila's answer, instinctively keeping watch of the surroundings. One glance at Isaac tells him the man is in shock at the sight, and Gam is not that much better, although the large man steels his expression and moves over to see if he can help, despite the sight of blood.

"Multiple shrapnel wounds; the vest caught a lot. Yeti caught a lot for him…" She pauses and clears her throat, and he grimaces, knowing she is forcing the dog out of her thoughts. "Shrapnel got through the side, though. Gia, torniquet his right leg. Gam, Isaac, Jax, I need the clotting pads from your med-kits. We need to stop the major bleeding before we move him to the truck to my med-pack."

Jax opens the emergency pouch in his molle vest and pulls out what she asked for, handing it to Lila. Even though he can hear her voice cracking a bit, her face is firm and determined, but he still sees the shed tears. Despite the adrenaline keeping him calm and functional, his own heart feels like it is in his throat.

"Let's get Nik out of here." Lila gets to her feet, her eyes glancing over to the injured dog.

"Alright, Gam, help me with Nik," Jax directs evenly. "Gia, can you carry Yeti? Isaac, you good? Cover the rear."

Gia nods and lifts the dog. Isaac numbly nods, his face almost as white as the snow around them, but he falls in step. Lila doesn't even wait to be asked as she knowingly takes lead on the trail.

After five minutes, they reach the truck, Jax and Gam get Nik into the back, and Lila climbs up, immediately grabbing her med-pack. She stops as Gia heaves the massive dog into the back, and Jax can see her struggling with herself.

"I've got the dog, Lil'," Jax assures her while he jumps in, and she nods without a word, returning to Nik's side.

"Gia," Lila calls out when Gia is about to go to the driver's side. "Get us to Vouna. If the clinic there is still intact, it will have everything we need."

"Copy that."

Jax doesn't say anything, but as he looks over the dog, bandaging the various lacerations to lessen the bleeding, he watches her as well. She is calm, focused, and the tears are wiped away, a streak of blood across her cheek in their place. Jax hopes it does not destroy her if they lose Nik, and he himself is resigned to the possibility but actively praying for otherwise. Isaac looks like he has turned to prayer as well, and he sits at the side, head bowed, hands folded.

With Gia at the wheel, they reach the debris-ridden town within fifteen minutes, and Lila doesn't waste time, immediately telling her where the clinic is. Once there, Lila grabs the propane heater and takes it with her into the building, pushing past rubble. She leads the way to a med-room, followed by Jax and Gam carrying Nik, and they set him on the steel table in the center. Gia sets the bandaged dog down to the side.

"Gia, we need an IV right away. Gam. Going to need you to hold the flashlight. It looks like they have the power out. I need to find a trauma scanner." She looks around the shelves as she sets up the propane heater to full blast, and then removes her helmet, balaclava, and rifle.

Jax locates the scanner and hands it to her, watching the way she deftly moves, directing Gia and Gam. Lila suddenly grabs his arm, and he looks down at her concerned expression, his brows furrowing.

"Jax, I'm not sure he's going to make it. If that's the case, I don't think Isaac should be here." She nods over to Isaac standing in the room, and Jax recognizes the man's frozen expression.

He nods and grasps her arm for a moment, surprised but impressed by her stability. "I'll take care of him. I'll be praying, Lil'. Let me know if you need anything else."

She nods and returns to Nik, meanwhile Jax takes Isaac by the arm and leads him out of the room. Sitting him against the wheel of the truck outside, Jax walks a few paces either way to check the surroundings before returning to him. Isaac leans against his knees and lowers his head to his arms.

Jax crouches in front of him, putting his hand on his shoulder supportively. "Isaac, you alright?"

"How do you guys do it?" Isaac speaks quietly, his usually upbeat voice cracking. "You're always stable. Gia has seen this many times. Even Lila... She used to look as shaken as I am now, but she's not."

"Not everyone is meant to be on the battlefield, Isaac. And it doesn't mean we don't struggle; it doesn't mean we aren't equally scared. We're just more prepared to handle it. I don't like bringing you out here because I never wanted to see you battle with what we go through."

Isaac nods slightly, and he tries to smile a little. "I still wish I could handle this better."

"How about we do something we both can handle together? We can sit here and pray while they're in there saving Nik," Jax offers, sitting beside him.

Isaac nods a little more firmly, and they begin praying, Isaac with his head bowed. But Jax keeps his eyes watchful while they continue.

# | 88 |

# Support

As the light of morning filters into the med-room through skylights, I slump back against the wall and sink to the floor, my right leg throbbing with the strain; my whole body exhausted. At one point, Jax had relieved Gia and helped me with Nik so she could attend to Yeti's injuries, which were substantial, but she assures me he is stable.

After that, Gia continued to help me while Jax went on patrol and updated headquarters. Isaac is more relaxed and resting in the other room, although I don't think he has slept yet. Gam has been sleeping for a couple hours now, and I am honestly impressed with how he stomached the entire procedure.

I silently watch Nik's chest slowly move up and down; an indication of him still hanging on. For respite I close my eyes and rest my head back, allowing myself to leave the hyper-focused state I have been in. After a moment, I realize someone is sitting next to me, and I know it is Jax when I catch the smell of pine.

"You asleep, Lil'?" Jax asks as quietly as possible.

"No. Just resting before we move Nik to the truck and head for the new base. Did you talk with them about a surgeon?" I lift my head to look over at him, and he stares at Nik before giving a nod.

"They'll have a medic ready to go with one of the recon teams. They'll drive Nik straight to the head surgeon in Vita Nova. How is he?"

Looking down, I realize despite wiping my hands, my arms, sleeves rolled up, are still covered in blood. Stains are on my molle vest and pants as well.

"I was able to remove some of the large shrapnel, but there are some near the spine I'm not skilled enough to risk, especially without the right equipment. His leg was the riskiest I was willing to work on, since a piece nicked his artery, but we have that stabilized enough for transport. I think he's going to make it, but I don't know what he'll be looking at long term."

I release a breath, and it comes out shakier than I expected. Jax hands me a bottle of water, and I take it thankfully, though my tired hands can barely function in order to open it, my fingers trembling. He reaches over and places his hands over mine until they stop shaking, and I look up. There is a mixed look of sympathy, approval, and something else that I am too drained to decipher, but I catch myself reflecting on how I could get lost in his eyes.

*And how much I admire this man.*

"You did everything you could, Lil'. It's time to take a rest." He smiles a little and opens the bottle before releasing my hands, even though a part of me wishes he wouldn't let go; it is calming to me. But I remind myself of his rule yet again.

"Thanks..." I answer tiredly and reluctantly shift my gaze away, taking a sip of water. "But we need to get going. I can rest on the way."

Jax nods and gets to his feet, pushing his rifle off to his side, and reaches down to offer me a hand. I accept it, and he pulls me up, stabilizing me until I find my balance on my aching legs.

# | 89 |

# Buried Feelings

Within a few more minutes, everyone is loaded into the truck and on the road with Gam driving, Gia sleeping in the cab beside him. Nik is secured on a stretcher from the clinic, Yeti is right beside him, and the propane furnace focuses mostly on the two of them. Isaac is somberly watching Nik from one of the side seats, but Jax can see he seems a little more at peace. He notices that Lila has strapped her rifle and helmet back on, yet her arms are still covered in blood and there is the streak still on the side of her face.

He had found himself wanting to wipe it off for her, and he is glad he didn't. It was one thing holding her hands, and Jax wonders if that was a mistake, because the look in her eyes was unsettling to him.

*It was akin to the look Gia gives Gam.*

The fact that he wants to see it again adds to his unease, and he acknowledges that it has become increasingly difficult to ignore how he feels about her.

*You're getting too close, Jax. It complicates things. Keep a clear head on the battlefield...*He tells himself again, feeling like a broken record.

At the same time, he reflects on how she has become indispensable to him in this team, and he wants to protect that. Sitting across from her, his rifle ever at ready, he listens and watches guardedly as Lila tries to sleep through the jarring of the vehicle.

*For everything there is a season, and a time...a time for love, and a time for hate; a time for war, and a time for peace...*

# | 90 |

# Praise and Respite

Five hours of driving straight north lands us at a former Defense barracks with an inner layout similar to that of the one near Vouna. Although it is much larger, of steel construction, and the windows are tinted. The surrounding terrain is extremely flat and almost unnervingly wide open, with very few trees to be seen. To me it feels like a security nightmare, but without their satellites and APA, we are at little risk from The Direction.

There is a dusting of snow, and the wind is bitingly cold, but the afternoon sun helps reduce the chill factor. A couple dozen trucks, bikes, and UTVs are parked within the fenced area, all confiscated from Defense, while two of our own guards are stationed in a tower by the gate.

Since the shutdown of APA, headquarters has directed their available teams along with a few militia groups to gather here to prepare for taking the main Oshana facility. Looking around at the assortment of vehicles and insulated tents, I wonder how many have arrived so far.

As soon as we arrived, we moved Nik to the waiting med-bus, and now Jax, Gia, Gam, Isaac, and I watch as they drive through the gate and head east, followed by one of the recon teams in a transport truck. The medic, a young man named Amos, has offered to take Yeti as well, so now Nik and Yeti are headed for Vita Nova.

*And hopefully a full recovery.*

I have a feeling it won't be that simple, but I pray it turns out better than I suspect.

"Father Malachi is taking Fae to Vita Nova so she can be there when Nik arrives," Jax informs us, after pulling his data pad from his vest and checking his messages.

"Good, he'll need that."

I nod as we turn and walk toward the building's front door. I notice Gam and Gia holding hands as they walk beside us, and I manage a slight smile. Suddenly, I realize my own hands are still on my rifle, so I lower it and shift it to hang down along my side.

"I'm going to need to sleep for a week," Isaac finally speaks in a tired but lighter tone, and it is a bit of a relief to me, since he had been silent the entire ride.

Jax smiles slightly, nodding, and I can tell it makes him relax a little as he hears his friend's voice. "You've earned it, Isaac."

Jax pushes the door open to the main front room, a lounge area much like the base in The Wilds, and we step in and stop in our tracks. Scattered throughout the various sitting areas, a couple dozen men and women, dressed in either cargos and combat jackets or full gear, suddenly stand at attention. Half of them salute properly; the others attempt to copy the effort.

I feel suddenly self-conscious. We must make quite the sight, since we are all covered in dirt and blood, half soaked from melted snow. Jax's face is resolute, and he returns a salute, which the rest of us feel obligated to give as well. Then the room breaks out in clapping, table pounding, and cheers before several of them move forward and give us handshakes and slaps to our shoulders.

My face flushes and then pales when I realize they are cheering and congratulating us on our success at shutting down APA. Gia's face breaks into a grin, and Isaac seems to cheer up a bit as they both recognize some faces in the gathering. Gam is a little out of sorts, but Gia grabs him by the hand and begins introducing a few people.

"You can smile, Lil'." Jax's voice is low, pulling me out of my stupor as he leans toward me.

"I don't feel I deserve it. I'm sure many of them have worked just as hard for us to get to this point," I confide quietly, after someone claps me on the shoulder.

"Let it happen. It's as much for them as us, Lil'. They all need this."

I comply and accept the remaining congratulations, still feeling tense; the level of noise in the room is a little overwhelming. I look over to see a grin break out across Jax's face while he returns a few final handshakes. The dirt, blood, and grime do nothing to dim the light in his eyes, and that somehow makes the awkwardness of the situation fade a bit. I am again impressed by his fortitude as a leader, and it makes me admire him even more.

Thankfully, things start to settle, and just in time because I feel I need to find somewhere to hide for a while. *And sit.* My leg is protesting every moment. I also want to process everything and contact Amos, the medic, to see how Nik is doing so far. It will be a grueling eight hours before he arrives in Vita Nova, and my mind is preoccupied with that thought as one last person approaches.

"Major Erricks." A man in his mid-forties, wearing combat cargos and jacket, greets Jax with a salute, and I see Jax flinch a little at the title. "It's an honor to meet you sir. I'm Sergeant Hann. I led the recon squad."

"In that case the honor is mine. Your team did damn fine work. It wouldn't have been a success without your recon," Jax compliments in return, shaking Hann's hand. "This is Captain Collins."

This is the first time I have heard him say my last name with a rank attached and it seems strange, but I greet the Sergeant and shake his hand.

"Any relation perhaps to Professor Hann?"

A grin spreads across his face, and he nods, his curly dark hair bouncing.

"Yes sir, that would be my wife."

*I'm not sure I am going to get used to this "sir" thing...*

Jax notes my discomfort and seems to smile a little at my expense, but it is quickly hidden.

The sergeant's face grows a little more serious. "I heard about one of your men. I hope it was not an error of ours that caused that."

"No, it was ours. A misstep. As I said, your intel was spot on," Jax reassures and then adds, "if you'll excuse me, I think I am going to find something to eat and then a place to clean up."

"Yes sir. Kitchen, med-room, and data center are down the left hall, and the sleeping quarters are down the right hall. Just pick a cot and throw your gear under it to claim it. Latrine, showers, and lockers are past that."

"Thank you, Sergeant." Jax nods to Hann and waits for the sergeant to leave.

"Will it always be that official?" I venture to ask, relieved that no one else is approaching, although I do wonder where Gam and Gia went off to.

He shakes his head, standing there for a moment while he watches the people around us leave to go about their tasks.

"That will be a while before General Miles can establish proper training and ranks. I know Hann was in Defense before. I never met him until now, but that's why he's formal."

"There you are, guys." Isaac approaches. "I just wanted to let you know I'm going to go get myself situated in the data room and then catch some sleep before my dad calls with the briefing."

"Sounds good. How are you holding up?" Jax asks, giving Isaac's shoulder a quick grip.

Isaac shrugs a little with a look of reluctance.

"Better now that we're here. But please let me know as soon as you hear anything about Nik, okay, Lila?" He looks to me and I nod.

"I will." I watch as he nods and heads down the left hall before I turn to Jax. "I think I'll go get my packs from the truck and wash up. You heading for the kitchen?"

"I'll get the packs. You've pushed it enough with your leg today. You need the rest." Jax gives me an almost accusatory glance and doesn't wait for my answer but ducks out the door.

I want to argue that he is probably about as tired as I am, but the door closes and I sigh, shaking my head.

*About as stubborn as I am, too...*

| 91 |

# Good and Bad

It is strange to him to be back in a setting where everyone sleeps in the same room. Jax has gotten used to his privacy; his ability to quietly reflect and pray before sleep. The banter, trash talk, and occasional throwing of things by the different teams in the room reminds him of his early time in Defense, and he is not sure he likes the feel of the memory. Part of him wonders if he will even want to be in an established military system once it is in place.

Laying in his cot in the still-dark hours of the morning, the room has finally settled into relative peace, although a few of the occupants snore loudly, including Gam in the cot next to him. Isaac had been sleeping the rest of the day once they had arrived, but his space is now vacant. One glance across the room to Lila's cot answers the other question on his mind: she isn't asleep either. The data pad in her hand lights up her face as she taps at it, and he forces his focus away.

Jax's own tablet beneath his pillow *dings,* and he reads a message from Isaac.

"Data room, new info. Plus, I have coffee for you."

Swinging his feet over, he sits up, puts his boots on, and looks over in the dimly lit room to see Lila do the same. She looks like she is rested, but he considers that could just be because she is no longer covered in dirt and blood, her hair freshly braided. As they wordlessly leave the bunk room together, he is grateful for his own clean set of cargos and shirt.

"Isaac message you, too?" He finally asks quietly, once they are clear of the sleeping squads, their path subtly lit by low lights at floor-level.

She nods, looking like she wants to say something, and he notes a small smile pulling at her lips. Jax doesn't pry, but the smile relaxes him, and they are soon entering the data room. The lights are down somewhat, but it still takes a bit for his eyes to adjust. Isaac is there with two mugs of coffee in hand, and he hands one to him and one to Lila.

"Good, now you can tell me, Lila." Isaac anxiously stares at Lila, his hands in the pockets of the sweatshirt he is wearing.

Lila's smile broadens, her eyes happier than Jax has seen in a while when she glances at the both of them.

"Nik just got out of surgery and pulled through like the champ he is."

Isaac's face lights up with a grin. "Nothing can keep that guy down."

"Praise God."

With genuine satisfaction, Jax smiles. Knowing Nik is going to be alright, and seeing Isaac coming out of his malaise is a respite from his concerns.

"What is the outlook for his recovery?"

He flinches inwardly as Lila's smile fades a bit.

"That's going to be the tough part." She pauses as she looks at Isaac's expression, and Jax knows she is holding something back. "But he's going to pull through that, too. Like you said, Isaac, nothing can keep Nik down."

Her face works into a grin, and she gives Isaac's arm a gentle grip. "Now, what's the info you've got for us?"

Soberly, Jax recognizes the effort she is making to keep Isaac's spirits up, which assures him again that he made the right decision choosing her as his second-in-command.

*And makes me all the more fond of her.* He again buries the recurring thought.

"Well, one of the recon teams picked up a transport bus making a run for it from Oshana, heading south. They had left the facility before I had it locked down," Isaac begins, and Jax sips his coffee, listening. "These ended up being the top board members of The Direction; the decision makers."

"And they were captured?" Jax interjects.

Isaac nods. "Well, mostly. A few of them offed themselves rather than be captured, but there are now four being kept in the holding facility in Gamal, awaiting interrogation."

Jax catches the grimace on Lila's face.

"The General doesn't use the same methods, Lila."

"Part of me wouldn't mind if he did, at least to those people," she admits, and the struggle is evident on her face, but she manages to settle herself. "But we need to be better than they are. Either way, you look like you have more to share, Isaac?"

"Yes," Isaac confirms. "The program I put in place of APA has allowed the remaining towns of Eden to view the history, various books, and current events on Consoles at their own discretion. Even members of Defense are willingly laying down their weapons and surrendering because of this. This has led to an increase of refugees in need of supplies and work."

"How is that being handled?" Jax finishes his coffee.

"The Gamal militias have taken charge. Since The Direction has pulled out of Gamal entirely, they are encouraging factories, facilities, and farms to bring in the people from Eden."

Lila nods as her smile returns. "That's fantastic! Well done, Isaac. What about at the Oshana facility?"

"It's not all me. My colleagues back in Vita Nova helped build the program and connected it to our satellites. But for Oshana, it looks like they have manually shut down all their devices so no one can view anything. I can control all the locks and have locked down the entire building, so when we move on them, they will probably be on pins and needles."

"And unpredictable to deal with," Jax muses with a little trepidation, and Lila nods in agreement. "Anything else, Isaac?"

"Yes, actually. Just a curiosity, though. APA sent out a data package before she shut down, and I am working on tracing where that went." He shrugs a little and doesn't seem too concerned, so Jax relaxes and nods.

"And that's about it." Isaac adds. "But there's more coffee in the kitchen if you need it. I have to continue the building specs for each of the teams and program more comms systems."

Isaac sits down in one of the chairs, several data pads and communication devices spread across the desk before him.

"We'll leave you to it. Good work Isaac." Jax claps him on the shoulder, and Isaac grins with an appreciative nod.

Lila follows him to the kitchen, and he refills his mug before topping hers off.

"You know, Fae might be right. As medic, I really should think of regulating this team's coffee intake. It can't be good." Lila muses, and Jax chuckles, shaking his head.

As though they are synced, they sit with their backs to the wall at a table off to the side in silence for a while. The room is still empty, and the lighting minimal since the sunrise hasn't quite begun. Jax likes these types of quiet times with her, it is peaceful, but he wants to know.

"What weren't you saying about Nik back there?" Jax keeps his voice low, sitting back in his chair, and watches Lila's expression go from thoughtful to concerned.

"I shouldn't even be surprised you caught that," she begins and leans her arms onto the table. "Some shrapnel was too close to his spine. There's a chance he'll never walk again."

"Damn," Jax mumbles under his breath, staring at the table and feeling like there is nothing else he can say to that.

"Yeah…my thoughts exactly."

| 92 |

# No More Loss

Jax stares down at the table in front of him, going over the details of the plans on his own, while Lila is outside helping Isaac load his equipment. The past few days have been hectic to say the least, but everyone is in relatively good spirits.

"Hey boss, can I speak with you?" Gia walks over, her hands in her pockets.

"What's up, Gia?" He asks, but suspects that he already knows, and he has honestly been preparing for this moment since the incident in The Wilds.

"After this assignment, after we take down the last hold The Direction has..." She hesitates, and Jax's smile is somewhat sad.

"You're leaving the team... with Gam," he finishes for her, and she only looks mildly surprised that he knows.

"I'm so sorry, Jax. I feel I'm losing my edge. I don't know if I can have your back the way I used to. And then Nik... that was the last straw for me." Gia's usually stern, determined face is apologetic, but somewhat content.

Jax shakes his head. "You don't need to apologize, Gia. I'd rather you be honest and quit before you get yourself hurt. Everyone reaches the end. Not everyone is honest about it, though. So, thank you."

She nods and looks at him studiously. "Just don't tell anyone else yet, please. I don't want them to be thinking about that during this last mission, but I owe it to you to give you a heads up."

"Thank you, Gia. We'll talk more about it after the mission and let the others know then."

Gia nods. "Sounds good, boss. See you in a few."

After watching her walk away, Jax plants his fists on the table in front of him, staring at the plans and pondering. He thought he would be prepared for her quitting, but the reality that he will be losing two more from his team hits harder than he likes. Especially knowing that Nik will likely never return. That leaves Isaac and Lila, and the dreaded process of selecting new team members. Looking over the specs and blueprints, his eyes land on those of Sublevel 20.

*Lil' isn't going back there...I can't risk losing her, too.*

Jax proceeds to scratch her off the list in the teams lined up for taking that level. He is not going to take the chance of losing her, whether physically or emotionally, to that damned place.

*You're going to regret not talking to her first...* Something tells him.

| 93 |

# Plans and Arguments

"Alright, as you heard, this is the prime time to clear the facility. The upper levels should be pretty easy, with mostly scientists and noncombatants. It's the last level that will be difficult. Comms will be spotty because someone down there manually disabled the signal booster and cameras. We can assume that is where the majority of the Defense will be held up, guarding any detainees we'll need to rescue. And without communications, they will have no clue that their bosses have abandoned them."

I stand off to the side as Jax addresses a few dozen men and women who are geared up and ready, standing in the main front room and eagerly waiting to finally put an end to this war. General Miles has put him in charge, along with Isaac, to organize and initiate the takeover of Oshana facility.

The General has already gone through the plan, and Jax has made a few changes, with Bram's approval of course. Any captured Defense, or anyone working for The Direction, will be taken to a holding facility in Gamal. All details have been sent to the team leaders ahead of time; this is just an overview and a question and answer.

Our team is the only one not fully geared up. I haven't even braided my hair yet, only wearing a shirt and cargos with my sidearm, but I am glad to not have the additional weight of the plate carriers and mags at the moment. Pushing my hair out of my face while I listen, I am reminded why I braid it all the time.

*I really should cut it like Gia...* I smile a little as I glance over at Gia, who has let her hair go fully to natural blonde, all the pink faded.

"We'll move from top to bottom, clearing one floor and one room at a time. Let's take our time with this."

"Sir. Lane, Tanners, Boeman, and I have teams that are set to rotate turns clearing all the floors, but none of us are involved with the last one. Is there a reason we're not able to assist with Sublevel 20?"

"Lieutenant Jenkins, I appreciate the offer, but Sublevel 20 is high risk, and the only two team leaders here who know that level are myself and Hann. We have both also run multiple extreme assignments, and no offense to your men, but most of you are new to the field. We can't jeopardize your lives like that.

"Me, Gia, and Gam will be joining Hann's team to tactically take out that level once the other levels are vacated. Captain Collins will stay with Isaac; she will take over command in my absence. We will have your team, however, escort anyone we capture up the elevator as we continue clearing that level."

Jenkins nods and seems to be pleased with this arrangement.

*But I'm not...*

Watching Jax's expression, I notice his glance shifts to me briefly, but he looks down at his tablet, and I know he sees the anger written all over my face.

*He never talked to me about this...*

The rest of the briefing goes by with me barely being aware of what is said. I want to brace him about keeping me out of the team, but I want to gain control of my anger first. I know he doesn't want me back in Sublevel 20, and a part of me is apprehensive about going, but he isn't even giving me a choice.

"Alright, everyone here but my team is geared up, so you all are clear to head out. We'll see you out there in two hours." Jax dismisses everyone and heads down the left hall toward the data room.

"Jax." I try to control the frustration in my voice as I jog after him, his long stride more than I can keep up with at a walk.

He stops at the med-room door, before the data room, and turns around to face me. There is an odd, but fleeting smile as he watches me before his jaw tenses.

"Lil', I know I should have told you, but I didn't want to fight about this."

"You didn't even give me a choice, Jax." I clamp my jaw, trying to avoid saying anything I might regret.

Glancing behind me and then behind himself, he grasps me by the arm and pulls me into the vacant med-room, flipping the light on and waiting for the door to close before releasing my arm and looking at me firmly.

"I can't let you go back there, Lil'. You *shouldn't* go back there."

"That's my decision to make, not yours," I argue, my eyes narrowing.

He looks almost offended, but he steels his expression. "First of all, it *is* my decision, as your commanding officer. And second, do *you* even think you should go back?"

Jax's statement is as good as a slap in the face, and I stare at him, flabbergasted, not at the second statement but the first. I can tell he instantly regrets his words as he lowers his head a little.

"What happened to friendship? And trust? The promise we made that we would tell each other if we've had enough? I'm not done, Jax. You can't bench me like that when I haven't said it's too much. Haven't I proven myself enough so far?"

"I'm sorry, I didn't mean it to come out like that. Yes, you have proven yourself many times over, and there is no other soldier I would want by my side in this. You're too vital to this team, though. To me as my partner in this unit. I don't want to jeopardize anything by putting you through that."

"I can handle it," I contest, determined, my jaw rigid still from his previous words. "Do you doubt me?"

"It's not that I doubt you. I don't like taking that risk," He clarifies.

"I'm willing to take it, Jax. You *know* I have changed, and I trust God will pull me through. Can you trust with me?" I challenge, watching his expression gradually go from doubt to approval.

"Alright," he answers calmly, nodding. "One more thing I need you to know, though."

"And that is?" My brows dip when I see him hesitate, as though he is battling with himself.

He watches my face, the way he does when he is expecting a certain reaction.

"Lil', I haven't told you everything, and I know eventually you would find out. You know there are a lot of things I regret doing for the Defense before I knew God. Do you know why I know Sublevel 20 so well?"

So, my suspicions are confirmed, but I wonder if he is using this just to test my resolve.

"I was in charge of interrogations. I trained Major Marc."

Unintentionally, I outwardly flinch, and he catches it, his brows knitting. I admit I wasn't expecting *that* much direct involvement, but it changes nothing for me, other than the fact that I am miffed that he hasn't shared sooner.

"Why didn't you tell me before?"

"Because you weren't ready for it then. And I wasn't even sure if you were ready for it now." Jax pauses as I lean against the table, and he leans against it beside me. "I thought that if you knew, you wouldn't want me near you, and you would have to struggle alone. I didn't want to see you go through that."

"Jax…"

I suddenly realize he might be right. Had he mentioned it right away, I may have been uneasy around him.

*But not now. Things have changed.*

"Maybe then, but not now. Things are different now…"

I don't continue. I want to admit how much I love and admire him, and nothing he did in the past could sway that, but I have a feeling it won't go over well.

"Do you still trust me, then, Lil'? Do you still want to go into that hell hole and fight alongside me?"

I meet his gaze and nod, saying what I know I can safely say from my heart.

"Yes. I know in my soul that none of that was you. What happened to me? Not you. God doesn't judge our past after our repentance; I can't judge you by your past. The man I see in front of me is Godfearing, confident, the best leader one could ask for, and sometimes cares too much for others at the cost of himself. That's the man I'll fight beside any day."

He doesn't say anything for a moment, just stares at me with a different light in his eyes than I am used to. I wonder if I said too much, or something wrong, but a smile finally breaks across his features.

"A lot of that could be used to describe you, too."

"I learn from the best." I smile when I see him visibly relax, although he still seems to study my face.

"And you're sure you will be alright to revisit that place, then?"

"I have to face and fight my demons someday, Jax, and it might as well be today. As long as I am fighting by your side. That's where I belong." I am resolute.

"You won't be facing them alone, Lil'," he promises.

"I know I won't." I smile, nodding.

"Hey Lil'..."

"Yes, Jax?" I raise a brow.

"I'm sorry I made that choice without you. I let fear influence my decision," he confesses.

"We're good, Jax," I assure him with a smile.

"Then let's finish this. It's time to put an end to that place." He likewise smiles and leads the way out the door.

# | 94 |

# Endearing

In fear he had tried to hold her back, thinking he needed to protect her again. He regrets that, but she didn't hesitate to confront him, convincing him otherwise, and it is endearing to him to have her justly challenge his decision. And then turn right around and forgive him.

The rest of the team finishes gearing up as he and Lila reach the lockers. Isaac, Gia, and Gam head out with their packs to get the transport truck warmed up and ready, while Jax and Lila get their own gear on. Opting to stay in their lighter cargos and don jacket shirts, since the facility will be heated, they each tug on their plate carriers.

The room empty, other than the two of them, Jax steps over and helps Lila fasten the sides of the molle vest and double checks to make sure the plates are secure. Pausing, he looks down at her and she returns a questioning look.

"You sure about this, Lil'?" He asks one more time, searching her eyes for doubt and involuntarily searching for something else as well.

*I love when her hair is loose...*

The thought distracts him without conscious choice, followed by the awareness of how much he has come to love her. Not just her appearance but her soulfulness, her resolve, and her faith. Jax suddenly doesn't want to ignore it, not right now.

"Yes. You can stop asking, Jax. Everything is going to be alright." With her voice low, her smile slight but confident, she holds his gaze calmly, and he finds what he is searching for.

It paralyzes his usual self-restraint, and he can't bury the emotion this time as he sees the determination and admiration; a resolute light in her amber eyes. To Jax, her fortitude and devotion is captivating, and in this pre-battle anticipation, fiercely enticing. On impulse, he does something he has wanted to do for some time now.

He leans down and kisses her, placing his hand at the back of her neck with his fingers entangled in her soft hair. The fervor with which she returns the kiss consumes him, and he relishes the warmth of her hand on his face. Before he knew God, he had been with a number of women, but this is something different to him: something pure and honest.

Jax pulls away after a while, his hand lingering at the side of her blushing face, until guilt hits him and he steps back.

"Lila, I'm sorry."

"Jax..." Lila steps forward, but he shakes his head, turning away and reaching for his rifle.

"No, I shouldn't have done that. It complicates things. I'm sorry. It makes things muddled on the battlefield." Inwardly he kicks himself while at the same time wanting to kiss her again.

"Jax." She repeats more firmly, but he continues, putting his combat helmet on.

"Lila, it was one thing with Gam and Gia. I didn't like the idea of it. I can't let myself get involved. It goes against what I believe is necessary for the stability of the unit. No involvements within the team. Even after we take down the facility, I know there will still be conflict, possible combat with stray Defense units, and we can't be distracted."

"Jax... It's alright. I understand." Her voice is quiet, almost sad, but he looks over and sees she already has her rifle and helmet on.

"It's OK." Her smile is faded somewhat, but she nods, shouldering her pack and walking past him while she braids her hair.

*God. What have I done?*

| 95 |

# Muddled Battlefields

Two gruelingly silent hours later, we are nearly at the facility. I can't bring myself to look at Jax, but I sense he is avoiding looking at me as well. The worst part was when he suddenly stopped calling me Lil'.

I close my eyes and breathe slowly, knowing he is right. It does muddle things on the battlefield. My mind can't help but go to that kiss, though, and how it felt like it was just me and him. Nothing else mattered.

*It felt right.*

Pushing the thought from my mind, I take another deep breath. With resolve, I know what I need to do, and I bow my head.

*God, even if Jax feels friendship is as far as this can go, please help me be there in that way. It has been too valuable to me, to us, to lose that. I promise to do my best to support him, even with his decision, but guide me, please. We need to have each other's backs on this.*

There is no more time for thought when the truck comes to a jarring halt, and we all step out into the cold early December air. I involuntarily shiver and look around at the all-too familiar paved lot surrounded by forest. Once the ground level is cleared, we will all go in and station there. We will have teams taking turns clearing the lower floors, while the transportation trucks haul the detainees away.

"Alright. First team, Jenkins. I have cameras active and will direct you through the main level to gather what are mostly civilians. You give me the go at each door when you're ready, and I'll unlock it from here. There are two officers in the entrance, but they don't seem to be prepared, they don't even have weapons, so I am guessing they are ready to surrender." Isaac is reviewing cameras, and I can see he almost looks excited and surprisingly calm.

Looking around at the six extraction teams, counting our own, they all have a low-level excitement on their faces. That makes sense considering this could be the final major conflict we will have to face, other than possible skirmishes later with Defense units still out in the field.

*Like Jax mentioned...*

"Don't make a bet on that though. Be prepared for anything," Jax cautions, and Lieutenant Jenkins nods.

Jenkins leads his team to the single entry and nods to Isaac. There is shouting but no gunfire, as Jenkins' unit clears the halls first, bringing captives, secured in tie-straps, to the waiting transportation. It takes twenty minutes more for all the rooms to be cleared, and the ground level is ours.

"You gonna be alright here, Isaac?" I ask while helping him set up his surveillance equipment and comms center.

"Yes." Isaac's voice is confident, with only the slightest trepidation on his face as he nods with a smile. "I have full control over locks, and this level is completely secure, so I'm good. Thank you for asking, Lila."

"No problem, Isaac. Just let me know if you need anything."

He nods again, but his attention is already fully on his job.

Through the morning, the first seven sublevels go smoothly; no Defense in sight. There are only scientists and civilians in various stages of panic or detachment, some of them not having eaten in three days, and they eagerly take the health bars given to them as they are loaded into the trucks. Gam and Gia continue to assist securing captives and loading them into trucks.

Sergeant Hann waits with his unit of four off to the side, looking anxious, and I can't decide if it is because he is back in the facility that he left long ago or because he wants to get in on the action. Jax is standing in the reception hall by the desk, looking edgy, and I watch his face tense when the other teams seem to relax into a routine.

Taking a deep breath and trying to keep my promise to God, I step to his side. "Everything alright?"

He seems a little startled, and his lips tighten to a thin line as he avoids looking at me, focusing on his own tablet and switching cameras to watch the maneuvers.

"It's too easy. The teams are getting comfortable with it."

I nod a little, wincing at his detachment, but I try to be considerate and step away a bit, turning to our studious tech. "Isaac, how are we looking on the lower levels?"

"That might be a little more tense. There's more Defense. They are still armed and definitely agitated from what little I can tell on the cameras."

"Jenkins." I call the team leader who is preparing for the next level while Lane's team wraps up Sublevel 7.

"Yes, sir?" His brow dips as he approaches, and I still won't be getting used to the 'sir' anytime soon.

"Remind your men to be alert. These next levels aren't going to be so easy. We can't risk any of our teams going down right now; we still have a lot of floors to clear." There is a strange feeling of confidence when Jenkins seems to appreciate the reminder.

"Yes sir." He gives a nod and returns to his team. "Stay frosty, guys, we might be going in hot this time."

I turn to also tell Boeman, whose team will go after Jenkins, and catch Jax eyeing me with a look of approval. He nods and goes over to remind the other two teams. I relax a little as he seems to settle back into the dynamics.

Isaac, sitting at the reception desk, keeps them all updated via separate comms per team, and I am impressed with how well he directs them. Jax only interjects occasionally to recommend different approaches to a few trickier situations, such as when teams run into combative, though unarmed, civilians.

"Alright, Jenkins ran into some issues this round on Sublevel 16. Gunfire was exchanged," Isaac informs.

"Any injuries?" I instantly inquire.

Due to a delay in the arrival of another combat medic, there is only one other medic in our platoon, Amos, who had immediately returned from Vita Nova. So, I am set as backup, my med-pack waiting at the reception desk. Jax hovers over Isaac, watching the various data pads logged into the cameras.

"Fortunately, no, but Sublevel 17 seems to have heard it, and Defense is getting prepared at both the stairwell and the elevator. This is the first floor I've seen more than a dozen."

With his statement, I can see uneasiness growing in Isaac's eyes, but he looks at Jax.

Jax puts a hand on his shoulder and nods firmly. "Boeman's team is next, Let him know what he's up against."

"Let my team go as well, Sir," Jenkins offers.

"You just did another round, are you still good to go?" Jax looks over the lieutenant, evaluating his current condition.

"Yes sir. We've got a good sweat going."

"Good. You take charge over that floor; you've got more experience." Jax nods, and I notice a brief look of apprehension.

There is a nagging feeling that this is going to be a bad encounter.

"Jax, I think we need to send a medic with them," I suggest, and he looks over at me, looking in my eyes for the first time since the locker room, but his expression is guarded.

"Copy that, Lila. Isaac, get Amos on comms and have him join Jenkins."

I cringe, but there is no time to think about it when the next few minutes quickly turn into complete chaos. Over Isaac's comms, we hear Jenkins barking orders through the sounds of stun grenades and gunfire. Viewing on the surveillance, I grimace as I see two from Boeman's team go down, but the medic pulls them back and quickly attends to them.

"They're losing ground." Isaac flinches, and Jax's face goes grim.

He nods a little. "We need to send in another unit. Defense is fighting like cornered rats right now."

Sergeant Hann has come over to watch, hearing Isaac's comment, and I note how ashen his face looks.

"Sir, what is my son doing down there? He was just supposed to be support medic."

Jax looks confused at first, but I know exactly who he means.

There is a certain dismay watching something take place when you can do nothing about it fast enough. And when I see Amos go down while trying to torniquet the leg of one of Jenkins' soldiers, the guilt of asking Jax to send him in hits me. Without thinking, I give a pointed look to Jax and grab my med-pack, shouldering it. I take off at a run for the stairs, shifting my rifle in front of me.

"Lila!"

# | 96 |

# Friendly Advice

He has been having a hard time remaining impartial and interacting with Lila the same as before, but her own conduct has been admirable, and Jax tries to amend his own. When she takes charge at one point, he supports her decision but still keeps contact to a minimum. It feels like he is battling against his own nature.

*And maybe against God's will?*

He has no time to think about any of that now, as Jenkins and Boeman's team land in hot water, and he is about to send Tanners' team for backup when Lila takes off down the hall.

"Lila!"

She doesn't stop, and he fights with himself for a moment, the desire to go with her weighing against the need to stay at his command post.

*And this is why you don't get involved...* He thinks ruefully.

"Let me and my team go, sir," Hann offers.

Jax knows the man is thinking about his son, but he nods and the Sergeant and his team run after Lila. While Lila and the Sergeant's team race down the stairwell, all Jax can do is watch on the screens, ignoring the tightness in his throat and opting for the numbness of battle. He barely notices as Gia and Gam come in from outside after getting water and food for some of the detainees.

"Where are the other teams and Lila?" Gam asks, looking around and seeing only Lane and Tanners' teams waiting on standby.

Jax gestures to the tablet displays, and the two of them come around. "Lila went to help."

"Oh shit," Gia comments. "Should *we* go down and help?"

No sooner does she say this, when Lila and the other team show up on Sublevel 17, and they watch as the tables turn in a matter of seconds, with Hann's team having far more experience. One-by-one, with the help of one of Hann's men, Lila pulls five injured soldiers, including the medic, into the open elevator under their cover fire.

"Unlock the doors, Isaac." She calls over the comms, although she does not need to, since Isaac already has the doors closing, and she slaps the button for ground level.

"Go help her." Jax nods to Gam and Gia, and they immediately head for the elevator.

He and Isaac are silent while they watch Hann and his team assist what is left of the other two teams, quickly resulting in the surrender of what is remaining of the Defense in that level. They only relax when the captured combatants are detained and brought up.

With the help of the stand-by teams, Lila and Gia have already set up an impromptu triage in one of the vacant rooms, assessing the injuries of the five and attending to one critical first. Jax glances at Lila, who is now speaking with Sergeant Hann, before turning to watch as Tanners clears Sublevel 18 with little resistance.

Level 19 is equally uneventful, and Jax feels the apprehension kick in. He and Hann nod to each other.

"How is your son?"

"He'll be fine, sir, just a hit to the plates. He's even insisting on taking over medic duties while the Captain and Gia join us." The Sergeant smiles with a hint of pride and relief.

"Good. That was fine work mopping up 17. Is your team ready for the final floor?"

"Yes sir." Hann nods firmly.

Lila walks up, wiping blood from her hands before situating her rifle in front of her. Gia and Gam are beside her, readying themselves for the final task.

"And this is going to be tricky," Isaac adds when he walks over. "Because the signal booster down there was manually shut down, I am switching you all to close range comms, which will unfortunately still be sketchy with all the concrete. There will be no way I can communicate with you once you're down there, so you will be responsible for unlocking doors with your tablets."

Jax nods and clears his throat. "Hann will take his team down the elevator and clear the west halls. We'll take the stairs and clear the east halls. Keep in contact. Once the halls are clear, any captives we have will be handed over to Tanners' team at the elevator."

"I thought that was going to be Jenkins' job?" Isaac looks up from his tablet.

"Jenkins was wounded. He's going to be alright, but out of commission for now," Lila explains.

"Tanners is good to go." Jax continues, barely even glancing at her. "After that, we clear room by room in pairs. Sergeant, divide yours however you choose. Gia. Lila. You two will team up. That leaves Gam and me."

Jax catches Lila's quick glance and tries to decide if she is angry or resolute, but he forces his focus on the task at hand.

"Alright, let's go."

"Jax, can I speak with you a moment?" Isaac prompts, looking over at the others and then to him, a worried look in his eyes.

"I'll meet you at the stairs." Jax nods and waits for his team to head down the hall. Meanwhile, Hann's team makes their way to the elevator.

"Is everything alright, Isaac?"

With an unusually forceful look on his face and his side of the comms off, Isaac lowers his voice.

"Shit, Jax. What the hell is up with you two?"

Surprised by Isaac's candor, and language, Jax hadn't realized Isaac was watching the entire time.

"Now is not the time, Isaac."

"Actually, now *is* the time. You need a clear head. You two always work together like you're mind-synced or something, but not today. You keep this up and one of you is going to get killed. What happened back at the locker room after we left you two?" Isaac is persistent, folding his arms.

His jaw tensing, Jax looks over, not even sure if he should mention anything but it escapes anyway.

"I kissed her, Isaac."

"Well, about time!" His friend throws up his hands.

"What?" Not sure if he heard him right, Jax continues, his arms folded above the stock of his slung AR. "It's *not* a good thing, Isaac! You know how that complicates being in combat together."

"*You* complicate combat, Jax. Have you ever thought that God meant for you and Lila to be involved, and that's why you two connect so well and make a good team? What is it you're afraid of?"

"I can't talk about this right now, Isaac." Jax goes to turn, but Isaac grabs his arm.

"At least pray about it, Jax, have you done that, yet?"

Suddenly, Jax realizes he hasn't earnestly prayed about anything else but this mission the past few days, and he feels a hint of remorse. He nods a little.

"Alright, fine."

"Thank you." Isaac nods, albeit still concerned. "Now good luck. I'll be praying up here."

"Thanks, Isaac."

Even with the mission at the forefront of thought, Isaac's words ring in Jax's mind, and a quote from a book he recently read enters his thoughts.

*"I held my heart back from positively accepting anything, since I was afraid of another fall, and in this condition of suspense I was being all the more killed."*

*Is my reason for rejecting her actually fear?*

# | 97 |

# I Need Her

It is disconcertingly easy and quick work for both teams to clear the dank concrete halls. The only Defense they encounter are eight of them, all thirsty, hungry, and readily surrendering. They're escorted by Tanners' team up the elevator, and the harder work begins.

When they go to split into pairs, Jax looks over at Lila and considers changing his mind about the arrangement. She seems more on edge than any of the others, and he guesses that the walls are speaking to her.

*You promised to help fight her demons...* A small voice reminds him.

"It's alright. We're good, Jax." She nods with a tense smile. "Let's finish this."

He nods firmly, feeling a twinge of guilt when she uses his own words, and he watches as she and Gia head for their assigned section.

*What am I supposed to do, God?*

*Two are better than one, because they have a good reward for their toil. For if they fall, one will lift up his fellow; but woe to him who is alone when he falls and has not another to lift him up.*

It dawns on him, not just that he won't be there as her backup, but she will not be there as his, and he feels a sudden vulnerability and hollowness inside.

# 98

# Securing

It is tedious but mostly uneventful. At each door Gam stands against the wall on one side and Jax the other. Gam unlocks the door, opens it, and Jax clears the room. This is repeated several grueling times.

Hann's team calls in with a few detainees, civilians held by the Defense, but no Defense. It makes Jax uneasy, and he wonders who shut down the cameras and booster. Only once does Lila and Gia call in, reporting six dead Defense, all from self-inflicted wounds, but the comms crackle in and out. He assumes they are near the tail end of their search area.

He remembers all these rooms clearly, and as they come to the final one in their section, he hears whispered voices inside. Nodding to Gam, they take up their positions and follow the process. Three Defense guards, already disarmed, beg for their lives and raise their hands.

"Out and on the floor!" Jax barks the order, and they comply.

He covers for Gam as the formidable man zip ties all their hands behind their backs. Pausing, Jax looks into the familiar room, and a thought comes to mind.

"Hold them there, Gam. I need to get something."

Inside, there are shelves upon shelves of boxes, meticulously labeled in alphabetical order. Jax quickly finds the box he wants and removes something from it, securing the item in one of his vest pockets.

With a small smile he steps out, and he and Gam shuffle the captured Defense back to the elevator.

# | 99 |

# Not This Place

I was miffed at first when Jax sent me with Gia, but I try to put my trust in God and pray for Jax's safety. Right now, it is not as much of a struggle as I thought it would be, although checking room after room is very repetitive. But I still want nothing more than to turn around and leave.

Gia is quiet but calm, giving me the occasional encouraging smile and it helps keep me focused. I am not sure if I have blocked the memory or not, but my recollection of these halls is hazy, and I just follow the map on my tablet. It is eerily quiet, and we do not encounter anyone.

*Both unnerving situations.*

At one point, we open a room to a putrid smell, and I nearly lose my last meal. After we say a quick prayer over them, Gia notifies Jax about the six individuals with self-inflicted gunshot wounds and we move on. We walk down the dead-end hall, reaching our second to final door, but as we unlock and clear the empty room, I am struck with the recognition of where I am.

I suddenly feel ill.

*The smell. The metal chair. The now-dark observation window.*

*I know this room all too well...*

I do not say anything to Gia, though, and she doesn't seem to notice as we exit the room, and I force myself to take slow breaths. I focus on the feel of my rifle's grip, trying to ground myself to this moment, when we approach the final door.

*The observation room.*

*Just one more room and then we can be out of here...It will be over.*

The uneasy feeling stays in my stomach, and my chest tightens. After we take our places beside the door, I take my tablet out, tapping the code and trying to pull myself back. We hear the audible *click,* but before I can put my tablet back and lift my rifle, the door cracks open and a can flies out.

"Flashbang!" Gia yells and turns to cover her eyes.

I am too late to react as it goes off right in front of me. My hearing is replaced by ringing, the impact to my equilibrium bringing me to my knees, and my vision goes blindingly white. After a few seconds, I see blurred images rushing from the room and one disarms me, removes my helmet, and pulls me across the floor by my vest's drag-handle.

I can see enough to recognize Gia trying to get up, and another figure elbows her hard in the face, sending her reeling backward. I can't hear the gunfire because my hearing is still out, but I see the handgun and then Gia hit the floor.

"Gia!"

A third, shorter figure stands at the door we had previously opened. I am dragged in faster than I can twist around and thrown into a corner by two pairs of hands. My head throbs, and a rush of warmth trails down the side of my face from the impact with the concrete wall. Gasping and rolling to get on my hands and knees, my vision slowly clears, but I would rather not see where I am.

"It's good to see you again, Lila. Now how about that code so I can get out of here?"

The familiar nasally voice reaches through my slowly returning hearing and hits me like cold water...

*To the face.*

I force my eyes to stay open, when all I want to do is close them and make this place go away.

*I fear no evil, for You are with me...*

They have the steel chair pushed against the handle of the solid door, and two Defense men with sidearms stand beside the short man I wish I would never see again. Hilam holds my tablet in his hand, looking at me expectedly.

"Lila, can you hear me?" Jax's voice comes through my still muffled hearing.

*I still have my comms!*

I push myself defensively back into the corner on one knee, eyeing the two larger men.

"Interrogation. Gia down. Three men."

I rattle off quickly, before one of them rushes over to yank the earpiece out, raising a fist to strike me. That is when I remove the boot knife I kept from Kain and slice at the inside of his leg, knowing immediately that I hit the femoral. He stumbles back and his partner watches him go down, the injured man pressing frantically on the wound to try to stop the gushing.

"Drop the knife!" The second officer aims his side arm at me, and I reluctantly let the knife fall.

"Don't kill her, just injure. We need the code!"

*Offer to help the officer...*

*What? I'm the one who cut him!* I almost argue more but realize there is a look of concern from the officer still standing.

"Your friend is dying; he's going to bleed out within two minutes if you don't compress it. I can help," I offer, and the officer looks nervous.

I am almost sure he will fold soon.

"I'll kill him myself if you let her help." The small aggressor threatens, taking the sidearm of the fallen officer, and it shuts down any look of doubt in the remaining officer's face.

With a vehement look and an evil in his eyes I have seen in someone before, he snarls at me.

"Good. Now the code! Or we can just use you as a hostage."

The handle to the door rattles, startling the Defense officer, and the distance between us is short enough to let me dive and knock him down. Scrambling past him across the floor on my hands and knees, I barely reach the leg of the chair blocking the door and yank at it as I hear the gunshot and feel the impact of a bullet on the left of my back plate carrier, knocking the breath out of me.

Gasping, I roll onto my back, the lights too bright, my head throbbing, lungs burning, and my ears ringing as subsequent gunfire sounds around me.

*I can't breathe...* I close my eyes, shutting out the brightness as I stop fighting, until I feel a hand grasping mine and hear a muffled voice.

"Lil'? You with me? Can you breathe?"

| 100 |

# This is the Way

"Gia!"

Just after he leaves the detained Defense officers with the escort team waiting at the elevator, a single gunshot from somewhere down the halls and Lila's yell over the open comms freezes Jax in his tracks. Gam looks to him, his dark features tense. Wishing he had changed the arrangement, Jax grimaces as he feels he is going to pay dearly for the poor choices he made in the past twelve hours.

"Lila, what's going on?"

He breaks into a jog down the hall to the section she and Gia were headed, trying to decipher where the sound of gunfire had come from. Gam follows right at his heel. With no answer and no idea which direction to take when they reach a crossway, Jax pauses and closes his eyes for a moment in prayer, his heart pounding in his ears with apprehension.

*And your ears shall hear a word behind you, saying, "This is the way, walk in it..."*

"I think it came from the left." Gam suddenly speaks from behind him, his voice nervous.

Jax nods and takes the left hall, asking again, "Lila, can you hear me?"

"Interrogation. Gia down. Three men." Lila says it so fast he can barely figure out what the words are before the comms crackle out.

*Interrogation...*

Grimly, he remembers four of those rooms down here, and only one of them is in her section. With a nod to Gam, he tucks his rifle against the front of himself and breaks off at a run until he comes to a turn. Slicing the pie, he sees Gia's body and Lila's helmet ten paces ahead but no one else in the dead-end hall.

"Gia!" Gam calls from behind him, and before Jax can stop him, the massive man rushes over and kneels by the short woman, looking her over.

"I'm good. Just took the wind out of me. Plates caught it." She grunts and rolls over, pressing her forehead down while she tries to catch her breath, and Jax feels relief for just a moment.

"Where's Lil'?" He asks, not even realizing he just used his nickname for her in front of them.

Gia, still trying to catch her breath, points to the door that he knows is interrogation, and he rushes over. Gam stands up wordlessly and follows him. Jax hears voices, and the two of them set up on either side of the door before he tries the handle. It moves, indicating it is not locked, but something is blocking it, so he pushes again.

It suddenly breaks free, followed by a sound of gunfire, and he takes in the scene in a blink of an eye. There is a bled-out Defense officer at one wall. Lila is on the floor right by the chair, gasping as though she can't breathe. Two armed men are hovering near her. One is extremely short, someone he regrettably recognizes as Hilam, and the other is a terrified officer who raises his sidearm. Gam doesn't even have to fire his weapon as Jax takes two quick shots, and both combatants go down.

Dropping to his knees by Lila's side, he feels like his heart is in a vice as he checks her over quickly. Though it seems the only blood is from a gash on the side of her head, she doesn't seem to be taking in any air, and she doesn't move.

*I promised to keep here safe, but I failed. I made fear-driven decisions. I give her over to you, Lord, but please keep her alive. I need her by my side...*

"Lil'? You with me? Can you breathe?"

Jax grasps her hand, at least feeling a pulse at her wrist. She gasps, her eyes opening, and rolls to her side with a groan of pain, which makes him exhale the breath *he* was holding.

"I'm good…Not good. OK, shit that hurts." She sucks in a breath when he throws her arm around his neck and lifts her to her feet, baring most of her weight while they leave the cursed room.

Gam likewise helps Gia, and they leave Sublevel 20.

*Hopefully for the last time…*

# | 101 |

# Holding On

"I'm fine. But maybe not pull on my arm so hard." I hiss as Jax supports my weight on the ride up the elevator. I feel like my left shoulder has been torn away from the shoulder blade and that is the arm he holds.

"Where does it hurt?" He sets me down and begins searching for injuries, taking off the molle vest.

"Is everywhere a legit answer?" I groan, managing a faint grin.

Though things around me feel like they are spinning, I catch a return grin from Jax.

"Wait, is Gia alright?"

"I'm right here. Just some bruised ribs."

Her voice comes from behind Jax, and I can just make out that Gam is supporting her. Something feels wrong, though, and I can't focus.

"I'm not sure I feel so good."

"Lil'? Stay with me Lil'..."

I feel like I am being held securely, and there is a strong smell of pine, but then everything fades.

*In peace I will both lie down and sleep; for you alone, O Lord, make me dwell in safety.*

# 102

# St. Mary's

I am first aware of the sound of a calming voice filtering into the darkness, chanting in that language Father Malachi sings. There is nothing else for the moment, just that. I listen while it feels like the strange words surround my soul, and I wonder if I am in Heaven.

"...cave, quaesumus, Redemptor noster, per gratiam Sancti Spiritus infirmitatibus hujus mulieris infirmitatis, et vulnera eius sana, et omnia peccata et dolores mentis et corporis dimitte, et ab ea repelle propitius. eamque interius et exterius plenam sanitati restituat, ut, misericordia tua adiuvante, pristino officio restituatur. Qui vivis et regnas cum Deo Patre in unitate Spiritus Sancti, Deus, per omnia saecula saeculorum."

Slowly other senses come into focus: a strange sweet, earthy smell followed by the feel of a soft material beneath my fingertips, like a blanket. I force my eyes to open, and although the lighting isn't too garish, I have the feeling my eyes have not been open for a while. I wait for my focus to adjust.

I see a domed ceiling, wood and plaster, with paintings of clouds and angels surrounding a beautiful woman in blue. I've seen her before: an image in Father Malachi's prayer corner. I realize it actually *is* Father Malachi's voice, as he continues the soothing chant, but now my senses slowly become aware of the rest of my body.

My head makes itself known with a throbbing at the temple that radiates around. My left shoulder and upper back aches, and I get the impression if I move I won't like the feeling. Although my mouth is dry, I am not particularly thirsty, and that's when I notice an IV above me.

*Well, I guess I'm not in Heaven...*

"Where am I?" I vocalize aloud, although it is not very loud and more of a croaking sound.

"My dear sister in Christ, you're in the side chapel, and the medical room, of St. Mary's. Also known as Vita Nova." Father Malachi's kind bearded face comes into view over me when he steps to my right side, an old leatherbound book in his hands. "How are you feeling?"

"I'm not sure yet. What happened?" I close my eyes for a moment, listening to the priest's voice.

"You had a concussion; you were in and out for a few days once they brought you here."

"My shoulder?" Opening my eyes again, I slowly begin to hear other sounds, voices in other parts of the room, but it almost seems like my hearing is muffled with an underlying ringing.

"Broken left shoulder blade. Your collar bone fractured again, and you have some bruised ribs."

Suddenly the memories of what happened all flood back to me, and I try to sit up, but the priest gently places a hand on my arm.

"Easy. Gia will scold me if I let you move around too much."

"Gia? How is she?"

"She is just fine. Would you like me to get her?"

"No, it's alright. She's probably exhausted."

He smiles and shakes his head. "She's had a few days to rest. Keep in mind, you have been here for a few."

"I want to sit up," I insist.

I don't like not being able to see my surroundings, especially knowing that I have been unaware of them for that long.

"You should rest more."

"I don't like resting."

"Would you like me to go let Jax know you are awake?" The priest offers instead.

"What? He's here?"

I hadn't thought to ask, partly because I am still trying to collect my bearings, and partly because I assumed he would still be assisting with the final stages of shutting down The Direction.

I close my eyes because my headache increases the more I try to focus, and then I notice singing from another room filtering in gently, soothingly. It is almost like one of the songs Father would sing back at Bear Base.

*I miss that canyon...I miss home.*

Father Malachi's voice sounds like he is smiling. "Jax has barely rested. I believe this is the first time I have been in here and not seen him praying by your side."

I mumble, feeling as though I am already half asleep. "Then if he is resting, let him rest."

"I'm here, Lil'. Are you still awake?"

I feel a warm hand on my arm, and I don't have to open my eyes to know who it is. Inopportunely, I fall asleep before I can answer.

| 103 |

# Vita Nova

The med-room bed is similar to those in the more advanced clinics, with programmed settings, and I relax against the raised back. The sitting position allows me to see my surroundings. Although the full ceiling of the room is visible, there are seven-foot-high wooden wall dividers around my area with a curtain in the doorway, and I am assuming there are other areas divided similarly for privacy. The floor is a beautiful but old stone inlay.

Yeti, who showed up the other day, is still recovering from his injuries and has taken up the left side of my bed. It feels good to have him back at my side.

"You gotta stop losing weight, Lila. As soon as you feel like you can eat, I am going to make the biggest feast ever." Gam grins from ear to ear, sitting on a chair to my right.

Sitting on the arm of the chair, Gia punches him in the shoulder. "You can't tell a woman she's too skinny. Anything about weight is not acceptable."

I grin a little. "Thank you, Gia."

"Now, may I continue, after you came in and so rudely interrupted?" Isaac good naturedly challenges Gam. "As I was saying, Lila, Vita Nova is essentially a large church that has been secretly repaired and maintained over the years. The population had their living quarters underground while The Direction had their satellites active, but ever since those were destroyed, they wasted no time in starting to build houses and fix roads.

"It's a bit of a mess right now, but construction companies in Gamal have arrived to help in exchange for their own solar power systems. Which leads to the next news. General Miles has the Professor working on new laws, with the help of Bishop Augustine, Father Malachi's superior. They have had basic laws before, but Gamal has agreed to consider Vita Nova as their authority, so advanced laws will be necessary to keep peace and order."

Isaac is speaking a mile a minute, eager to share the history and plans for the future, but I am barely able to take in all the information with the side of my head aching. I nod, trying to acknowledge Isaac in his excitement, but I pinch the bridge of my nose, closing my eyes.

"Isaac, take it easy, man. I think you've broken her."

I hear Jax's voice and look over to see him leaning against the frame of the opening, his arms folded and a smile on his face.

*The smile I love.*

"Oh gosh, I'm sorry, Lila. I just didn't want you out of the loop," Isaac apologizes sheepishly, and Gia gives him an accusatory look.

"It's alright, Isaac, I appreciate it. Where have you been?" I address Jax.

I have a vague recollection of him being here the first time I woke up, but I haven't seen him for the past two days. I begin to wonder if he has been avoiding me. He shrugs a little, and to my surprise, he comes and sits on the bed by my side, facing me.

"I'm sorry I haven't been here. I came by a few times, but you were always asleep. Otherwise, the General has kept me pretty busy with meetings and discussions."

"I'm only here all the time because I took a position with the medic staff here," Gia mentions, and I raise a brow.

"Really? What about the team?" I never pictured Gia as anything else but a soldier or maybe a combat medic, but I guess things have changed.

"I guess I decided I am done with taking lives; it's time to save a few." She shrugs, her tone holding no remorse, and I watch as Gam grasps her hand with a wide smile.

I look at Jax to see his reaction, but it seems to me he has already heard this news from her. He smiles a little and nods, as though answering my unspoken question.

"And Gam is going to be opening up a culinary school here in Vita Nova," Isaac adds with his ever-present grin.

"That does not surprise me." I grin over at Gam, and he laughs.

Isaac keeps going. "Oh, and did I mention we have seen Nik recently?"

"Oh?" This piques my interest, and I shift to sit up more. "How is he?"

"The doctors say he has a good chance of walking again, but it will be a long road to recovery," Jax answers, and I can see his relief as much as I can feel my own.

"Good. How is Fae holding up?"

"She is happy to have her husband alive, thanks to you." Gia replies with a smile.

"Thanks to *all* of us, Gia. And God. I couldn't have done anything otherwise."

I press my fingers to my temple for a moment, prompting a pointed look from Jax.

"Alright guys." He looks around and nods to them. "I think that's enough news for the day. Let her take a break before she's discharged from here this afternoon."

They each in turn say their goodbyes and leave, but Jax stays.

"How are you feeling?" His sage-green eyes seem concerned but relaxed, and I am happy he is here, acting mostly like himself.

"My head hates me, and I have one cardinal complaint."

"What is that?" His brows furrow.

"Why does it have to be my left shoulder again? It was finally feeling normal."

I smirk, and it takes Jax a moment, but he laughs, a real, genuine laugh that makes his eyes light up and makes me smile.

"You should just stop getting yourself in trouble."

"I tried that. It seems to find me anyway." I give a one shoulder shrug and rest my head back for a moment.

"I have to apologize for the shoulder part anyway. I'm afraid in my hurry to get you out of the facility I damaged it more." Jax frowns a little.

"It's fine, Jax." I absently rub Yeti's ears. "I was glad to be out of there. A shoulder is a small price to pay."

He still looks remorseful, but I change the subject.

"So, Isaac mentioned something about an honors ceremony in a week?"

"Only if you're up to it. The General insists that you are there, too, and he'll delay if necessary."

I scrunch my nose. "It's going to be all pomp and circumstance, isn't it?"

The look on Jax's face tells me he is not exactly thrilled either, but he nods, and then an unexpected impish grin crosses his features.

"You'll have to wear a military dress uniform too."

"Well, shit..."

| 104 |

# Reality Hits

Fae had helped Lila get settled into temporary living quarters once she was released from the clinic, but other than a few meals shared with her and the others, including Nik, Jax hasn't been able to spend much time with Lila. The past week has been a flurry of activity in preparation for the ceremony, and the overall relief of finally having The Direction shut down has had everyone in a general state of jubilation.

He notices, however, that Lila still seems detached and out of place, like she is waiting for the next assignment. She even keeps her sidearm always on her hip.

*Like me...*

Although Vita Nova is an attractive community to be in, he feels equally out of place, and hasn't yet stopped feeling like there is something more he needs to do.

Eyeing himself in the mirror, he analyzes his appearance. Although he isn't keen on uniforms in general after the Defense Industry, Jax approves of the new design: dark grey, almost black, and complete with a beret. Rubbing at his clean-shaven chin, he inwardly ponders growing a beard again someday.

"You coming, Jax?" Isaac pops his head into Jax's officer's quarters at the newly built barracks and then gives a low whistle. "Looking good."

"Shut up." Jax scowls.

"That's alright. Just wait until you see Lila." Isaac himself wears a grey suit with a bow-tie.

"You're incorrigible, Isaac." Jax grins, but he has to inwardly admit that he is anxious to see her.

He grabs something off his desk and slips it into the pocket of his uniform jacket before following Isaac down the hall and to the outside. They walk alongside a large lake and then turn east to head for the twin belfries rising above the trees. The mid-December air is crisp and refreshing, with it being a warmer winter, and Jax is glad to not need his heavier coat, since he forgot it.

*Keep focused...*

"You alright, buddy?" Isaac asks, and Jax gives him a side-glance.

"I'm fine. Just don't like fancy ceremonies."

"Ah, sure." His friend grins but doesn't harass him, and Jax gets the impression Isaac knows the other reason for his nervousness.

Once they arrive at the impressive red-brick structure, he is struck by the beauty of it despite its age, and impressed at how carefully it has been maintained over the years by the hidden community. Stepping through the narthex, they walk into a massive space filled with old worn pews, the floor a mosaic of polished tile. Columns line the far sides of the central pews, climbing far up into the ceiling way above them. There is gold inlay everywhere and beautiful statues throughout.

Even though Jax has seen this before, it still takes his breath away, but he has little time to appreciate it now as he walks to the front pews where a crowd of similarly uniformed men and women gather, most of the faces recognizable. It takes a moment to find her amongst the others, but her left arm in a sling makes her easier to spot.

There is no room to sit beside her, though, because Fae is sitting next to her with Nik in a wheelchair in the aisle. The young medic, Amos, sits at her other side. Jax resigns himself to sit between Gia and Isaac. Slowly, the church fills up behind them with civilians, and then General Miles arrives, stepping to the front. All the uniformed people who can stand do so and salute.

"At ease." Bram returns a salute. "As you all know, it has been a long, grueling, road. Many have paid the price for this freedom, and in the generations to come we may still be paying the price. That is the curse of human nature in a mortal world. But we come here today to honor those who have passed, and those still with us today who have battled long and hard to give us the ability to step outside without fear. And so, we begin…"

In groups of ten, non-ranked men and women are called and given medals, and then individually the officers are called up. Jax hesitates when his name is called, it being a reminder of the medals he had earned for deeds he would rather forget, but he tells himself this is different. Standing at attention, he receives the medals and shakes the General's hand before stepping down, trying not to look at the crowd as they applaud.

When Lila's name is called, he catches himself leaning forward a little, and he smiles at her nervousness. She looks sharp and attractively trim in the uniform, even with the arm sling, and her beautiful hair is in a bun at the nape of her neck.

*The beret makes her look cute…*

But this thought is soberingly dismissed in the next moment.

The medal ceremony complete, General Miles begins reading from the list of lives lost over the years during the battle against The Direction. Jax hadn't prepared himself for this moment, and he is solemnly aware of how many names he knows on that list. Names he has pushed into that part of his mind where everything he doesn't want to think about goes. Now it is like they are here in front of him, and he can almost see their faces. It is unsettling, humbling, and after a while he bows his head in prayer and does something he hasn't allowed himself to do for years: he lets the tears fall.

Suddenly, he feels a slender hand grasp his left hand, squeezing gently, and looking over he notices that Lila has switched places with Isaac. She does not say anything; doesn't expect anything. Just quietly sits there in solidarity with him, and there is no one else Jax would rather have sitting by his side.

The General finishes with another short speech which Jax barely hears, and Bishop Augustine begins a memorial Mass for the deceased. Lila seems reluctant to do so, but she releases his hand as she watches attentively. He himself has only seen a couple times what Father Malachi told him is called a Latin Mass, and he understands how she is enthralled.

After the ceremony finishes, the uniformed men and women process to the narthex, followed by the civilian crowd which presses in on them, thanking them for their service. Jax watches as Lila tries to keep up with the individuals vying for her attention, but eventually he sees the stress building from the number of people, and he feels it too.

Gam and Gia seem to thrive on it, and he realizes this truly is where they belong, with this vibrant community. Fae and Nick are equally suited it seems. One look at Isaac reminds him that the man loves telling stories and pretty much speaking in general, but he also knows the tech genius would be equally happy to be working on a computer.

Having had more attention than he desires, Jax locates Lila again and leans in beside her.

"You mind meeting me at the lake when you get the chance?"

One look from her tells him she has been hoping for an excuse to leave, and she nods before finishing her conversation with Gia's sister.

"It was nice to meet you, Meg. Please excuse..."

Her voice fades behind him, along with the rest of the crowd, while he leaves out a side door and makes his way through the trees to the lake.

# | 105 |

# I Need Him

Uncomfortable would be an understatement, when I heard my name called. I received the medals numbly, trying to avoid noticing the crowd. When the names were being read, though, the embarrassment turned into humility, and I looked over across the aisle to my right.

It was odd for me to see Jax in tears. I always knew everyone comes to the point they need to cry, even men as confident as Jax, but it still took me by surprise; and made my heart ache. I wasn't even sure if it would be crossing the line that was put in place by him before the facility take-down, but Isaac seemed strangely eager to offer his seat when I went over, and on compulsion I held Jax's hand. Him not pulling away was a relief, and it felt natural to be at his side.

The memorial Mass was fascinating. I had no clue what was going on, but it was breathtaking and felt sacred. I was at peace in the quiet reverence. The civilian crowds were another story, and I was more than happy for the excuse to leave, because I felt myself more on edge with each encounter.

*Not to mention the increasing headache.*

Now in the quiet, cool air, the noonday sun filtering through the leaves, I have time to think as I walk through the massive trees. Yeti, having waited outside the church, now quietly pads beside me. Jax had sounded serious, and I wonder if this has to do with his multiple meetings with the General. Another thing I ponder is where Father Malachi has been the past few days.

The trees thin out, and I see Jax standing at the shore with his hands in the pockets of his uniform slacks. I notice that even in the safety of Vita Nova, he carries his sidearm, as do I.

Because of the warmer winter this year, there is barely any ice on the lake, and the gentle waves make a rhythmic sound against the sand and stones. It doesn't cover the sound of my approach, though, or Jax somehow senses, and he turns slightly with a smile. I am reminded again of how good he looks in a uniform, especially with that smile, but I unwillingly push it to the back of my mind.

"Hey, there. I had to get away from all that," he confides in a low voice.

"As did I. Thank you."

Jax turns back to face the lake. "Anytime, Lil'."

I smile a little at the familiar exchange, waiting in silence for a moment, although he doesn't seem to be in a hurry.

"Where has Father Malachi been? I thought I would see him today." I start first.

"He left for Bear Base to get it ready." He responds quietly, his expression not giving me much to go by, unfortunately.

"Ready for...?"

Jax glances over only briefly. "I told General Miles I need a few months off before I go on the next assignment he gave me."

Trepidation holds my breath for a moment. I have not heard of any assignment, and I wonder if it is because I am not involved. I don't want to be left here, and I am ready to argue for my place at his side in whatever mission.

*Even if it means I have to ignore how I feel about Jax.*

"What assignment?" I fight to keep my voice steady, and I stare across the water, trying to let the lapping of the waves ease the anxiety creeping in.

"Isaac traced the data package APA sent out from The Wilds, and it was received somewhere in a country far south once known as Mexico. Recently, Vita Nova linked with satellites capable of aerial imaging, and there seems to be a massive compound where the data went. The General wants me to pick a new team for a long-term mission to recon what's going on."

A lump forms in my throat, and my gaze lowers to watch Yeti playing at the water's edge.

"A new team?"

There is a bit of sadness in his voice as he continues, but I can't look up. "Gia and Gam are getting married. She's done with fighting, and he was never meant to carry a gun. This is their home now. Nik already said that even if he can recover fully, Fae is where he plans to be. Father Malachi will join me, but Isaac has yet to decide if he is ready."

The news about Gia and Gam does not surprise me. I know Nik will be several months in recovery anyway, and part of me wonders if Isaac really wants to go through that again, but so far Jax has said nothing about me.

"Jax..."

"Let me finish, Lil'..."

His gentle firmness and the warmth of his tone catches me off guard, and I lift my eyes to see him facing me, his green eyes with a light of determination as he holds my gaze.

"I need to start building my team with the most important asset, and I have prayed ardently about this. Lil'... I want to know if you will be not just my medic, but my second-in-command, my confidant, and most significantly..."

Jax pauses while he removes something from his uniform jacket, takes my hand, holding it, and places the items in my palm. I look down and see two well-worn, simple metal union bands, one with a familiar chain still attached.

"...My wife." He completes his sentence.

"Jax... how did you...?"

I am silent for a moment, trying to take in everything he just said and what he just handed me, almost not believing. I realize he must have taken time to find my ring at the facility. Looking up, I notice his expression has a hint of concern at my delay.

"Lil'...?"

"Yes. Yes, Jax. I will. There is nowhere else I'd rather be but by your side. Always."

The widest grin I have seen yet crosses his features, and he removes his beret and mine simultaneously, dropping them to the ground. He steps closer, nearly against me. Sinking his fingers into my bundled hair at the base of my neck, he pulls me even closer and leans down in a fervent kiss.

And just like that, everything around disappears, and I know that this is the only person in this broken world that I want to sit beside, stand beside, and fight beside. Until death do us part...

*And beyond, God permitting...*

# EPILOGUE

Out in a meadow covered in wildflowers, just outside of a place called Bear Base nestled in some canyons, a trim woman with sparkling amber eyes and long dark hair holds the hands of a man over a head taller than she. With tousled sandy blonde hair and sincere sage-green eyes, he boasts a strong build.

"Jax Erricks, do you take Lila Collins to be your wife? Do you promise to be faithful to her in good times and in bad, in sickness and in health, to love her and to honor her all the days of your life?" A bearded man in ceremonial attire questions.

"I do." Jax grins.

"Lila Collins, do you take Jax Erricks to be your husband? Do you promise to be faithful to him in good times and in bad, in sickness and in health, to love him and to honor him all the days of your life?" Father Malachi continues.

"I do." Lila replies, her eyes focused on Jax.

"What God joins together, let no man put asunder."

The priest blesses two simple union bands, worn and faded, but irreplaceable.

"Lil', receive this ring as a sign of my love and fidelity." Jax places the ring, the one that remained around her neck for so long, on her finger, and it fits perfectly.

"Jax, receive this ring as a sign of my love and fidelity." Lila takes the ring that has been with Jax through the years, and places it securely on his finger.

"I told you the rings would fit us one day," she whispers, and he grins, recalling hearing that from a little girl a lifetime ago.

As Father Malachi pronounces them man and wife, the cheers of Isaac, his best man, and Gia, her maid of honor and a small handful of their closest friends fade into the background.

He leans down over her, one hand at her lower back and the other at the nape of her neck, tangled in her loose hair. Remembering the words of their youth, he quietly recites them.

"No one can take you away from me, now, Lil'."

Jax presses a kiss to her lips, and she wraps her arms around his neck, her fingers in his hair; neither of them wanting to be anywhere else.

*Then the LORD God said, "It is not good that the man should be alone; I will make him a helper fit for him."*

# FINDING FORTITUDE

After their teams file into the back of the transportation truck, Jax and Lila stand facing each other, dressed in light military gear. He smiles down at her with his hand against her cheek, his gaze searching her eyes.

"Are you ready for the next assignment?"

"Only if you're there at my side, Jax."

"Always and forever, Lil'."

"Then yes."

He gives a playful grin.

"We can call it our honeymoon."

She raises a brow at him.

"Jax. I don't think you can honeymoon in a warzone."

"You're cute when you do that."

"Do what?"

"Raise one eyebrow."

"You might be biased."

"I'm allowed to be, Lil'."

She goes to reply, but he grins and kisses her. Opening the door for her first, they climb into the cab of the truck and begin their long journey south together.

To Mexico.

# ACKNOWLEDGEMENTS

First and foremost, I want to thank God for the inspiration He gave to me for this book. This was a work in progress since I was 16 years old, based on a dream. I tried to keep it non-religious because I was afraid to tie God into the action and romance of the story, wanting instead to cater to the general populace. How will I have a successful book if I paint myself as blatantly, unabashedly Christian in my writings? After all, people just want action, villains and heroes, not the heroes confessing to God how they are nothing without Him, admitting they have to face their issues with God. Over the years, I wrote bits and pieces but there was never a clear plot that tied everything together. Until now, twenty years later, God inspired me to base the entire book on having faith and trusting God. This tied every bit of the story together, everything I struggled to match came into place, and "The Direction" became clear to me.

So, thanks be to God, completely!

My other thanks go to:

Nicholas, who helped encourage me into the frightening world of self-publishing.

My friend Mary, with her insight on immunizations and medical questions.

My brother, Benedict, with his knowledge of geomagnetic impact on electronics, and the enthusiastic support from him and his wife, Jackie.

My brother Gregory and his wife Bethany with their insights on faith and their encouragement.

My daughter Maggie, who faithfully cheered me on and critiqued my writing every step of the way.

My Dad, Patrick, and his off-grid systems expertise. But mostly for the faith he raised me in, teaching me to be confident through Christ and trust that God will bring me through everything that life throws at me.

And the most important thanks (other than God of course, but God did send this man into my life so, technically I am thanking God too.):

To my husband, Benjamin.

My greatest critic (because I can trust him to be honest), my support, my one-man cheer squad, the man who keeps me grounded and sane (or keeps me company in my insanity), the man who has my back 100%, my prayer warrior, my hero, my "us against the world" partner…

Pretty much *my* "Jax".

Thank you for your insight and for being here every bit of the way and enduring my endless days of fretting over this first book, Husband, even though I probably drove you crazy and asked you way too many questions.

You are "…the only person in this broken world that I want to sit beside, stand beside, and fight beside. Until death do us part…"

www.ingramcontent.com/pod-product-compliance
Lightning Source LLC
LaVergne TN
LVHW041739060526
838201LV00046B/858